HOME

HOME

H.L. ANDERSON

CONTENTS

FRACTURED REALITY

Publishing

ISBN

Paperback: 979-8-9862244-0-4

Hardcover: 979-8-9862244-1-1

Digital: 979-8-9862244-2-8

To George, Linda, Ken, and Hallie
for always being supportive of my writing.

To Brian,
for always challenging me.

To Amadea for endlessly listening to my plot twists.
The sled ride is for you.

KATIE

Something was wrong. Something was very wrong.

Katie stared at the sunlight flickering through the trees as the Jeep zipped past. She ran her fingers over the gold embossed letters of the leather book she held in her lap. The light danced with the leaves and filtered into the car. The letters of her book glittered as the light slid across them.

It was the kind of day when the world felt new. The air smelled fresh and clean, the sun felt warm, and the breeze was gentle with a lingering nip from winter. The temperature was that perfect spot between hot and cold. Just stepping into a day like this should make Katie feel alive and free.

The trees had a handsome new coat of green. With the sun burning behind the leaves, they glowed as if radiating their own light. Life was blooming in every corner, but nothing *looked* alive. The trees were nothing but sticks, the leaves just brittle paper ready to blow away with a stiff wind. Wind, her favorite element, held no appeal for her now.

Reality, for her, had been altered, and she couldn't shake it. She saw the world as if her soul still hovered above the nameless planet in the dream. She didn't need to close her eyes to see the glowing blue horizon and the flat, fanned rays of the sunlight stretching across the surface. *Something was coming.* She felt it in the fiber of her being. But she woke just before she saw it—a single phrase repeated in her mind of its own volition. *I almost saw...*

What was coming? Whatever it was, was coming—and soon. She knew they had to prepare, but how do you prepare for the unknown? Was it good? Was it bad? What *was* it!

Her father pulled the Jeep into the small meadow near their bomb shelter, built over one hundred years ago, well before her family bought the property, by an old recluse who had stocked it during the War of 2018. He had been prepared. He would have been all right when *it* came, but he died before *it* arrived. He had no family. The shelter sold "as is." Her parents had spent days cleaning it out, taking inventory, stocking fresh supplies, and getting it ready for a rainy day. Now they would be prepared, thanks to one old man and a war that sank continents and drove people underground.

Katie climbed out of the Jeep; her eyes were drawn to the blinding blue sky so vast and so—empty. She saw how bright and vibrant the colors were, should be, but somehow were not. They were muted. Her parents had already opened the back hatch, and Mary raced for the trees.

"Not too far, Mary!" her mother cried. Katie turned, slow, like a ballerina in an old music box, and took a bag from her mother's arms, the paper somehow coarse against her skin, yet distant. Like a memory of the feeling.

Concern clouded her mother's pretty face. Her smile seemed forced. Katie knew her mother was worried, but that knowledge didn't sink far enough into Katie to affect her. Katie couldn't tell her. How could she describe this feeling? How could she explain she felt detached? Like a balloon tethered to the earth by a thin, frayed piece of yarn? Any second now, it would snap, releasing her into the arms of that limitless space.

She avoided her mother's vacant eyes. They were empty, dead, as if her soul was strangling in her body. Same with her father and sister. They were shells—future ghosts.

Her motions were automatic as she helped spread the picnic cloth on the ground, the classic checkered pattern bright against the new spring grass. They would wait to eat once Boon got there. Boon? How would he look? Would he be a shell too?

She should feel something, right? Horror, fear, *something;* some form of reaction to what she was experiencing, but there was only emptiness inside her. She looked at the world through new eyes and felt nothing. No connection to any of it. Was this how God saw the world? Was this how He saw the souls of His children, suffocating in these shells? Were they simply "shell people" to Him? No, God loves His children. He *feels* for them, but still, she felt nothing, not even the fear of being stuck in this altered view.

She went to the shelter, found the door in the tall grass, and lifted it. The air got noticeably colder as she descended the stone steps into the darkness. She left the hatch open to let the light fill the depths of the room. There was little dust as her parents took regular care of the shelter. She set the old tome on a table and picked up a can. Even this cold, hard, metal thing felt strange to her. She was an alien to her world, and this daze kept her at arm's length. What would it be like to be locked in here? The door, once locked, would not open until the preset time had elapsed. How long? Months? Years? She had no idea. Presumably, a safe length of time following a nuclear blast. She set the can back down and looked back at the light streaming in, illuminating the shadows. She wasn't a part of this world anymore, and she didn't know why. She climbed the stairs, letting the hatch fall shut behind her, forgetting her book by Poe on the table.

⤙Z⤚

She knelt by the stream. The water was high from the melted snow and fast. She stuck her hand in the water, deeper, up to her elbow. It was icy and strong as it pressed against her hand. She focused on the feeling of the water stretching her hand wide, how it made her palm feel round and smooth. She willed it to connect. To feel real, but this too was distant.

The crystal water shimmered in the light, mesmerizing her. She stared until her vision blurred, and her bones ached from the cold. She wiped her hand on her jeans and stood. What was wrong with her? She should feel frustrated, but she felt nothing.

She closed her eyes, felt the breeze brush her hair off her shoulders. She filled her lungs with a long breath of clean, damp spring air, but even this was somehow too far away to fully enjoy.

She needed to snap out of this daze! But try as she might, when she opened her eyes, she still saw the same dead world. She was the living, witnessing the dead walk. They were just memories doomed to repeat the same day, a video playing on a loop, and she was on the outside watching.

Impatient flowers shoved their way through the debris left by winter. She drifted to a grassy spot by the picnic blanket and flopped onto her back. Though the grass was dry, the ground beneath was still damp from the snow that had melted just weeks before. Her clothing absorbed the moisture. She ran her hand over the silken threads of the new green grass. She breathed in the fresh earthy smell, then let her lungs release the air in one long sigh. It didn't feel real. She couldn't make it feel real.

She rolled her head to the side and looked at her family. Her father lay sprawled under an old oak, his eyes closed. Her mother ducked branches as she chased Mary through the trees. Mary giggled as she ran close to her mother, only to dart away at the last second. Katie's mother made an exaggerated grab at Mary, purposely falling short. Mary squealed.

Katie turned her head at the sound of Boon's truck. Sitting up took effort, forcing a smile, trying to appear normal took even more. Could she tell him? How do you tell someone you almost saw something, and now you see too much? How do you explain that your soul feels detached from this world? That everything is muted and muffled as if she was viewing everything through water?

His hair was still long, brown. He was wearing his habitual fake coon skin cap and boots, which earned him his nickname. His jeans were old, tattered; his t-shirt sported the logo of his favorite rock band. His eyes were still the color of milk chocolate, but they were vacant as well. She felt she should cry, she should be upset by this, but still, there was apathy in her heart.

He pulled her into a hug and tipped her chin up for a kiss. He pulled back at her lack of reaction. She tried a smile, but she again had to reach down into herself to force the corners of her mouth up, and she knew it looked just as false as the rest of the world looked to her.

His dead eyes narrowed a touch, anger? He leaned close, whispered harshly in her ear.

"Are you still mad about that stupid fight?"

Fight? How could he think of the pointless spat when *it* was coming? Before she could answer, her mother called them over to eat. Boon replaced his look with a smile that didn't make it up to his eyes—his vacant eyes.

This will all fall away.

They didn't get to sit. The world went dark as a moonless night. Like the world before light pollution. As if the filament in the sun snapped, killing the bulb. The darkness was thick, almost tangible.

The shock of it burst the bubble that had enveloped her. She landed back in reality with a jolt. Before she could say anything, an eerie green light blinded her. She squeezed her eyes shut and, painfully, forced one back open. The light spread until everything glowed green. Not a vibrant new green like the sun through leaves in spring. No, a dark, sickly green. The color of poison and long-lasting illness.

Katie looked at her hands, then at Mary and Boon. She softly touched Boon's cheek.

"You're glowing," she whispered.

"So are you."

"Mom, Dad?" Katie asked. She held up her hands as if they couldn't see the green.

"What's going on?" Mary asked. Katie took her sister's hand and squeezed it. It was real, soft, young. What was dead before now teemed with life. There seemed, now, to be too much life. Life oozed out of every tree, rock, and stick. It moved and breathed. Colors, dull before, were now too sharp and clear. She was suddenly and completely interwoven with this planet.

"It's here," Katie whispered. She knew this with every fiber of her being. The apathy shattered like delicate glass, feelings churned inside her; the strongest of all was dread. The dread from the dream engulfed her.

"This is weird," Boon said.

"We have to—" Katie started.

Boon cut her off with an elbow to the ribs and pointed. "Look!"

A fat squirrel fell out of the old oak. It hit the ground with a thump, staggered to its feet, and stumbled around. It made an awful whining noise, a moaning screech that pierced Katie's ears.

"What's wrong with it?" she shouted, crushing her hands to her ears to muffle the awful sounds. Everyone was doing the same, their faces distorted in pain and fear. Her family exchanged confused glances. Her father shook his head.

"I don't know," he shouted. He had his face inches from hers when he answered, but she still had trouble hearing him. The squirrel gave one final shriek, then a soft popping sound, and the squirrel was no more. For a split second, there seemed to be a fine powder in the air, then nothing.

"Where did it go?" Katie asked. She dropped her hands to her sides, her ears still ringing.

"Did it explode?" Boon asked.

"I don't think so," her father answered. "There would be pieces of squirrel if it had exploded, right?"

"I would think so," her mother said.

"So, what happened?" Katie asked. Her stomach twisted.

"It's as if it," Boon paused, seeming to search for the right word. "Instantly evaporated?"

"You watch too much sci-fi." No one laughed.

Before Boon could reply, the old oak started groaning as if a high wind were trying to rip it from the ground. It didn't move, and there was no wind. It creaked and moaned, then that same faint popping sound followed by the idea of fine powder. The tree was gone.

"This is nuts," Boon said. His voice held a note of disbelief. Mary whimpered. Katie tugged on Boon's arm.

"I think we should go." She barely finished her sentence when individual blades of grass started popping. More trees popped. Birds shrieked as they fell from the sky, popping before hitting the ground. Insects popped in mid-air. A deafening wailing lifted around them, louder than a stadium of people. Each howl seemed more tortured than the last.

Boon's lips moved as if giving an order, but Katie couldn't hear what he said. He looked frustrated and grabbed Katie's hand, jerked her with him. Her parents started to follow, but her mother stopped. Katie looked back and saw her mother pressing her hands to her head.

Katie pulled free and ran back. Tears streamed down her mother's beautiful face.

"The pressure..." she gasped.

"I can't... take... the pressure..." She looked into Katie's eyes. Her father took her mother's arm.

"You have to run. You have to try." He pleaded, pulling on her arm. It's the first time Katie had ever seen her father cry. The first time she had ever seen the abject terror in his eyes. Her mother shook her head, dropped to her knees, and howled. She curled into a ball and screamed into her knees. Then she lifted her head to look at Katie.

"Baby—" she popped, just like the tree, just like the squirrel. Just a hint of dust remained, like blowing off an old book, then nothing.

"Mom!" Katie screamed. She shook her head, staring at the spot her mother had been. She couldn't think. This was a joke, right? This couldn't be happening! What's that noise? Was someone screaming?

Stop screaming! I need to think!

Why did her throat hurt? That's when she realized she was the one screaming. Boon grabbed her around the waist and dragged her with him. She was still shaking her head.

"Dad!" Katie tried to pull away from Boon. Her father was holding his head now. Mary stood by the spot their mother had been. Fat tears slid down her pale cheeks.

"Mommy?" Mary whimpered. Her father threw his head back and howled. Then he was gone.

Katie jerked free and raced toward her sister.

"Daddy?" Mary asked. She looked so small, standing there in the growing emptiness, small and scared.

"Mary," Katie cried. Mary dropped and squirmed on the ground screeching at the top of her lungs. The horrible sound would stay with Katie for the rest of her life. Katie dropped to her knees by her sister, flinging her arms around Mary's tiny shoulders. Too late, just as she was closing her grip, Mary popped. Her arms closed around air. For a second, there was a slight surprise of not touching anything like trying to step up on an extra step that isn't there.

"No!" Katie howled. She kept reaching into the empty air around her. As if she could collect the microscopic pieces of her family and fix them.

"I'll save you. I'll save you." She chanted; her voice was oddly flat. Tears streamed down her face, dripped off her chin onto the quickly disappearing grass. They had to be here; people don't just disappear!

Boon grabbed her under the arms and hauled her to her feet.

"We have to go, now!" he growled. He half-carried, half-dragged her with him.

"Mom," Katie mumbled. She stared back at the spot her family had been. The grass was still popping all around their feet. He tripped, and they both fell. The impact knocked the breath out of her. A ball of dust kicked up as they landed on dirt. She looked around—no more grass, trees, or flowers. Spring was gone. Life was gone—everything was gone. In the distance, a whole mountain disappeared! She discovered just how painful it was to be ripped from the fabric of life. Moments ago, she was hopelessly interwoven, and now she was a tattered fragment of material caught in this rogue wind.

He leaped to his feet and pulled her with him. He grabbed her by the shoulders forcing her to look at him. He shook her hard.

"We have to run, now!" he growled. She nodded, and together they raced to the shelter. Her lungs heaved. It was getting harder to breathe. What was wrong with the air? She felt as if she were breathing through a tiny straw. No matter how hard she tried, she couldn't get enough air to satisfy her lungs.

He jerked the hatch open and pushed her toward the black hole. The green light spilled down the staircase like an insidious poison.

"What good is this?" Katie sniffed hard. Tears still drenching her face, she wiped them away with her sleeve and heaved another painful, disappointing breath.

"It's everywhere! You can't hide from this!" She tried to yell, but it took all her strength just to breathe. Her voice came out hoarse and weak. She hit his shoulder with her fists. Each hit was softer and more pitiful than the last.

"It's better than waiting to die!" He caught her fists and pushed her farther down the steps. He pulled the hatch closed behind him, then pressed buttons on the keypad and cursed under his breath. Katie stood a few steps below him.

"What's wrong?" He looked back at her. His eyes were dark and angry. His jaw clenched.

"The keypad won't..." He sighed and crushed her in a hug.

"Won't what?" she asked. He kissed her hard.

"I love you." He shoved the hatch open and was out before she could react.

"Boon!" Katie leaped forward. Too late, Boon slammed the hatch and locked it from the outside.

Not one ray of that horrid green light could touch her now. She placed a hand on the hatch and closed her eyes. Hot tears squeezed out, slid down the pre-made tracks on her cheeks, and dripped off her chin.

"I love you too." She whispered.

KAT

The rock burned Kat's hands as she pulled herself up onto the plateau. The sharp rim cut into her palms; she ignored the pain and grunted as she dragged herself over the lip. Her Kur turned its strange alien head in her direction for only a moment before looking away. It looked like a cross between a kangaroo and a mule, but that didn't matter to her. It was loyal—and her only friend.

"Glad to see you too." She muttered as she looked over the cliff's edge she had just ascended. The climb out of Neptune's Hollow got more brutal every year. The single massive ocean that had once occupied its mysterious depths had been called the Ocean of Atlantis. Sure, they borrowed from mythology, but it was aptly named. The ocean swallowed continents as it had swallowed Atlantis. So, from one myth to another, the hole left behind had been deemed Neptune's Hollow. She cocked her head, and stared across the deep empty canyon. The wind sang a haunting, sorrowful tune.

Neptune's Hollow had been a great source of bargaining materials over the years. What the ocean had eaten over the centuries now yielded gladly in the harsh light of the sun. All its secret's laid bare for all to see.

It's a treacherous climb into the depths. The steep drop, leading to the next ledge, would intimidate most of the people left alive, which is probably why no one had found her secret water source. Those brave enough to attempt the journey were either determined or crazy. She was pretty sure she was one of the crazies.

Of course, there were very few people left alive to even worry about finding her secret treasure. Even if they stumbled across the entrance, they would have to be willing to go deep underground to locate the water. She heaved a sigh and picked up the sack she had thrown onto the plateau prior to climbing up and slung it over her shoulder. The trinkets she had found, half-buried in the sand, clattered together as they thumped against her back.

"I used to know so many stories from Mythology," Kat mused. She stroked her Kur to calm it. All the stories had faded from her memory in the face of this harsh dry land. All she had left was her dear friend Poe. His stories had sustained her sanity through the years. She chuckled at the irony.

Her Kur didn't move as she tied the sack to its back. It shifted from foot to foot as she tightened the straps. She patted its long neck. "Yeah, we'll go soon."

She turned her attention to the limitless horizon, hating the flat bleakness of it. The sky had hardened to a matte, dull, immovable gray. There were no clouds to shield the poor bruised Earth from the scorching rays of the sun. A harsh and constant wind scoured the land.

She closed her eyes and let her mind's eye show her the world as it had been five years ago. She could still see the clear blue sky lit with the golden rays of the sun. She remembered the feel of the breeze when it was still gentle. If she concentrated hard enough, she could see the spring grass and feel the green silken threads. The memory was distant, faded like an old photograph, but it was there. The memory burned away as soon as she opened her eyes to look at the hot, dry world that surrounded her now.

The memories that never burned away were the tortured faces of her family, the agonizing moans before they died. Awake or asleep, she heard them. They played on a loop in her mind, her constant companions these five years, driving her to the brink of madness. She never did forget the detached feeling she had had that day, nor the dream that preceded the nightmare. If she had figured out what "it" was sooner, perhaps... The familiar anger boiled deep inside her, heating her blood, and poisoning her stomach. Her nails bit into her palms as she fisted her hands. *It all falls away.* She closed her eyes and shook her head. Slowly she unclenched her fists; her nails pulled from her skin. She took the chains of the Kur. Strolling down the "what if" path would be pointless. She couldn't go back.

"Come on." Her voice was sharper than she had intended. "Let's go home."

She didn't cry as she walked, and she wouldn't. Tears were for the weak, and weak she was not.

She leaned into the harsh wind, felt the heat through her protective silver suit. It would be nice to have a cool breeze just once. No such thing on this dust ball they called Earth. Wouldn't Poe be delighted at such a dreary dead planet? What would he say to describe it? *During the whole of a dull, dark, and soundless day in the autumn of the year...* Oh, but he couldn't say *autumn*, could he? No, for it was never autumn. Never winter. Never spring nor summer. There were no seasons on a dead planet. It should be embalmed and buried or cremated, and the ashes spread throughout the limitless universe. Yes, specks of Earth to dust a different world.

Despite her hermetically sealed helmet, she still squinted as the clouds of dust scraped from the hard ground and pelted her face shield.

Far across the dim horizon, she could barely make out the low dome of the nearest colony. It was the only object to break the monotony of the landscape. The government of Camexus had long ago collapsed. It evaporated with all the people, animals, and plants. Now all that remained was a handful of colonies sprinkled across the nameless land.

Each colony had its own set of laws, and Kat was familiar with all of them.

She reached the shelter, which had been her home for the last five years. She left her Kur standing outside, knowing it would be there when she came back. Kurs were fiercely loyal creatures as long as you treated them well.

She hefted the hatch to the shelter and tossed her supplies into the darkness. Darkness she had endured for three years; three long, lonely years, an endless time waiting, never knowing when the door would open and release her, not knowing if she wanted to be released.

She made her way down the steps into the cool darkness. She tapped the release button on her collarbone and her helmet dissolved. She took a breath of stale air and touched her torch; it glowed, a gift given by an alien race, one of many after the attack. She made a point of staying out of intergalactic politics, but she knew the Caparians had killed the planet. She knew other alien races took pity on Earth and helped the pitiful humans survive in the airless, dead world. She gritted her teeth against the surge of anger, picked up her sack of debris, and heaved it onto a shelf. It clattered harder than she had intended. She unloaded her bottles of water and neatly lined them up next to the bag. Trinkets fetched a high price at market, more if the bauble happened to spark nostalgia in the buyer, but not as high as water. Water was the new platinum.

She had long ago run out of canned food and bottled water from a time before the attack. Now she was forced to trade in the colonies for food and air. She never knew what she would be bringing home to eat, always strange alien foods, foods with weird colors, and stranger textures. The strangest of all was food brought from an unpronounceable planet. To the human eye, it appeared as just a shade of gray. It was an unappetizing gritty blob and had no flavor. Sure it was packed with nutrients. Sure it kept her filled for days; it didn't matter. She didn't buy it again. Life was too short to waste on disgusting food.

She missed cheeseburgers and milkshakes. None of the alien food came close to the delicacies of Earth. She even missed Brussel sprouts and cabbage. Not coconut, though. She'd never miss coconut.

The air tank on her back beeped three times. She pulled it out of the pouch on the back of her skin-tight suit. She admired the smooth flat tank that was the same size and thickness as her hand. It was the latest in air tanks; smaller, lighter, and could hold more air, a full two days more. It had one day of air left. She would have to make a trip to the colony. She slid the tank back into the pouch. If she could get her oxygen generator working again, she wouldn't have to depend on the colonies to refill her tank.

She opened her bottle of water and took a sip. The cool, clear water slid down her parched throat. She felt the cold slide down her esophagus into her stomach, like a long thin ribbon chilling everything it touched. Her lips tingled to taste more. Her throat begged, her body demanded, but she put the cap back on the bottle. She paused, stared at her hand. Her fingernails rimmed in black grit, and the dirt ingrained into her skin, highlighting every imperfection, every tiny crack. Suddenly she was aware of all the filth on her body. Her scalp itched, her skin felt brittle and dry. She grabbed a scrap of cloth from the shelf and scrubbed her hands, uselessly. Not enough water to wash properly, barely enough to keep hydrated, she couldn't afford to waste it on a bath. She flung the rag against the wall, frustration wanting to burst from her in a scream, but she gritted her teeth.

A noise outside stilled her every movement. She hit the button on her collarbone and her helmet reformed around her head. She put out the torch. Her fingers found her staff in the dark. It was only twelve inches long now, but it could extend six feet. It had been costly. She had traded thirty bottles of water, a pack Kur, and the last of her canned food for it, but it was worth every drop of water, every morsel of food, and every coarse hair on the Kur. Tuned to her brainwaves, she was able to release it with a single thought. It had a second release which added blades to each end.

She held her breath, listening. She willed her senses to grow stronger, stretching them beyond normal human abilities. A line from a

Poe story drifted across her mind. *Above all was the sense of hearing acute.* Such was the way she listened. Nothing. Only the sound of her heartbeat in her ears. *It was a low, dull, quick sound—much such a sound as a watch makes when enveloped in cotton.* She felt her pulse throb in her neck. She strained to hear past the beating heart. The chains on her Kur's harness rattled. The stomping became persistent. The Kur was in distress! Her instinct to protect her property, her only friend, kicked in, and she bolted into the light. She leaped from the door with a shriek, extending the staff just as she cleared it.

In a quick sweeping glance, she saw the wagon, the two extra Kurs, and a lean man. She kept her eyes on him. He was emaciated. She wasn't sure how he could even stand. He was the walking definition of skin and bones. A long greasy beard hid most of his face. His head was nearly bald, save for a few black streaks that might pass for hair if it ever met water and soap. His eyes were ice blue, piercing, calculating. Perspiration glistened on his forehead. What might have been a smile revealed a few blackened teeth. Though she was a good twelve feet away, she caught a whiff of his breath, or was that just his general stench? Suddenly, she wasn't so thankful for the ability of this alien helmet to allow scents through. She hit another switch on her collar, and the helmet filtered out the offending odor.

"Well, hello," he said.

She didn't like his tone. She kept her stance and spun her staff as a warning. He held up his hands, but he took his time to look her up and down. Kat raised an eyebrow.

"Would you be interested in trading?" Kat kept her voice professional and confident but didn't let her guard down.

"I don't do business with children."

She pulled her shoulders back. "I see no children here."

"You eighteen?" he asked.

"Legal age to trade," she responded.

He looked her up and down again. His gaze made her feel exposed. She resisted the urge to shudder and instead lifted her chin. He climbed down off his wagon with more agility than she expected, took a swaggering step toward her, glanced at her Kur, and made a move to grab its chains. The Kur swung its head around and slammed the man in the stomach. He fell back and skidded across the hot ground. Kat smiled. Her Kur would remain loyal. The man got back to his feet and slapped the dust off himself. He swore at the Kur and raised his fist to strike it, but Kat leaped forward and swung her staff hard.

The blow connected with his stomach; he grunted and dropped to one knee. Kat pulled her staff into a helicopter spin and brought it down in a fast arc aimed for the nape of his neck. She stopped the swing inches from the mark. She brought her staff back to a neutral pose and waited. He sucked in a few more gulps of hot air before getting back to his feet. His amused look hardened into annoyance.

"What's your problem?" His voice was sharp.

She glared at him. "We can trade, or not. I don't care either way."

"Spirited young thing, eh?" His revolting grin had returned. When he smiled, his head looked like a skull.

"If you aren't going to trade, move along." She spun her staff again.

"All right, sweetie," he crooned. "Whatcha got?"

"What do you need?" she countered. He laughed as if she had said something hilarious.

"I need," he took a step closer. "—a woman!"

He lunged for her, but she was faster. She spun the staff in a head strike, around again to strike the opposite side of his head, then brought the butt end up under his chin. He staggered back with a growl. He touched his face and brought his hand back to examine the blood on his finger.

He pulled a gun, but she didn't give him enough time to aim. She swung the staff knocking the weapon from his hand. He grabbed his wrist with a sharp bark, and she struck again. The next blow caught him in the side, followed by the loud crack of breaking ribs. She brought the other end around and took out his left knee. He dropped to the ground in a penitent pose. She took the staff into a helicopter spin again and brought it down on the nape of his neck. This time she did not take pity. He dropped the rest of the way. She pocketed his gun then checked for a pulse. He was unconscious and bleeding but still alive.

She searched his pockets and found nothing. She pulled a medallion, with the symbol of the Droplet, off his neck. The only thing Kat knew about the Droplets was that they had helped after the attacks, and they only gave out these medallions to special friends. She had never seen one.

She doubted he was a "special friend" of the Droplets. He most likely stole it from an alien delegate. She slipped the medallion into her pocket and searched his wagon. He had nothing worth trading. Deep in the back, she discovered a trunk. It wasn't locked and was oddly silent as she lifted the lid. She shuffled through photos of people and animals. She paused over a picture of a golden retriever puppy. Where in the world? How did these survive the attack? She ran a finger over the image.

"A puppy," She whispered. She shook her head and tossed the photo aside. Photos of the past would only make her melancholy. She tossed out a few shirts and realized she must have accidentally deactivated the filter because the shirts stunk like rotten cabbage. Hidden in a small compartment at the bottom was a key.

"Well, well, well, so you have an escape pod," Kat murmured. She never understood the whole escape pod concept, as if *that* would save them from another attack. *Let's jettison ourselves into space, and then we can die a slow death instead of a quick one!* Sometimes it wasn't better to survive. Sometimes it's better to die with the rest. She pocketed the triangular key. She would be able to fetch a reasonable price for an escape pod.

She climbed back out of his wagon, glanced at the crumpled and snoring figure. It would be a while before he awoke. She went back into the shelter, picked up her travel sack, and filled it with some things to trade.

She picked up her old tome of Poe stories and poems, running her fingers across the black leather where gold embossing used to exist. The leather worn with constant use, and the pages frayed at the edges. The print was fading, and she mourned the day it would disappear completely. She gently slid it into the sack. She slipped the strap over her shoulder and wrapped her long cloak around her.

The cloak would protect her from the winds and keep her cool under the burning sun. The unique alien material was softer than fur and stronger than silk. She collapsed her staff and slid it into the sheath on her belt. Once she had gathered all she needed for a day's journey to the nearest colony, she climbed back out and locked her shelter. She pondered briefly before setting a bottle of water and some food next to the man. She eyed up his Kur.

"I could use a Kur for riding," she mused. She looked back at the unconscious man. "And you could use a lesson."

She gave a slight bow to the Kurs hitched to the wagon. "Would you permit me to ride you?" One Kur gave her a sideways glance, and the other ignored her. The one looking at her finally nodded its kangaroo-like head. She unhitched it from the wagon and mounted it. She took up the chains from her pack Kur and headed for the horizon.

"Pleasure doing business with you!" she shouted over her shoulder.

As she rode, she examined the key. The tag attached to it read Beta Alpha Quadrant Four. Impossible. He was nothing—a waif on the wind, a shade that took advantage of the weak and uninformed. Only high-ranking alien delegates had escape pods in Beta Alpha. He was *not* a delegate.

Kat scanned the horizon. It would be farther than she had planned to travel, but it was doable. She turned her Kur.

"Looks like we may need to visit this Beta Alpha escape pod," Kat said to her Kurs. They hummed in response.

BETA ALPHA COLONY

The oxygen dome in Beta Alpha dissolved around Kat as she passed through and reformed behind her. She entered the colony in time to hear the sirens fill the air with their ominous shrill screams, a death cry on the wind. She watched with sickening dread as the sky filled with escape pods. Wave after wave lifted from the ground like a swarm of angry bees. They blackened the sky like an oppressively low thunderhead. She gasped when two collided and watched in horrified silence as the burning remains plunged to the ground. She had to keep a tight hold on her Kurs. They stamped their feet and tossed their heads; the explosions drowned out their distressed humming.

She hit the release on her helmet as she headed for the Observation Base, rising from the middle of the colony like a giant silver boil, to find out more about the evacuation.

Her Kurs danced about before finally taking a step in the right direction. The colony was deserted. The hot wind, funneled by the buildings, whipped her cloak roughly and twisted her hair into her face. With the facilities all domed and the ground hard-packed, there was nothing to slow the wind. Her cloak and hair seemed to be the only thing moving. Everything else was oddly still.

The silver domes reflected the light, blinding Kat no matter which way she looked. She reformed her helmet and darkened it against the brilliance. She didn't cringe at the next round of explosions as more and more pods crashed. Flaming flowers like a Van Gogh painting scarred the sky. Memories of fireworks mingled with the burning blooms above her. The increasing explosions soon drowned out the sirens.

A sizeable flaming section of an exploded escape pod landed on a building right next to her. The impact popped the dome like a soap bubble and knocked her off her Kur. The chains from her other Kur ripped from her hand; she felt flesh tear. Her palm bled. Her pack Kur bolted, eyes wild with fear. She rolled to her knees, got a foot under her, and pushed off, just catching the harness on the other Kur. She held tight and watched as her pack Kur ran into the horizon with all her things clanging together. Its shrieks faded. She closed her eyes and sighed.

The building was on fire now. Several minor explosions added to the inferno. Kat mounted her Kur and headed for the Observation Base as fast as she could get the Kur to run. The fire seemed to be every-where now. Smoke thick in the air around her. She coughed, choked, sputtered. She slammed her palm against the filter button. The air inside her helmet cleared. The sooner she got inside, the better.

She turned a corner and spotted a motionless figure lying on the ground. She hopped off her Kur.

"Hey," she knelt by the body. "Are you all right?"

She rolled the body over and gasped.

He couldn't be more than ten years old! His face was bloody, and he had footprints on his chest. His brown eyes stared at her in an eerie fixed death gaze. She closed his eyes.

"I'm sorry," she whispered. She pulled the child out of the street and laid him by a building. Another explosion shook the ground. She climbed back on her Kur and raced for the Observation Base.

The noise was deafening. Pieces of pods rained down around Kat. She urged her Kur to go faster. She focused on the base of the observa-tion dome. A massive section of a burning pod landed directly in front of her. She pulled hard on the reigns of her Kur. It flipped over back-ward, and they both hit the ground hard. The Kur was up on its feet and running before Kat could catch her breath.

Each new explosion stabbed at her ears, causing her eardrums to pulsate. Another fit of coughing doubled her over. Her lungs burned with the heat and smoke. She hit the filter button again, but the air didn't clear. It must be damaged. She gave up.

Kat gripped her satchel and scrambled to her feet. She skirted the burning debris and ran as fast as her legs could carry her. There were no guards at the door. She didn't slow down as she burst through the door and slammed it shut behind her. She was alone again. Her ears rang with the sudden silence. She strained to hear past the ringing, but it was useless, and it was too dim. Kat hit the release and her helmet dissolved.

"This ringing can stop anytime now," Kat muttered. Her voice echoed down the empty hall. She felt foolish, as if she had just burped in church.

She slipped the strap of the satchel over her head and strode down the hall. Her steps silent, though she wouldn't be able to hear her boots over the ringing anyway.

"This is ridiculous!" she hissed.

"Hello?" she called. If her voice was a gun blast, the silence was its casualty. She sucked in a breath and held it. The ringing had subsided enough for her to hear the reply.

"Hello?" The voice sounded miles away and underwater. Kat let out her breath in one loud whoosh.

She followed the voice into the command center. She entered to find a young man standing at the window. He wore a suit similar to hers, only black.

He had his back to her. The dim light was enough to catch the red streaks in his brown hair. He was lean and tall and seemed solid. Kat cleared her throat, but he didn't turn around.

"Do you know what's going on?" Kat asked.

"Didn't you hear the sirens?" He said with a sigh. He sounded tired. Not just tired, profound soul-weary fatigue that only permeates those who have lost everything and can't find the strength to keep fighting.

"Somewhere in the explosions, I think I heard a siren," Kat replied dryly. He finally turned to her and stared at her for an uncomfortably long time as if deciding if she was real or not. He walked closer. His eyes were the most crystalline blue she had ever seen. Like the brightest hurt-your-eyes blue the sky could sometimes get, yet dulled by pain.

"You need to leave," he said.

His skin was much darker than hers. Kat was painfully white. No matter how long she spent in the sun, she never got any darker. Even covered in dirt, her skin was still a stark contrast to his dark skin.

"Well, I'd be glad to, but first tell me what's going on," she demanded. She put her hands on her hips and tapped the toe of her right foot. He grinned at her. His two front teeth were slightly crooked, which somehow complimented his face.

"All right, asteroids are about to demolish this ugly little planet, and unless you leave, they will have the pleasure of taking you with it." His voice was flat, his grin gone. She decided she didn't like him.

"Then why are you still here?" She pulled herself to her full five-foot, seven inches which didn't help since she still had to tilt her head up to look him in the eye.

"None of your business," he towered over her by at least five inches, maybe more. He looked at his watch.

"You have an hour to get off this planet."

"What about you?" she asked.

He shrugged and faced the window again.

"Fine," she pulled out the key and squinted at the tag. "Can you tell me how to get to Beta Alpha Quadrant Four?"

He spun around, eyes wide, mouth open. Had she impressed him?

"That's where your pod is?"

"Yes."

"Come on!" he grabbed her hand and yanked her toward the door. She jerked free.

"What?" she asked.

He spun to face her.

"That's an hour and a half away," he said impatiently.

"Oh," she pushed him out the door. "What are you waiting for?"

He growled but kept running. Kat stopped once they got outside.

"This way," he pulled her with him. He half dragged her to a small garage, letting go only to jerk the wide door open, revealing a land roamer. Kat had only heard about land roamers. It was a sort of hover-craft that could travel great distances at very high speeds. This, however, looked as if it had seen better days.

The once red paint was chipped and faded. The sides dented from several accidents, fender-benders, perhaps?

"Old demolition derby car?" she asked. He rolled his eyes.

"What's that dusty adage? Never judge a book by its cover?"

"Yeah, a book, land-roamers on the other hand..." She let her statement hang.

"Just get in."

"Is it yours?" she asked as she settled into the seat.

"Nope!" He kicked it into gear; they zipped out of the garage. Kat jerked backward, making a weird sound like a squeaky toy. She had never ridden in one of these things before. Even though she may be about to die, she couldn't help but enjoy the speed and the wind in her hair.

The first meteorite hit far off, but the ripple of energy still impacted the land roamer, forcing it to the side. "The small ones will hit first," he said. "It's the big ones we have to worry about."

Another meteorite hit, then another. Soon it was raining meteorites like a hail storm from hell. He whipped back and forth, dodging them. He leaned way over the wheel. His face set in grim determination, sweat beaded on his brow.

Kat leaned back and resisted the urge to hide her face. With each impact, the ground became more scarred. He was right; these were tiny. They did little more than poke holes in the surface.

She was thrown from side to side with each lurch he made. Each impact carried a deafening blast that penetrated deep into her poor ears. She covered them, a vain effort to protect her hearing.

Clouds of dirt filled the air like fog. Her throat was thick with grit. She clamped her mouth shut, but she had already breathed in the dust of the earth. She fought the urge to cough, her lungs convulsing in her chest. Her shoulders shook with the effort. She pounded the button on her collarbone, and her helmet reformed.

"Almost there," he said through gritted teeth. When had he formed his helmet?

"How can you tell?" But her voice was swallowed up in the blast beside them. She lurched forward as the land roamer abruptly stopped. Her palms slapped hard on the dash. If it was a dash, she didn't know much about the technical terms used on these things. If it had been a car, it would have been the dash.

"We're here," he said as he climbed out. Kat jumped out the other side. Her legs shook.

"Where's your escape pod?" he asked. The ground shook hard with another impact. Kat lost her balance, but he caught her.

"All right?" he asked his face inches from hers. Close enough for her to notice the stubble on his chin.

"Yes," she pulled herself up. She looked at her tag.

"Quadrant four," she read.

He took off, and she stumbled more than ran after him. All the buildings looked the same to her. She hoped he knew where he was going. A nearby explosion sent a shower of dirt over them. Kat ducked, covered her head with her arms, and kept running.

The rusted door squealed as he jerked it open and started down a narrow hall. There were four pods left. Kat had no idea which one it was. The ground shook again, followed by a loud explosion. The light flickered.

"Which one?" he shouted.

She shook her head and spread her hands. "I don't know!"

"How can you not know which escape pod is yours?"

"Because it isn't mine." Her voice was raw with all the yelling.

"You stole it?"

"Yes! From a thief!" she shot back. She felt a pang of guilt for the defenseless man she left in a heap.

"Let me see that," his voice was sharp. He snatched the key from Kat's hand. He ran from pod to pod, trying it in each one. The ground was constantly shaking now. The explosions all ran together, sounding like one long peal of thunder, only louder and more pronounced as if she were in the tallest tower of a castle where the thunder could surround her.

"This one, hurry," he exclaimed. The lights flickered and went out.

"No!" he cried, pounding his fist on the door.

"Please, God..." she prayed. The lights flashed back on.

"Yes!" he hissed. "Get in!"

They climbed inside, and he launched them into space. They were far from safe. He had to dodge the meteors hurtling towards them.

Even the slightest nick would send them spinning out of control and plummeting to their graves. They burst out of the atmosphere.

"What's that?" Kat pointed, knowing very well what it was. "Hang on!" he cried. The meteoroid loomed in front of them, getting bigger by the second. Kat closed her eyes. *This is it!*

CHAR

Char jammed his thumb down on the button till he felt his thumb would snap. The escape pod lurched to the right. Slowly, too slowly, they rolled out of the way.

"Come on!" he growled. They slipped around the side just as the meteoroid passed. He expected the girl beside him to scream. Her knuckles were white as she gripped the arms of her chair, but she didn't make a sound. Soon, they were floating a safe distance from the flow of asteroids. They watched as the asteroids slammed the once beautiful planet. Each impact sent massive plumes of dirt into space. There was no break; one plume would melt into another. Soon, there wasn't a difference from one cloud to the next, as if the Earth had floated into an interstellar fog.

Char imagined the Earth breaking away, under that cloud, one chunk at a time. His hope seemed to break away with the planet. Finally, the asteroids quit coming. They stared at the debris. The few stars they could see through the dust glittered harmlessly against the devastation.

A hole seemed to open in Char's chest. He couldn't pull enough air, couldn't control his thoughts, couldn't stop the one phrase from repeating in his mind. He couldn't stop himself from muttering it, breathy and hollow, *"Not possible. Not possible. Not possible."*

Hand over his mouth, he stared into the ever-expanding Earth debris. Dead. The whole thing. Dead. Gone. He couldn't grasp the magnitude of the situation. He dragged his gaze away from the screen and looked at the girl. He had never seen hair so black. A strange thing to notice, but he didn't want to think about the emptiness.

"I heed not that my earthly lot / Hath little of earth in it— / That years of love have been forgot / In the hatred of a minute:—" she murmured.

"I'm sorry?"

"Poe," she replied. The silence stretched. Those haunting words hung in the air between them, making it hard to breathe. She was the first to break the silence.

"You'd think they would have learned," she whispered.

"Who?" He raised an eyebrow. She didn't look away from the fragments of Earth.

"It's actually kind of ironic. All those movies, books, and stories we used to watch and read had 'us' completely prepared when the aliens would attack."

"What are you talking about?"

"Or if we weren't prepared, we at least were able to thwart their attacks by combining our intelligence." Her voice was quiet and bitter. "But when you come right down to the reality, we were nowhere near prepared, and we were nowhere near intelligent enough to save our own hides."

"Did you get hit on the head?" he asked. Just his luck, the last woman on Earth—what was he thinking? The Earth was gone; the last woman *alive*, period, had to be a nut job.

She closed her eyes and sighed, and edge creeped into her voice. "What's your name anyway?"

She turned to look at him. Her eyes were large, dark, and haunted. Her thick lashes made her eyes seem larger and her skin whiter.

"Char," he replied, forcing himself to look back at the controls.

"I'm Kat," she continued. "Like the animal, but spelled with a 'k.'"

She held out her hand; he took it in his. Her grip was firm, her hand cold and small, folded in his.

"Do you see any other escape pods?" she asked as she withdrew her hand. Her fingers left cold spots on the back of his hand.

He looked at the vast emptiness extending before him. The stars aren't so pretty when stranded, floating helplessly amongst them.

"All I see is dust and stars," he replied.

She leaned closer to the screen. "There must be other survivors. It can't be just us."

"Maybe they're hidden in the dust cloud." He tried to sound hopeful. The cloud thinned, but no other escape pods appeared.

"There must be more..." he mumbled. He fiddled with the controls and scanned the area for other pods. No pods registered.

"Are we the last?" she breathed.

Char swallowed against the lump forming in his throat. The last two humans. The last of a species. Their planet was gone. There were no words to express what he was feeling, no words to relay the magnitude of that realization.

His voice strained with his reply. "We are now endangered."

The pod lurched.

"What was that?" he cried. His heart slammed into his ribcage. He flipped switches, changing the view until he could see what hit them. When he saw the ship, his heart skipped, his blood chilled.

"What is it?" Kat asked. She sounded strangely calm, but her eyes were wide.

"I think it's a Caparian battleship," he swallowed.

Her eyes narrowed at the name, her lips pursed.

"I have to get us out of here," he flipped switches and pressed buttons. He knew full well there was no outrunning a Caparian battleship, but he had to try.

"Nothing is responding!" he slammed his fist on the control panel in frustration. He looked at the screen. "We're dead in the sky."

The speaker crackled to life, delivering the nightmarish voice of a Caparian. Grated, garbled, it shouted something at them. He instinctively reached for the cross that used to hang from his neck. He realized what he was doing when his fingers didn't find it and dropped his hand. If she saw, she didn't say anything.

"What's it saying?" Kat asked. She leaned forward as if that would help translate.

"How would I know?" Char growled. "The translator must have been damaged in the hit."

"You don't have to snap!" she shot back, then mumbled, "I don't think he's happy."

"He's a Caparian! They *never* sound happy!" He gritted his teeth, regretting his tone.

"You don't have to be a jerk," she snapped. "Try to respond."

"Respond? With what?" he shouted. "Even if I had the power, which I don't, I don't know the language!"

"I don't know! Maybe they know our language!" Her eyes shrank to slits as she glared at him. The pod lurched again then started moving in the direction of the battleship.

"Don't go *toward* them!"

"I'm not!" he bellowed. "They're pulling us in!"

She paused, the irritation slowly melted off her face, replaced by a cold, calculated stare at the screen. Her voice, when she spoke, was eerie calm, "Perfect." She sounded pleased. "Rig this thing to blow, and we'll take down the enemy in one glorious blaze."

"Are you nuts?" he cried. "If we blow this thing, it will only scratch the paint, not disable it. They would be sitting in their chairs laughing at us as we blow ourselves to nothing."

"At least we would die fighting!" The fire was back in her eyes. Strange; he had been so prepared to die on the planet. He had urged everyone else to escape, fully prepared to go down with the ship—as it were. Yet now he found himself nose to nose with this mini tyrant trying to convince her suicide was not the answer. She looked at the monitor.

"What's that?" she pointed.

He grinned.

"That, my dear, is a Zortentearthian war ship!" He cheered and threw his arms around her hugging her hard. Her body felt small and surprisingly solid. She wiggled free without returning the hug.

"How do we know they're not here to kill us as well?" she asked. There was no mistaking the suspicion in her voice.

"Droplets are a neutral race. They were the first alien race to respond to the attack five years ago. They helped us build the oxygen domes as well as design that suit you're wearing."

"You don't have to tell me how they've helped. I *have* been around these past five years," Kat replied. Her tone was sharp, indignant.

"Then how can you not know they're peaceful?" He forced his voice to remain calm.

"Well, if they're going to help, they had better do it soon," she said, ignoring his question. He looked back at the screen. They were nearing the Caparian ship; a door on the side began to open. Red light seeped out around the edges.

More voices filled the speakers. A high melodic voice clashed with the grating voice that had been talking previously. They seemed to be arguing, their voices entwining like a twisted opera, one voice harsh and coarse the other ethereal; demons and angels fighting for the last two souls from Earth.

The pod lurched again, and their advance on the Caparian ship stopped. The pod groaned.

"Oh, good," Char said. "Now we're the rope in a tug-of-war."

The pod pulled away from the battleship, but only slightly. "This is bad," Char mumbled. "The Caparians are a warring race. A single battleship is a force to be reconded with, whereas the Droplets are a peaceful species."

"If they're peaceful, why do they have a warship at all?" Kat asked.

He shot her a sideways glance, "Even Switzerland had an army."

"So, what are you saying? We're doomed anyway?"

Before he could respond, the Droplet's ship shot the battleship with a blue laser. The lights went out in the battleship, and the pod veered away from the Caparians.

"Interesting," mused Char. "That shot must have disabled something important in the battleship, or they would have shot back by now."

"They're leaving," Kat said. She sounded disappointed. Relief washed over Char like a warm wave. He hadn't realized how tense his muscles were until he let them relax.

The Droplets were pulling them in; Char leaned back and laced his fingers behind his head. He glanced at Kat. She continued to watch the retreating Caparian ship.

"What are you doing?" Kat asked. "Try to break free."

"Even if I could, which I can't, I wouldn't. We can't sit out here forever, and they," he gestured toward the warship, "may be able to help us."

"Why are you always so quick to give up?" she asked.

"Why are you always so quick to pick a fight?" he shot back. Kat folded her slender arms and glared at the wall.

A door on the side of the remaining ship opened, releasing a much more inviting blue light. Char felt less like he was being pulled into the gates of hell and more like he would get to glimpse heaven if heaven truly existed. He resisted the urge to touch his missing cross. The pod finally settled, and they were permitted to climb out. The inside of the ship was large and airy. The ceiling was high, and the walls shimmered like the reflection of water. Except there *was* no water.

All around them were short green humanoids with wild short blue hair. The creatures ignored them and scurried back and forth, each seeming to have its task. Their green skin was flat and dull, and their dark blue hair appeared brittle.

"What are they?" Kat whispered.

"I believe they are called Sprouts," Char replied.

"Shh," she hissed, her elbow jammed into his side.

"Ow!" he whispered. "What was that for?"

He looked up and noticed another being approaching, "Oh, a Droplet."

The Droplet was tall, nearly eight feet. His skin was blue, but all different shades of blue, which seemed to change every time he moved. He flowed like water and seemed to glow. His light green hair fell to his waist. Silver objects intertwined with his green hair and glittered in the soft blue light. Char couldn't tell what their purpose was; helmet, crown, simple decoration? The Droplet moved with confidence and authority.

"Why did you bring us here?" Char asked. Kat elbowed him again.

"Quit doing that!" he snapped, keeping his voice as low as possible.

"He can't understand you," Kat mumbled.

"On the contrary, I understand you perfectly." The Droplet had a voice like the hum of a gentle wind.

If she was embarrassed, it didn't show, her ghostly skin didn't change color at all, and her set expression just about emanated distrust.

His voice sang to them, but the English words came from the speaker overhead.

"I am Captain Gar. What may I call you?"

"I'm Char, and this is Kat," Char said. Captain Gar nodded his head. He had large gray eyes and no nose. At least no nose that Char could see.

"We will take you to our planet. The Princess wishes a word with you."

"What if we don't want to go?" Kat asked. She kept her back ramrod straight but was no match for the Captain's eight feet.

"You, of course, have the option to leave. But before you go, that Caparian Captain is looking for you, and he will be back. When he does come, how will you fight?" His voice could soothe a lion, and he spoke the truth.

"He has a point, Kat," Char said. "Where would we go? What

would we eat? We don't have to set up permanent residence on this planet, but it is a place to start."

Kat seemed to consider this, then nodded.

"Fine," she replied.

Captain Gar motioned to one of the short green creatures.

"Elici will take you to a Suspended Hibernation Capsule. It will be a long journey; you will be most comfortable sleeping through the trip." He turned and left, more floating than walking.

"Come," Elici beckoned for them to follow.

"What's a Sprout?" Kat whispered. Char put a hand on her back and gently pushed her in the direction Elici had gone. He leaned down to speak in her ear. She smelled like sweat and dirt. He wondered if he smelled the same.

"They're the less intelligent beings on planet Zortentearth. They are strong and feral and hard workers. The Droplets take them in, train them, and put them to work," he said.

"So, these Sprouts are slaves?"

"Not really."

"How can you 'not really' be a slave?"

"The Sprouts are incredibly primitive; if left alone, they fight and kill each other like wild animals, but not for self-defense or food like wild animals. They simply fight and kill just to fight and kill. Once the Droplets adopted them and taught them how to work, the fighting stopped. Now the planet is peaceful."

"Why not teach them more? Then they won't have to be servants," Kat said.

"They learn manual labor by sheer repetition but are unable to memorize two plus two."

"Has anyone tried?" Kat asked. Char rolled his eyes.

"Listen, we're not going to this planet to start a civil war. The Droplets have helped us in the past, and we are not going to spit on their doorstep, understand?" He had stopped and taken hold of her arm. He squeezed a little too tight. She glared at him and yanked her arm free.

"*I can* memorize two plus two," she said and started walking again.

Elici stopped walking and opened a small round hatch.

"In," Elici grunted. Unlike the Droplet's, Sprout's voices were low and rough. Nowhere near as ugly as the Caparians voice had been, but still far from pleasant.

"You first, so I can make sure he doesn't do anything funny," Char said. Kat got an amused smile on her face; her eyes twinkled.

"What's to stop him from doing something after you're asleep?"

Char pressed his lips together, "Just get in." He balled his hands into fists. Why did she have to be so stubborn?

Her grin widened as she climbed into the capsule. Char watched as Elici closed the hatch and spun a dial.

"In," Elici grunted after stepping to the next capsule. He towered over the Sprout.

"Thanks for your help," he said. Elici just grunted and pointed at the capsule. Char nodded.

"Right, in," he climbed inside, feeling like a giant rat in a small shoebox. He took a deep breath and let it out slowly, waiting for the sleeping fog to roll in.

Z

"So, you're going to be a Pastor, huh?" Her red hair glowed like fire in the sunlight. They walked along the dirt road outside of town. She stuffed her hands into the pockets of her blue jeans.

The limbs on the trees were already starting to bud. The sun was bright, but the air was still cool with the last gasp of winter. Each breath was new and clean; a feeling of starting over hung in the air.

"What's funny about that?" he asked as he kicked a stone.

Her cerulean eyes sparkled with good humor.

"Pastor Charlie sounds funny." She bumped into him with her shoulder. The breeze caught a wisp of her hair and slapped it in her face.

He gave her a playful shove. "I think it sounds fine."

"You think getting in good with God will make up for shutting me in the dryer when we were six?"

"You deserved it! You dumped paint in my shoes!"

"Oh, very Christian of you," she giggled. "That's the eye for an eye part, right?"

"So, I need to work on a few things," he shrugged. "Nobody's perfect."

"Least of all you!" She laughed and danced out of range of his swinging fist. Not that he would ever really hurt her. Her white shirt fluttered as she danced. She flung her arms out and spun in circles.

"Spring is here at last!" She screamed at the sky. Her long hair was flung straight out by the force of her whirling. He stopped walking and looked at her, shaking his head.

"Will you ever grow up?" he asked. She stopped spinning.

"Never! Life ends when you grow up."

Something was wrong. Why was her shirt suddenly green?

"Tracy?" he asked. She gave him a curious look.

"Why is your face green?"

He touched his face as if he could feel color. The black limbs of the trees caused an eerie effect against the green sky.

"I think we should—" He stopped when he heard a howling. A stray dog stumbled out of the bushes. He staggered and whined.

"Aw, what's wrong?" Tracy crooned. She dropped to her knees by the tortured animal.

"Don't touch him; he may have rabies," Charlie cried. She ignored him, as usual, and placed a gentle hand on the dog's side. The small comfort seemed to bring him more pain; he growled and snapped at her. She jerked her hand back. The dog continued to whine.

"He needs a vet," she murmured. There was a hissing, like air escaping, then a faint popping sound. The dog was there one moment, and the next, he was gone. There was the faintest hint of dust, then nothing.

"Where did he go?" Tracy asked. She looked around her. Charlie stared and stared at the spot the dog had just been. His eyes had seen it, but his mind refused to accept the conclusion.

"He— just—disappeared," Charlie breathed. "It's as if he —evaporated."

"That's nuts," Tracy got to her feet. "Animals don't just evaporate— at least not on a cool spring day—not even in the desert on the hottest day —animals don't evaporate!"

A tingling of unease started at the base of Charlie's spine and crawled up his back to tremble at the edge of his skull. He had an uncontrollable urge to run and didn't fight it. He grabbed Tracy's hand. "We have to get out of here!"

They ran for their town. Trees began popping all around them. There was chaos in the streets as people, animals, and buildings popped with no rhyme or reason; there was no warning; no way to know who was next. Children sat crying in the streets. Adults gripped their heads and dropped to their knees, shrieking about the pressure. With each new explosion, which wasn't an explosion, another building, another tree, another life was gone. The town was dissolving before their eyes, slipping silently away amidst the shrieking of the dying.

"We have to get to the shelter," Charlie said. She pulled away and ran to a child. She scooped him up; he must have been about four. His chubby face was wet with tears, his cries drowned out by the wailing around him.

"We have to save them!" Tracy cried. "Help me save them!"

"We can't possibly save them all!" Charlie shouted. The inhuman howling was deafening. He could barely hear himself over the noise. He pulled on his sister. Her eyes flashed fire as she lashed out at him.

"I won't leave them!" She grabbed another child by the hand. The child in her arms began to squirm and whimper. She lost her grip, and the child toppled out of her grasp but never landed. He was gone before he hit the ground.

"No!" She shrieked as the tiny hand of the other child disappeared. She looked at her hand as if it had betrayed her.

"Come on!" he shouted. He dragged her with him. They got to the shelter. She kicked and fought the whole way there. She jerked free at the door.

"We have to save them!" she shouted. She held her ground, hands on her hips like she used to do when they were ten. She looked like Grams when she did that.

"Look around!" Charlie cried. "There's no one left to save!" She didn't look. She leaped forward, shoving him in the chest. Caught off guard, he toppled back into the darkness of the shelter. The air whooshed from his lungs, and his vision went hazy. The chain of his cross pulled tight for a moment before jerking free.

"I love you, brother," she said as the door slammed, shutting out all of the hideous green light.

Charlie scrambled to his feet and staggered up the steps to the door. He pounded until his fists ached.

"Tracy! Tracy!" His voice grew more frantic each time he said her name.

"Traccccccy!"

⹋Z⹌

"Tracy!" Char sat straight up, slammed his head into the ceiling then collapsed. He held his throbbing head as he sucked in a sharp breath and hissed it back out.

"Tracy," he mumbled. That was the last time he would ever see his sister and that cross she had given him. The door to his capsule whipped open. Char jerked to the side and crashed into the wall. His heart beat in his ears.

"Out," Elici grunted.

"Oh, yeah," Char said. "Forgot."

He rolled over and squirmed out of the tube. He tripped, fell out of the capsule, and landed hard on his shoulder. The rest of his body seemed to fold up like a blanket. A slow clap followed his tumble.

"That was graceful," Kat said. She stopped clapping long enough to offer him a hand up, which he took.

"That's me, Mr. Graceful." He rolled his shoulder, testing for pain. It popped.

"Come," Elici grunted. They followed the four-foot-tall Sprout. Elici led them to a room where they were able to get washed up and changed.

Char scrubbed at the ingrained grime that had become a part of his flesh until his skin tingled and felt new. He reveled in the feeling and ran his fingers through his hair, which had grown longer while in suspended hibernation, and realized how much softer his hair was now that it was clean.

He found a new suit waiting for him. The material was light gray, soft yet durable, and very expensive. It was unlike any material seen on Earth. The design was similar to what they had been wearing when they boarded the ship. He pulled on the fur-lined boots, which laced up to mid-calf.

He stepped out of the cleaning chamber to find Kat waiting in a similar suit and boots.

Another Sprout led them to the bridge.

"Sir, I have Captain Mrah."

"On screen," Captain Gar replied. Mrah's emaciated head appeared on the screen. His gaunt face dripped with sweat and drool. His yellow teeth, razor-sharp, protruded from his mouth. His hot, red eyes, trapped in a permanent glare, stared hard at Gar. His mustard yellow skin had patches of long hair the color of dried corn silk. It appeared matted and coarse.

"Captain Gar," Mrah bellowed.

"What is it you have come for?" Gar asked.

"What is that?" Kat whispered. She leaned into Char's side.

"That is a Caparian," Char responded.

"You know what I came for, and you have them," Mrah answered. "If you do not give them over to me, I will destroy your ship. Then I will destroy your planet as I did theirs!"

Char felt Kat tense beside him. Her face had hardened, her eyes narrowed, fists clenched at her sides. Rage flowed off her in waves, almost tangible. He put a hand on her shoulder, but she stepped away and maintained her rigid pose.

"You can try, but you will not succeed."

"Then you leave me no choice." Mrah's face disappeared. Captain Gar turned to face them. His eyes reflected kindness as he addressed them.

"They have come for you. This ship is no match for theirs, but that does not matter. Follow me." Captain Gar walked quickly down the hall and entered a small room lined with doors. He opened the air lock on one of the doors then turned back to them.

"This is an escape pod."

"Another one," Kat grumbled. Char nudged her, willing her to be silent. She glared at him and rammed her sharp elbow into his side again.

"It has shields stronger than this ship," Captain Gar continued. "They can withstand four hits at maximum power before they give out. You will have controls with which to navigate—" The ship lurched.

Kat staggered. Char tried to catch her but was too slow. She slammed off the wall with a loud crack and a sharp gasp. She gritted her teeth, and her expression tightened into one of concentration.

"You okay?" Char asked as he helped her to her feet. She nodded but didn't say anything. She felt up and down her arm.

"Nothing seems to be broken," she said.

He put his arm around her, but she shrugged it off.

"Damage report," Captain Gar calmly spoke into a small box on the wall.

"Direct hit, sir."

"Shields down."

"Incoming."

Each voice was calm and musical. As if death itself didn't scare any of these beings. They could just as easily be reporting tomorrow would be sunny. Another hit shook the ship. Gar stood firm with the impact. Char managed to keep his balance, but Kat bumped into him.

"Get in." Gar grabbed two long smoky gray cloaks and handed them to Kat. "Here, you'll need these. It is winter in some areas. Now listen; engage the cloaking device as soon as you launch. Head for

Zortentearth, and no matter what happens, *do not come back.* Do you understand?"

They nodded.

"You must survive," Gar said, then shut the door. For a moment, they could see his glowing face then he was gone.

Once again, they were jettisoned into space.

KAT

K at watched in terrified silence as the Caparian warship shot the Zortentearthian warship. Captain Gar's ship shuddered on impact; black burn marks scarred the silver surface.

"Do something," her voice was barely a whisper. She pulled on Char's sleeve and demanded, "Do something!"

"Like what?" he asked. He was looking all over the control panel. His hand would hover over one button then flit to the next without touching it.

"I don't know, go back!" She hated the burning at the corners of her eyes. She balled her hands into fists. By sheer will, the burning subsided.

"I can't go back," Char's voice was low, with an underlying rumble. The muscles around his jaw pumped in and out.

"Why not?" She wanted to punch him. He pushed buttons and tried levers.

"I'm following orders," he mumbled, then more irritated. "Where's the cloaking device?"

"They need help." Kat, her voice just as irritated, punched a button, and their pod disappeared.

"How did you know that?" he asked.

"The picture on the button kind of looked like a coat," Kat replied. "Now go back and help them!"

"You risked our lives because the picture *kind of* looked like a *coat?*"

Another blast rocked the Droplets' ship. The pod shuddered in the shock wave.

"Help them!" Kat shrieked. She started flipping switches and pushing buttons, trying to get the pod to return.

"We can't help them!" He shouted as he grabbed her hands and held them tight in his own.

"Don't yell at me!"

Before he could react, a blinding white light filled the pod. He dropped Kat's hands; she raised one to shade her eyes and squinted into the brightness.

"What is it?"

"I think it came from Gar's ship," Char replied. The light condensed and formed a solid beam that connected with the Caparian ship. The whole ship went dark.

Then everything flamed red. The force of the blast shook the pod. Kat braced herself. The flames died, leaving an empty place with only pieces of the Droplet's ship floating in the darkness. The white flash burned into her vision, creating the annoying phantom light that followed her line of sight.

"No," Kat whispered. Her blood ran from cold to hot to cold. She couldn't tear her eyes away from the horror.

Char cleared his throat but didn't speak.

She forced herself to turn from the remnants of the ship to look at Char.

He stared in stunned silence, swallowed, tried to speak, closed his eyes, and shook his head.

"The force... of their own laser... too much for them..." His voice was deep, rough.

The tears burned again at the corners of her eyes. She hardened her heart, and the tears sank back into her body, burning the whole way down. Her fear and sorrow formed an icy hot ball in the pit of her stomach. Tears never brought people back from the dead. Her voice, when she spoke, was deep and flat.

"Get us to the planet."

⇝Z⇜

"We're coming in too fast!" Kat cried. Char's muscles strained to keep the pod under control. The shock wave from the blast had damaged the pod's controls. They careened toward the planet below.

"Hang on!" Char grunted. The tops of the trees rushed up to meet them. Kat braced herself for impact. Despite the speed at which they fell, it took an eternity for them to collide with the trees. There was too much time to think; to know pain, possibly death, was mere heartbeats away.

The pod crashed into the thick web of branches. The camera was the first casualty. The sound of wood colliding with metal filled the pod. Each branch slammed the pod, scraped, snapped, and dragged. There was a brief feeling of release as they broke through the canopy before they hit the ground.

Kat imagined a wave of dirt flying up over the pod. She squeezed her eyes shut. Everything inside her crunched up like an accordion; she was sure her joints were all molded together. Her head jerked down on impact, forcing her chin into her chest. She became acutely aware of her collar bone as her chin pressed against it. The downward motion was interrupted as the pod lurched and toppled end over end. She hit her head, and everything went black.

The slow climb back to consciousness began with the pain in her neck. Each new pain announced itself like a ripple from that center point. Gradually, she became aware of a throbbing in her head. She couldn't feel her left arm, and there was a sharp pain in her calf. Why was it so hard to breathe?

Something, somewhere, was ticking. Kat opened her eyes and saw only her hair. She tried to flip her hair but only succeeded in aggravating the pain in her neck. She wiggled her fingers and found she could move her arms with no problem, though her left arm was beginning to tingle. Good, it was just asleep. She brushed her hair out of her eyes and realized she hung by her seatbelt at an awkward angle. The pod must be on its side.

Her muscles twitched all over. The pod's front crushed down on her legs. She wiggled toes, shifted her legs a little, and groaned. The sharp pain in her left calf sent a burning streak to her brain, a warning not to move again, which she ignored.

"Char," Kat's voice cracked. A light in the back flickered. In the strobe effect, she could just make out the shape of Char's body. He wasn't moving. She cleared her throat.

"Char, are you awake?" She stretched to touch his shoulder and managed to skim his torn shirt. He didn't move.

"Please, God..." She aimed her left hand for the side of Char's seat, unbuckled her seatbelt, and managed to guide her body as it fell. She landed behind his seat rather than on top of him. Her legs jerked from their prison, and her right calf now had a wound to match the left. The searing pain was all she could think about as she crunched into a ball and gulped air. She gritted her teeth; the air hissed in and out. Beads of sweat formed on her forehead.

She checked her legs for damage. Both had gashes in them, but the left was longer than the right. The bones seemed sound. "At least I don't have broken legs."

She wiggled around until she could see Char. She grimaced against the pain but didn't groan.

The ceiling had Char severely pinned. His breath made a wet spot on the section of metal closest to his mouth. His head tilted at an odd angle. She felt around his ribs and discovered a sharp point that had pierced his left side. She brought her hand back covered in

Char's blood. She felt his wrist and breathed a sigh when she felt the pulse.

"Don't you dare die," she ordered. How was she going to get him out? If she undid his seatbelt, he would collapse completely onto the spike. She pushed at the metal surrounding him, but it wouldn't budge. He needed to be awake so he could help her support his weight.

"Char," she placed a hand on his shoulder. "Wake up. I need you awake now."

When he didn't respond, she turned her attention to finding something she could use to wedge against the metal. She snatched her satchel out of a pile of broken glass and searched for her staff. She extended it carefully and slipped it gently between Char and the metal.

She used it as a lever to bend the largest chunk of metal away from Char without injuring him further. His breathing became a pitiful wheeze.

"Kat..." Char followed his whispered word with a gut-wrenching groan.

Kat pulled her staff back and leaned in so he could see her. "Hey."

He turned his head and appeared to be assessing his injuries. Blood seeped down his forehead and coated the puffed skin around his one swollen eye. He winced when he discovered his punctured side, "Ow."

"Who taught you how to drive, huh?" She let out a shaky laugh. The relief that flooded her almost warmed her fingers.

"I didn't see you taking over the controls." He muttered as he tried to shift his weight. He sucked in a sharp breath.

"Of course not," she replied. "I didn't want to crash. Don't move! We need to figure out how to get you out of this mess."

"I think my legs might be broken," he said, ignoring her order to keep still.

"That will complicate things," Kat said. "I'm more worried about that skewer under your left side. How are your arms?"

He moved them and flexed his fingers. "They feel fine."

"Can you support your weight while I unfasten your seatbelt? Then I can help you move away from the spike."

"I think so, but I don't know if I can move my legs."

Kat worked at bending the metal back to free his legs. He grunted, and his face was tense, but he didn't complain. When she was sure his legs would pull free with no problem, she looked him in the eye.

"Are you ready?" Her voice was gentle.

He took a couple of deep breaths and nodded.

Kat slipped one arm around his back and found a safe place to put her hand on the left side. Char put his weight on his hands and used her arm as support. She reached around his front, released the seatbelt, and held tight around his waist so he wouldn't sink further onto the spike. She lifted with all her strength, ignoring the pain in her own body. Together they managed to get Char safely away from the protruding metal.

His legs couldn't support his weight, so she half carried half dragged him to a clear spot behind the seats.

As the pod was on its side, Char sat on a cabinet. He stretched his legs out across the wall, and his back leaned against the floor. He tipped his head back and closed his eyes.

"I think I pulled about forty muscles lifting you," Kat muttered as she examined his legs.

The right leg had a bone protruding from his torn flesh, definitely broken, but the left leg seemed sound, perhaps severely bruised. They each had black bruises already forming in various places all over them.

"I'll look for bandages," Kat said. The cabinets and shelves had vomited their contents on impact. She sifted through the debris, rescuing bandages from the broken glass and twisted metal,

and tossing away the crushed and useless medical ointments,

The light still flickered, making it difficult to see, but Kat was able to find everything she needed to make a splint. She crouched by Char and suppressed the gasp of pain.

"I'm going to have to set this," Kat said, not knowing how she was going to do it.

"I know," Char said as he braced himself.

Kat handed him a rolled-up cotton bandage to bite and looked into his eyes. His nostrils flared as air hissed in and out, beads of sweat formed on his forehead, a white line formed around his lips as he clenched his teeth on the bandage. With his single nod, she set the bone. The cotton muffled his howl as he passed out. The bandage fell free and unrolled harmlessly across a cabinet door.

Kat's hands shook as she splinted his leg. She was cold, and her fingers ached with every movement. It wasn't just her loss of blood; there was a crack in the hull somewhere letting in cold air. She remembered Captain Gar had mentioned it was winter in places.

The air inside the pod was filling with smoke. They wouldn't be able to stay here. She quickly filled her satchel with extra bandages, her collapsed staff, and anything else she could find that looked useful. She discovered a tent and noted it had straps in the fashion of a backpack. She also found a rock she was about to throw away, but her gut told her to take it, so she tossed it in the satchel. She looked at Char, still unconscious, and realized he wouldn't be able to walk. She needed a way to transport him. She leaned over him and whispered in his ear. "I'll return."

She stacked anything that appeared stable enough to hold her weight until she could climb up to reach the opposite wall, which had become the ceiling. The door was dented and wedged. She pulled her staff back out, extended it, and used it to ram the door until it broke free.

A cold blast of wind pulled the air from her lungs. She felt the remaining heat in her body dissipate. She pulled herself up through the hatch and closed her eyes against the wind and icy flecks hitting her face. She forced an eye open and stared in amazement. She caught some of the floating crystals in her palm.

"Lavender—snow?" Kat whispered. It appeared to be snow. It coated every limb, every stone, every protruding object like a thick quilt. Two or three feet deep, drifts just like winter on Earth, except it was the shade of lavender.

The gash in the forest made by their pod was already heavily coated in lavender. Broken limbs hung from the trees by splinters. Kat had never seen trees so enormous. Each broken branch was large enough to be a tree in its own right. The gouge they had made would have given her a clear view of the sky if the falling snow wasn't so thick. Black earth, turned up by the pod's skid, was quickly being swallowed by the snow. Visibility was only about five feet. Would it still be called a "white-out" if the snow was lavender?

"'Lavender-out' doesn't have the same ring to it." Her voice was loud in the stillness of the snow-laden forest. Her fingers were already red and numb. She needed to find something to help Char.

She slid over the side of the wreckage and landed in a deep, soft snowdrift. It absorbed most of the shock, but she still grunted in pain. Each tiny injury demanded attention. The sudden stop sent another jolt of pain from her whiplashed neck to her skull, intensifying her headache.

She scrambled out of the pile and trudged over to the nearest tree. She was grateful to Captain Gar for the fir-lined boots. The wounds on her legs burned like fire, and she realized she had forgotten to bandage them while she tended to Char. She passed low bushes, rounded and heavy with snow.

"Fascinating," she murmured. She touched the bark of a tree which resembled a Maple from Earth, except the bark was yellow, and the direction was horizontal rather than vertical. The most significant difference was the tree still had broad flat leaves, not in the shape of maple leaves. They were narrow at the stem and widened into a teardrop.

"A deciduous tree which retains its leaves even in winter," Kat mused. She blew hot air into her frozen hands and mumbled, "Should have grabbed the cloak."

She almost forgot the cold as she walked deeper into the forest. She kept looking back to make sure she could still see the pod. She found something like a coniferous tree with the longest softest needles she had ever seen. Not only were they long, but the tips were dull. She wrestled with the lower branches until she had broken enough of them off to serve her purpose. At least these branches were thinner than the massive limbs she had spied from the pod. If every limb had been that large, she would have had to carry Char.

By the time she had enough branches, nothing more than twigs on the grand scale of the whole, her fingers were cracked and bleeding. They ached just to bend. She couldn't feel her toes, and she sniffed hard against the real or imagined runny nose.

"I've gathered what we need to travel," Kat said as she climbed back into the pod. Her legs throbbed, and she resolved to bandage them before completing another task.

"How does it look outside?" Char asked. He was attempting to stand on his one good leg. He wasn't successful in hiding the grimace.

"You won't believe the color of the snow." Kat pulled her boots off to see the gashes better. Each wound started below her knee and ended mid-calf. She cleaned her wounds, bandaged them, and shoved her feet back into the boots.

She put the long strap of her satchel over her head. Her single treasure thumped against her hip bringing her comfort as it had for so many years. She picked up the tent and climbed up to the opening to toss it out into the snow. She pulled her satchel back off and tossed it out as well. Every movement throbbed, ached, and burned. She looked down at Char, "Getting you out is going to be fun."

Kat braced herself on the edge of the door and reached down through the opening to grasp Char's hand. Char's face turned red with the effort to pull his body weight up and through the door. Kat felt the sharp slice of metal cut into her left hand as it slipped along the edge of the door frame. She gritted her teeth but held tight. The tower she had built collapsed. Kat, in a burst of adrenaline, jerked Char through the door.

His upper body flopped over the edge; his legs still dangled over the empty space. They were both breathing hard, their breath revealed in frozen puffs. His hair was drenched with sweat and dotted with the lavender snow.

"I'm sorry," he whispered. He took Kat's left hand and placed his hand over the fresh wound. A strange fluttering started in the pit of her stomach. She pulled her hand back.

"I'm fine." She swung her legs over the edge of the pod and slid off into the snow drift. Char poised to follow but paused.

"Why is that snow darker?" He pointed to where the lavender had blackened with her blood, turning it to a muddy violet.

"That's my blood," she replied, vaguely wondering if there were dangerous animals in the area. "I forgot to bandage my legs before venturing into the forest."

"We should hurry, then," Char said. "We don't know what kind of animals are out there, but if they follow the scent of blood, we probably don't want to meet them."

He tried to drop over the edge without landing on his leg but yelped as he landed at an awkward angle in the snow. His face contorted, his voice a twisted gasp, "Think I twisted the good ankle."

"Didn't feel you had enough injuries?" Her tone was wry. She helped him get comfortable on the sled she had made from the branches. She covered him with the cloak that Captain Gar had given them and wrapped the second around herself. The capes were not only long but had many folds of thick warm fabric. She was warm seconds after donning the cloak, covered from head to toe, and the hood provided extra protection.

She lined up the forks from the several branches, got a good grip, and hauled Char along. The snow was deep enough, so she was able to pull him with no problem. He argued only a little. The pain and loss of blood dulled his sense to fight.

They trudged into the woods. The little light that made it through the trees was fading quickly. Kat found a clearing and set up the tent. Her fingers and toes had long ago gone numb, and she realized she was starving, but the need for sleep outweighed her desire to eat. Char had fallen asleep on the sled. She checked him every so often to make sure a little puff of air still appeared around his lips.

She finally got the tent up. Visibility was dropping at an alarming rate. She needed to get him inside before he was buried alive in the snow. She woke him, and together, they got the supplies into the tent.

"It's cold," Char said.

Kat blew hot air into her frozen fingers, leaving her nose buried in her palms, but the warm breath didn't last long enough to help the icicles in her nostrils melt. She picked up the strange rock she had found in the pod. It was familiar; she realized she had once seen a trader selling them. It was a heating apparatus, but she hadn't seen the need to learn about it since Earth had been so hot.

"This thing is supposed to heat up, like a fire, but I don't know how..." She trailed off as she focused on her task.

"Here, let me," he held out his hand.

Kat raised an eyebrow but handed it over without comment. The tent swayed with the wind; it whistled and whined. On Earth, the wind could howl, and it never bothered Kat, but somehow, it had a whole new eerie effect on this foreign planet.

"Did you notice the snow?" Kat asked. Char didn't look at her.

"Yep," his answer absentminded as he concentrated on the fire rock.

"Lavender," she said.

"Uh, huh."

"I suppose it's pretty in its own right," she continued. In her mind, she was picturing the soft white fields of her childhood. She saw her sister trying to run in the deep drifts. She would be up to her waist and struggling for all she was worth. Kat would laugh and hold her hand. Once she tripped, and the snow had swallowed her up. Kat dove in to save her, and they came up giggling. They dug tunnels and made igloos. "But I prefer the white."

Char looked at her, "So do I."

The rock glowed red, and heat filled the tent. They huddled close to it. It cast a reddish light across Char's face. Kat checked their bandages and replaced those saturated with blood. Char's wound on his side appeared to be getting infected. She didn't know what to do about it. There had been no salvageable medicine in the pod, and she didn't know the first thing about plants and herbs on this planet. She kept her face blank while she worked. Char seemed to be watching her, but she pretended not to notice.

"What's that book?" Char asked, pointing to the corner peeking out of her bag. She smiled.

"My single companion for the three years trapped in that bomb shelter," Kat said as she pulled the old leather-bound book from the sack. *"The Complete Works of Edgar Allen Poe."*

"Poe? Rather a depressing book to keep you company," Char said. "It's a wonder you didn't commit suicide."

Kat glared at him and stuck her nose in the air. "Do not insult my dear Mr. Poe."

Char laughed at her mock snobbery. "Come now, I'm sorry. Please read something."

She considered him a moment, not sure if he was serious. He grinned, which had a gruesome effect with his cuts and bruises, swollen eyes, and the reddish glow on the whole lot. "Please?"

"Very well," Kat said. She looked at the cover of the book but didn't open it. She didn't need to; she knew every word by heart. *"In visions of the dark night / I have dreamed of joy departed; / But a waking dream of life and light / Hath left me broken-hearted. / Ah! what is not a dream by day / To him whose eyes are cast / On things around him, with a ray / Turned back upon the past?"*

"Please," Char whispered. He stared at the glowing red rock, his voice trance-like. "Something else. That one depresses me. How about *The Raven?* I've always liked that one."

Kat smiled. "I like that one too." She covered him with a blanket and tucked it up to his chin. She wrapped one around herself and curled up. *"Once upon a midnight dreary, while I pondered, weak and weary, / Over many a quaint and curious volume of forgotten lore..."*

KAT

Kat closed her eyes and tipped her head back so the sun would warm her face. A fresh spring breeze filled her lungs and fluttered her hair. She opened her eyes and saw her family in the distance. They were having a picnic under the old oak. She laughed with joy.

"I knew you weren't dead!" Kat called. Her family smiled and waved. She ran to them. They kept smiling. She kept running. She ran until she couldn't breathe, but she never got any closer. Her family kept waving—mechanically—strange mannequin smiles on their faces.

"Mom?"

"Dad?"

"Mary?" Kat ran harder, but the distance didn't diminish. A white speck floated before her eyes. She stopped running. "A snowflake? But it's spring!"

"Mom?" Confused, Kat stared at the white flake in her hand. A lavender stain started in the center and spread to the edges. She looked back toward her family. They stopped smiling, stopped waving, and stared at her.

Her voice was small, "Daddy?"

They stared at her for an eternity while the white flakes fell around them like confetti at New Year. Finally, they turned and began packing up the picnic basket; their movements slow faces sad. Desperation welled inside her, drowning the previous joy. She started running again. Her family turned their backs on her and walked away. They took haunted steps, drifted like ghosts, but still, she couldn't catch them. The air seemed thick as mud, and she strained to push through it. A panicked, "Wait!"

They kept walking. Kat called to them, begged them, but they didn't turn around. The snow swept in, thicker, swallowing her family. Horrified, she realized all the snow touching her had been bloodied with lavender, and she was alone.

Kat opened her eyes. The remnants of the dream still clung to her like an invisible sticky web. She had the mild urge to brush them away, but that would be as useless an effort as brushing away actual spider webs. She had always hated having an invisible web wrap around her face in the middle of the woods. No matter how much she wiped at it, the feeling never went away.

She realized she was curled up close to Char, with her head on his shoulder. He didn't budge, but his gentle breathing assured her he was still alive.

The tent still glowed with the red rock, but she could tell it was light outside as well. The wind had stopped blowing. She could see the snow line around the tent and realized they were half-buried. It would be interesting getting out without getting snow inside the tent.

She sat up and stretched. Her loud exhale woke Char. He winced as he sat up and rubbed his eyes. He tried stretching but jerked his arms back down, cutting the stretch short.

"Ow," he growled. He pressed his hand against the wound in his side. "Forgot..."

"Looks like we're buried," Kat mused. She crawled to where the door of the tent should be, but without a seam, she was simply guessing.

She touched the top of the "door," and it peeled away but stopped as it got to the top of the snow. "How about that…"

"What?" Char asked. He leaned forward. Kat looked back at him.

"The door stopped opening once it met the snow line. Ingenious technology or frozen mechanics?"

"Beats me," Char shrugged. He tried moving his legs. His face turned white, and beads of sweat broke out on his forehead.

"Would you quit!" Kat scolded. "You're going to do more damage."

"Well, I can't just sit here!" Char snapped. He cringed again as he shifted his weight.

"I'm going out," Kat said, ignoring his irritable tone. "We need food and water."

"You can't go out alone," Char argued. "You have no idea what dangers are out there."

"We don't have much of a choice. You can't walk, and we can't survive without food."

"I don't like it," Char grumbled.

"Look, I survived for years on my own in that barren wasteland we called home. I think I can handle this place."

"Earth didn't have any wild animals to eat you," Char countered.

"It had vagrants who'd kill me!"

"But a vagrant could be reasoned with; animals can't!" Their voices rose with each shot. They glared at each other.

Kat pursed her lips. Fighting was pointless. She shoved her feet into her boots, wrapped her cloak around herself, and grabbed her staff. She crawled out through the small opening in the tent.

"I'll be fine," she bit.

Char started to protest again, but she touched the top of the opening, and it closed on his voice.

She stood on the surprisingly solid snow. It must have had a very thick crust of ice because her feet didn't sink as they had yesterday. Her steps were silent as she made her way deeper into the forest. The air was still and cold. Her hood slid off her head as she looked up. The trees towered over her, taller than even the mighty sequoias. The massive trunks could have housed two or three of the enormous redwood trees. Other trees were shorter, thinner, and of a different species. Even those were massive compared to most of the trees on Earth.

Each tree had an unusual color and texture. Some trees resembled coniferous; others resembled deciduous. Again Kat marveled at the deciduous trees and their ability to retain broad leaves in the winter-like climate. Some of the trees had needles so long and thick they resembled spears. The colors were like nothing seen on Earth. Yellows, reds, and oranges adorned the trunks where various brown, white, and gray shades would have been.

Every step seemed to pull and stretch her wounds. They burned, ached, and throbbed. She hoped her legs would go as numb as her fingers then she wouldn't have to feel the pain. A noise halted her.

"What was that?" Kat paused. Her breath appeared in little puffs before her face. She sucked her breath in and listened. "Water?"

She started to jog toward the sound of flowing water and skidded, flapping her arms wildly but to no avail. She fell on her hands and knees, staring at her hands as she slid helplessly across the ice. Mini ripples raced away from each finger as they plowed through the thin layer of water covering the surface of the lavender snow. Her white skin was a sharp contrast to the color. She could do nothing to slow her slide. She waited, body rigid until she came to a stop at the base of another gigantic tree.

She decided *walking* toward the sound of water was a better idea. With the help of the sturdy tree, she pulled herself to her feet. She tugged at her wet clothing, breaking the suction to her skin, and tucked her freezing hands under her arms. Her knees ached with the cold.

The bubbling of the water grew steadily louder, but the river never popped into view. The massive trees obstructed everything, and skirting them took so much time.

"Stupid trees," she mumbled as she trudged around yet another tree that would put the mighty sequoia to shame. She slipped again, caught herself on the tree, pulling a muscle in her side as her feet shot out at a crazy angle. The bark on this tree grew horizontal and thick. It offered good hand grips and seemed much stronger than the bark on trees on Earth. She looked up into the branches high above. "Thanks."

Finally, she broke free of the trees. The lavender snow thinned, and the hard crust gave way underfoot. She plunged up to her knees, sighing as she pushed her way through the deep snow, lifting her legs ridiculously high to take a single step. She continued to follow the roar of the water. The snow continued to thin until it only covered her ankles. She almost laughed when she saw the stream. It thundered like Niagra Falls but trickled like a stream and was—purple?

"Purple water?" Kat stood and stared at the rippling water. "A trick of the light?" Even as she said it, she knew that wasn't correct. There was lavender snow on this planet; why not purple water?

She knelt by the stream and dipped her freezing hands into the icy water. She cupped some and brought it to her nose to smell. Her nose was too cold to smell anything. It was definitely purple. She dropped the handful back into the stream and swirled her hand around in the water. It had the same consistency as water on Earth; it was just the wrong color. She shook her head and stood.

"I wouldn't want to try it," she whispered. She turned to head back into the woods when a thump caused her to spin back around. It came from the other side of the stream, which was too wide to jump. Another thump had her curiosity piqued. She cocked her head, tried to gauge the distance across the stream, and extended her staff. She backed up, got a running start, stuck her staff in the middle of the stream, and pole-vaulted across. She landed steadily on the other side. Either she was getting used to the jolts of pain, or her body was going numb. Either way, she hardly noticed the aches and pains from the crash.

She kept her step light as she approached the thumping. She backed against a tree and edged her way around a little at a time, crouching as she got to a point where she could peak around and see what was causing the noise. A creature resembling a lemur, but with lemon yellow fur and no stripes on the tail, knocked strange fruit from a tree. The shape of the tree resembled an ancient oak. The fruit was the size of a cantaloupe but seemed more pliable as it struck an object. None of them broke open as they landed. The lemur-like creature dropped by one of the hard-earned prizes and scratched at the surface. After creating a slit, it seemed to drink from the fruit. The sides of the fruit collapsed, and the lemur tossed it aside where it lay like a deflated and forgotten basketball.

Kat didn't hear a sound, but the bright yellow lemur sat up on its haunches and looked around. At first, she was afraid it had realized she was watching, but it didn't look her way. It turned and bolted. It was gone before she could process the danger it must have felt. She stepped away from her hiding place and looked around. She still didn't hear anything, but that didn't stop the tingling on the back of her neck. She did a front spin with her staff as she scanned the area for danger.

Another creature the size of a German shepherd stepped into view. It was cat-like in body structure and fur, but the snout was longer like a dog's, and the ears were large and pointed. It had cat-like paws, but the tail was bushy like a squirrel. It took a step closer. Kat kept her footing ready for battle. She spun her staff again.

She didn't want to have to fight, let alone kill, any of the life on this planet. Her mind raced. Should she back away slowly? Keep her eyes averted? Was this like meeting a bear? Would playing dead work? The creature lifted its nose to the sky and howled like a wolf. Kat shivered at the eerie sound. She swallowed hard as she realized more of the alien animals were surrounding her.

"Great. Pack hunters," she mumbled. She took an involuntary step back as she surveyed the area. They were all around her, six that she could see. Not all were as large as the German shepherd, but they were still big. She spun her staff again. They seemed to take this as a threat because they attacked. She didn't think, just let instinct take over. She spun her staff till it was impossible to tell which end was about to strike.

She caught one under the chin and sent it flipping backward. Another she rammed in the soft underbelly as it was leaping at her. All she could see was fur, teeth, and claws. They came at her from every direction. Still, she fought. She felt the thud of each strike and heard the muffled thump of metal against furry body. The creatures would land hard but be back on their feet and leaping like a rebounding rubber band. Her arms tired quickly under the weight of the cloak and the trauma over the past couple of days.

She had no choice. She extended her blades; the flashing metal sang as it cut the air. She caught another under the chin, but with the blade, it cut the snout in half. The creature staggered back, coughing and choking. She didn't have time to analyze it, as another was flying at her. She impaled it as it leaped for her head; she continued the motion over her head in an arc. It slid off her blade on the other side and rolled across the ground.

One landed on her back. Her cloak did little to protect her from the sharp needle-like claws as they dug into her skin, rather like having a cactus jammed into her shoulders. Kat growled at the pain and backed the creature into one of the massive trees. She heard a loud crunch, and the screech cut short as she crushed it against the coarse bark. The claws dug deeper for a moment then pulled out. It fell off as she stepped away.

She spun her staff faster and faster until she imagined herself a cyclone of flashing, singing metal. She stopped. Everything was still. She was standing in the middle of a bloody battlefield. The blood mingled with the lavender snow creating a deep red-violet like crushed mulberries.

She felt sorrow for the lives she had taken. Strange yet beautiful creatures cut down like they were pests. "I am the first human to step foot on this planet, and the first thing I do is slaughter a herd of animals. Typical of my species." Kat said bitterly.

Her muscles twitched all over with the last of the adrenaline. Her staff felt heavy in her aching fingers. She jammed one blade into the ground and leaned on the weapon. She didn't remember receiving the injuries that covered her, but her shredded cloak exposed the blood that traced crooked lines down her limbs. She felt bone-deep exhaustion. If she were to lie in the blood-stained snow, she would sleep in seconds.

Her mind, numb, struggled to decide what to do next. The cold seemed to penetrate to the marrow of her bones. Her cloak was worthless against the icy air. A thin layer of sweat covered her entire body, making her uncomfortable. They needed the fruit, but did she have the energy to retrieve it?

Heavy breathing sent a jolt of dread through her system. Like an electric current, it sizzled down every nerve in her body. She turned to face another creature; only this one was much larger. She felt the blood drain from her face and ice in her veins.

It stared at her with yellow eyes. Its fur was white, with black patches like a leopard, but the white was darkening to an angry red. It rippled and pulsed like a heartbeat. Yellow eyes and pulsing red fur were intimidating enough, but when it opened its mouth to growl at her, it exposed long, sharp teeth, stark white against the pulsing red.

"No," Kat whimpered. No time for thought, it attacked. Kat stepped to the side, ripping the blade from the ground, and brought the staff up under the creature's underbelly. She cut a long red slit, but it wasn't deep. The beast howled but landed solidly on all four paws. Crimson drops speckled the ground under the beast.

Kat ran for the stream, the beast snapping at her heels. A massive paw hooked her cloak, clotheslining her. Her feet flew out from under her, and she landed hard on her back. She immediately slipped her head free as the creature jerked the cloak away. It stuck to the paw for an instant before being flung to the side. The sudden burst of cold sucked the air from Kat's lungs. She gasped and coughed but ran again. The creature leaped, and Kat turned to block the attack with her staff.

The creature hit her like a sledgehammer. She flew back and landed in the stream. The creature's front paws were on the staff, the only barrier between her and the gnashing teeth. She pressed up with all her might but only managed to keep the creature's teeth a breath away. The weight of the beast pushed Kat under the water, her bottom sinking into the riverbed. A sharp stone pressed painfully into her lumbar.

Her head slipped beneath the surface of the cold water. Every sound became muffled, except for the bubbles, her bubbles, her precious air escaping to the surface. She lifted her head to get air, but the teeth snapped in her face. She snatched a breath and jerked her head back away from the teeth, submerging her head again. More bubbles. It was a game, a sip of air, a taste of purple water which burned in her lungs and dodging deadly teeth. She was getting dizzy.

She pushed again and grabbed another gasp of air, but too soon. Water filled her mouth; she swallowed some, the rest filled her lungs. She coughed and sputtered, but she submerged again, so only more water filled her lungs. With one last burst of strength; she shoved the creature off.

She staggered to her feet, blind from the icy water and coughing up purple sludge. Her arms were cold and stiff with fatigue. She tried to force her eyes open, but they burned. She swung her staff, awkward and unsteady, and prayed she'd hit the beast. She felt it strike something, and the beast howled. The impact knocked the weapon out of her near frozen hands. Her fingers stung as the staff jerked free, and she heard the splash where it landed in the stream.

Kat abandoned her weapon and ran for the nearest tree. She used the horizontal bark like a ladder. Her fingers and toes were numb from the cold, but she forced herself to climb. Her adrenaline was fading, even amidst danger. She had reached the limits of her body. Her limbs were frozen, and her teeth chattered. Her muscles didn't want to cooperate; she pushed herself to climb higher but knew she'd never make it to the branches. She was out of reach of the creature but not high enough. She had nowhere to rest; all she could do was cling to the side of the tree. She pressed her face into the coarse bark. She was so tired, so cold. Her head ached like the worst brain freeze *ever*. She looked down when she heard the scraping. It was climbing!

She saw blood on the left paw. It was a deep wound that slowed the creature down, but it was still coming. Kat faced the tree again and whimpered. She had to climb, but her mind was sluggish and her body stiff. She was going to die. What would happen to Char? How long would he wait before searching for her? What would he do when he found her dead? *Would* he find her?

A deep throaty growl warned her it was close. Would it be fast? Would it hurt much? It raised a paw. *Father, please!* She closed her eyes. *Here it comes!*

The creature grunted, followed by cracking as the bark gave way, then a loud thump. Kat opened her eyes and saw the beast motionless on the ground. She released the breath she hadn't realized she had been holding.

"What?" Kat couldn't figure out what happened.

"Kat," Char's voice had never sounded so good. "Kat, it's all right. You can come down."

"Char?" Kat whimpered. This time she didn't mind the weak sound in her voice. She twisted around till she could see him. He leaned on a crude wooden crutch and held a gun in his free hand.

"Come down, Kat," he said again. Her fingers were locked, frozen.

"I-I d-don't th-think I can." Her teeth chattered so hard her vision jumped. As tired as she was, she couldn't let go. Her muscles started to shake, a deep tectonic vibration that started in her core and rippled out. She concentrated and managed to climb down a couple of feet before she couldn't hold on any longer. She fell the last few feet and landed on the soft furry body of her near executioner.

Char helped her get to her feet and wrapped his cloak around her shoulders. She shivered and leaned against him. He rubbed her shoulders and arms. She closed her eyes and let herself lean on him. He hugged her, rocking her gently, shushing her like a baby.

"It's all right," he soothed. "You're safe now."

The warmth he surrounded her with only accentuated the cold in her bones. With an effort, she pulled away from the heat of his body. The cold swept in around her again. She pointed to his crutch and managed a grin, though it felt as if her face would shatter with the effort. "What's that?"

"I thought this would be more useful than just keeping the tent warm," he said. "Like it?"

"It'll do." Her laugh was breathy and weak. She shook her head and stepped back into the water. By now, the cold in the water seemed warm.

"What are you doing?" Char asked. "You'll catch a cold."

"I'm already drenched, and I need my staff." She kicked around until she found it and collapsed it, tucking it back into her belt. Her cloak lay in a tattered heap on the other side of the stream.

"Purple water?" Char asked. Kat nodded.

"It probably isn't good for us."

"I should think not." Char said, "Purple is the color of poison.

"I thought it was green?"

"Take your pick."

"I like green," Kat shrugged and continued. "I found strange fruit on the other side of the stream." The idea of crossing the stream again and walking through the slaughtered bodies of the strange creatures silenced her.

"Kat," Char put a hand on her shoulder. "We should get you back to the camp and rest. We'll come back for the fruit later."

Kat shook her head. "No, we should get it now while we can."

She lifted her chin and stepped into the stream. Char limped along behind her on his crutch. Kat kept her eyes on the strange white fruit and ignored the battlefield. Char let out a low whistle.

"You took down all these by yourself?"

"Yes," Kat didn't look at him. She concentrated on each step. It was getting more difficult to move.

"Remind me never to get on your bad side."

"The fruit is up there." She pointed. The lowest ones were not high, but they might as well have been on the moon. She was too weak to climb, and Char could barely get around on his crutch. His face was pale. This fun little excursion into the forest was proving too much for him. "Are you all right?"

"I'm fine," his reply was clipped. "Any ideas how we can get the fruit down?"

"Nope."

"What about your staff? How long will it extend?" he asked. "It might reach the lower branches.

"Good idea," Kat said, pulling her staff from her belt and extending it; she released one of the blades. She sighed and touched the back of her hand to her forehead. Her stomach rolled, and she felt clammy.

"Are you all right?" The concern in Char's voice was unmistakable.

"I'm fine," Kat whispered, but she wasn't. Her stomach rolled again, and she was afraid she was going to be sick. Sharp pains shot through her insides as if she had swallowed knives. Something was carving her up from the inside. With an effort, she forced herself to focus on the task at hand.

Her staff felt heavy, but she managed to lift it high enough to clip the lowest branch. She severed one of the fat fruits. It fell with a strange fleshy thump. Char retrieved it and put it in a sack he had brought with him. She cut another and another. They gathered all the fruit she could reach with the staff.

"I hate to ask this, but," Char said as he looked at the dead creatures. "Do you think they are edible?"

"What?" the very idea of eating the creatures that tried to kill her turned her stomach again. She gagged and covered her mouth.

"Come on," Char said. "It isn't that bad."

Kat tried to get out of view before getting sick, but she didn't quite make it. Her hair fell on her face, and tears filled her eyes. She hated getting sick. She had always hated it. For some reason, it had always frightened her; solitary, helpless, and small. This time it was worse than ever. Her insides felt shredded, and she was afraid she would bring something up that was supposed to stay on the inside. The pain was agonizing, and every nerve in her body seemed to echo the pain. She stayed on her feet, willing herself not to fall to her knees. The next wave came, and she was helpless against it.

Char stepped up behind her and pulled her hair back. He wrapped one arm around her middle and squeezed; this, for some reason, eased the pain. Feeling his arm around her made her feel less alone and less scared. He didn't say anything. Finally, the waves passed. She felt weak and drained. He helped her sit by the tree and told her to rest.

He went over to one of the creatures and used her shortened staff as a knife. She saw his back as he worked. He seemed to be blocking her view intentionally. She knew what he was doing and didn't want to think about it. When he finished, he cleaned her staff with a chunk of snow. He was awkward in everything he did, with his leg in a splint. Hobbling around with that crutch, but he got the job done.

She felt wrung out like an old dish rag. Her body, limp, with no resiliency left, molded to the tree. The longer she sat, the more she felt as if she were becoming part of the tree. She couldn't move her arms or legs, and her eyes felt like cold marbles. Is this what it felt like to be a statue? She was just a sculpted piece of marble in a museum left over from an ancient civilization—the last standing testament to what once was. Proof Earth had existed, that man had existed. Years from now, beings from this planet would happen along and find her frozen here against this tree, part of this tree. She would be part of this alien planet forever. Her vision was dimming, and Char seemed to be worlds away. She wanted to call out to him, to say goodbye, to thank him, to tell him he was the last, but her vocal cords had crystallized, and any attempt at sound would shatter them completely.

"Kat," Char's voice was sharp and clear in her addled brain. "Kat, wake up!"

Her face exploded with a stinging jolt of pain. She couldn't figure out where it had come from or what had caused it. It felt as if it had dislocated bones in her skull. With more effort than it was worth, she managed to blink. Char was staring intently at her. His nose was inches from hers.

"Kat!" He shook her, sending shock waves throughout her body.

"Stop," she managed to mumble, though her voice didn't sound right.

He helped her to her feet, ripping her from the tree that was her tomb, and she felt the loss. She felt detached from everything, from the world, from her body, from life.

CHAR

Char grunted as he strained to keep hold of Kat. She was unconscious, limp, and heavy. He half carried, half dragged her back to camp; no small feat with a broken leg, not to mention the hole in his side. He leaned heavily on his homemade crutch. It supported both their weights quite well, though the ice made balance difficult. His leg sent urgent pain messages to his brain, translating into beads of cold sweat on his forehead. He fought off the dizziness, knowing, if he passed out, they would both freeze to death. The hole in his side stretched with the effort to carry the load, but he gritted his teeth and ignored the pain.

The sunlight never made it through the thick branches overhead. It was perpetually dusk in the forest, but the little light that seeped through was fading and the temperature dropping. Char just hoped the hard icy crust on the surface of the snow stayed strong. The last thing he needed was to sink knee-deep in the snow with a broken leg and an unconscious girl.

He stopped and heaved an icy breath that chilled his lungs, making him cough. His teeth ached with each breath, and icicles formed inside his nostrils. He curled his lips around his teeth to protect them from the cold, didn't help. His fingers and toes had long ago gone numb.

They were nearing camp, awkward and slow, as his grip around her ribcage started to slip. He had to get her inside and warm. He jerked her up and caught her, adjusting his hold. He immediately regretted the action as pain shot through his side. He may have ripped his wound anew.

"We're almost there, Kat," he couldn't tell if she was still breathing or not. "Hang in there."

Finally, they reached the tent, and Char managed to open it without dropping Kat or falling over. He dragged her inside the tent and promptly put too much weight on his broken leg. An electric shot of pain raced up his leg, jolted through his spine, and slammed his head like a battering ram. His growl rumbled deep in his chest like distant thunder. In his agony, he dropped Kat and collapsed beside her. He landed on his wounded side, sending a whole new wave of pain whipping through him. He clutched his injured leg, squeezed, and jammed an elbow into his side to press on that pain. He could *feel* the jagged edges of bone scraping around inside his leg, sparing with each other. With eyes clamped shut and gritted teeth, he waited for the throbbing to subside.

As the pain subsided, he released the breath he had been holding and gently let go of his leg. When he could move again, he inspected his bandages; blood had seeped through them. He wished he could change them, but they would have to hold out until he could find more or a suitable substitute.

Kat, the bags, and his crutch lay tangled in a heap. He rolled onto his good leg and pulled Kat closer.

"I'm sorry," he said, but she was still unconscious. Her breath was so shallow he couldn't feel it, but her chest rose and fell; she was still breathing. He had to get her warm. He got the wet clothes off her, wrapped her in his warm cloak, and piled blankets on her. He got the hot rock warmed up and pushed it closer to her. One at a time, he freed her hands and feet, rubbing them until they turned pink. Her hair thawed and dripped. He rubbed a blanket on it, sopping up most of the moisture. Only when she seemed to be warmer and her breathing stronger did he scoot back to rest. He leaned back and closed his eyes for a moment.

"Boon!"

Char bolted upright. He rubbed his bleary eyes, and mumbled, "Must have fallen asleep." The jolt of adrenaline faded as soon as it appeared.

"Mom!"

Char dragged himself over to Kat. She rolled her head from side to side, her brow damp with sweat. He put a hand on her forehead and snatched it back in surprise. She was hot enough to heat the tent on her own, forget the hot rock.

"Kat," he said. "You're burning up. Wake up," He wiped her forehead with a dry cloth. She didn't respond or indicate she had heard.

"What do I do," he wondered out loud. "Is it feed a fever, starve a cold or feed a cold, starve a fever?" Was that even a thing? Why was a tired cliché from every movie he's ever seen the first thing he asks himself?

She moaned and twisted. Her blankets getting tangled in her arms and legs.

"Forget movie cliches; think logically!" He scolded himself. "You're too hot. I need to cool you down." Char said. He ripped the blankets off her, shoved the hot rock away, and packed purple snow around her. She shivered and whimpered.

He mopped her face again with a clean rag. She grimaced. Whatever she was dreaming was torturing her. He brushed her damp hair away from her face and stroked a thumb across her brow. Her dark lashes were stark against her pale skin.

"When I saw you against that tree," Char whispered. "I thought that was it, that you were dead."

He closed his eyes; she had sat so motionlessly. Her unblinking eyes were staring through him. His heart had frozen in his chest.

"Fight this, Kat," he pressed his forehead to hers. "You survived for years on a dead planet. You survived when that planet was obliterated. You can survive this. This is nothing. *Nothing* compared to what you have already survived. So fight."

By the tree, when she was freezing to death, he had been so scared he'd slapped her to bring her back. That barely audible "Stop" was the sweetest sound he had ever heard. Now she was in danger of burning up.

"It's from one extreme to another with you, isn't it?" He shook his head and skooched back to his place by the hot rock. Staring at her would not help her. He needed to get some liquid into her.

His body demanded rest, but he shook the fog from his head, pulled one of the strange fruits from the bag, and examined it. In the back of his mind, he wondered what was causing her illness; was it simply cold, fatigue, and lack of food? Did she eat any berries while she was out? Did she try to drink any of the purple water? He tried to focus his thoughts on the task at hand. He needed to find a way to hydrate her.

The fruit was white and fleshy, large as a melon but not as firm. He pressed a thumb into the side. The rind gave like a water balloon and bounced back. By the pressure it took to squeeze the fruit, he could tell the skin was thicker than a water balloon but not as thick as a cantaloupe. He dug around in one of the packs and found a sharp instrument, something like a knife, but with an alien design and alien carvings on the hilt. He pressed it into the flesh of the fruit, and a clear liquid oozed around the blade. He withdrew the knife and stabbed it again, pulled it free, and repeated the process until he had a hole like the eye of a jack-o-lantern. He sniffed the opening, but there was no odor to the fruit.

The liquid inside appeared free-flowing, with no cell-like pockets trapping each drop as with fruit on Earth. He dipped his pinkie in the clear liquid and touched it to his tongue, a slight hint of bitterness like a green grape. His tongue absorbed that single drop like a starved desert floor. He found himself wanting to suck the melon dry, but a slender thread of caution wrapped around his mind. It's alien fruit; would it poison him?

He found a large empty water bottle in Kat's bag and poured the water-like substance into the bottle. The bottle filled to the brim as the rind hollowed like the sunken cheeks of a consumption victim. He cut the hollowed shell open; inside was the color of a plum. He sliced a small piece off and chewed it. He gagged on the extremely bitter flavor and unsavory fatty texture. He spit out the nasty tidbit almost as soon as he bit into it. The entire melon appeared to be hollow and without seeds. He tossed the rind aside and turned his attention on the bottle of juice. There was only one way to test the liquid. He would have to drink it.

He took a deep breath and let it out slow, before putting the bottle to his lips. The cool liquid coated the inside of his mouth; he held it, enjoying the feeling. He felt the refreshing cool liquid touch every surface the whole way down. When it reached his stomach, it seemed to spread out and line the entire organ like a fresh coat of paint. He took a single drink but felt refreshed as if he had never been thirsty in his life.

"Mary..." Kat mumbled. Her head tossed back and forth on her pillow. Sweat glistened in the soft light of the fire rock. Char looked at her. How long should he wait for the effects if it were poison? Should he sleep? What if he never woke? He dug around until he found the book she had kept with her. The weight felt familiar in his hands, reminding him of another book he had carried so many years ago. He shook his head at the memory. That was a lifetime ago. That Char was dead.

"Shall I read to you?" he asked.

Kat moaned and tossed her head. He flipped through the worn pages of the old tome. "How about a short story, *The Tell-Tale Heart?*"

He looked at her, but she made no response. "You're right. We shouldn't read about going insane. After all, the situation in which we now find ourselves is insane enough. How about a poem? I have just the one *To Helen*." He scrubbed at his eyes and began reading.

"*I saw thee once—once only—years ago; / I must not say how many ——but not many. / It was a July midnight; and from out / A full-orbed moon, that, like thine own soul, soaring...*" He trailed off, staring at the page without seeing the words.

"July..." He let the book fall closed on his lap. His eyelids felt heavy, and fog seemed to fill his mind. "I remember July with the hot sun and green grass. And... Tracy..."

Char lay back and put an arm behind his head. "Tracy..."

Flickering light. Char opened his eyes. The branches of the trees slipped by; the sun played peek-a-boo in the leaves. The rocking of the truck lulled him. He rolled his head to the side and saw Tracy. She was twelve again, and she watched the branches go by too. Tracy looked back at him. She smiled and laughed. This was her favorite part; laying in the back of the pickup while their father drove them out to the fields. The flickering of the light stopped with the tree line. They were out in the open sun now, warm on their skin. He sat up. Rows of corn, knee-high, zipped past. "Knee-high by July" ran through his mind. This was going to be a good year for corn. He looked at his hands. They were a boy's hands, not a man's.

The truck stopped, and Char jumped over the closed tailgate. Tracy stood in the bed; her face turned toward the blue sky. A breeze caught her hair and spun it. Later she would complain about the knots, but now she turned her face into the wind. She loved the wind. Her hair glowed like fire in the afternoon sun. She hopped out of the truck; it was time to get their hands dirty.

"Tracy..." Char wanted to touch her, but his arms wouldn't move. He felt too old for this body. A grown man crammed in a child's form. "Dad!"

The man with the same red-brown hair turned to face him. He smiled. "Here, son." Char ran to him. Father! Alive! He's just the same!

He still had the farmer's tan. His muscles still bulged under his shirt. Whenever he hugged his father, it was like hugging a boulder. He was solid.

"Dad," Char cried. "You're alive!"

Rows of corn whipped past as he ran faster, but he wasn't getting any closer. His mother stepped from the corn field and put a hand on his father's shoulder. Her hair, just as flaming red as Tracy's, was pulled in a long ponytail, ready for work. Her eyes, the same cerulean blue as Tracy's, shone with love. His father looked at her and lost his smile. Hers wilted as well. They both turned to Char.

He stopped running and stared at them, "No..."

Their stare became eerie. A shiver ran down Char's spine, and he felt cold in the hot sun. Their skin paled then turned pink with the rashes. Bulbous protrusions thickened their necks and under their arms, twisting them, turning them into grotesque creatures. They stared back without a word, tears in their eyes. His father put an arm around his mother, and they leaned on each other. His muscles atrophied in seconds, thinning him till he was a mere shadow of himself. His mother, thin to start, soon became a literal interpretation of skin and bones. The emaciated bodies created a sharp contrast to the hideous swelling lumps from their lymph nodes. Then the color drained out of them, and they were gray against the green corn stalks. They shriveled, their faces became hollow. They withered like a delicate plant in the harsh noonday sun.

He wanted to move. He wanted to run to them. He wanted to stop the inevitable, but all he could do was watch in horror as they crumpled like ash, and the breeze blew them away as if they never existed. A hand grasped his, and he looked at Tracy. She stared at the spot their parents had been. She looked at him with tears in her young eyes. In a single moment, he was suddenly responsible for another life—he aged decades in seconds.

"Don't let me die," her mouth moved, but the wind had increased. It snatched her words and whisked them away unheard. It spun around them like a cyclone. It picked the truck up and jerked it away. Corn *stalks ripped from the ground and splintered before them. The wind grew dark, angry, with dirt and debris. Tracy kept staring at him. Her red hair wrapped around her face, but her blue eyes peeked through and burned into him. They said she needed him, depended on him. He was the only one left to protect her.*

His sister clung to him. They were the same age, but she seemed so much smaller, so much frailer. They watched as the twister destroyed everything they had ever known. Then her eyes went wide. The twister had latched on to her, too, with the strength of a thousand bears. It wanted her. It wouldn't be satisfied until it had swallowed his whole world.

He held her hands as her feet lifted from the ground. She shouted his name; her voice lost in the roar of the cyclone. The same wind which she so loved now would be her destroyer. The pull was too great, and his grip was slipping.

"You can't have her," Char screamed. He gritted his teeth and pulled hard, throwing the full weight of his measly twelve years into it, but the wind was stronger. Her delicate white fingers slipped from his grasp. "Tracy, noooooo!!"

Char jerked to a sitting position. Sweat drenched his body. The dream clung to him like a vine. It grew over him, anchored him, imprisoned him in his nightmare. It was his job to protect her, and he had failed. Anger, deep and black, filled his body and mind. Its Stygian color infused his soul, coated it, swallowed it whole. It steeped inside him. He had let her down, just as God had let him down.

He shook his head and rubbed his face. The past is the past, and that Char was dead. Someone else depended on him now, and he wasn't about to fail this time. And he wasn't about to rely on a God who would claim love then turn His back on an entire planet of "His people."

He forced the dream to the back of his mind as he dragged himself over to Kat. She still slept fitfully. He realized he had slept through the night. He thought about the juice. "Well, I'm still alive. Must not be poison."

He took the bottle with the juice and lifted Kat's head. He poured a bit into her parted lips. She coughed and sputtered. He waited till she stopped and poured a little more. Again she coughed. He rubbed a few drops on her lips and lay her head back down. She wasn't getting better and needed medical attention that he couldn't give.

Once upon a time, he would have prayed, but now he knew that was pointless. After all, all those long nights he spent on his knees praying for his parents then, in the shelter, praying that somehow Tracy would have survived, went unanswered. He brushed a lock of hair off Kat's forehead. His hand was so dark compared to her pale skin; night and day, yin and yang.

"I will have to risk moving you," he whispered. He wrapped his cloak around him, feeling as stiff and achy as an old man. He gathered the small alien blade, a sack and climbed out of the tent. "I'll be back."

He leaned on his crutch and trudged through the snow. The upper crust had weakened, and periodically a leg would sink up to his calf. Each sudden drop jolted his injured leg and irritated a thousand other aches and pains all over his body. He gritted his teeth and kept going. He needed to find something on which to drag Kat.

"I need a sled," Char mumbled. He wasn't likely to find a sled randomly hanging out in the woods, so he would have to find an alternative. He stumbled across a large dead animal. A chill went down his spine when he thought about her out here all alone fighting the pack. The pelt would help keep her warm. He managed to get himself relatively comfortable beside the dead beast and worked at cutting away the coat of white and black fur. It was more difficult than he expected. There always seemed to be sinew or gristle or some stringy substance refusing to cut. He sawed away at each fibrous gooey string. The stench made him gag, and more than once, he had to stop, struggle to his feet and get away before he got sick. He was determined, though, and kept going back.

Finally, he got the pelt free of the carcass. He did his best to clean it using snow and rough bark to scrub it before folding it to carry. He was about to get up when he noticed how large the creature's canines were. They resembled the long teeth of a saber tooth tiger. He touched the tip; it was very sharp like a talon. He may be able to use it as a tool. He went to the stream and found a rock. He took it back to the dead creature and smashed the snout above the tooth. With a sickening crack, he was able to pull the tooth free. He hated mutilating this creature in such a way, but he needed what it had.

He walked until he found a tree with vertical bark rather than horizontal. He fingered the thick, coarse bark and figured it would slide through the snow rather well. It had some cracks in it, which he might be able to use to his advantage. He jammed the alien blade in a fissure and wiggled it. The bark snapped and popped but didn't come free. He spent the better part of an hour working at it. It was slow, exhausting work, but he needed that section of bark.

A loud, piercing cry shook the ground. Char dropped to his stomach and covered his head, not noticing the pain as he banged his bad leg off the tree. *What was that?* It was like the cry of a hawk but much louder. It boomed like thunder. Whatever it was, it sounded big. Bits of twigs and leaves fell from the trees like rain. After the debris had settled, he looked up at the trees, but the branches were too thick to see the creature. It was somewhere above the treetops.

He waited in the snow, freezing his belly, afraid to move. Something pointy was pressed into the hole in his side. The sharp pain brought tears to his eyes. They burned at the corners, adding another tiny sting to his list of agonies. The cry didn't repeat, and he dared climb to his feet. His hand shook as he whittled at the bark again.

Finally, he managed to liberate a large chunk of bark from the tree. It fell, like a door, across the snow. It was large enough to carry Kat, plus their supplies. He just needed a way to drag it. He left the "sled" and the pelt next to the tree and went looking for some vines.

He stopped by the stream and looked around. He didn't see any vines and hadn't seen any vines anywhere the whole time they had been on the planet. He spotted something crumpled on the other side of the stream and worked his way over to it. It was the cloak Kat had been wearing when she fought the creatures. It was useless as a cloak, but the material was still strong; he might be able to braid a rope.

He rolled it into a ball, gathered his supplies by the tree, and headed back to the tent.

⁓Z⁓

He spent the next day ripping the cloak into thin strips and braiding them. It took longer than he expected. He had to take frequent breaks; his fingers kept cramping. While he rested, he would read more Poe to Kat. She wasn't improving, and he felt a growing urgency to get moving. Finally, he had all the strips braided. He measured it by using his arm span as a guide. He had just under four arm-spans of rope.

"That should be long enough," he said. He took the saber tooth out to the large piece of bark he had dragged back to camp. He would use it to bore a hole through the bark. Just like cutting the pelt free, this turned out to be more difficult than he thought. He hammered on it with the rock from the stream and rolled it between his hands in a drill fashion, all of which seemed to make little progress. He worked at it till the light faded. He gave up for the night and crawled back into the tent.

His stomach growled. He pulled out the chunks of meat he had sliced from the dead cat-like creature. He had yet to try it. He worried it would make him sick, but if he didn't get some food in him soon, he would get sick anyway. He heated the hot rock. He hoped it would get hot enough to cook the food. He sliced the meat as thin as possible with the alien blade, laid the strips of meat on the hot rock, and was rewarded with a pleasant sizzle. The comforting sound reminded him of a better time, frying eggs and bacon, fresh toast with homemade jam, and fresh-squeezed orange juice. His mother had been obsessed with old-fashioned cooking, insisted on doing as much of it herself as possible. She wouldn't hear of buying a carton of orange juice or a loaf of bread. She'd get up extra early to bake and squeeze oranges. His mouth watered at the memory, and his stomach growled louder.

He poked at the meat with the tip of the blade. It was browning nicely. He stabbed it and flipped it. It smelled good. The juices from the meat seeped and bubbled on the edges. When it seemed thoroughly cooked, he cut off a piece and put it in his mouth. It melted on his tongue and had a buttery flavor, rich and tender. He barely had to chew. The meat liquefied and coated his tongue. The flavor of this meat truly deserved the title of umami. There was nothing on Earth to compare to the taste of this meat. He ate more. He ate as if he had never eaten before, as if he would never eat again. Only when he had eaten over half of what he had brought back from the kill site did he stop.

He washed it down with the melon juice. This flavor mixed and harmonized with the flavor of the meat. It sent his taste buds to a whole new level of enjoyment. He thought about the rest of the carcass in the woods. Would it still be good? Would it be decaying, or, due to the snow, would it be preserved? He would have to look tomorrow.

He checked on Kat again and lay down for the night. The lingering taste comforted him as he drifted into a dreamless sleep.

⁊

The following day, he discovered the bodies were not only frozen to the ground but iced over. No amount of poking and prodding would release even the tiniest morsel. He gave up and went back to camp. They would have to make do with what they had.

He worked all day on boring holes in the bark. He finally succeeded as dark fell. He quickly laced the ropes he had braided through the holes. He tied a buntline hitch and pulled it tight. He did the same with the second hole. Once he had his knots secure, he stood and gathered the rope and held it over his shoulder, testing the length. It was a good length, and he even had several inches to spare.

Now the sled was ready; they would be able to leave in the morning. He crawled back into the tent and packed everything up. They would move at first light.

Kat moaned and shivered. Her fever wasn't coming down. Char

packed fresh snow around her, then bundled himself up in the blankets and tugged the hot rock closer to keep warm. He stared at her face and hoped they'd find help soon.

⹇Z⹉

When he awoke the next morning, he noticed Kat seemed to be sleeping more peacefully. She didn't moan or shout out names he didn't know and lay curled in his arms like a child. When had she moved closer to him? He was careful to disentangle himself without waking her. He packed everything and loaded the sled he had made.

He wrapped Kat in as many layers as he could spare. Now that her fever had broken, he was determined to keep her warm. He tucked her into the sled and laid the cat pelt across her. Buried in material, very little of her face showed, just enough to allow her to breathe. He didn't want her getting frostbite in the cold.

He broke down the tent and used the straps to carry it like a backpack. He wrapped the last cloak around him and pulled the hood up to protect his head. He leaned on his crutch and pulled on the rope. The sled held fast at first, but once it gave, it moved easily across the snow.

They made slow progress. The sled seemed to catch on everything; tree roots, stones beneath the snow, got wedged between two trees, and each time he had to tug the sled free, he pulled the muscles around the hole in his side, or he put too much weight on his bad leg. There was no end to the pain. The ground was slanted; more than once, the sled shot forward and rammed his good leg. The snow seemed to be thinning as well. More and more stones were protruding from the lavender carpet, which only slowed them more.

"Are you doing this *on purpose?*" Char growled as he tugged it free yet again. The ache in his side competed only with the pain in his leg. All the other million minor aches and pains paled in comparison. He pressed on.

They traveled till they lost the light. Char set up camp, ate, gave Kat a little juice, read to her, and then collapsed in a stupor. They went on like this for days. They were running low on food and liquid. He worried Kat would soon die without food, and the juice might not be enough to keep her hydrated.

On the third day, they finally reached the tree line. Char noticed the light getting brighter and the trees thinning. He dragged the sled close to the base of another massive tree but didn't want to pull it out into the open until he knew it was safe. He laid some branches around the sled to hide it, then headed for the light. He didn't have to walk far before warm sunshine engulfed him. He sucked in a breath.

The sky was green! It shone a bright Easter green, like new spring grass. It rippled like water. He couldn't see any clouds, and he was surprised to see a single sun in the sky. "Aren't alien planets supposed to have two or three suns?" he asked aloud.

He could now see they were on a mountain. The lavender snow extended down the slope but stopped suddenly, as it collided with—water? It was blue with white caps. It didn't move like water, though; it swayed like wheat but looked like ocean waves. It couldn't be an ocean; he could see across to the other side. A valley filled with blue water?

The horizon was pimpled with red mountains. Another forest carpeted the base of those mountains. The wind whipped by, chill on his already frozen cheeks. In the midst of the far forest, he saw towers of some kind. They glinted in the sun like a beacon to a weary traveler.

"Well, we're weary, and we're travelers," Char mumbled. "So, that's where we will head." The side of the mountain seemed to be clear of any dangerous obstacles. Char considered riding down the side on the sled. It would be difficult to drag the sled down the side and control its descent with his injured leg, so riding it seemed to be a better idea. "But what if there's a drop-off I can't see?" Char mused as he cleared out the branches and pulled the rope. "What if we need to stop?"

He pulled the sled free of the trees and stood considering. He couldn't see any hazards to prevent a smooth ride down. He looked at Kat. He imagined her scolding him. She would probably be halfway down the hill already. The thought made him smile, "All right, have it your way."

He lifted Kat into a sitting position and sat behind her. He leaned her back against his chest, so he could hold her as they descended. Perhaps he would be able to control the speed or direction with his crutch. He was about to push off when that same piercing cry shook the trees. He ducked his head and covered his ears. It was much louder in the open. A shadow covered the sled and extended down the side of the mountain. Only a cloud could make such a large shadow, but when Char looked up, what he saw wasn't a cloud. It was a massive bird that looked like a falcon but was the size of a Roc. It was circling them like a vulture!

Char used the crutch to shove off, and they started down the mountain. He prayed they would go fast enough to outrun the bird. In his mind, he knew this to be impossible; still, he couldn't give up. They picked up speed. He tried to use the crutch like an oar to help them along, but it jerked out of his hands the first time he tried. The shadow still hung over them, oppressive like the clouds over the *House of Usher*.

Massive talons dug into the snow on either side of the sled. A lavender spray surrounded them, peppered his face, but the sled slipped by without injury. Another ground shaking cry and the bird took to the sky again. The down burst from the wings felt like a hurricane wind. Char did his best to protect Kat's face. He couldn't watch the bird and where they were going at the same time. The shadow fell across them again. The snow was thinning, and the ground was getting bumpy.

The snow line abruptly ended. It raced toward them. Like noticing a deer too late to swerve, the sled bolted toward the inevitable. They hit the snow line just as the bird made another grab at them. Talons slammed into the ground, sending up clumps of earth flecked with lavender snow. The sled hit the dry land and flipped. He held Kat tight as they rolled and was acutely aware of every rock punching his side as they tumbled. The wound ripped open after hitting a huge stone. A loud splintering crack punctuated the death of the sled. The cry of the falcon drowned out the crunching of wood as it mounted the sky again. Another down burst of wind rolled them along faster. His head bounced off something hard.

Char couldn't tell which way was up and which was down as he rolled. He had no idea how close they were to the bottom; it was all he could do to hold tight to Kat. Another impact vibration as the talons struck again; in front of them, behind them? A loud ripping sound signified the grass tearing from the earth, or was that his flesh? They were still rolling. Another cry and the bird took flight. Another burst of wind caught them and, this time, sent them flying.

KAT

Dark. Cold. The darkness was tangible, like liquid, but Kat could breathe. She wasn't standing or sitting but somehow suspended. Adrift, somewhere between the bottom of a murky pool and the surface of the water. She strained to see, opening her eyes wider and wider, yet the darkness engulfed her. Seeped into her, becoming part of her essence.

Bubbles. The sound of a stone dropped in deep water—unseen gurgling in the dark.

Where am I? More bubbles and heat. Searing heat. The liquid around her roiled. The sound of hundreds of stones dropped in deep water. I'm being boiled alive!

A light—dim at first, then brighter. In the light was a face. Fuzzy, unfocused, but a face Kat knew. Mom? The face faded back into the dark.

So hot. Why was it so hot? Another face, her father, faded away. More faces, coming faster now, appearing for only moments then vanishing again. Her parents, Mary and Boon. Friends, family, and loved ones; scenes from Earth; swirling around her, lighting up the dark, and *fading just as quickly. New buds in spring. Green trees under a hot July sun. The burning colors of fall and the cooling white of winter. Life, breath, and home. All while she boils to death.*

Am I dying? Is this what it was like to have her life flash before her eyes?

"Kat..."

A voice! Not familiar. Beautiful, like a song. All the faces dissolved, and darkness swooped in to blind her.

"You must swim, Kat."

Where? How?

"Swim for the surface. Swim!"

Kat released a breath, and bubbles formed. They rolled down her chin. Suddenly she couldn't breathe; pressure on her nostrils, the feeling of water fighting against the air in her nose. If the bubbles rolled down her chin, she must be upside down! She swung her arms in a wide circle, tucking her butt down and keeping her legs straight. She curled her legs in and thrust them down. She blew more bubbles, releasing precious oxygen. Her lungs pumped, strained, but she refused to give them what they needed.

The bubbles rolled up her face, bouncing off her nose, and sliding across her eyes. She tipped her face up and kicked. She pointed her hands up and drew a horseshoe around her as she pulled her way up. She kicked and pulled and climbed. She felt the buoyancy pushing her up, faster. Her lungs burned. Where was the surface?

"Swim!" Involuntarily her mouth opened, an explosion of bubbles, and her lungs sucked in water. Then she was choking. Coughing, but more liquid filled her lungs.

"Not yet!" the voice ordered in her mind.

"Keep swimming!" Kat felt dizzy, but she forced herself to give one last kick. She launched through the surface and sucked in the sweet air.

Kat opened her eyes. Lines; weird straight lines towered over her. Like lying in a field of wheat and looking up at the tops of the stalks; the strange illusion of falling, fast. The smell of hay, yet the peculiar tall grass was deep blue at the base and gradually got lighter toward the top.

Her head hurt. When she tried to sit up, she felt dizzy. She pressed the butt of her hand to her temple.

"What happened? Where am I?" She touched one of the blades of grass with her free hand. It had the same look as bluestem grass on earth, only it had minute barbs all over it and was ten or twenty feet tall. She stopped looking up; the optical illusion made her dizzier.

She climbed to her feet and promptly fell to her knees. Her muscles were weak, unsteady from lack of use and illness. How long had she been asleep?

"Char," Kat rasped. Her voice wasn't working. She crawled a little way, but it was too hard to navigate through the thick grass. She climbed to her feet again, unsteady, and the world swooped under her. She closed her eyes, but that made the spinning worse. She cocked her head to the side, which seemed to help.

She pushed the grass aside, it was thick, close, but she managed to squeeze through into the sunlight. It was warm, and the snow was gone. No, the snow was still there, but it was part way up a mountain.

"A snow line?" She saw bits of debris. Their things scattered down the mountainside. "What the hell happened?"

She climbed the side of the mountain to salvage what she could from their scattered belongings, but she soon realized her vertigo was too intense to continue. She breathed a sigh of relief when she found her staff intact.

In a flash, she remembered the creatures, the fight, and how Char had saved her—limping up like a battle-worn hero to kill the last alien cat just in time.

She found the crutch splintered against a rock. Cold sweat beaded on her body. *Where was Char?*

She looked back down the hill, but the field of blue grass seemed unbroken. She couldn't even tell where she had been lying. It was a breath-taking effect, the deep blue lightening till it white-capped on top, giving the whole field the illusion of ocean waves.

She worked her way down the hill. The tent was shredded. Massive gouges in the ground sent chills down her spine. What could cause such enormous cuts in the dirt? Had they been attacked? Had Char been carried off? Was he dead?

Her throat constricted at the thought as she stumbled back to the edge of the field. Her muscles were twitching from the effort.

"Char!" Kat shouted. Her voice sounded shrill. A wave of panic washed over her, and she had the urge to rip the tall grass from the ground with her bare hands. She balled her shaking hands into fists. She needed to calm down. It wasn't as if she had never been alone before. She just had never been alone on an alien planet before.

It wasn't just that she would be alone. If Char were dead, she'd be the last. The very last human. Her entire race, extinct because of aliens. Her heart pounded in her ears, and her head swooped. She pursed her lips, the corners of her mouth twitched.

"Kat." The voice was faint. Her heart leaped!

"Char!" She cried and bolted in the direction of his voice. "Keep calling! I'm coming!"

"I'm here." The voice was closer and to her left. She staggered as she ran. Every couple of steps had her careening in a bizarre direction. She nearly fell on her face three times. The grass grabbed at her, scratching and catching on her clothing. She tripped and rolled, almost landing on Char.

"Char!" Kat threw her arms around him and squeezed.

"Gaaa," he grunted in pain, but he wrapped his arms around her and squeezed back. Her throat closed again, and it was several seconds before she was able to force her voice through.

"I was so scared when I woke, and you weren't around."

His voice was weak, "Welcome back. I thought for sure you'd be dead."

Kat pulled back and looked at him, cocking her head. "What happened?"

His eyes were barely open, and his breathing was shallow. There was so much blood. Was it all his? She had to turn away from his leg, which was twisted at a grotesque angle. His head was bleeding profusely.

"You've been unconscious for days. Or has it been weeks now?" He shook his head. "Can't remember. The days here are longer than back home."

Fatigue sapped most of the energy from his voice. His eyes rolled, and his head dipped as he tried to talk. "I had to move you. You were dying. Had to..." His lids slammed shut, and he seemed to force them open only to have them rebel again and close.

"Shh," Kat crooned. "Rest now; you did well."

He shook his head. His lids snapped open; a flash of determination brightened his eyes.

"No, you need to know. We were attacked." He doubled up with a painful cough. She put a hand on his back. It was warm and sticky from the blood. She saw a flash of red on his palm before he closed his fist to hide it from her. "Attacked by a massive falcon-like bird."

"A falcon?" Kat asked. Char shook his head and held his arms out wide.

"Huge—" The word was distorted by his next round of coughing. It was obvious he had severe internal damage and probably internal bleeding. He was going to drown in his blood, and there was nothing she could do about it. Her insides quivered from more than just her injuries and alien illness.

A deep, piercing cry shook the ground. Kat ducked and clamped her hands over her ears. She turned her head to look at Char.

His eyes widened in fear. He pulled Kat close to him as if he was in any condition to protect her. A down burst of wind shoved the grass to the side. They were exposed for moments before the grass came snapping back up to cover them once more. Just before the waves of grass came crashing over them, she caught a glimpse of the falcon. She had never seen anything so huge! She had heard of mythical Roc's, but this seemed bigger.

She looked at Char. He wouldn't survive another attack. She had to lure the bird away from him. He seemed to read her mind and shook his head. His eyes widened again, this time with worry for her. He put a feeble hand on her arm. His eyes seemed to plead, "stay."

"I'll be all right. You've protected us this far. Let me protect you." She stood with staff in hand.

"You're... no condition..." another round of coughing. Kat cringed at the sound, touched his shoulder, and turned to force her way out of the field where she could see clearly. She spun in place, looking for the falcon, but didn't see it. Her spin was opposite the spin inside her head. The sun went behind a cloud. She watched the shadow drift down the side of the mountain before gliding over her. That's when she realized it wasn't a cloud but the falcon. She staggered as another screech shook the ground. It dove.

She extended her blades and aimed up as it descended. *Please, God, just a bit more strength.*

The staff connected with the bird, and it shrieked before taking off. The air pressure from its wings was like a hurricane blast. She jammed her blade into the ground and held tight.

She felt queasy, and her muscles didn't want to work with her. She slipped into a crouch, trying to catch her breath. She noticed the wound on her side. She must have lost a lot of blood. When did she sustain this wound?

She looked for the bird. It circled her but didn't attack again.

"What are you waiting for?" she screamed. "Attack!"

It responded with another piercing cry but didn't attack. The ground shook again, and Kat dropped to one knee.

"'Be that word our sign of parting, bird or fiend!' I shrieked, upstarting – ... 'Leave my loneliness unbroken! –'" Blood ran down her legs, and her hands slipped on her staff. That last attack, the bird must have made some kind of contact because she didn't remember waking with all this blood on her. But why hadn't she felt it?

The falcon swooped again but landed rather than attacked.

Kat pulled herself to her feet, yanked the staff from the ground, and spun it as a warning. It was all she could do to stand, and she had no idea if the spin was straight or not. The bird had every feature of a falcon. Quick short movements, cocking of the head as it looked at her.

It was simply massive. She saw a tiny cut where her staff had made contact. A trickle of blood flowed from its wound.

"What do you want?" Kat swayed on her feet. *No, mustn't... mustn't pass out...* Her vision blurred. *"Quoth the Raven, 'Nevermore.'"*

Something was coming; other creatures. Tall, blues, greens, reds, yellows all mixed, making Kat's vision into a kaleidoscope. She squinted, trying to make sense of all the colors. One of the creatures seemed to walk up to the falcon and touch it.

The world tipped under her, and her vision went dark. *Char...*

⌐Z⌐

Kat stretched, enjoying the feel of silk on her skin. Her eyes snapped open. Silk? No pain? Yards of fabric hung above her head like a lavender sky. She pulled herself into a sitting position and gasped. No pain! Her wounds were all healed! She moved her arms and legs. She felt her side where her last injury had been, and she was sound. But how? And where was she?

Sheer lavender drapes surrounded her; she swung her legs over the side of the bed and shoved the filmy curtains back. Her feet dangled, making her feel like a child again.

She looked across the large room at another bed. It was empty, and the covers were half off the bed. They spilled across the floor like melted chocolate.

"Char?" She slipped off the side and landed on her bare feet with a soft slap. The tiled floor was warm. Her night gown was long with excess fabric. It swept the floor, her sleeves met her wrists, and the collar was lace. It was old-fashioned but beautiful.

She padded over to a door where she heard voices. She knocked.

The door swung open, and a female Droplet slipped out, shutting the door quickly behind her. Kat caught a glimpse of Char soaking in a mountain of bubbles just before the door clicked shut. His head leaned against the side of the tub; his eyes were closed.

"Come," the Droplet whispered.

"Who are you, and where are we?" Kat asked.

The Droplet was tall, as is the nature of her race. Her hair was long and brushed the ground. She had ribbons woven into it, holding it back in a long, thick, intricate braid. She wore a long flowing gown, white, with long wide sleeves which nearly touched the hem. Her eyes were a soft gray, with a prominent darker gray pupil and no iris.

"My name is Calypso," she replied in her sing-song voice. She drifted toward a door on the opposite side of Kat's bed.

"Nice to meet you, Calypso, but you still haven't answered my other question. Where are we?" Kat asked. She stood her ground, refusing to follow Calypso like a puppy. Calypso opened the door and paused in the doorway.

"Coral City. There will be plenty of time for questions later. First, I shall draw you a bath." She entered the room.

Kat looked around at the expensive antique furniture, which seemed brand new; cherry wood canopy beds, matching chest of drawers, and even a wardrobe. At a glance, she saw willow leaves and rose petals carved into the fine wood.

She peeked in the room Calypso had entered and found a large porcelain tub with golden claw feet. The room was small, at least compared to the bedroom, but still, it was larger than her bedroom from home. The walls had a serene picture of a waterfall hidden back in the woods. The sound of chirping birds and other earthly wooded sounds drifted in the air. Kat rubbed her eyes, thinking her vision was blurring again. Was the waterfall really moving?

Calypso filled the tub with warm water and poured in a lilac-scented bubble bath. Kat wandered over to the waterfall and touched the dry paint. It didn't appear to move this close, but once she stepped back, the illusion was back. "Fascinating."

"Calypso," Kat turned. "How are my wounds all healed?"

Calypso smiled and gestured Kat should get in the tub. "Where did all that furniture come from?"

"We made it," she replied. "Come, your bath is ready."

"From what?" Kat asked as Calypso drifted out the door without responding. The door shut with a click. Kat sighed and slipped out of the night gown and into the mountain of suds. Her muscles relaxed in the warm water, and she felt safe for the first time in years. She hugged her knees to her chest and stared at the waterfall for a few minutes.

She leaned her head back with her eyes closed, but as soon as she lay back, her bottom lifted, and she floated to the surface of the water. She sat up and forced her backside back down. She lay back and popped to the surface again. It was no use; she was too buoyant.

She pressed her hands and feet to the sides of the tub and walked her body down to re-submerge, but it took more effort than it was worth. How did other people just lay back and soak? She tapped her toes against the bottom of the tub. She eyed the dress hanging on a hook by the door. She was never one to soak in a bath, not even on Earth. She was more of a shower girl, and even then, she didn't spend undue time in the shower. She got in, got clean, got out.

Her fingers drummed on the side of the tub. How long was she expected to soak? The dress was a rich deep emerald green that shimmered in the light. The white trim sparkled like diamonds. She stood and grabbed a silver towel. How can they expect her to sit in a bath when there were so many things to see and do in this strange new world?

She quickly dried with the towel and slipped the dress over her head. It slid over her frame, molding perfectly to every curve. As if the dress self-altered. It was the perfect length. She twirled and looked down to watch the skirt flare. The bodice was form-fitting and a darker emerald than the skirt and the sleeves. The neckline was squared and trimmed in sparkling white. Next to the dress was a cloak of deep royal blue; the trim also sparkled like diamonds. She found slippers below the hooks, which matched the dress. She draped the cloak over one arm as she slipped out of the bathroom.

The door to Char's bathroom was still closed. She decided not to bother him. She peeked into the hallway. The corridor was long, with vaulted ceilings and massive windows which came to a point near the top. She stepped across the hall to peer out the window. She could see the city. The buildings interested her most. They appeared to be a type of coral, like pillar coral, only taller and more slender. They branched like trees, reaching their dainty fingers for the green sky. If a rainbow cried, its tears painted this city; each building had a different color, each vibrant hue.

Kat looked back at the door to her room and hesitated only a moment to wander down the hall. The floor felt angled as if she walked down a gentle hill. She took a few steps down, then a few steps up. Which way should she go? Up, she decided. She passed many doors on her right and just as many windows on her left. She climbed higher and higher. The slope never increased nor decreased. The incline was so gradual it required no more effort than walking on flat ground.

The long corridor ended in a single tall white door with silver trim. Kat brushed her fingers over the alien markings carved into the surface and tried the silver coiled handle. The door swung open without a sound. She stepped onto an expansive balcony. Slender stone, like blades of grass entwined like ivy, created an elegant railing. She put her hands on it and peered over the edge. She appeared to be in the tallest tower of an enormous castle.

She gripped the railing as the wind whipped hard against her. Far below stretched Coral City, and beyond that stretched a forest. Like the city, the forest trees were a variety of colors—splashes of pink and white, mixed with blues and violets making her think of spring. In contrast, the burning red, yellow, and orange felt like fall. The red mountains, the shade of blood smeared across white, far in the distance, created the backdrop to the rainbow forest. To her left, she spotted the lavender-capped blue mountains where they must have crash-landed. She could not see the scar their pod had created when they hit.

She swept the city again, taking in all the colors and strange shapes. She sucked in a breath; her heart thundered in her chest. The wind whipped her hair into her eyes. She impatiently swept the strands into a fist and stared at the island of green trees. In this ocean of color, a single island of green trees floated like a promise. Every nerve in her body demanded she go there. She needed to stand among the trees that reminded her of home. From here, she could make out the dark greens of conifers and lighter greens of the deciduous trees she so adored. Green! Green where it was supposed to be, on the ground!

She flipped her cloak around her shoulders as she spun and ran for the door. She followed the corridor back the way she had come. With each step, she ran faster; the incline helped move her along. The green isle floated in her mind. Green trees! She skidded to a halt when the hall branched in several directions; with no idea which way to go, she took the path that sloped down.

Blindly, instinctively, she ran. She let her heart pull her in the direction she needed to go. Each new branching intersection, she would pause for a heartbeat then take off again. In the lower passages, she saw more Droplets. None of them stopped her. She didn't know any of them and didn't care; she had to see the trees. She found the main door, a massive thing, fitting of a castle. The door was heavy but opened with little trouble.

On the other side, she found herself in a corridor of trees. This stopped her. She heaved a breath as she stared at the leaves. The trees were blue; the trunk a deep rich blue; the leaves a delicate blue glass. The light that filtered through the sparkling leaves colored the air in the corridor. She filled her lungs with the cool, crisp, and sweetly scented air. The trees were breathtakingly beautiful. Truly alien and deserving of praise in their own right, but they were wrong. All wrong! They needed to be green! They needed rough brown bark and vibrant green leaves! The bark on these trees was smooth as glass, and the leaves clinked like champagne glasses, like thousands of champagne glasses, like fancy wind chimes.

She ran again. She was huffing by the time she reached the end of the champagne trees. She leaned against the last blue tree and sucked in air as if she had just burst from the depths of the ocean.

Droplets and Sprouts passed without acknowledging her existence. She merged with the masses and was swept along in the current of life. She passed through something of a market. Colorful stalls filled with the vendors' wares lined the streets. Droplets bartered for their goods while Sprouts stood by awaiting orders. Banners, of all different colors and lettered with strange alien characters, flew over each stall.

She stopped by a Droplet and watched as he bartered for a bolt of cloth. After some dickering, the Droplet purchasing the bolt handed over a tool resembling a shovel, with a pick-ax at the other end and a bag of something. The Droplet selling the bolt handed the bolt over to the purchaser. The material glimmered like fine silk; the ends fluttered like feathers on the wind. Kat walked away. There was no exchange of money; interesting.

She passed stands selling farming tools, fruits, jewelry, and more goods that she didn't recognize. Nothing caught her fancy; nothing held her interest; nothing dampened her desire to see those trees. Not that she had anything with which to barter, even if she found something she wanted.

She had to find those trees. But the buildings were taller than she expected. They were not shabby little huts but slender tendril-like mini castles. She turned back to see the main castle she had left and caught her breath again.

It was much larger than she had imagined. Hundreds of towers reached for the sky. All the colors of this planet shimmered across the surface of the palace. Violet would beat deep, and hot then fade to lavender nearing white, only to have pink blush the surface and deepen to red, pulse out, lighten, then be taken over by the next color. She had never seen anything like it.

If she were a tourist, she would have been content to stand and watch those colors pulse across the castle, but what she wanted most to see was the green trees of home. She closed her eyes and visualized the welcoming green she had seen from her tower.

When she opened her eyes, she spotted a Sprout carrying a hoe and rake. The tools looked so earth-like that she followed. The Sprout seemed unaware of her as she followed him through the narrow, confusing streets of the city. Finally, they came to the trees.

They truly were Earth trees! She spotted maples, oaks, and pines just from where she stood! The Sprout disappeared into the forest. She ran after him, but as soon as she neared the tree-line, she hit something and fell back, landing hard on her tail bone.

She climbed back to her feet and took slow steps forward with her hands outstretched. Her fingers touched a wall she couldn't see; a barrier? She pressed her palms against the resistance and slid her hands up, but she couldn't find a top. The leaves rustled; she could hear them, but she couldn't touch them. Her throat closed, and she pounded her fists on the invisible wall. She kicked it, but nothing worked. It held firm.

She stood back and stared at the trees. Home seemed so close. If she concentrated, she could imagine she was in a forest on Earth; the trees before her, all that was left of a dead planet. It wasn't fair! Tears burned at the corners of her eyes, but she forced them back down. She added them to the ball of anger and hatred she kept hidden in the pit of her stomach. Poe again filled her mind as she longed to touch those beautiful trees.

"'The happy flowers and the repining trees / Were seen no more: the very roses' odors / Died in the arms of the adoring airs. / All – all expired save thee – save less than thou... / I saw but them – they were the world to me.'" Kat whispered the words. Her heart ached, her soul ached; every fiber in her body ached at the cruelty of the situation.

A Droplet stepped from the shadows in the forest. He stared at her for a long time. She stared back. He was not as tall as most Droplets, and his features seemed off a little. She couldn't quite put her finger on what was different. Individually, all the characteristics of a Droplet were there, but still, something about his air was different.

He stepped through the barrier as if it wasn't there. He watched Kat like an exotic bird and was afraid he would spook her into flight. The way he stared at her made her feel like flying. She stood straighter and squared her shoulders. He circled her, and she turned in place to keep her eye on him.

"Human," he whispered. His voice was melodic like a Droplets, but his English was his own, not a translator.

"Obviously," Kat said. "Why are you staring at me?"

"I've never seen a female human."

"Well, congrats," Kat replied. "Check this off your bucket list."

She wanted to be irritated, but she was staring as hard at him as he was at her. What was different about this Droplet? He seemed to have more muscle definition than other Droplets she had seen. He was beautiful in a way that was not the same as the beauty of the other Droplets. She looked into his eyes, and her heart skipped a beat. Unlike a typical Droplet, he had black pupils, blue irises, and pale gray where the white should be. She gestured to the trees and forced her eyes away from the depths of his gaze.

"Why?" she asked.

He looked at the trees briefly before turning his searching eyes back on her.

"Preservation," he said.

"May I see them?" she asked.

He shook his head slowly. "Restricted."

"Are you giving me one-word answers because that is all the English you know, or because you're coy?" she asked. He cocked his head.

"Coy," he repeated. "I do not know this word."

"Are you intentionally answering my questions in such a way as to reveal as little information as possible?" she asked, actual irritation tainting her voice. He smiled a wide, warm smile.

"I apologize," he said. "I did not mean to offend you; it's just when I am intrigued, I forget to finish a sentence."

She raised an eyebrow. "Well, I suppose, since I am not allowed to see the trees, then I will go back to the castle."

"Castle?" he said. "You must be one of the humans they rescued from the wilds."

"Sharp aren't you?" she asked as she turned to walk away. He put a hand on her arm. She looked at the blue skin against her pale white. His skin was different somehow as well.

"Wait," he said. "What is your name?"

"Kat," she replied. "Yours?"

"Alexander," he said. "You can call me Alex if you like."

"Alexander? That's a strange name for a Droplet." Kat said before she thought. She kept her face solid, but on the inside, she cringed at her brashness. He smiled again. He held his arm out like a gentleman and asked, "May I escort you back to the palace?"

She had no idea how to get back to the palace and hesitated only a moment before taking his arm. They walked back through the narrow streets of Coral City and talked. She looked back only once as the green of home once again disappeared.

CHAR

Char opened his eyes. The water, once hot, had grown cold. The mountain of bubbles had long since sunk to a thin layer of suds floating on the surface. He lifted a hand from the water and looked at his wrinkled fingertips. The cold began to seep into his skin and wrap around his bones. He must have fallen asleep. He sighed and pulled himself into a sitting position.

He looked around the small room. The walls donned a serene earth scene, a field of wild flowers with running horses. The flowers were so life-like they seemed to sway in a breeze. The sky, painted bright blue, had wispy cirrus clouds smeared across the blue surface.

He eyed the clothing hanging from hooks by the door. They can't possibly expect him to wear such garments. He climbed out of the claw foot tub and dried with a silver towel. He didn't know much about clothing, but these clothes looked ancient, like something from a Robin Hood movie; sixteenth, seventeenth-century – maybe. He pulled on the deep royal blue, tight-fitting pants. He sighed as he pulled the light blue shirt over his head. It fell to just above his knees. He pulled on the matching royal blue tunic, noticed it was slightly longer than the shirt, and wrapped a lighter blue belt around his waist to cinch the tunic. Last he pulled matching boots over his feet. He tossed the emerald green cloak over his arm and put a hand on the door handle. He shook his head.

"If Kat laughs at this ridiculous outfit..." He mumbled as he jerked the door open.

He found Kat's bathroom empty, and she was nowhere in the room. His heartbeat quickened, and a drop of sweat ran down his spine. "She wouldn't have left on her own, would she?" he asked aloud. The answer was obvious; of course, she would.

He ran to the door and burst into the hall. The floor felt slanted but didn't look slanted. He stepped to the window, not noting the breathtaking view but judging the location of his current position. Even if she was within sight, he was too high to spot her. Would she have gone up or down? He tried climbing up. He found the balcony at the top, looked out long enough to see she wasn't there, then shut the door and retraced his steps. All the doors lining the corridor were locked, save for his room.

He quickened his pace as he descended. Where could Kat be? He came to a fork in the hall. Which way? He shrugged and took a left. He followed the path and at every split, feeling more and more like he was in a maze, trapped in a labyrinth straight out of Greek mythology.

"I'll meet the Minotaur next," he grumbled. He passed a door that blended so well with the wall he nearly missed it. The only indication of a door was a slender silver handle attached abnormally low on the door. He looked over his shoulder at the empty hall. Where was everyone? Why was he allowed to wander the halls unguarded? He hadn't seen anyone the whole time he had been exploring. He shrugged and opened the door.

He found himself standing outside. The heavy sweet scent of flowers filled his nostrils. Tall walls and the towers of the castle enclosed a beautiful garden filled with pink and white trees. They were eerily silent as their soft petal-like leaves swayed in the breeze. The pathway appeared to be maroon moss. Black and white flowers lined the path.

On either side of him stood tall trees that resembled evergreens on earth, except these were a deep purple. They towered over him by at least five feet. His steps were silent as he followed the soft mossy path.

Songbirds filled the air with their breathtakingly beautiful song. Char's heart ached at the sound. One of the soft gray birds landed on a branch nearest him and seemed to sing only for him. A lump swelled in his throat, and tears burned at the corners of his eyes. As he listened to them, he felt calm, safe, as if he were in the presence of God.

The path led him to the center of a garden, then split and circled a pond with three statues in the center. The trees continued to line the walkway all the way around. There were openings every few feet where a new path broke off from the main stem.

Directly in front of him was a small rectangle of ground, which extended into the pond. A stone bench, more suited to kneeling than sitting, rested in the center of the rectangle.

The water in the pond was dark and still. Something luminescent shone in the depths of the water like trapped stars. In the center of the pond was a brilliant white statue glowing in the light of the sun. The figure was of a Droplet, wearing a white robe, with its arms held straight out at the sides. The long sleeves of the gown draped down like wings. The head lay back facing the sky; the eyes were closed. To the right and left, and slightly behind the center statue, stood two more figures. Each with its arms held out but without the draping sleeves. They faced toward the center statue, pleading, with water pouring from their eyes.

"The statues cry," Char whispered. He circled the statues, taking each new path he found. Each branch took him to an identical clearing with a stone bench, tall enough to sit rather than kneel.

After exploring every path, he made his way back to the center.

He stopped to look at the statues again. The center figure looked familiar to him, but he couldn't figure out why.

"Why do they cry?" he asked, his voice, still, barely a whisper.

"Because they know the truth," the musical voice answered. Char spun around.

"Calypso! You startled me." he gasped, putting a hand over his heart. He had never heard her walk up. "What truth do they know?"

Calypso smiled at him, drifted by, and knelt in front of the statue. She bowed her head; after a few moments, she made a sign in the air and stood.

"Calypso?"

"You already know that story," she replied. "The question is not, what truth do they know? The question is, what did you learn from the truth?"

"What?" he asked, but she did not clarify. Instead, she held out her hand, palm up. In the center of her palm was a small round piece of metal.

"What's that? A metal tick?" he asked.

"A universal translator, it fits inside your ear canal. You will need it."

He took it and stuck it in his ear.

"Thank you."

"Remember your lessons, and understand." She turned and drifted away. Her words hung in the air, dissolving slowly. He turned back to the statues and sat on the soft maroon moss. He brought his knees up and wrapped his arms around them.

"What story? What truth?" He stared at the statue in the center.

"Do I know you? Do I know your story?" He closed his eyes, reaching instinctively for the cross that used to hang from his neck. He remembered one story. It seemed like ages, centuries since he'd heard it.

"I don't understand," he whispered.

"The grass withers, the flower fades, but the word of God shall stand forever."

His eyes snapped open, and he leaped to his feet. He spun, searching for the voice which whispered those words. He was alone in the garden.

"Who said that?" he demanded. His voice was loud in the still garden.

"The fool hath said in his heart, 'There is no God.'" A deep voice boomed in his mind. It was angry, scolding. It was not his mind's voice but another more tangible voice. It was inside his head and outside all at once. It filled him to bursting, spilled out of him like water, and surrounded him until he felt he would drown. A chill shot down Char's spine like a jolt of electricity. He turned and bolted from the garden.

He ran blindly. The words echoed in his mind. How had the voice known? He ran harder. He crashed into a wall as he turned a corner. His shoulder throbbed, but he kept running. *The fool hath said...* The fool! It was him! The voice was talking about him! But what was it? *Who* was it?

He had never said the words to anyone, not anyone. No one had heard the words from his lips! *No God. No God. No God.* His own words thrown back at him! He had never actually voiced them, never put them into such an absolute sentence in his mind, but that's where his heart had been.

For five years, since the day his cross ripped from his neck, that's where his heart had been, lying dead in the dust of the Earth, consumed by the vague notion that God did not exist. He had turned his back on God and walked away.

The fool hath said... The fool hath said... He slapped his hands over his ears.

He found himself near the door to the balcony again. He rushed through it, slammed it shut behind him, and leaned against the door. His skin was damp with sweat, and his clothing clung to the moisture. His heart thundered in his ears, but it couldn't drown out the words. He stumbled to the railing of the balcony.

"Leave me alone!" he screamed at the sky.

The wind, furious, gusted and shoved him to the side. He gripped the railing with all his strength. He squeezed his eyes shut against the blast. It was unnatural. The wind was like a thing; a beast determined to sweep him off the balcony. It wrapped around him like a blanket, jerked him hard. He was holding the railing as he had held his sister in his nightmares. His grip was not strong enough to save her, and neither was it strong enough to save him.

"Please..." Char forced the word out against the wind. The wind stole the word and whipped it away, taking his breath with it. "I'm... sorry..." he managed to push out, just as his strength gave way. The wind died almost instantly. He stood with his eyes closed for some seconds longer. His muscles twitched all over from fading adrenaline and the effort to hang on to the railing. Finally, he opened his eyes and, the first thing he noticed was the patch of green in the vast forest of color. His heart skipped a beat.

"Green trees!" he cried. That's where Kat went! He ran back into the castle. The echo of that voice tickled his mind and followed on his heels. He wasn't sure if he was running toward Kat, or from the voice, or both. The memories of the sound still vibrated every nerve; would it ever truly leave?

After following one endless identical corridor after another, he finally found his way to the main door. He sprinted toward it, but Calypso blocked him with a hand.

He skidded to a stop, irritated at her obstruction, and looked past her to the door. What if Kat was in trouble?

"Princess Aurora Jima requests your presence in the throne room," Calypso said in her native song-like voice.

"I can't right now," his muscles twitched all over, and he felt a thin veil of sweat coating his body. If Calypso noticed his state of unrest, she did not comment. "I have to find Kat."

Though her expression didn't change, the air in the room suddenly became oppressive. He shifted his feet and glanced at the door again.

"Why?" Char sighed. He couldn't decide which would be worse, offending the princess of this planet or losing Kat.

"About the future of the Earth."

His muscles went still. He narrowed his eyes at Calypso. "The Earth is dead. What future could it possibly have?"

Before she could answer, the door swung slowly open, indicating the weight of the massive structure. The sound of laughter drifted in, followed by Kat, and a Droplet Char had not met. All the days he had spent with Kat, he had never seen her genuinely smile. It spread across her face like a rainbow, touching her eyes and making them sparkle. Her whole face lit up. If she was beautiful before, she was breath-taking when she smiled.

She was so focused on the Droplet that she nearly collided with Char. Her eyes darted from the Droplet to Char, to Calypso, and back to Char.

"Oh, hey," she said brightly. Char had never seen her act so light and happy. He felt another burst of irritation and something twisted in his stomach.

"Char, this is Alex – short for Alexander. Alex, this is Char," Kat said.

She didn't say what his name was short for; then Char realized she didn't know. All that time and they never talked about themselves.

Char forced a smile that he didn't feel and shook the proffered hand. He hated how his hand was engulfed by the Droplets as if he were a child shaking the hand of an adult. He forced his voice to stay level and polite, "Alexander."

"It is a pleasure to meet you, Char," Alex replied in English. Char kept his expression neutral but was amazed at the response in his native language. The words had a more musical quality but, it was obvious, Alex didn't use a translator. There was definitely something different with this Droplet.

If Alex noticed Char's tense civility, he didn't react.

Calypso held out one of the universal translators to Kat. Kat took it and looked at Char.

"It goes in your ear. You'll be able to understand them." He nodded in Calypso's direction.

She nodded and stuck it in her ear.

Calypso smiled, "If you would follow me, please."

She turned and drifted away. Her long white gown trailed behind her.

Char was annoyed to see Alex fall in step beside them as they followed Calypso. Alex offered his arm to Kat, and she took it with a smile.

Char stared straight ahead and forced his jaw to relax. They walked in silence. Calypso led them to the throne room, where Aurora awaited in all her silver splendor. She sat upon a silver throne sparkling all over with diamonds. When she rose, she revealed a vibrant blue velvet cushion.

She wore a dress similar to Calypso's, except it was silver rather than white. Her sleeves were just as long, and the train poured down the three steps like a silver waterfall. Her soft green hair shimmered like silk and flowed from her head to the floor and pooled around her feet. She was a blue and green Rapunzel.

A pendant hung around her neck on a silken cord. Char recognized it as the Zortentearthian symbol resembling a "Z" with a "T" down through the center. Upon her head sat a silver crown with the same emblem interwoven with alien leaves and berries. Magnificent jewels of strange colors made up the leaves and berries. Colors with no names, colors never seen on Earth. Vibrant colors that would dull any color found on Earth.

Char noticed the royal blue walls rippled like the surface of a lake. The ceiling was so high he couldn't see the top. The floor was like marble, and their steps echoed in the massive hall.

Calypso knelt before the Princess and bowed her head. "Your Highness, I present to you the Chosen One," she made a grand gesture toward Kat, "and her friend," she gestured to Char. "Sole survivors of Earth."

"Very good, Calypso, you may go."

Calypso stood and drifted toward the door.

"Hold," Aurora's voice, though firm, was melodic, and the word danced around the room before fading.

Calypso turned back and bowed.

Aurora pointed at Alex. "Who is this?"

"He is my friend," Kat said. She placed a protective hand on Alex's arm. Char looked at her before turning back to Aurora.

"My name is Alexander," he said. He lifted his chin. Something about his pose seemed familiar to Char.

"Alexander," Aurora said his name slowly. "I know of you. You are not a full-blood Droplet, and therefore have no voice in this hall. Calypso, escort Alexander from the room."

"Wait," Kat took a step toward Alex.

Alex put a hand on her arm, "She is right. I have no place here." He winked at her and followed Calypso out.

Kat set her jaw and glared at Aurora. Whatever Aurora had to say, Char was pretty sure Kat would be far less receptive to the idea.

Kat folded her arms across her chest.

Not a full-blood Droplet; that would explain why Alex seemed different from all the others. Char felt his shoulders relax as Alex left the room.

After the room was clear, Aurora turned back to Kat and Char. "Welcome to Zortentearth. I apologize for not greeting you sooner."

"Why did Calypso call me the Chosen One?" Kat asked.

Char nudged her and whispered in her ear, "Your Highness."

Kat ignored him.

"I understand you left your room before eating," Aurora ignored the question. "You must be hungry. Come, we will fill your stomachs. Time enough to speak once we are all satiated."

Aurora beckoned them to follow and drifted through a small side door. Char looked at Kat and wasn't surprised to see the annoyed look on her face. Her sunny smile was gone as if it had never existed.

A massive silver table filled the smaller room. Not a blemish marred its shining surface. Char and Kat stood by the chair indicated and politely waited for Aurora to sit. She did, and they followed.

White pillars lined the walls, between windows, reaching to the twenty-foot ceiling and weaved through each other in an intricate design, which reminded Char of the Celtic designs on Earth. The windows had long, sheer white curtains that rustled with the breeze from one of the open windows. Floor-to-ceiling windows allowed the sunlight to enter and glisten on the table.

Char squinted against the glare. Aurora noticed and motioned to a Sprout standing nearby. The Sprout touched a seemingly smooth wall, and the windows darkened, dimming the bright reflection.

"Thank you, Your Highness," Char said.

Aurora nodded. She motioned to the same Sprout, and he left. The Sprout soon returned with a copper tray laden with fruits and vegetables. Kat gasped, and Char stifled his exclamation.

The food was Earth food! He met Kat's eyes over the tray. Was it real? She picked up a strawberry and bit into it. Her eyes widened in surprise. She popped the rest in her mouth and reached for more.

Char chose a piece of watermelon. He couldn't imagine them being able to recreate the fruit exactly as it had been on Earth. He had lived on a farm. He remembered cold watermelon on hot summer nights, spitting seeds at his sister and dodging her backlash. He bit into the watermelon. It splashed inside his mouth. Sweet and cold, as good as he remembered. They greedily ate carrots and broccoli, each piece perfectly ripe and ready to eat, but how? Where did they get food from Earth?

"Let us retire to the relaxation area," Aurora suggested after they had eaten their fill and the table cleared. The large room had a nook with three overstuffed chairs facing a blank wall. Aurora waited until they got settled in the chairs before pressing an invisible button on the wall. Char was amazed at how comfortable the chair was, like sitting on a giant marshmallow. The wall in front of him lit with an image of Earth.

It was the cliché image of a mountain with a cap of white snow and a green blanket of tall pines. A lake surrounded by wildflowers at the foot of the majestic hill mirrored the mountain. Birds sang sweet Earth songs, and cicadas chirped incessantly. Char felt a tightening in his chest. He couldn't seem to pull in enough air. He had so many questions, but he couldn't seem to fit the words into coherent sentences.

"How? Why?" Char managed.

"That is not important," Aurora replied.

"I know of your tragedy, of how the Caparians used their Particle Separator to destroy your home; also, of the second attack, when they snapped the asteroid belt and sent hundreds of asteroids straight to Earth. I also know why they decided to annihilate your planet."

"Why?" Kat asked.

"Mrah," Aurora let that one word hang in the air for a moment before continuing, "is a murderous creature. He cares little for life and less about the pain he inflicts on others."

"So, what is he? An interplanetary serial killer?" Kat asked.

"Oh, no, he has a reason for attacking Earth," Aurora said.

"Then what is his reason?" Char asked.

"He came to me for an answer," Aurora said. "And he did not like my answer."

"Why would he come to you for an answer?" Kat asked. "And that doesn't answer the question."

"We, as a race, know the future of every race, save our own."

"So, you guys are like cosmic fortune tellers?" Char asked. Kat jammed her elbow into his side. He suppressed a grin.

"What was his future?" Kat asked.

"One Earthling has the power to destroy the entire Caparian race."

"If one Earthling can destroy the entire Caparian race, why destroy plants and animals?" Char asked.

"Or even all the people?" Kat added. "Why not just kill that one person?"

"He did not know which being on Earth had this power, so he killed them all."

"He killed grass," Char raised an eyebrow, his voice flat.

"Just because you can speak does not necessarily mean you have the most power. There are many planets where the most powerful life-forms are small leaves similar to blades of grass on Earth," Aurora explained.

"Why didn't you just lie to him?" Char asked.

"We are incapable of telling falsehoods."

"So, don't tell him anything!" Kat leaped to her feet, her hands balled into fists. "You let him come to Earth and kill billions of people! And for what? To kill one person!?"

"I could not stop him," Aurora seemed unfazed in the face of Kat's outburst. Char put a gentle hand on Kat's arm. She looked at him and sat.

"You could have tried," Kat muttered.

"I knew he would not be able to kill the power."

"Well, you were wrong," Char was bitter. He had an urge to put his arm around Kat.

"No, I am not."

"Then who?" Kat asked. Aurora stared at Kat. Kat's hand fluttered to the base of her throat.

"Me?" She asked. Aurora nodded. Char looked from one to the other.

"So, Earth was destroyed because of me?" Kat slowly got to her feet and wandered over to the nearest window. She looked so small against the massive window, like a toddler in a mansion.

"In a sense, yes," Aurora replied, her voice still a silvery melody, neither loud nor soft. "But there is a way to save Earth, a way for you to go home."

"How?" Char jumped to his feet. He paced like an expectant father. "The Earth has been completely obliterated. There is nothing left to save!"

Kat's back was to the room as she stared out the window. He didn't know what she was thinking, but he was thinking of his family, his sister, his friends, and life as it had been on Earth. A life before vengeful aliens, before death, before the stripping of the once green planet. Was she thinking of family too? Of lost love? Was the hideous green staining her memories as it did his? Did she have nightmares of the asteroids punching holes into the defenseless planet? Why did they never talk about it?

Aurora ignored his outburst and kept her eyes trained on Kat. Kat was slow to turn from the window. She looked Aurora in the eye and whispered, "What do I have to do?"

"You would have to time travel into the past, to a time before the first Caparian attack to stop it," Aurora said. There was a fast flicker of something in Aurora's eyes when Kat responded. It was gone too fast for Char to figure out what it meant. Her voice did not change. It neither implied approval nor disapproval.

"Time travel isn't possible," Char replied.

"Oh, but it is," Aurora said.

"How?" Kat asked. She sat hard, and the soft cushion nearly swallowed her whole.

"You will have to go through the Zortentearthian Soul Separation ritual. It will allow your soul to move freely from your body. You will then leave your body behind and travel to the nearest black hole and enter it."

"Hold up!" Char had just sat back down but was on his feet again in an instant. "You can't send her into a black hole! She'll die! Nothing can escape a black hole; not even light!"

"You are correct. No *matter* can escape a black hole, but when Kat enters the black hole, she will not *be* matter, she will be—"

"—energy," Kat finished. Aurora nodded. Her silken hair shimmered with the motion.

"Yes, energy," Aurora continued. "In all of Time, you are the only one who has a life force strong enough to make the time leap through the black hole. You must use your energy to harness the energy from the black hole and propel yourself into the past."

"This is crazy!" Char felt a drop of panic spreading like a flood throughout his system. He looked at Kat. "You can't, seriously, be considering this."

"What will I be in the past?" Kat's eyes flicked to Char then back to Aurora.

"You will exist in spirit form. A ghost, if you will."

"Ghost of Christmas Future?" Kat quipped.

"There are no ghosts," Char muttered as he flopped back in a chair. He glared at his toes.

"Yes, there are, though not in the way you imagine. There are very few 'dead' ghosts. Most are just other beings who have attempted time travel and got lost or stranded. They 'haunt' your world, searching for someone to help them find their way home."

"You said Kat was the only one who could do this, and I quote, 'in all of Time,'" Char challenged.

"In all of Time, she is the only human who can harness the energy and control where she lands. Others can try, but all will fail. That is how they end up lost in time."

"What if she can't?" Char asked. "What happens then?"

"Then the Earth will stay dead, other planets will die at the hands of Mrah, and humans will become extinct," Aurora answered.

"No pressure," Kat snorted.

"There is a risk, though," Aurora said.

"*A* risk?" Char stretched the first word.

"If her body dies here, she will be trapped in the past, with no way to come home. Her spirit will ascend to the great being that created all."

"Oh, great," Char mumbled. He moved closer to Kat.

"You will, also, have little time. The human body is fragile and cannot withstand the separation from the soul for very long."

"How long will I have?" Kat asked.

"One Zortentearthian week, two Earth weeks, to accomplish your mission or your body will die." Aurora paused, then looked directly at Char. "The Caparians are sure to attack while she is in the past. It will be up to us to protect her body."

"How are we supposed to do that when they have the Particle Separator?" Char asked.

"The Particle Separator has limits. The operator can target specific people or items, but it cannot 'dig' below the surface. He could do it a layer at a time, but that would take too long. It is most effective when the green light can surround the target on at least three sides. Anything less requires more power and hits."

"That would explain why everyone in underground shelters survived," Kat whispered. Char looked at her. She stared at her feet, her toes moved inside the slipper, and one cracked.

"Yes," Aurora replied.

"What about the ocean?" Char asked. "How did he take out the entire ocean? Wouldn't that be like digging underground?"

"Water, being fluid, will absorb the light. If you swim underwater, you will see shafts of light coming from the surface. Essentially, the green light not only surrounded the water on three sides but filled it as well." She looked at Kat. "If we hide you below the surface of this planet, he will be forced to come to the surface to find you."

"No," Char was on his feet again in one smooth motion and stood over Aurora. His voice was gruff. "What right do you have to risk the lives of the only two humans left?"

He gritted his teeth and willed himself to stop shaking, but it was no use. His muscles were jumping as if electrocuted. Aurora did not reply. A gentle hand on his shoulder turned him to face Kat.

Her black eyes looked into his. Silver flecks in the irises reminded him of the stars in the night sky. He tried to swallow past the lump forming in his throat. He barely got his voice around it.

"This is insane. You could be..." Char couldn't finish the sentence.

"Killed, I know," Kat said. Her voice was kind, as gentle as her touch. "What do we have if I don't try?"

"We'll have each other."

"And what would we do? Run from planet to planet? Always looking over our shoulders for the next attack? Endangering any friends we make?" Kat shook her head. Char pressed his lips together. Kat didn't look away.

"I'll do it."

KAT

"What's your problem?" Kat asked.

Char shrugged. He stared out the window and took one step away from her.

"Are you mad that I agreed?"

"No," he mumbled.

"That was convincing." She faced the window, sighed, and took a step closer to him to close the distance. A dark-gray bird landed on the sill, chirped once, then flew away. Kat smiled a sad smile.

"I miss so much, you know?" Her voice was faint, far away, lost in her memories.

He nodded.

"I miss the way the green in the trees looked against the dark gray sky of an impending storm. I miss the way the air felt when it was heavy with rain."

"Yeah, and the days when the sky was so blue it hurt your eyes and the grass so green and soft, you could almost give up sleeping indoors," he added.

"Or the feel of the ocean waves and the wind so strong it could almost pick you up," Kat said.

He grinned now.

She liked his smile. She put a hand on his cheek and turned his head to face her.

He looked into her eyes. He seemed to look into her very soul and lost his smile.

"What are you going to do?" He asked. "How are you going to stop him?"

"I'll wing it," Kat shrugged. "It's what I do best."

"You can't just *wing it!*" Char cried. "You have to have a plan!"

"All right," Kat said. "I'll go back and stop him."

"That's not a plan! That's a goal!" His voice rose with each word. "You don't even know if you'll be able to communicate with the people around you. You'll be a *ghost,* for crying out loud!"

Kat shrugged again and, in a playful tone, added, "I'll think of something. I'll move stuff, write creepy words in the fog on a mirror, throw things, haunt my family until I get one of them to listen. I'll get them to notify the military."

"How can you be so nonchalant about this?" He grabbed her by the shoulders, forcing her to look at him. "There isn't enough fire power on the Earth to stop that ship."

"Maybe the military has a secret weapon."

"*Maybe,*" Char pushed away and paced. "That's your great plan? *Maybe the military has a secret weapon?*"

"You're ranting," Kat said. She might find this whole conversation entertaining if she couldn't see the pain she was causing him etched into his face.

"Look," she caught his arm to stop his pacing. "I could stay. Mrah could stop hunting us tomorrow. We could live for a hundred years, but we would have to live every day for the rest of our lives *knowing* we had this one chance to go back and *do* something about this crime, and we didn't take it. We would have to live with the knowledge that we could have saved them. We could have *tried,* but we just walked away. Do you want to live with that? Do you want to face *every day* knowing you could have saved lives, but you let them die?"

His eyes filled with tears, the muscles in his jaw pumped. There was anguish in his eyes that didn't come from her words. He seemed to struggle with his thoughts but didn't give voice to his internal battle.

"Even if I can't save the whole planet. If I can save just one more life. Just one more, it'll be worth the risk." She paused. He leaned closer. Her voice was just a breath, "I'm doing this so we can go home."

He nodded. Any closer, and their noses would touch. Her lips tingled, and her heartbeat quickened. He pressed his forehead to hers.

"I know." His voice was thick.

The door swung open.

"It is time," Calypso said. Kat stepped back, let out a breath, and nodded to her. She could still feel his forehead on hers.

"We're ready," Kat replied.

They followed Calypso down the serpentine halls. They didn't look at each other as they walked, neither did they speak. After, what seemed like twenty minutes, Calypso opened a door and gestured them through. Behind it lay steep steps. They descended into the darkness. Every few feet, an orb glowed, lighting the stairwell.

Kat lifted the hem of the silver ritual robe to prevent tripping. The last thing she needed was to tumble down a bottomless stairwell. They seemed to descend for hours. A light scrape had Kat spinning to look behind her. She focused on the sound. The others stopped as well.

"What is it?" Char put a hand on her shoulder. Then with underlying hope, "Second thoughts?"

She shook her head. "No, I thought I heard a footstep behind us."

"We must continue," Calypso urged.

Kat took one last long look back up the stairwell, willing her eyes to see what had made the noise. She shrugged and turned back to her ever downward spiral.

"This place is huge," she whispered to Char. He nodded.

She wondered why he was allowed to wear tight black clothing that moved with him, and she got stuck in this billowing robe. They finally reached the bottom only to begin another long winding tunnel.

" *'These vaults,' he said, 'are extensive,'*" Kat whispered to herself.

"What?" Char whispered back.

" *'The Montresors,' I replied, ' were a great and numerous family.'*" Kat let the words hang in the air for a moment before answering Char. "It's from *The Cask of Amontillado* by Poe. These tunnels reminded me of that story. Do you think they'll brick us into a wall too?"

"That's creepy, Kat," Char replied.

"Lucky for us, this place isn't as creepy as the catacombs in the story."

Calypso suddenly stopped. Kat looked for a door, but the walls were smooth.

"Calypso?" Kat asked. She smiled to herself at the thought Calypso may have forgotten the way. Calypso ignored Kat and pressed a spot on the wall. A door materialized.

The room they stepped into was soft gray, like the gray of the birds in the garden. A table engulfed the center of the room, with a single chair to one side. They were all the same color as the walls. There were no windows and only one door. Calypso motioned for Kat to lie on the table. Her heart thundered in her ears. What if this was a mistake?

She lay on the table, and Calypso arranged the silver robe around Kat. A line of Droplets drifted into the room, all with the same watery skin, the same silky green hair. They each wore a different colored robe; red, green, blue, violet, orange, and yellow. Aurora floated in wearing a black robe. The color of death? Great.

"We are ready to begin," Aurora said and then began to sing. Something slammed against the door that had just de-materialized. Aurora stopped her song at the sounds of scuffling and shouting.

Kat sat up; her heart nearly exploded with the shot of adrenaline.

Char, who had leaned against the wall, now stood straight. His muscles pulsed under his skin.

The door materialized. A wall of guards stood between the occupants of the room and— "Alex!" Kat gasped.

Alex shoved his way through the guards and stepped into the room. "Aurora, I demand you stop this!"

"You have no voice here," Aurora responded. She seemed neither afraid nor flustered by his intrusion. The rest of the robed Droplets stood unmoving. Creepy.

"Kat," Alex looked at her. He was not at all as calm and collected as his adversaries. "Don't do this. Let me take you someplace safer. The forest! I can take you to the forest!"

"Guards," Aurora ordered. They stepped in and took hold of his arms.

"No," he shouted. He struggled against them, but four of them had a hold he couldn't break. They began pulling him from the room.

"Char!" Alex bellowed. "Don't let them do this! I know you care about her; protect her! Stop this!"

Kat looked at Char's unreadable expression. His jaw muscles clenched and unclenched.

"I know why you're doing this, Aurora! *I know the truth!*" The guards jerked him from the room.

Kat shook all over; every muscle twitched.

"What did he mean?" Kat asked.

"Forgive him. He is half-human and allows his emotions to interfere with God's message," Aurora responded. "He does not understand."

Aurora placed a calming hand on Kat's forehead and pressed it until Kat was lying back.

"I don't know about this," Char said. "Kat, maybe we should discuss this."

"We will continue," Aurora replied.

"I said wait!" Char stepped forward and placed a hand on Aurora.

"We need silence to do this. If you cannot contain yourself, you will be removed until we are finished." Aurora did not get angry or flinch at the touch, but her voice took on a slight edge.

"It's all right, Char," Kat said. At least on Char's part, the growing tension was making her nervous, and it was difficult to keep her voice steady and sure. "I've made up my mind. If I have even the slightest chance to save Earth, I'm taking it."

Char's eyes narrowed, and his jaw clenched again, but he stepped back.

"Aurora, please continue," Kat said.

Aurora began her song again. It was in the Zortentearthian language. The mishmash of meaningless sounds that made up the words that were not words was full of meaning and emotion. The others joined in the song, each new voice – like ocean waves – undulating together, weaving a fabric of sound so tangible it wrapped around Kat's heart, making it ache at the beauty. Tears burned at the corners of her eyes. Her chest felt tight with agony, the kind of pain felt at the reunion of a mother and lost child. A sweet, uplifting pain of hope so dense it forms a hard pressure in the lungs.

Aurora took her place at Kat's head. Kat didn't look up at her. She kept her eyes focused on Char. He stood at her feet, his jaw set, his arms folded across his chest. He will be so alone once she is gone. She tried to send strength to him through her eyes. He didn't look away.

"For the strength of the mountains..." Aurora said in English. Her voice had taken on a deep mesmerizing hum. The Droplet wearing the blood-red robe sprinkled a liquid on Kat. It was warm like fresh blood but transparent like water.

"For the durability of the ground..." The Droplet wearing a blue robe to match the ground on Zortentearth, sprinkled a liquid on her right arm. The fluid was cold, like ice, but the color of fire.

"For the knowledge of the trees..." The Droplet wearing a yellow robe, matching the trees Kat had seen when they landed, sprinkled hot liquid on her left arm. Kat gasped and tried to sit up, but she couldn't move!

"For the freedom of the sky..." The Droplet with the sky green robe sprinkled a fine white powder across her chest.

"For the warmth of the sun..." The Droplet wearing orange covered Kat's body with a blue sand-like substance. Her whole body warmed.

She felt drowsy and had trouble keeping her eyes open. She tried to keep her eyes trained on Char. Stone-faced, he stared at her.

"For the hydration of the waters…" The Droplet with the dark violet robe dipped a thumb in a silver container and rubbed a black greasy line across Kat's forehead. Kat felt a wave of dizziness sweep over her. She wanted to wipe away the feeling of the Droplet's thumb from her forehead. She shifted inside her body, wanted to giggle because it tickled. The voices already seemed miles away. The deep hum seemed to vibrate her soul. She tried to talk, to at least say good-bye, but she couldn't connect that thought with her mouth.

"For the vast darkness of space and time, may they be at your command." Aurora dipped her fingers in a blue liquid and ran her fingers over Kat's lips. The liquid seeped through her lips, sealing them. Kat had the vague impression of the fluid being sweet.

She was unable to keep her eyes open any longer. She still felt fully conscious. She wiggled again and tried to sit up. The hum of Aurora's voice filled her and lifted her. She managed to sit up and gasped as she looked back down at her body. Aurora had put the blue liquid on her eyes as well. The black streak across her forehead glistened. The Droplets filed out of the room.

Aurora stopped to whisper to Char, putting something in his hand as she did. He nodded and walked around the table to Kat's head. He put a medallion around Kat's neck, which wasn't difficult since her body was hovering ten inches off the table!

"Remember, never remove the medallion from her body; she would come out of the trance too quickly and die." Aurora left, the door dematerialized behind her.

Kat looked closely at the medallion. It was the Zortentearthian symbol of a Z overlapping a T.

Char looked at Kat's body for a long time before sitting in the chair.

"What are you supposed to do?" Kat asked, her voice sounded hollow. Like an echo. Char shook his head, rubbed his face in his hands, then let out a deep, tired sigh.

"Guess you can't hear me, huh?" She stepped closer to him and snapped her fingers by his ears. He didn't move.

"Great, and I forgot to get directions to the nearest black hole!" Kat complained, her voice still sounded hollow. She closed her eyes, or she imagined closing her eyes. Did ghosts close their eyes?

She looked up at the ceiling; could she float through it? She jumped, nothing happened.

"That worked well," she said.

"I," Char's voice was thick, and he paused. Kat turned her attention back to him. "...didn't want you to go."

His eyes glistened with unshed tears. "Kat..."

Kat knelt beside him and placed a hand on his cheek. His eyes widened, and he brought his hand up to cover hers. His fingers slid through her hand to touch his skin. She pulled her hand away and stood back up.

"Goodbye."

She climbed on the table. "Excuse me—me," she giggled and tried jumping again. She still didn't go anywhere.

"How am I supposed to get out?" she asked. She looked back at Char. He sat with his head in his hands.

"Maybe I'm going about this the wrong way." She mused as she closed her eyes and took a deep breath. She pictured herself getting lighter and lighter until she just floated off the table. She gasped when she opened her eyes. She was floating near the ceiling!

She paused. Slowly, she touched the surface, smooth and solid.

"I must be able to," she mumbled. She tried to imagine it disappearing and touched it again. It worked! She closed her eyes as she floated through with little resistance, like swimming underwater, then she broke through the surface. Behind her, she thought she caught a whispered goodbye from Char.

Zortentearth was breathtaking. Or it would be if she had a breath to take. She saw it all at once; the tall red mountains, sheltering the valley of blue grass. A herd of unicorns of all different colors raced through the blue valley and gathered around the deep violet waters of a lake.

In the center of the large violet lake was an orange dragon-like creature! It lifted its massive head; purple water poured off in streams as it seemed to look right at her before snorting and dipping its head back in the water. Its long pointed snout snapped at something beneath the shimmering surface.

The bright green sky darkened as the sun dipped below the horizon to rest for the night. A gray bird brushed by on its way to its nest, seemingly oblivious to her presence. The tall yellow trees waved to her in the breeze. She floated down and touched a tree. She didn't hear a voice, inside her head or out, but she suddenly knew where to find the nearest black hole. She floated away from the tree, thinking how strange it was to have a tree know more than she.

"But it's one light-year away," Kat said out loud. How would she be able to get there before the Zortentearthian week was up? She didn't have time, or did she? Was time real, or was it an illusion? Was it man's creation? A way to measure the number of seconds he had to spend on Earth? Not happy with simply day or night, but he had to break it down into hours, minutes, seconds, even unto milliseconds. He was continually slicing time until it was rice paper-thin, measurements so small you couldn't fit a blink in between the segments. Filling his days with billions of moments smaller than a breath of a hummingbird; still, he cries *not enough time!*

She closed her eyes and tried to imagine the distance between her and the black hole disappear. Her mind's eye pictured the black hole, or what she thought it might look like, expanding as she flew closer. She opened her eyes and was surprised to see a black hole looming before her. She could still feel her heartbeat, but it was weak and far away. Her whole spirit pulsed with the rhythm. Would she be able to feel her heartbeat in the past?

She felt a strong magnetic pull and realized she was being drawn in by the black hole. Fear crackled through her. Her spirit popped and snapped like static electricity. What if she couldn't harness the energy? What if she was trapped in the wrong time forever? Or worse, trapped in the hole for all eternity?

Time seemed to stretch and bend all around her. It seemed to take eons to cross the event horizon, but suddenly, she was past it. She felt as if she had fallen into the maelstrom, spinning out of control. She was being swept away in the power of the hole. She tried to fight it, but it was too strong. She swam against the current, fighting, paddling as a swimmer paddles away from the inevitable waterfall.

"Don't fight it," a voice whispered.

"What?" Kat asked. She stopped paddling, letting herself get swept away in the current. It was faster than she had expected. She listened hard, but the voice did not return. Did she imagine it? Or had there been an actual voice in this vortex?

She closed her eyes again, focusing on the energy she possessed. She felt it pulse inside her. First small and weak against the power of the hole, but it grew. It became tangible, something she could hang onto, like a racing stallion. It pulsed around her, threaded with her energy, combining and dancing until the two were indistinguishable.

She focused all of her thoughts on the faces of the loved ones she had lost. Her desire to see them again filled her, overflowed from her. Faces and memories spilled from her like photos falling from the pages of an album.

Then there was a wind, strong and fast, whipping past her. She opened her eyes. The wind was time itself unwinding before her. Numbers and dates, tiny like sand, flowed past too fast to read; not around her, more like through her. Her mind, like a filter, sifted through the sand. The numbers morphed into faces. Millions of faces full of smiles and tears, joy and anguish. Centuries of faces rushed through her like a tidal wave. How would she ever find them in this ocean of faces?

She concentrated on one of the faces she wanted to see most. The one that had simultaneously saved her life and doomed it. She etched his face in her mind, coloring in his brown eyes and shoulder-length brown hair. Smiling at the nickname she had always called him because of his fake coonskin cap.

"Boon," Kat said. With that one word, the world came into sharp focus. She had a sensation of landing, a brief impact that didn't hurt. Happiness shot through her like an adrenaline rush.

The sun was shining. The sky was blue with lazy white clouds. The grass was green, and a breeze she couldn't feel rustled the leaves in the trees. She remembered days like this where the sky was blinding, but there was something wrong. The colors seemed muted somehow. As if she stared at a faded photograph. They were the memories of color, of life, but they were still a world away. She was Alice on the other side of the looking glass, and she couldn't touch this world for all her efforts. Pain welled in her chest from realizing that she was still as far from home as she was moments ago on Zortentearth, a phantom pain for a phantom body.

Boon brushed his hair back when the breeze tossed it in his face.

"I've missed you so much," Kat said.

He didn't respond, didn't seem to see her. Then he broke into a smile. Kat always liked it best when he smiled. She used to tease him, how he looked like a stern old black and white photo of a man in a stiff suit, but his whole face changed when he smiled.

He waved. Relief washed through Kat, but it was short-lived. He called someone else's name.

"Mary, hi," he called and ran right through Kat!

She gasped as she felt his body travel through her spirit. He paused and looked back, confused. He opened his mouth to speak but shut it quickly. Shaking his head, he turned to face Mary as she ran up.

"How's little Mary?" he asked.

"Quite contrary!" She giggled as he caught her.

This was their private joke, and they never would tell Kat what it was all about.

Kat smiled, then laughed. She stepped closer and touched Mary's face. The pain in her chest tightened; she wanted to cry, but no tears would come, not even phantom tears. How could she feel pain without a body? Was she like a soldier who suffered phantom pain in the lost limb? She had lost her whole body, but did her spirit remember pain?

"Oh, Mary, you'll never see ten," Kat whispered.

Mary lost her smile for a moment as Kat touched her, then suddenly her face warmed, and she smiled again.

"Katie?" Mary asked. Kat jumped back. She looked at her hand, turning it over to stare at her palm. Boon looked just as confused as Kat felt.

"Katie's not here," Boon said.

"Yes, she is," her tone free of doubt.

Boon shook his head and set her down. Kat felt a glimmer of hope, they couldn't see her, but they could feel her! She touched Boon. He shivered in the warm sunlight and looked over his shoulder.

"Come on, Mary, let's go inside. I'm getting spooked."

Kat followed them home. She stared up into the leaves of the trees as they walked. The sunlight slipped between the leaves, creating the glitter effect she so loved, but the glitter was dull. Her street looked the same as she remembered, bicycles dumped on their sides carelessly tossed aside by children as they chased after a new adventure. Spring was just new but already flowers were pushing through the soft mud. Children, released from their winter prison, ran about tossing off jackets. Kat watched them as she might watch an old home video; life replicated, yet life never again.

She followed Boon and Mary into the house. Mary ran ahead shouting, "Mom! I'm home!"

Kat touched the notches in the door frame where her mother had measured her as she grew. She knew the coarse surface so well, but she couldn't feel it now.

"Hi, honey, how was school?" Her mother mumbled as she focused on the collage she was piecing together. A photo fluttered to the floor. Swooping like a hawk, her mother scooped it up before it could touch the tile. Her brown hair swirled around her face and shoulders. Kat sucked in a breath, then another and another, forgetting to breathe out.

"I won the race at school today!" Mary held up her first-place ribbon with pride.

"Mom," Kat mouthed the words, the sound wouldn't come. Phantom tears burned at the corners of her eyes. Maybe she could cry?

"What?" Boon cried. "You didn't tell me that!"

He ruffled her hair, "Good job, squirt."

"That's great, honey," their mother smiled at Mary. "Good job! Did you show Daddy?"

Mary shook her head, her grin ready to split her face. "Where is he?"

"He's in the garage working on his latest project." Their mother mumbled as she snipped around a person in a picture and spread glue on the cutout's back.

Boon leaned over to look at the collage as Mary raced out the door to show off her award. Kat saw him point, but she didn't hear what he said as she followed Mary out the door.

Her father hunched over his workbench; a bright light illuminated a small figure in his large hands. His hand was steady as he carefully painted a delicate face on the tiny head.

Mary bounced up next to him and shoved the ribbon in his face. She jostled his arm, and a streak of blue paint made a gash from the eye to the ear on the figurine. Her father, always the patient one, sighed and set his brush and figure on the table.

"Look, Daddy," Mary squealed. Any touch of annoyance her father had, melted at the look on Mary's face.

"What have we here," he took the ribbon and held it under the light as if he needed to examine the shiny blue ribbon closely. "First place!"

"I won the race!" Mary cried. "Even though Buddy tried to trip me, I didn't fall, and I kept right on running."

"Well, this calls for a celebration!" He shut his light off and took Mary's hand. "Should we frame this?"

"Yes! Yes!" Mary bounced in place.

"Then let's go find a frame." They walked into the house. Kat followed behind. She felt as if she had swallowed an orange, and it lodged in her throat. They entered the kitchen, and her father looked from Boon to her mother and then to Mary.

"Where's Katie?" he asked.

"Dad," Kat croaked. She stepped closer to her father. Her voice still sounded hollow, "I'm right here, Daddy."

It'd been so long since anyone had called her Katie. She covered her mouth. "How can I feel so much when I don't have my body?"

"Oh, she's at the Dojo. She said she wanted to sign up for some tournament." Boon answered. He was sifting through photos in a box. He pulled one out. "Here, this one would look good right here." He pointed to an opening on the collage.

"I'm home!" Katie burst through the door. Kat turned to face her past self. Was she ever that young?

It had only been five years, but it seemed like centuries. This girl, standing before her, was fresh and young, barely seventeen. Kat stepped closer to Katie and touched her hair. It was so long, longer than she remembered, and shiny. Her cheeks were round with a healthy weight. Not gaunt as Kat was now. She wore blue jeans and a bright yellow top. Her dark eyes sparkled with an innocent light. Nothing had ever hurt this girl, and she showed it.

Kat felt impossibly old next to her younger self. She was only twenty-two but felt more like sixty.

"Katie!" Mary snatched the ribbon from her father's hand and raced over to Katie. She waved it in the air. "I won the race!"

"What race," Katie asked. She let her backpack slip off her shoulder and slam on the floor. She took the ribbon and read it.

"We had a field day at school, and I had to race against *four* other kids, and I beat them *all!*" Mary had to suck in a deep breath after rattling all that off at the speed of light.

"It's a lovely ribbon," Katie said. She pretended to admire it from every angle. "We should do something special with it."

"Daddy's gonna frame it!" Mary puffed her chest out and held her head high.

Kat felt trapped in a trance. In a memory that wouldn't shut off like a song stuck on repeat. She remembered this day. Mary talked about that race for days. It was the first time she had ever won anything. Mary was never really athletic, but this one event turned it all around. She began talking about joining track when she was old enough.

Kat drifted over to her father.

"Daddy," Kat touched his arm. He shuddered and rubbed his arm with his other hand. "Dad, did you feel me?" Kat cried.

"What are you working on, Mom?" Katie asked. She studied the collage.

"It's a collage for Aunt Lilly," her mother said. "She's in the hospital again and is missing the family. I thought I would make this so she had something to look at that would remind her of everyone."

"She'll love it," Katie said, then rocked on her heels, hands jammed in her pockets. "Sooo, then we're on our own for supper?"

"Supper," Kat cried. "No! Supper is not important! You should be thinking about the aliens!"

Kat stepped between her mother and Katie. She waved her hand in front of her mother's face. Her mother's eyes went wide.

"Supper," she gasped. "I completely forgot!"

"You can't hear me, can you?" Kat asked. She groaned and stomped her foot. Of course, they couldn't hear her.

"Fine, then I'll just have to scatter a few of these memories." Kat swiped her hand across the photos spread across the table. Her hands sailed through them as if they weren't there. "This is so frustrating!"

She tried again, but there was barely a flutter. "I probably didn't even do that. This house always was drafty." Kat pouted.

"It's okay, Mom, I'm not starving or anything," Katie picked up a photo and handed it to her mother. "This one is my favorite; we should put it there."

As they bent over the collage, Kat turned back to Boon and caught the briefest shadow cross his face. The look, though short, gave her a chill. It was gone so fast she wasn't sure she had seen it at all. Was he annoyed? Angry? At what? Katie's suggestion?

Kat leaned in close and whispered in Katie's ear, "Soak up all the love you can because soon you will never feel love again."

If Katie felt her presence at all, she didn't react. Boon rounded the table, snatched Katie around the waist, and swung her around. Katie screamed. He plopped her down, "Come on, let's go get some dinner for everyone."

Kat watched as her family shouted out orders. Katie scribbled them on the back of an envelope. How she longed to join in, to tell them she loved them. She had never said it enough.

"How can I save you?" Kat whispered. Her words echoed into eternity, unheard and unanswered.

CHAR

"**W**e have to save them!" she shouted. She held her ground, hands on her hips like she used to do when she was ten. She looked like Grams when she did that.

"We can't; they're all dead!" Charlie shouted back. Viper quick, she shoved him in the stomach. Caught off guard, he toppled back into the darkness of the shelter. Only this time, he kept falling.

"I love you, brother." Her voice spun away from him as he fell. Into a vast darkness, he plunged, a darkness with no walls and no bottom. An oubliette in his mind where he would be forgotten, but he alone would never forget. The wind whipped by, forcing him to close his eyes. He stretched out his arms, groping in the darkness, but there was nothing to grasp.

Then there were voices, or was that the wind? No, they were definitely voices.

"Char," They called from all around him. They chanted his name, their voices coming from everywhere outside and inside his head. His mind seemed to expand until his skull felt too small to hold it. It grew and strained to connect to the vastness around him.

The words echoing through him felt scattered as if they, too were, falling through empty space like confetti. He tried to call out, to answer them, but the wind forced his words back down his throat. He choked on them, his cheeks puffed and rippled as if he were on a roller coaster.

"You must help," More voices, deafening, like the roar of a crowd at a concert. All of them talking at once, each saying something different until the individual words became a jumbled mess of incoherent sounds, like grains of sugar through a sifter the words poured through his mind.

"I don't understand!" He tried to shout over the din.

The voices all pulled together. Like liquid in the dust, they drifted together, joined, and molded into one deep rumbling voice, chanting.

"Help her! Help her! Help her!"

The voices swirled around him, faster and faster. Then, all at once, they stopped, and he landed.

Char sat straight up in bed. He tugged at his shirt, drenched in cold sweat. The fear of the dream still clung to him like a wet fall leaf. He flopped back onto his pillows and stared at the canopy above his bed, focusing not on what he saw but the feel of his hammering heart. He patiently waited for it to slow to a normal rhythm and disappear back into his chest.

With the curtains drawn, he couldn't see Kat's empty bed. Only half a day had passed since she left, but it seemed longer. Anxiety oppressed him from the inside; it seeped into his bones, twisted his muscles, and turned his stomach sour. He squirmed and curled into a ball. Moments later, he stretched, flipped onto his stomach, and buried his face in his pillow. He lay there for a few seconds before he rolled back onto his back only to flip onto one side then over to the other. Finally, he sat up, unable to finish his afternoon nap. Unable to shake the apprehension filling his soul.

He shoved the curtain out of the way and dragged himself out of bed, feeling the heaviness of being tired. His eyes ached, his head throbbed. His muscles twitched, each flex an irritating tickle.

"Maybe if I get something to drink," Char mumbled. He scratched his head and yawned. His bare feet slapped the floor as he stumbled across the room with his eyes half-closed. He pulled a door open and stepped inside the bathroom.

He blinked several times before realizing he wasn't standing in the bathroom but the hall. He saw a flash of blue skin disappear around a corner. He followed. He reached each turn in time to catch a glimpse of blue skin or green hair just as it disappeared from view. They continued in this fashion until he found himself outside the door to the garden where he had heard the voice.

He hesitated at the threshold. The memory from that voice still shook him to the core. How had it known? He lifted his foot and stepped within the garden almost against his will. He drifted, silent as the exhale of a flower. The purple pines lined his path, making his destination clear. The serene atmosphere enveloped and cradled him, soothing him like a nervous child. With each step, the tendrils of anxiety tying up his soul loosened and fell away.

He stopped before the statues and stared into the face of the center being. He waited for the voice, but silence filled the air around him.

"Speak to me," he said. Silence. Abandoned. Again. All the faces of those he watched die, faces of children, crushed in around him. The pain in their eyes pierced him again. A new pain filled his chest. It started small but grew. Larger and larger, it filled his lungs and rolled up his throat to choke off his breath. Tears burned at the corners of his eyes. His legs gave way, and he dropped to his knees.

He gasped, pressed a palm to his chest, fisted his hand in the material. Their screams filled his mind, spilled out through his ears, and shattered the silence of the garden. They were all around him, the children he didn't save. The children his sister died trying to save. They wanted to know why he turned his back on them.

Amid the faces of the children, he saw the gaunt faces of his family, eaten away by disease, his sister slamming the door forever in his face. The injustice of the unprovoked attack by a species the humans had not even known existed. Anger surged through him, and he slammed a fist into the soft moss. That single strike was like puncturing a water balloon. The hot tears fell from his eyes like tiny bombs, exploding on the maroon moss. He punched the moss again and again until bits of soil from beneath speckled his wet face and scattered before him, a raw wound in the pristine groundcover. The pain in his chest ripped from him in a long howl.

"Why?" He clenched his fists in his hair, screamed into his knees. His insides burned and expanded until he felt he would fly apart. *"Tell me why!"*

He would shatter like delicate glass. Millions of shards of him would litter the ground in this beautiful garden. They would be absorbed into the soil until he was indistinguishable from the moss. He shrieked until all the pain and anger drained out of him, leaving him empty of all emotion. Like the pouring out of a jar till not a drop of water remained.

He collapsed on his side, beside the wounded moss, and rolled his eyes to look up at the statue. He lay still as the dead. The last tear slid from the corner of his eye to his ear. "I didn't want her to go." His whisper was little more than a breath.

In the emptiness of his mind, in the stillness of his soul, a voice touched him. Light as a zephyr, it brushed his thoughts, words spoken more than two millennia ago. *You are not mindful of the things of God but the things of men.*

Five years have passed since he last thought of that scripture. Did he think it now, or was it someone else? He sat up, feeling light, weak. He was a balloon floating away on the wind. He touched his collarbone where his cross used to hang.

"God, be merciful to me, a sinner," Char whispered.

Lo, I am with you always, even *to the end of the age.*

"How can this be?" Char asked.

"He speaks."

Char turned. The spell broken; the voice gone. Calypso, in all her splendor, stood before him. With great effort, like waking from a drugged sleep, he stood up. He looked at his hands; soil lined the cracks in his skin, packed under his nails. His scalp throbbed where he had pulled his hair, and he felt the grains of dirt stuck to his face. She did not mention the scarred moss nor his haggard appearance. He looked into her gray eyes and knew she understood.

"I don't understand." Char rasped, his throat sore from the scream. She nodded and began to follow one of the paths. Char climbed to his feet, unsteady, and followed.

"What is the name of your God?" Char asked.

"Our God has no name," she replied.

"No name?" Char repeated. "Then what do you say if someone were to demand a name?"

"The same thing you would say."

"Me, why?"

"Because the God you serve is the God I serve. He created all," she smiled. "Does this surprise you?"

"I guess I never really thought about it. That's why you told me I already knew the story of the statues. Did God send someone to save you as he did us?"

"No, these statues represent the Crucifixion on Earth. You are a blessed people to have a Savior; you need only to believe, and you are saved. You have a great Teacher to guide your footsteps. We are not in a position to be saved. God granted us the vision to see the universe as he sees it; the beginning and the end of time. Yet, he wanted us to have free will, so he reserved our future for Himself to see only."

"I don't understand how that keeps you from being able to be saved," Char said.

"We know God exists, we have seen Him, and can talk to Him easily. There is no faith on our planet. He simply is. Without faith, we are held more responsible. Try to see it this way. On your planet, you have parents. Your parents love you and want you to be safe. So, they tell you not to play with fire. You see them; you know they exist. You know, absolutely, that you are not to touch fire, yet should you play with fire anyway, your parents would punish you." She paused, then continued.

"Now, imagine your parents are invisible. Others have told you they exist, but you can't see or hear them. You read in a book that your parents wouldn't want you to play with fire. Still, that fire is there, and all your friends say play with fire. They tell you you can't believe everything you read; you don't really have parents, so go ahead, play with fire. So, you do. Your parents would still be mad you disobeyed them, but they would also understand you don't know what to believe. You have so many people telling you what to do that you don't know which way to turn. Therefore, you require saving."

"I think I understand," Char said. "So, my parents would want to help me understand. That's why they would send someone who knows all about them; someone who could guide me in the right direction. Then all I would have to do is believe."

"Exactly," Calypso stopped walking and sat on a bench.

"You don't need saving because you can see the parents." Char mused. He sat beside her. Even sitting, she was taller than he.

"Correct, it would be foolish for me to disobey God because I can see Him. There is no doubt of what He wants of me when I can see and hear Him."

"What does God look like?" Char asked. He reached instinctively for his cross again then dropped his hand when he realized it was still gone.

She smiled and sang words Char couldn't understand. They were powerful and painful. Beautiful and terrible. The song ached inside him, making him want to cry and laugh. He felt joy and sorrow. Every emotion he had ever felt churned inside him like a vortex. It filled him with awe and wonder, and terror.

He couldn't handle it. He didn't understand the words, but he felt as if he suddenly understood the passages in the bible where it said if one saw God, he would surely die.

He put a hand on her arm and gasped, "Stop, please."

She smiled. "There are no words in your language to describe God."

"You could have just said I didn't need to know, or that information is classified or something." Char felt weak as a new kitten.

The sun had already gone down, and now the world glowed with the brilliant white of the moon. One more day shuffles off into the past; he wondered how Kat was doing.

"You had a calling on Earth, did you not?" She asked. Char shrugged.

"I guess so."

"There has been much talk of the Chosen One and how she will save the Earth. There is little about her companion, you," she continued. "But you are every bit as important as she is, maybe more."

"How?"

"What was your calling?"

"I had this foolish idea to be a pastor, but I wouldn't call it a 'calling,'" Char used finger quotes when he said the word calling. "It isn't as if I heard a voice saying, 'go be a pastor.'"

"You felt drawn to the word. You hear God."

"What? I don't *hear* God. I just did what the bible said, or tried anyway." Char replied. He stared at his bare feet. His toes were cold. "Didn't matter anyway. The second I had my first test, I failed."

"You may not hear God the way we hear God, or the way you sometimes hear Him when you are in this garden, but you do hear Him. When your compassion tugs at your heart, or when you feel the urge to say something you may feel is out of place in a conversation *that* is God guiding you."

"I don't know," Char said. Calypso stood. She turned to him and placed a hand on his shoulder. He looked up into her face, feeling like a child.

"You've shut that door. You stopped hearing Him because you let the rage close off His voice."

"Then why do I hear Him now?"

"Because you are here, in this garden, where He loves to visit. He sees your soul in turmoil, and He cries for your pain."

"Then why does He let it continue?" Char asked. Calypso shook her head.

"That isn't the question you should be asking."

"Then what should I ask?"

"If you cannot figure that out on your own, telling you will do no good." Calypso turned to walk away.

"Wait!" Char grabbed her arm; he was back on his feet. "That's it?"

She was slow to turn back, *"A faithful friend is a strong defense: and he that hath found such an one hath found a treasure.* You are a treasure, Char, never forget that."

She drifted away as silently as she had come. Char watched her leave then retraced his steps.

∻Z∻

"A faithful friend is a strong defense," Char mused as he made his way back to his room. He was about to enter it when he spotted Aurora drifting around a corner.

"What is she doing up?" Char flinched. He hadn't meant to say that out loud. He hurried down the hall and peeked around the corner. She disappeared around another corner.

"Is this a Droplet thing?" He mumbled as he raced down that corridor to catch another glimpse. He followed her for a while before she finally stopped in front of an oval door.

The yellow door had a strange design carved into it. The pattern was vaguely Celtic in its looping, endlessly interweaving lines. Aurora opened the door, paused, and entered.

Char hurried to slip in before the door closed. He stood in another corridor; this one was straight with no curves. Char waited until Aurora was a fair distance down the hall before following. She never once looked back. At the far end of the hall were two large pillars. Char hid behind one. He was able to see Aurora walk up to a very old Droplet.

"I seek audience with the all-knowing Elders," Aurora said respectfully.

"Plenty of time, our dear Aurora. What seems to trouble our young princess?" The Elders had a voice that was many voices and one, high and low at the same time, male and female. The voice resonated with time and knowledge. Aurora knelt in front of the strange being.

The Elders was thin, almost emaciated, but appeared strong. Char couldn't tell if the Elders was male or female. Its skin was midnight blue, much darker than any of the Droplets he had seen so far. Its hair was dark green, darker than hunter green on Earth, and pooled around the sitting body.

The Elders wore a violet robe with silver trimmings, which folded and overlapped with its hair.

"I wish to know if the Chosen One will succeed," Aurora said.

"She came but had to depart –First a battle within a heart. Time is long but short to one. Home is lost, but new will come. When time is broken, she will fight. First for wrong, then for right. A body and soul, from each other, are torn. In order for a world to be reborn." The Elders replied.

"I know the prophecy," Aurora said, frustration tainting her voice. "I want to know more; will she succeed? Or will we be lost?"

"Our child, time will reveal. You are young and are learning still. Soon the knowledge of ages will fill your mind and make you great for all time."

"I don't want to wait for time to tell me. I want *you* to tell me." She said.

"Our dear Aurora, time is the sand we all must sift through. What really troubles you?"

"You know what troubles me!" She stood, towering over the shrunken form of the Elders, her voice rising with every word. "He could attack again! He must be stopped, or more Droplets will die!"

"Death comes to us all; why do you fear the fall?"

"Why doesn't it trouble you?" she shrieked.

Char jerked, just managed to stifle the gasp. Droplets do not lose control like this.

"Our dear Aurora, you lack the control of your peers. You should suffer no fears. These outbursts call for concern; we shall convene a meeting your course to discern." The Elders may be concerned, but it did not appear upset, and its voice remained neutral.

"My course?" Aurora's voice dropped lower than Char had ever heard from a Droplet. A low guttural rumble below the melodic voice sent a chill down his spine. There was something seriously wrong with Aurora. "And just where would you guide my course?"

"Lack of control shows you are weak, little else of which to speak. For the throne you are unfit, we shall deliberate and reassign it," the Elders said.

"Weak?" She tilted her head down, her hair falling around her face obstructing Char's view.

"I'll show you weak!" she screeched. She raised her hand to strike the Elders but stopped. Her hand trembled in the air. After a long moment, she lowered it.

The Elders never flinched as it stared Aurora in the eye.

She pulled her hand back and stared at it. She shook her head, her lips moved, but no sound came out. She turned and ran from the room.

Char held his breath, waited, then followed Aurora. He stuck to the wall until he was sure the Elders couldn't see him.

He slipped through the door and closed it silently. He was pleased with his tracking skills until he felt a hand on his shoulder. He turned to find Aurora's burning eyes inches from his face.

"Tell no one what you saw," she hissed. Her eyes seemed to glow with an inner light, and they weren't the customary solid gray of the other Droplets. They had altered, but Char couldn't figure out what was different about them.

"I-I'm confused," Char stuttered. "I thought you knew the future."

"Walk with me," She demanded, more than requested. "I know many things, but my mind has yet to open to all the secrets of the universe."

Char fell into step with her. He wanted to ask her what had happened in that room. He wanted to ask her why she was the only Droplet that couldn't control her emotions. He wanted to know if it was a mistake to trust her. He didn't ask any of the hundred questions circling his mind.

"When will that be?" he asked instead.

"When the Elders die."

"Why?"

"Think of it as an inheritance. When the Elders die, all of the knowledge in her mind will transfer to my mind. Such is the way in all the families on Zortentearth. The oldest member in the family retains all of the knowledge. The younger Droplets will learn from the older until the older die."

"So, you don't know how this will all end up?" Char asked.

"No, I do not," Aurora said. Her voice calmed; she was beginning to sound more in control, like a proper Droplet. "Even if I had all the knowledge, there is no guarantee I would know what would happen. If another species' future gets too entangled in our own, it clouds our vision."

"Are you afraid?" Char asked. She didn't answer for a few minutes. Her mouth formed a solid line as if she were agitated.

"No, Droplets do not fear death." The control in her voice seemed forced. She stopped walking. "Here is your room. I suggest you get some sleep. We do not know when the Caparians will attack, but I believe it will be soon."

She left without another word. Char waited until he was in his room before releasing the breath he had been holding. Was it a mistake to trust Aurora?

I know why you're doing this, Aurora! I know the truth! Alex had shouted that in the soul separation room. What was it Aurora had said about Alex?

Forgive him. He is half-human and allows his emotions to interfere with God's message. Char gritted his teeth. He had to find Alex.

If Alex couldn't control his emotions because he was half-human, does that mean Aurora wasn't full-blood either? If not, what was she?

Char dressed quickly, foregoing the sissy outfit reminding him of a Shakespearian play and, instead, donning black pants and a black tunic. He wrapped the royal blue cloak around his shoulders and waited until he was sure Aurora was gone before slipping back into the hall. He swiftly climbed the tower to the balcony where he had spotted the green trees. He noted where they were before descending. The entire castle was sleeping. There were no guards posted at the doors, and he was able to escape outside undetected.

City center was quiet and still. The moon was bright enough to see by, and he had no trouble navigating the winding streets by its light. He kept his hood pulled over his face on the off chance someone was out for a moonlit stroll. He reached the edge of the city and kept his eyes up, looking for the familiar leaves. Finally, he found the coveted island of green.

He ran to the trees; joy expanded his chest at the prospect of touching a thing from home. He hit the barrier, bounced off, and slammed into the ground. The air whooshed from his lungs. His hood flipped off his head, and he lay sprawled on the cold blue grass. He stared at the trees, wondering what had just happened.

A twig snapped beyond the barrier, and he strained to see what had made the sound. A tall figure stepped into the moonlight. A hood obscured the face, but Char was sure he had found Alex. The chuckle started low, then grew louder and turned into a full-bellied laugh. Blue hands pushed the hood back, revealing Alex's face.

"My friend," Alex laughed as he stepped forward and held out a hand. "You should have seen the look on your face when the barrier set you back."

A slow grin spread across Char's face. He couldn't help but see himself from Alex's standpoint. Soon he was laughing along with Alex. He took the proffered hand, and Alex effortlessly pulled him to his feet.

"What brings you out on such a lovely night?" Alex asked. A chilly breeze swept through, and they both pulled their cloaks tighter around them.

"I have some questions for you," Char said. "About Aurora and what you know."

Alex looked at him a long time before nodding and beckoning him to follow.

Char followed him into the forest. There was a slight tingling as they passed through the barrier then they were amongst the trees of Earth. Char ran his fingers along the trunk of a maple then through the long needles of a white pine. He stopped to smell the pine needles, a breath of home. Somewhere in the trees, a crow cawed. He spun on his heel, searching for the bird. A crow!

Alex had stopped and looked back. "Please, follow."

"But," Char glanced at Alex and went back to scanning the trees, "A crow!"

"We have little time." Alex continued walking.

Char followed, making each slow step count. He inhaled all the sweet scents of Earth. He could almost forget where he was; almost forget this was Zortentearth. He knelt and swept away the pine needles and discovered rich dark soil. He dug into the dirt and pulled up a handful, inhaling the rich earthy scent.

"How can this be?" Char asked. The dirt slipped through his fingers, leaving a dark line beneath his fingernails.

The trees thinned, and they stepped into a small clearing. Nestled against the trees was a modest log cabin. Inside there was a warm fire and handmade wooden furniture. Alex hung his cloak on a peg by the door, and Char did the same. They sat in comfortable rocking chairs by the fire. The chairs were not as high as most of the chairs Char had seen on this planet. Alex was not as tall as most Droplets.

They rocked for a bit, warming their hands by the fire. Char stared at the orange flames as a log snapped in half. The sparks glowed and flew up the chimney. All of this was so familiar, so homey; tears burned at the corners of his eyes.

"From childhood's hour I have not been / As others were—I have not seen / As others saw—I could not bring / My passions from a common spring." Alex stared at the flames as well. His voice was low and melodic.

"That sounds familiar," Char said. "Where have I heard that?"

"*Alone* by Edgar Allan Poe," Alex replied.

"You know the works of Poe?" Char asked. He thought of Kat's worn old tome lost somewhere in the wilds of Zortentearth.

"I know many things of Earth," Alex said. "You see, my mother was a Droplet, but my father was human."

Char leaned forward. "How can that be?"

Alex stood and filled a kettle with water. He spoke while he worked. "On Zortentearth, every Droplet born is paired with another Droplet." He hung the kettle on a hook by the fire.

"Like an arranged marriage?" Char asked. Alex shook his head as he sat.

"No, more like—wait." He stood and walked out of the cabin.

Char looked around the room. The hearth, the mantle, the simple design of the cabin was reminiscent of pioneer log cabins. A ladder led into a loft. A blanket with a brightly colored pattern full of triangles and straight lines colored with teal, orange, red, black, and white lay folded on the back of a couch. Cast iron skillets hung from hooks on the walls.

Everything here seemed modeled after a time long before Camexus and the war that sank continents. Camexus was all that was left of a continent called North America, at least, according to his history books.

Alex walked back in carrying a leaf.

"This is a leaf from a white ash," Alex held the compound leaf up for Char to see. It had seven leaves on a thin stem, each with a mirror image on the opposite side. All except for the one at the tip, this was alone. "See how they have matching counterparts? If one falls away," He plucked one of the leaves from the stem. "A new one will not grow back, and the counterpart is left alone. On Earth, humans speak of a soul mate; on Zortentearth, this is literally true. If that Droplet dies, their counterpart will face life alone. Like this leaf."

"So, when Gar died, that doomed his counterpart to a life of solitude?" Char asked. Alex nodded.

"Yes, Calypso will spend her life alone." Alex laid the leaf on the rough-cut wooden table by his chair. The kettle screeched, and Alex poured tea for each of them.

"I had no idea," Char whispered. Not that he could have saved Gar. "Poor Calypso."

"My mother was different. She wasn't born with a mate," Alex continued, either not hearing Char's musings or ignoring them. He handed a steaming cup to Char.

"Like the leaf at the end with no counterpart?" Char asked. He shifted the hot cup in his hands, gripping the large handle with one hand and patting the scalding side of the cup with his other hand. He held the rim close to his lips, not daring a sip, but relished the warm steam on his nose. Alex nodded.

"She had always felt different. She was not as tall as other Droplets, and she had a yearning to move beyond her borders. Most Droplets are content to live on this planet. They have no need or desire to go anywhere else. My mother kept her eye on the horizon, always wondering what lay beyond." Alex took a sip of his tea.

"What was your mother's name?" Char asked.

"Nemoria," Alex said. "In 2117, Earth years, she had the opportunity to go to Earth to study the plants and animals of your planet. She jumped at the chance."

"Which is how she must have met your father," Char said.

"Correct," Alex said. "When she met my father, she was masquerading as a human professor of botany. My father was a professor of literature. She knew he was her mate the moment she met him."

"Why would her mate be on a foreign planet?" Char asked. Alex shrugged.

"I suppose God must know something we do not and set it up this way," Alex continued. "My mother never truly fit in around here, but it was worse for me. I am a half-blood. In a way, I am shunned. Not as you, humans, shun each other, but I am forbidden to hold council in the castle. I would never be allowed to wear the crown. I cannot speak directly to God, as other Droplets can. Like my mother, I am one of the leaves on the very end, the one without the mirror image."

"You don't have a match?" Char asked.

"Not on Zortentearth." Alex looked him in the eye as he said this. Char felt a twist in his stomach. Nemoria's match was on Earth, and there was only one Earth girl left. The twist in his stomach tightened, and he leaned forward in his chair. He couldn't hide the irritation in his voice.

"I'm sorry, as fascinating as all this is," Char snapped. "I don't see how this pertains to Aurora and why you burst in on the Soul Separation Ritual."

Alex stood and paced, tapping a hand against the side of his mug. "I can't speak directly to God. I don't know all the things other Droplets know." He stopped pacing and looked directly at Char. "I can't *control my emotions* like other Droplets. I *feel all the passion* you humans feel. I am *much like my father*."

Char stared at him. He felt his blood run cold.

"Do you understand what I'm saying to you?" Alex asked.

"I think I do, but why?"

"Because Mrah killed Aurora's mate," Alex said. Char felt sick.

"But, the Droplets accept their demise like no other race I've ever seen," Char said.

"Yes, Droplets do, but if I were her, I would want to take revenge on Mrah for taking my only mate," Alex said.

"Fine, let's say she isn't a full-blood. Let's assume she wants revenge on Mrah, but what has that got to do with Earth?"

"I think Earth was a tool. A weapon, if you will."

"A weapon?" Char jumped to his feet. "Why would they use Earth as a weapon?"

"Zortentearth does not have a strong military, as you have probably noticed. We could never survive an attack from the Caparians. Humans, however, do have a war mentality. You've proven this, repeatedly, for thousands of years," Alex said. "I imagine Aurora used this information to her advantage."

"How do you know any of this?" Char asked. He began to pace; his cup of tea sat on the table, forgotten.

"I don't," Alex replied. "I just know she tends to fall out of character, as you might say."

"Well, what do we do?" Char asked.

"We have to get Kat out of there. I have a place built where she will be safe. Mrah won't think to look there; then we can work on a plan of getting you off this planet and safely someplace else."

"How do I know I can trust you?" Char asked. "You are half-human. At the risk of putting down my species, humans do tend to have ulterior motives."

"You have no reason to trust me, but can you look me in the eye and honestly tell me you trust Aurora?"

Char looked Alex in the eye. He thought about Aurora's outburst at the Elders and shook his head. "So, what's the plan?"

"I know of a forgotten passage under the castle. My mother showed it to me once, long ago. It's how I was able to sneak in to crash the soul separation ritual."

"Which bombed," Char replied as he sat back in his chair and picked up his cold cup.

"Nobody's perfect," Alex shrugged. "At least I tried." He looked pointedly at Char.

"Hey!" Char cried. He put a hand up in mock defense. "I *tried* to talk her out of it. Do you have any idea how hard it is to change her mind?"

Alex held his gaze for a beat longer before continuing. "Anyway, I can work on gathering supplies in the event of a siege. I'll need you to figure out the best time to put this plan into action, then contact me with the information as soon as possible."

Char nodded and took a swallow of his tea. "I can do that, but are you saying that *nobody* in the castle knows about this secret passage?"

"I don't know that *nobody* knows about it. The royal family may know about it, but it seemed pretty forgotten when I used it. The last known usage was a thousand years ago." Alex replied. "I'm counting on it being—little thought of, how's that?"

"Are you telling me that castle is *thousands* of years old?" Char raised an eyebrow.

"Looks good, doesn't it?" Alex asked. "We build things to last."

"You're telling me!" Char paused, "Why isn't it used anymore—the passage, I mean?"

"A long, long time ago when this planet was in civil war, the Droplets were not as we know them today." Alex leaned forward and set his cup on the table, then settled back in his chair. "We built better and better weapons, determined to win the war at any cost. The intended use of the passage was to be an escape route for the royal family, should the war take a turn for the worst. It is my understanding that it leads deep under the castle where the royal family stored their weapons."

"I thought you guys could talk directly to God," Char said. "How did he feel about this civil war?"

Alex smiled, "That was before God spoke and made us His people."

"God brought peace to Zortentearth?" Char asked. Alex nodded. Char sipped his, now, icy tea. "Someday, I'd love to have a long discussion about the history of your people, but for now, tell me about Mrah. How do we fight him?"

"Excellent question," Alex said. He stood and walked to the kettle and poured more hot water into his cup. He held the kettle up, a nod toward Char's cup. Char shook his head and held a hand over it. Alex put the kettle back by the fire and sat.

"Caparians are battle-trained but fight with honor."

Char snorted, "Yeah, I've seen their 'honor.'"

"No, you haven't." Alex shook his head, stood, and paced. "How can I explain... well, for one, did you know Caparians consider guns a weakness?"

Tea went down the wrong pipe, Char coughed. "No! Why?"

"Since they far outmatch any creature in this corner of the universe, they feel it is an unfair advantage over their opponents."

"So, they don't use guns at all? What about the particle separator?"

Char asked. He set his cup on the table and leaned forward in his chair, elbows on his knees.

"Caparians train young. Children are allowed to use a gun until they train with a blade. To move up in the ranks, a Caparian must prove his skill with a blade. To reach Captain, he needs to demonstrate his ability to battle an armed opponent with a gun, fighting with nothing but his knife. If he fails to disarm and defeat his opponent, he will be stripped of all rank and forced to climb the ladder again from the bottom."

Char let out a low whistle, "Harsh."

"In fact, if you really want to insult a Caparian," Alex leaned in and winked. "Offer him a gun before you fight."

"Good to know," Char chuckled. "But, again, what about the particle separator? It's like a great big gun that destroys planets."

"I don't know much about the particle separator. You'll have to ask a Caparian about that." Alex replied.

"Maybe I will," Char drained his cup.

KAT

Kat crouched by the bed and watched Katie as she slept. Her memories of sleeping in this room were still so fresh she could almost feel the bed sheets. She remembered cursing herself for the entire week it had taken her to paint the walls and ceiling like the bright blue sky, complete with fluffy white clouds. To say it was tedious would be the understatement of the century. But the effect opened her room and made her feel free and happy.

Her room was a cluttered mess with books stuffed on shelves and her desk strewn with papers, pencils, and tablets filled with random ideas and favorite quotes. The disarray of her desk reflected the chaos in her head. Jumbles of thoughts piled high in her mind, packed tight, till the words fairly spilled from her ears.

Kat turned her attention back to Katie. Asleep, she appeared even younger than her seventeen years, maybe fourteen. She had a soft smile on her slumbering face. Her dark lashes lay against impossibly pale cheeks, her black hair pooled around her head. It was so much longer than she remembered. Kat touched the silken strands. She couldn't feel them, but she remembered how soft it was. Katie cringed and rolled over, turning her back to Kat.

"I hope this works," Kat mumbled. She had decided to try and communicate with her past self through dreams, though she wasn't sure that was possible or even how to do it. After all, basic poltergeist activity didn't seem to work for her; why should possession?

She took a breath as she stood and leaned over the sleeping form of her past self. She pulled a wisp of hair back so that she could see Katie's face again. The soft smile was back.

"Dreaming sweet dreams?" Kat asked. "I'm sorry, but that will have to change."

Kat gently touched Katie's face. Katie grimaced again and pulled her covers tighter around her shoulders. She pulled her knees up to her chest and tipped her head down into them.

"It's time," Kat whispered. She crawled on top of her counterpart and said a quick prayer for this to work. She imagined her soul was like water and allowed her spirit to seep into the body. She felt a jolt of resistance. Katie's spirit did not want to share Katie's body.

"But it's my body, too," Kat argued. "Actually, it's also my spirit if you want to be technical."

She felt confusion from the other spirit. They were the same, yet different. They were of the same energy but ages apart.

"Don't worry, we are the same," Kat soothed. She focused on mirroring the other spirit. The resistance started to fade, but the confusion remained.

"I'm a friend," Kat cooed. Could the other spirit understand her? She sensed a growing curiosity from the other soul, which began to outweigh the confusion. She concentrated on projecting love. Little by little, Katie's soul relinquished its claim. Kat slid in like sand through the waist of an hourglass.

At first, there was nothing, just darkness. Serene darkness only found in dreamless sleep. Kat found she could control the area with her thoughts. She chose altocumulus clouds that rippled across the sky interrupted by breaks revealing electric blue skies. It was so beautiful it made her phantom heartache.

Kat hovered, cross-legged, with her eyes closed. She relished the feeling of weightlessness and allowed the serenity of the dreamscape to envelop her. It filled every fiber of her being with a peace she hadn't known since before the dream warning her of the impending attack. When she opened her eyes, she saw herself.

She felt as if she were looking into a mirror that only showed images of the past. Katie sat wide-eyed, staring back at her. Kat gave her a reassuring smile.

"Who are you?" Katie asked.

"I am you," Kat replied.

"No, you're not," Katie said. "My hair is longer."

"I am you, and yet, I am not." Kat stifled a giggle; she was enjoying being cryptic. Katie did not reply.

"I am you in the future, and I am here for your help," Kat paused. How much should she tell her?

"My help?" Katie asked. "With what? Hair advice? Here's a tip, don't cut it. It looks better longer."

All the amusement Kat felt evaporated. Suddenly she was back in the bunker; the door shut against the green light. Her family was dead. Never day, never night, just endless darkness and the weak glow of a lantern by whose light she hacked her hair short. Each strand that fell silently to the floor was another stab at the life she had known. Another death toll for the pieces of her soul she'd left behind in the dust with her family. By the last strand, she was no longer Katie. Katie was dead. Katie died in the green light. She was simply Kat, a stray with no past and no home.

Katie snapped her fingers in Kat's face, effectively bringing her back to the present, as well as annoying her. *"Hello?"* said with attitude.

Kat gritted her teeth and straightened her legs till she was standing, though she still hovered five inches off the ground. She balled her hands into fists and spoke with thinly controlled fury.

"An alien species, known as the Caparians, are determined to destroy our world, and in fact, already have. I and one other were the only humans to survive."

"Then how can I possibly help you?" Katie asked as she picked at a fingernail as if that was more interesting than an impending attack. She looked up from her nails and looked around. "Where are we?"

"You can stop it before it starts," Kat replied. She ignored the second question.

"Am I dreaming?" Katie asked.

"You need to take this seriously!" Kat snapped. She dropped to the ground, took a quick step forward, and grabbed Katie by the collar.

Katie jerked free.

"Would you take a dream seriously?" Katie asked as she straightened her collar.

Her rage broke free, and Kat bellowed, "Then see what will happen!"

She launched into the air, flinging her arms wide obliterating the clouds. Trees closed in around them. New spring grass sprouted under Katie's feet. Kat stared at Katie even as the memories of that day washed over her. A day when the sun still shone, when the world was still beautiful and love still existed. Shadows of the past drifted before them; Katie and her family and that doomed picnic.

Kat, not wanting to dwell on the painful memories, rushed into the disaster. The world turned the hideous green that permanently colored her memories, followed by the squirrel and its tortured cries. The dreamscape magnified the screeching.

Katie slapped her hands over her ears. It didn't matter if Kat did or not because she heard the screeching inside her head, and no matter how hard she pressed her hands to her ears, it never muffled. No one can silence a memory.

Then came the horrible popping sound followed by the vague idea of dust, then nothing. The squirrel was no more. The trees and grass disappeared.

"What's happening?" Katie screamed. Kat didn't answer with

words; like a mute phantom, she pointed at the family as it ran for the shelter.

Kat had trouble fighting the tears as she watched her mother pressing her hands to her head. She looked at Katie as their mother dropped to her knees. Katie had white knuckles pressed to her mouth. Tears flowed freely down her cheeks.

"I can't... take... the pressure..." The words seemed to come at them from all angles then echoed into the distance.

"You have to get up; you have to try," her father pleaded.

So real, it was all so real. Kat's memories painted across this dreamscape, threatening to consume her. She lost control, and the images appeared faster as if she was stuck on fast forward. New memories rolled and collided with the previous. Glimpses of pained expressions, shots of anguished cries, and bursts of destruction created a medley of sorrow from which there was no escape.

Her mother curled into a ball and screamed into her knees. She lifted her head to look at her.

"That look will haunt us for the next five years." Kat's voice came from the sky, rumbled like distant thunder. She gritted her teeth and managed to regain control of the feral images.

"My baby—" She popped, just like the tree, just like the squirrel.

"Mom!" They both screamed, the Katie from her memory, and the Katie Kat currently held captive in this nightmare. Katie, from the memory, kept screaming. Boon was dragging her away.

"They all die," Kat said. Her words held the hollow sound of eternity.

"What?" Katie asked as she dragged a sleeve across her face, leaving a red streak where the tears had been.

Kat didn't respond. She needed to drive the point home and brought her hands above her head; her body lifted straight up, her legs formed a point. She hovered in the air forcing Katie to look up. Kat paused, then dropped her arms in a sharp motion. Like a shock wave, the ground rippled, leveling everything around them.

"A mere five years later," Kat said. She showed what the world had become.

Katie didn't move or say a word as she stared at the dry, barren desert, with its scorching sun and flat baked ground. With another wave of her hand, Kat showed the weird Kurs she had owned, the domes of the colonies, and how hard it was to get water.

"There is no living in this world, only surviving, and we survived," Kat continued. Her words boomed all around them. *"Alone."*

Then she showed the meteors, each larger than the last. The planetoid objects as they careened toward the Earth. The fire-flowers burst across the sky as hundreds of frightened people tried to flee the doomed planet.

Again, Kat lost control of the images. Exploding escape pods mixed with meteorites crashing into the ground. The face of the trampled dead boy appeared in the sky, larger than life, then exploded in a fire-flower. Bits rained down around them.

"Stop!" Katie cried. "Stop! Stop! Stop!"

Katie tried to escape but had nowhere to run. Every direction showed more destruction. She didn't bother to wipe away the tears soaking her face. Her hands still covered her ears as she tried to block out the explosions. She dropped to her knees and wrapped her head in her arms. Her long hair draped around her like a cloak, protecting her from the images. Kat moved in, still hovering over Katie, and leaned down to shout at her.

"That's what you will go through; what the *world* will go through *if you do not help me!*" Her voice thundered, mixed with the explosions around them. Katie rocked herself; her shoulders heaved with sobs. Kat rolled her eyes.

"Oh, all right," she swung her hand again and replaced the fire storm with clouds. The noise ended abruptly, leaving a deafening silence in its wake.

"I want to wake up," Katie mumbled. She didn't look at Kat. She continued to rock and chant. "I wanna wake up. I wanna wake up."

"Katie," Kat started.

"Wake! Up!" Katie screamed.

～Z～

Kat paced the room as Katie took her shower. She didn't know if she had made any progress with Katie at all. Perhaps she had overdone the dramatics a bit. She balled her hands into fists, her arms folded across her chest. If Katie had just taken her more seriously, she wouldn't have had to be so rough.

She stopped by her bookcase and read over the volumes. She ran a finger down one spine, tilting her head to read it.

"Poe... my one friend in the dark," Kat whispered. She wandered over to her desk and ran a hand along the messy surface.

"I really should get more organized." She shrugged, "Maybe next time around."

She smiled over her stuffed animals and all the fond memories they brought back. She shook her head; her smile vanished.

"This is no time to get caught up in memory lane!" she scolded herself.

"Come on! Aren't you clean by now?" she shouted at the bathroom door. The door swung open, releasing the fog trapped inside. It rolled across the floor.

Kat leaned against the wall and watched Katie flit around the room, picking out clothes and brushing her hair.

"Come on, you're beautiful," Kat said impatiently. "Didn't I scare you enough last night? Don't you want to run and tell Mom and Dad?"

Katie's hands shook as she finished braiding her long hair. She was paler than usual and stared at her reflection with huge scared eyes. Kat snapped her fingers in front of Katie's face. It had no effect, but Katie did seem to focus again. She finished getting ready and headed downstairs.

"Finally!" Kat cried. They got to the kitchen, where their mother was already eating breakfast.

"Good morning, sweetie," she said.

"Morning, Mom," Katie said as she took a bowl out of the cupboard.

"There! Here's your chance!" Kat said. She hopped a few times and made wild gestures towards their mother.

"Herrrreee's Mom!" Kat said in her best announcer's voice.

Katie made her bowl of corn flakes and sat at the table beside her mother. For the next few minutes, the only sound was crunching. Kat sat opposite Katie and stared at her. She slapped her hand down on the table, a wasted effort as her hand slipped through the table without a sound.

"Say something!" Kat shouted. A horn beeped outside, and Katie leaped to her feet, the half-eaten bowl of cereal forgotten.

"That's Boon, gotta go!" She kissed her mother on the cheek. "Love you, Mom."

Kat raced outside with Katie and leaped into the car with her. She sat in the backseat while Katie sat in the front.

"Well, at least I can't get car sick as a ghost," Kat said dryly. She leaned back and looked out the window. The trees were budding green, the ground littered with winter's debris. Moist mud with soggy fall leaves created a carpet the spring grass had to push through to reach the sunlight.

"I had a bad dream last night," Katie mumbled. Kat leaped forward, sticking her head between the seats so she could hear.

"What?" Boon asked. He glanced at her before focusing back on the road.

"I had a nightmare last night." A whimper escaped.

"Yes, yes, tell Boon, he'll help," Kat said. Her spirit crackled with anticipation.

"About what, Hon?"

"Nothing major, I guess," Katie replied. Kat slapped her hand over her face, dragged it down until her face stretched, and her lids pulled away from her eyes. Or, at least, she imagined she did since she didn't have a face, or hands, or skin to stretch.

"Then why bring it up?" Boon asked. His eyes narrowed on the road.

Kat cocked her head and raised an eyebrow.

"That's it?" Kat asked. "You're not even curious?"

"I dreamed about me... Well, I dreamed about a future me, and I was telling myself the world was going to end." Katie said. She stared out the side window, so she didn't notice Boon rolling his eyes. Kat felt the urge to punch him.

"That's a start, but it's confusing," Kat coached, even though Katie couldn't hear her. "Try again."

"Well, what ended the world?" Boon asked, his tone patient as if talking to a child.

"Aliens," Katie said. Boon exploded in laughter.

"Aliens?" He howled. "What kind? Were they little and green?"

"I don't know what they look like," Katie giggled. "I didn't show them to me!"

They both roared in laughter.

"Okay, I admit, this whole conversation sounds a little ridiculous," Kat's voice was calm and even, then shouted, "But it's true!"

"So," Boon said, choking on suppressed laughter. "Do these aliens have names?"

"Yes, Cakerians... no, Kripto... no, Tapeworms," Katie struggled with her giggles. Each attempt made them laugh harder.

"Caparians!" Kat screamed. Her entire spirit reacted to her temper, snapping and crackling. She felt a burst of power emanate from her core, shooting out like a shock wave. The car lurched and swerved.

Boon cursed. He wrestled with the wheel. They fish-tailed and swerved into the on-coming lane; a semi barreled towards them. Katie screamed and covered her face with her hands.

Boon jerked the wheel, and the car lurched out of the way, spinning toward the edge of the road. The front tire slid easily into the ditch. A tree stump brought the vehicle to a halt with a loud metallic crunch. Boon and Katie sat in stunned silence for a few minutes. Kat sat with her mouth hanging open.

"Did I do that?" She asked. Of course, no one answered.

"What the hell?" Boon hollered. He pounded the steering wheel with his fist.

"*My new car,*" He leaped out of the car to inspect the damage on the front end.

"I don't think this hunk of junk qualifies as a *new car,*" Kat mumbled.

He furiously kicked the crushed in front bumper, swearing and spitting in his rage. Kat jumped out, followed him around the car, and shouted, "Hello! I'm still in the car! I might be hurt! Shouldn't you be more worried about me?"

He finally realized Katie was still sitting in shock. He moved around to the passenger side, his face tight with anger more than worry.

"You all right?" His voice was a little too sharp. Katie slowly nodded.

"Yeah, I think so. What happened?" Even as she was responding, Boon had already turned back to mourn over his precious car.

"You're kind of a jerk," Kat said. Katie was visibly shaking, and all Boon could think about was a stupid car.

"All I have to say is that dealer had better have a good reason for this!" He said the word dealer as if it left a bitter taste. "Come on, help me push it out."

Katie got out of the car and put shaking hands on the hood.

"Not like that!" Boon snapped. Katie jerked back as if the car burned. "Like this." He roughly repositioned her, and together they pushed the car out. He managed to get the mangled hood open and checked the engine.

"Shouldn't we call someone? Report the accident?" Katie asked.

"Don't be an idiot." He snapped. "Get in. It's drivable."

He got behind the wheel and turned the key, nothing. The engine didn't even try to turn over. He tried again, but it didn't even click. He slammed his hand down on the steering wheel and cursed again.

Katie jumped as if he had hit her. He jerked himself out of the car and whipped the hood open, then stormed around the car and ripped the trunk open. Katie got back out of the vehicle and timidly took a step toward Boon.

"What are you doing?" he snapped. Katie flinched. He pulled a jump pack out of the trunk. Katie tried to put a calming hand on his arm, but he shook her off. "Get in the car and stay there."

"What are you doing?" Her voice was small.

"I'm checking the stupid battery," he growled. "What's it look like?"

"Hey, you can't talk to us like that!" Kat yelled. Of course, he couldn't hear her. Katie bowed her head and got back into the car.

"Why are you just crawling away like a scared mouse?" Kat wanted to shake some sense into Katie. Katie pulled her knees up to her chest and wrapped her arms around them. Kat shook her head and got back in, seething in the backseat. After a few minutes, Boon slammed the hood and got back in the car.

"The battery is dead." His voice still had an edge. "The stupid battery is completely dead."

CHAR

Char's mind kept drifting back to his last conversation with Alex. The danger they were in and how they would keep Kat safe. Right now, Alex was gathering the supplies for a siege. He had already strengthened the barrier around the green isle in preparation for this inevitable attack. It was as strong as it would get; they had to pray for the best after that.

Char forced his attention back to what Aurora was saying. She had pressed a button on the table, and a hologram of a galaxy appeared suspended over the white oval surface. Not a disk shape like the Milky Way, but a spiral galaxy. Aurora swiped her hand across the hologram and massive planets zipped by as she zoomed in on a green and purple smudged planet.

"This is Zortentearth," Aurora said. Orbiting the planet was a massive moon. The moon could have been the size of Earth, yet it dwarfed in comparison to Zortentearth. She waved her hand again, and Zortentearth diminished in size until another planet appeared. "This little fire ball is called Lebrac, from whence Mrah hails."

Char leaned in closer to the hologram. The coloring of Lebrac was similar to that of Mars, but it was much larger than Mars. Lebrac was closer to the Sun than Zortentearth. "How hot is it on Lebrac?" Char asked.

"The coolest areas of the planet dip as low as four hundred degrees, that would be by your Fahrenheit measurements. The hottest areas are even inhospitable to its inhabitants at over a thousand degrees." Aurora replied.

"Over a thousand?" Char gasped. "That's pretty hot."

"Now, Mrah's ship was severely disabled in that last attack by Captain Gar. It would have taken him longer to get back to Lebrac than normal."

"How far is Lebrac from Zortentearth?" Char asked. He looked through the hologram to Aurora. The colors of the planets mixed and muddied her shimmering blue skin.

"Distance has little meaning when you have such fast ships, but about four of your AU's from this planet."

"Four Astronomical Units, that's what?" Char looked at the ceiling and ticked his fingers while he calculated in his head. "Something like 372 million miles, right?"

"Close enough," Aurora said. "But as I said, Mrah has a fast ship. He can normally span that distance in mere days."

"How many days?" Char asked. A cold drop of dread made its way down his spine.

"With a good ship, three Zortentearthian days."

"That's only six Earth days!" Char cried. "How long have we been on this planet?" He tried to remember how many nights had passed since the crash. Was it three? Four? He couldn't remember.

"I said with a *good* ship, but his was crippled; it would take him longer to get home. So, let's assume it takes him twice as long—"

"We can't assume!" Char interrupted. "We have no idea how badly his ship was damaged. It may not have been able to fight back, but that doesn't mean its warp drive – or whatever – was damaged. For all we know, he's already been home, gotten himself a new ship, and is within a breath of this planet already!"

Aurora glared at him from across the hologram. Was it a trick of the hologram, or was she shaking? She opened her mouth to speak, but Calypso spoke first.

"His argument is sound," Calypso said. She drifted across the room and touched a button dissolving the hologram.

"We have to plan for the worst," Char continued. "What is the shortest amount of time he could realistically take to get this task done?"

"Three days to Lebrac and three back," Calypso said.

"If we're going to assume anything, let's assume the worst. Let's say everything lines up for Mrah. He has a ship waiting for him when he gets there," Char said. "It's all ready to fly; he just has to run a quick check and transfer anything from his damaged ship to his new one. That would take, what, a day?"

Char looked from Aurora to Calypso. Aurora had pressed her lips together; a dark line formed around the edges. Calypso appeared calm. When neither contradicted him, he continued.

"That gives us at worst seven days, right?" He asked. Calypso nodded. His stomach turned sour. "That gives us about two or three days before he attacks."

"We have little time and no way to defend ourselves," Aurora said through tight lips. Char thought about Kat's body and the plan to keep it safe. He had to find Alex and tell him how little time they had.

"I can fight," Char said. Aurora shook her head.

"No, you must protect the Chosen One."

"Her name is Kat. Why can't you just say her name? She's not an object. She's a person!" Char pounded his fist on the table. He tensed his muscles, trying to calm the growing wave of anger. He suddenly hated this world; hated Aurora and her stupid prophecy; hated the fate that forced them to risk everything.

"I. Can. Fight." He ground out each word through clenched teeth. He was *not* going to hide like a mole this time. This time he would make a stand.

"She will only be safe from the Particle Separator, but not from

Mrah." Calypso was as gentle with her words as she was with her light touch.

"Mrah would come for her?" Char asked. "Why not obliterate this planet as well?"

"The risk is too high. Mrah will not take the chance of you two escaping again. He will kill enough of us to teach us a lesson, but he will not kill all of us. He would not want to lose his—what did you call us—fortune tellers?" Aurora asked. Was it his imagination, or did she sound bitter?

"Well, I'm not just going to hide while everyone dies." He crossed his arms.

"You must seal yourself with *Kat's* body," Aurora put particular emphasis on the name. "We will fight for as long as we can. You must protect her body at all costs. You are our last hope."

⁂

Char held his hood tight to his head as he ran through the streets of the city. He tripped on nothing and stumbled a few paces but caught himself and kept running. He dug his toes into the ground, pumping his legs hard. His cloak flapped behind him. Each gasping breath stung, his lungs tight. He had to find Alex.

He reached the edge of the green isle. He didn't hesitate as he blew past the barrier. He didn't notice the slight tingling sensation as the barrier deactivated in that one spot for him to enter. The deactivation device Alex had given him did its job. He raced through the trees ignoring the chipmunks and squirrels. He didn't notice the whitetail or the fox, so focused was he on getting to the cabin in the middle of the woods.

He took the steps two at a time, crossed the porch in a bound, and burst through the cabin door. It was empty!

"Alex!" Char yelled. He sucked in a breath and bent to put his hands on his knees. The only sound was his heavy breathing. His heart was pounding so hard it pulsed in his skull.

"Alex!" Char called again. The muscles in his legs twitched, and sweat coated his body.

He stumbled over to the stairs leading to the loft, but he sensed Alex wasn't in the cabin. He slapped his hand on the banister, hitting a nerve that shot a jolt of pain up his arm. He bolted back out the door and crashed into Alex. The basket Alex held hit the floor; Meadow and Horse Mushrooms rolled and bounced around their feet. Char stepped back, crushing one under his boot.

"What's wrong?" Alex asked as he knelt to pick up his scattered treasures.

"Forget them!" Char grabbed Alex by the shoulder and pulled him back to his feet. "Mrah is coming!"

"What? When?"

"I don't know when, exactly, but I just left a meeting with Aurora and Calypso. We did the math, and it seems Mrah could strike literally at any moment."

Alex narrowed his eyes and nodded. "I understand. The shelter is all prepared. We'll need to get Kat tonight."

"I have to go back to the palace," Char said. Alex had knelt again to pick up the mushrooms but stood, dropping the few he held.

"Why?" He asked. "I thought we decided to get her together."

"Aurora wants me holed up with Kat so I can protect her from Mrah. She seems to feel Mrah will invade in person. Kat will need a body guard."

Alex nodded again. He knelt and tossed mushrooms into the basket. "This could work to our advantage. Aurora will suspect less if you play the part she wants you to play. I'll sneak in, and together we'll get Kat out of there."

He stood and set the basket on the table, then put a hand on Char's shoulder. "Get back to the castle. I'll come tonight."

⇒Z⇐

Char had just made it to Coral City when the hideous green light once again enveloped him. The buildings stood tall and somehow wispy in the viridescent light. His stomach twisted, a sour taste invaded his mouth. Next to him, a blue tree groaned. A strange alien animal stumbled out of the underbrush, keening in agony.

Suddenly it wasn't an alien animal; it was a whimpering dog. The one Tracy tried to help.

"Why is your face green?" Her voice, her glowing red hair. Crystal clear as the day it happened. She dropped to her knees by the tortured animal.

Char staggered back, not wanting to see her, not wanting to relive the nightmare. His fingers touched his collar bone where his cross used to hang. Tracy had torn it from his neck.

He leaned over, hands on his knees, gulping air as if he'd just emerged from the water. He focused on his fingers. Counted them, trying to ground himself in the present. Taking deep, deliberate breaths.

A tree exploded into the signature nothingness of Mrah's weapon of mass destruction. It snapped him back to the present. The alien creature was already gone.

"Kat!" Char's heart nearly exploded with the adrenaline rush. He had to get to her! He raced through the streets, running toward Kat as much as he was running from his memories. Warning sirens went off all over the city. Droplets drifted out of their homes.

Char slowed then stopped. He gaped. No screams. No stampeding. No pushing. No shoving. Everyone was calm. He wove his way through the crowd, which wasn't even a crowd. The mass of bodies formed a single line.

"We have to get underground!" He shouted at them. "We need to hurry!"

Not one Droplet increased the pace. Not one acknowledged the urgency in his voice. He growled and stepped forward to snatch a child who appeared to be about the size of a five-year-old from Earth. Her skin was soft blue; her hair was pastel green. Looking at her made him think of Easter. He spotted Calypso.

"Help me save them!" As he said the words, it wasn't his voice he heard; it was Tracy's. Her voice echoed in his memory, so familiar it brought tears to his eyes. He squeezed his eyes shut, then looked down at the child he held in his arms.

Her fearless gray eyes stared back at him, seeming to question him. A question he couldn't figure out, one he couldn't answer. There was a thump in front of him; he looked up and saw a Droplet on her knees. She made no sound, didn't even squirm as every other creature had, just knelt there for a few seconds before popping.

He looked back at the child in his arms. Her skin darkened. It became more of an aquamarine while her hair glistened like an emerald. She put a slender hand on his chest.

"I can walk," she whispered. Her voice was much deeper than he expected. Not deep as a man's voice, yet not quite like a child's. She sounded much older than she appeared. He set her down and watched her walk away, rejoining the line.

Textbook controlled evacuation, with everyone calm and in single file. A chill ran down Char's spine. It was too quiet. Too calm. It was creepy. Where were the screams, the pushing, and shoving? The panic? They were future ghosts drifting to their death.

Calypso glided up next to him.

"I don't understand," he said. Buildings disappeared all around them, animals, plants, Droplets, all popping at an alarming rate, still no one panicked.

"Everything dies, and everything has its time," Calypso said. "We understand and accept this. If our life ends this day, running will not extend it. Come, we must inform the Princess."

They headed back to the palace. Char wanted to run, but Calypso's steady pace forced him to slow his gate. His muscles twitched; he clenched and unclenched his fists. A howling arose in the stillness. He gritted his teeth as sweat broke out all over his body. The sound was worse than anything he had heard on Earth. He spun around, looking for the owner of the insufferable sound.

They turned a corner and found a horde of Sprouts, fighting and convulsing in one great massive pile. They bit and kicked at each other while others writhed and made the most horrible demonic noises before popping.

Calypso touched Char's arm, and he turned from the horrific scene to follow her into the palace. They found Aurora, pacing, in the throne room, mumbling to herself. The green light fell in shafts from the tall windows. Aurora paced through them as if she didn't see them.

"It must surround me to hurt me," Char whispered as he positioned himself between two shafts of light, making sure none of it touched him. He looked at Aurora. "You're highness?"

She stopped pacing and stared at him as if she didn't know him.

"What's going on?" she asked. Char raised an eyebrow.

"The Caparians are attacking," Calypso replied.

"That can't be," Aurora's laugh was sharp and high. She waved her hand absently at them as if brushing away a fly. "Mrah couldn't possibly make it back here this soon. He still has a whole day."

"Must have broken a speed limit," Char mumbled. Two Droplets in uniforms entered the room. Calypso motioned for them to stop by the door.

Aurora glanced out the window and twirled her hair around her long fingers. Her skin twitched, and her eyes darted from one thing to the next.

"You're Highness, I assure you, it is confirmed," Calypso replied.

"We have to fight," Char said.

"No! Mrah cannot be here yet!" Aurora snapped. She turned back to the window, still mumbling to herself. The green light enveloped her whole body. "This wasn't supposed to happen. This isn't the way it's supposed to happen." Her voice didn't sound right. It was a little too coarse for a Droplet.

"What wasn't supposed to happen?" Char asked. Did he want to know the answer? His stomach soured at the unknown implication. He took a single step toward her. Her sudden shrill scream ricocheted off the walls. Char jumped, his heart leaped in his chest, and his head seemed to clear. Every object came into sharp focus as if his eyes suddenly remembered how to see.

"What?" He cried. His heart slammed against his chest, causing real pain.

"It's all disappearing!" She ran her fingers through her hair, balled her hands into fists, and tugged on the long strands. "My home!"

She pounded on the glass and yelled at the window. "Leave them alone! Stop it!"

She spun around, tears streaming down her face. "It wasn't supposed to happen like this! It was supposed to be different!"

"What are you saying? What was supposed to be different?" Char demanded. She started walking in one direction, twirled on her heel, and went the opposite way; another step or two, then turned back as if she didn't have enough room to pace properly. She wrung her hands, mumbling again.

"Make them stop!" She paused her pacing long enough to shriek, then in a breathless whisper, "What do we do? What do we do?" Her pacing resumed.

"You're Highness, perhaps I should—" Calypso started.

"No!" Aurora shouted. She spun to face Calypso fully, her arms straight at her sides, her hands balled into fists. "You cannot have my throne!"

A singular hatred burned in Aurora's eyes, unlike anything Char had ever seen. A chill shivered through him; he took a step back. Droplets were incapable of hatred, or so he had always thought.

She seemed to grow taller as she walked closer, her head bent down, her glowing eyes stared out at them from the cave her hair made around her face. Her eyes were sunken, her cheeks hollowed. Her lips pulled back from her teeth in an animal-like snarl. Char had never noticed her teeth before, perfect white pebbles glowing in her mouth as if she were under a black light.

"I do not seek your throne. I was merely going to offer—"

"*I said no!*" she shrieked again. Char flinched at the razor-sharp pitch. She paused, seemed to listen, then slowly, a serene smile spread across her face. She lifted her face to the ceiling and looked down at them out of the corner of her eyes.

"I can handle it," she said with a childlike voice. She flung her arms out at her sides, tilted her head back, and spun in slow circles. Some of her long tresses covered her face, and the rest twirled around her. She started singing what may have been a lullaby, but her voice sounded like she was a fifty-year-old smoker. It would hardly put a child to sleep, give it nightmares maybe.

Char rubbed his sweaty palms on his pants, his muscles twitched all over his body, but his blood felt cold in his veins. Had he entrusted Kat's life to this creature? He glanced at Calypso and gasped.

"Calypso, look!" He pointed at her darkening arm. She looked down. Her skin slowly darkened to a midnight blue. Her hair turned a dark hunter green. She looked into Char's eyes. Her dark gray pupils grew until her entire eye was dark gray. Her voice, when she spoke, sounded centuries old, just like the Elders, a voice which was many voices.

He looked at Aurora, who lowered her head again, dipping it into her chest. Her hair slid down to enshroud her face. If she had had eyelashes, she would have been staring at Calypso through them.

"The aging process has begun," Calypso said. Then looked at Aurora and nodded. "I understand, now. You have Sprout blood in you."

Aurora didn't move, her face contorted in rage, hideous as the devil. Her skin darkened slightly, but not as much as Calypso's. Deep lines formed around her once beautiful features, accenting the anger and hate. She shook her head, slowly at first, then faster.

"No," she rasped. She cocked her head, letting her eyes roll in Char's direction. Her toothy grin made him shudder. He wanted to look away, willed himself to look away, but he couldn't even blink. She was still somehow hauntingly beautiful.

"Our dear Aurora, it is time," Calypso said. Calypso seemed unaffected by the change in Aurora. She stood firm, unyielding, unshaken.

"You can't have my throne." Her voice was guttural, like a Sprout's.

Her shrill screech filled the room as she flung herself out of the green light and at Calypso. Her long fingers wrapped around Calypso's slender throat. Calypso stood still and let her.

Char leaped at the two and tried to pull Aurora away. He couldn't get a grip. Her skin was as slippery as sea slime. She was also at least two feet taller than he. He managed to wrap his arms around her waist, only to slide off. He was a child trying to stop an adult. She whipped one arm around and, with more strength than he expected, flung him aside.

A shock jolted up his spine as he landed on his tailbone. Air whooshed out of his lungs. He coughed and rolled onto his knees. He sucked in air as fast as he could, but none of it seemed to be enough. Still, he staggered to his feet. He took one shaky step toward them when he noticed the soldier's spring into action.

They jerked Aurora back and stepped back into a shaft of green light. Calypso, still calm, looked Aurora in the eye.

"By Zortentearthian law, we now assume the throne."

"Noooo," Aurora moaned, shaking her head so hard, her hair flung out and wrapped around her face. She snatched handfuls and yanked on them. White blood oozed from her scalp and ran down her forehead. Some of her hair broke when she ripped it from her scalp. Short tufts stuck out at wild angles amidst the long silken strands. She looked more like a Sprout with every passing second. A trickle of blood followed one of the deep lines in her face until it reached the tip of her chin.

"I know just as much as you," Aurora said it more like a threat than a statement.

"It's a stupid law! I can handle the throne!" Aurora squirmed in the grip the soldiers had on her upper arms.

"Ask the Elders! Ask the Elders! She will tell you." Aurora's voice became light and breathless, desperate.

"Our dear Aurora, the Elders, is dead, as you well know," Calypso replied, then looked at the soldiers. "Take her somewhere safe."

"Yes, you're Highness," The soldiers said in unison.

"No!" Aurora fought, but they would not release her. She kicked and thrashed, her head whipped back and forth. Her body flipped and jerked in such ways; it seemed she had no skeleton. She grunted and moaned like a caged animal.

"She sounds like a Sprout," Char said. Calypso nodded.

"That is because she can no longer control the Sprout blood in her veins."

"You don't understand! He killed him! He *murdered* him!" Aurora raised her forearms to grab her head; her legs gave out from under her. She would have fallen if the soldiers had not had a firm grip.

"The pressure!" she wailed. She twisted hard. The soldiers lost their grip, and she dropped to the floor like a tattered old blanket. She writhed on the floor; awful noises emanated from her throat. No creature Char had ever heard made sounds like that, not even the fighting Sprouts he had just witnessed. Aurora popped.

"Follow the others," Calypso ordered the guards. They bowed and left.

"What did she mean, 'He murdered him'?" Char asked in the sudden silence.

"No time to explain; we must get you to the chamber," Calypso said to Char. They entered the hall and fell into step with the other Droplets from town. They walked, single file and slow. Char was ready to pull *his* hair out.

Finally, Calypso broke off of the main line and headed down the long hallway to the chamber where Kat's body was. Char wondered if Alex had escaped. Had he made it to the underground tunnel? Was he already with Kat? Or had he fallen victim to the green light? They reached the door. Calypso opened it.

"Remember, what we do, we must. You may not understand at first, but one day you will. Then, it will not matter at all." Calypso said.

"I can fight," Char insisted.

Calypso shook her head. There was no fear in her eyes, no uncontrolled emotions, just sheer age.

"Save us."

Char sat with his head in his hands. How long had he been sitting in this chamber? Where was Alex? Was he dead? Was he on his way? Char's hair had gotten longer in the time he had spent on this planet. The long strands tickled the backs of his hands. He thought about getting a haircut the first chance he got. Then, who would cut it?

He thought about how Tracy used to cut his hair. She always insisted she cut it. She used to joke that was why she was born his twin to give him free haircuts. Her face flashed through his mind, her long straight hair around those blue eyes and her smile; her innocent yet wise smile. She was always so kind and generous. She never thought of herself first, always the other person, whomever it may be.

"I'm sorry, Tracy," he mumbled into his hands.

"I should have helped you. I should have done more." He stood and paced the room. Guilt nearly crushed him. He was always amazed at how heavy guilt could be, how it pressed on his lungs.

"What kind of Pastor cares more about saving his hide than that of his flock?" he cried. A rush of anger shot through him. It seemed to take on a life of its own. He punched a wall before he could think. He grunted in pain and clutched his throbbing hand.

"Well, guess the walls are harder than they look." He cradled his wounded hand and sat in the ugly chair again. Kat hovered above the table, completely unaware of his presence—or was she?

"Kat," Char whispered. He stood and leaned over her. Her black lashes made dark lines across her closed eyes. Her hair fell away from her face, leaving the pale orb free to show off its painfully perfect features. His hand shook as it touched her sable hair. It was as soft as it appeared.

"Kat, if you can hear me... warn me..." He choked as the tears burned at the corners of his eyes. "Please, Kat, warn me. Help me save them. Even if I don't get them all, I want to try."

He stopped as a sob jerked through his chest, making him gasp for air. He fisted his hands, knuckles white, squeezed his eyes shut even tighter until they ached. All the faces of the people he had run past, had dragged Tracy past, flashed through his mind in an endless morbid parade. So many faces—young and old, crying, dazed, pained—people he ignored to save himself and his sister. They surrounded him now, forcing him to acknowledge them. Then the faces distorted, glared at him, accused him of abandoning them.

He lifted his head, stood, and fixed his eyes on Kat's slumbering face. His voice was solid, unapologetic. "I am not going to cower in the dark this time. This time, I fight!"

He crossed to the wall with the invisible door and felt around the smooth surface. He didn't feel anything, but a section of wall dissolved into an opening. He peeked into the deserted hallway, stepped out, and ran his hand down the outside wall. The door closed, leaving a wall just as smooth as if the door never existed. He hoped he would remember where it was after he found Alex.

He ran down the hall as quietly as possible. The corridor was eerily silent. Deep black shadows alternated with pools of lights from the orbs in the ceiling. For the first time, he noticed the pillars lining the long hall. Amazing the little things, he noticed now that his life was in danger. He saw the world anew. Ornate objects became less about beauty and more about how they could help him.

He kept expecting explosions and screams to echo throughout the building but was constantly disappointed. He slid a hand along the wall at about the level of the invisible switches, hoping to activate another door. He needed to find a weapon, and he needed to find Alex.

He passed the stairwell that would take him up and out, but he figured Alex wouldn't be coming from above. His secret passage was down deep. Just as Char was about to give up on finding another switch, a door finally opened, and he peered inside the dark room. Nothing moved nor jumped out at him.

He slipped into the shadows and felt around the wall, but he couldn't find a light. He stretched his hands out in front of him like a blindfolded man and took tentative steps into the darkness. His eyes adjusted till he was able to make out lumpy outlines. His imagination turned them into the stuff of nightmares, but his rational mind told him they were just stacks of boxes. He bumped a pile, and it collapsed. The sound of the spilling contents reverberated as they clattered across the floor.

He ducked his head and froze. Nothing. Stillness. Several heart-beats later, he knelt by the toppled boxes and dug through the mess. He found what felt like a gun. He grabbed it and hurried back into the hall to examine his find.

It was black, sleek, and heavier than he expected. It had a trigger like a gun, but it was unlike any weapon he had ever seen on Earth. It didn't even look like the gun he had used from the escape pod. At least *that* one had looked like a gun. On Earth, before all this madness, he had never handled one. He had had no need. No desire. He had saved Kat but considered himself lucky he hit the giant creature without hurting Kat.

How would he figure out this alien gun with all its smooth lines and round edges? He ran his fingers over the muzzle, and five green lights lit up. It made a sound like it was powering up. A slight vibration told him it was ready to fire—or explode, how would he know? He stared at it and wondered if he would be able to pull the trigger on a being more like a human than an animal.

Now that he was armed, he felt better about hunting for Alex. Not that a gun would do anything against the green light. He closed the door, listened for any sounds, and hurried down the hall. The tomb-like silence was so thick he almost didn't hear the scrape.

He sucked in a shallow breath and pressed himself into the crevice between a pillar and the wall, deep in a dark shadow. His heart thun-dered in his ears. It had sounded like someone scuffing their feet. He adjusted his grip on his new weapon. The scrape didn't repeat, but soft slapping footsteps did. Char sensed someone was there, just out of sight. He was equally blessed and cursed with his hiding place. He was as blind as his hunter. He wondered if it was Alex but didn't want to risk a look.

Footsteps moved down the hall toward Kat's room. After the steps faded a bit, he risked a glance and spotted a Caparian! It didn't take long for the Caparian to reach Kat's door. Char slipped down the hall, keeping to the shadows, trying to remain silent. He had to get closer. He didn't want to risk missing his target.

Char almost cried out when the Caparian rammed the door with his shoulder.

Char slid along the wall in a long shadow, thankful he was wearing black. He just needed to get a little closer. His heart thumped against his ribs, and blood roared through his ears.

Another crash left his ears ringing. He inched ever closer. His injured hand ached as he tightened his grip and cursed himself for being so foolish as to punch a wall at a time like this. He knelt and steadied his grip with his other hand, just as the third crash succeeded in breaking down the door. The Caparian stumbled in with the debris. He lost sight and silently cursed himself again, this time for not being faster. He raced for the door, gun up. He fired as soon as he saw yellow.

The Caparian dodged the shot, turned, and glared down at Char; his red eyes burned like hot coals. His yellow hair hung limp against his mustard-yellow skin. His browned banana peel grin revealed revolting teeth. He was the visual representation of all things evil and satanic. He looked as if he wasn't born with enough skin to cover his skeleton. It pulled tight around his bones and resembled leather.

Char's stomach flipped inside him and gurgled in protest to the sight. He could feel the bile working its way up his throat. He swallowed, but nothing could get past the lump. His sweaty hands were slick on the gun. His knees trembled under his skin. It was all he could do to keep from collapsing. There was no doubt in his mind this Caparian was the same one he saw on the screen in the ship. This was Mrah.

"Pitiful human and your silly toys," Mrah growled. Faster than Char expected, Mrah had closed the distance. Char fired another shot, but it went wide. Mrah pinched Char's wrist between two fingers and twisted. Char growled as a sharp pain shot up his arm and dropped the gun. Still using his two fingers, Mrah flung Char against the wall. He bounced off the wall and collapsed beside the chair.

"You can't have her," Char said through gritted teeth. He climbed to his feet and stared defiantly into the blazing red eyes of his foe. He gripped the chair and swung it as hard as he could. It shattered on impact. He was left holding a single jagged chair leg—little more than a stick. Mrah didn't even flinch.

He raised the chair leg, but Mrah grabbed his hand holding the stick and squeezed. Char's bones molded around the wood, the corners cut into his flesh. He heard his bones snap like sticks of candy, felt a pain that burned like hot iron spikes. He howled in agony and felt dizzy and sick. Mrah flung him against the wall again as if he were nothing more than a three-week-old puppy. His head bounced off the wall with a fleshy thump. He collapsed and lay there a few moments, trying to find the breath to move. Finally, he managed to lift his head to look at Mrah as he leaned over Kat's body.

"Stop," Char rasped. The room blurred, and he struggled to stay conscious. Where was the gun? He had to find it.

A Droplet raced into the room and full-body-tackled Mrah. Alex! Char tried to sit up, but the room spun, and he slumped back down. Blood trickled into Char's eyes. He wiped it away and squinted at the two aliens fighting.

Alex and Mrah crashed into the wall, bounced back, and hit the table. It released a loud groan as it slid across the floor. Some of the precious sand slipped off Kat's body.

Kat! Char forced himself back to his feet. He staggered toward Kat. Alex slammed a fist into Mrah's face. Green blood spurted from his nose.

Mrah howled and shoved Alex back against the wall. He pinned Alex with his forearm across Alex's throat. Char tugged on the table, gasping at the weight. He pulled as hard as he could and managed to get it under Kat again.

Alex's eyes bulged, his mouth moved, but he wasn't getting any air. Feeling like a child attacking an adult, Char rammed his shoulder into

Mrah's side, throwing all his body weight into the hit. Mrah staggered to the side a step. It wasn't much, but it was enough to break the hold on Alex.

Alex squirmed his way free and sucked in a lungful of air.

Char scanned the room for the gun, but Mrah was faster. He grabbed Char around the throat and lifted him off the floor as if he weighed no more than a dried leaf, then just as easily flung him against the wall again. At this point, Char almost wished Mrah would just punch him. Getting tossed around like a rag doll was just embarrassing.

He fell in a heap by the gun. Char wrapped his good hand around the gun but couldn't lift it. There was nothing he could do as Mrah picked up the broken chair leg and rammed the pointed end into Alex's chest.

"No, Alex!" Char whispered, then the swooping darkness claimed him.

KAT

Kat stood over Katie's sleeping form, hands balled into fists. Their laughter still rang in her ears. Their mocking of her warning burned in her veins like acid. She made a conscious effort to relax her hands. Uncontrolled anger would not serve her now. She needed to stay calm, to think. She needed to find a way to prove to Katie this wasn't all just a silly dream.

She whispered a quick prayer and dove into Katie's body. Kat sensed fear as she shoved Katie's spirit to the side.

"That's right, no games this time," Kat said. "I mean business."

"No clouds, either." Kat waved a hand across the darkness, transforming it into the unmoving steel gray sky she had had to stare at for so many years.

"You will endure what I had to endure for five years," Kat said though Katie had not yet, arrived. "Well, minus the three years of darkness."

She walked across the baked brown plains, all of it still so real in her mind. It was easy to recreate the unforgiving heat of the sun on the parched land. She raised a hand to send the hot, dry wind whipping across the planet. The unbridled wind shoved its way through anything and everything that stood in its path. She stopped walking and waited for Katie to appear. She didn't have to wait long.

"Not you again," Katie whined. She stomped her foot on the packed dirt and folded her arms like a petulant child.

"Yes," Kat replied, her voice calculated and cool, "me again."

"I'm leaving," Katie said and spun on her heel. She stuck her nose in the air, arms still folded across her chest, and stalked in the opposite direction.

"Where will you go?" Kat asked.

Katie shrugged and kept walking. Kat lifted her hand, strengthening the wind; it thrust Katie back with all the fury of a hurricane. She staggered back, and Kat grabbed Katie by the upper arms and squeezed. Then, she released one hand to snatch a handful of dark hair, jerked down, forcing Katie to look at the sky.

"Look at this!" Kat hissed in Katie's ear. She squeezed her fingers deeper into Katie's arms until Katie gasped. Kat concentrated on the sky, forcing it to form the image she wanted.

Mrah's emaciated head filled the sky. His gaunt face dripped with all the sweat and drool Kat remembered. His yellow teeth, razor-sharp and protruding from his mouth, appeared close enough to bite them. His hot, red eyes glared at Katie.

Katie wiggled in the tight grip, whimpering like a child. She shrank, in Kat's grasp, away from the hideous face that loomed over them.

"This is what you wanted, isn't it?" Kat growled, "For me to show them to you?"

"This is a... what did you call it? Kakarian? Kripto? Tapworm? *Caparian!*" Kat roared. Katie flinched and tucked her head down further, squeezing her eyes shut. Kat showed no mercy. She spun Katie around and brought her nose inches from Katie's face. Katie's hair swung around her and slapped Kat's arm. Long dark strands stuck to Katie's face accenting her huge dark eyes.

"Look into my eyes, Katie!" Kat ordered. She stared into Katie's eyes, seeing the dark depths, like miniature black holes. "You know it's true!"

"No," Katie whined, shaking her head. Katie's eyes glistened with unshed tears. Kat shoved her away. Katie stumbled and fell, landing hard on her back. She lay still for a moment before propping herself up with her elbows.

"I want to wake up," Katie mumbled.

"Not this time," Kat said. She stood over Katie, hands on her hips, shaking her head. The wind whipped her short hair around her face, blocking out one eye. She ran her fingers through her hair, but it fell right back in her face.

"You can't force me to dream," Katie replied. Her eyes lacked the confidence her voice tried to portray.

"You're here until I release you."

"No!" Katie shouted. Now her eyes flared with defiance. Kat smiled.

"Think you can laugh this dream off tomorrow?"

Katie's eyes widened.

"How, how did you know?"

"Because I'm real!" Kat bellowed. "I'm not some specter your mind created. I'm with you *all the time*. I follow you *all day*."

Katie closed her eyes, slowly shook her head, and pulled herself to her feet. She was calm and logical when she spoke, like Scrooge trying to explain away Marley.

"No, you're just my sub-conscious—"

"Katie!" Kat shouted. "Listen to me! I heard you laughing; I *caused* the *accident!*"

"You?" Katie cried. "Why?"

"Because you didn't even *try* to help me!"

"How dare you risk my life just because I didn't help you!"

"How dare I risk *your* life? Excuse me; it's *our* life! I told you who I am!"

"So, what?"

They stood toe to toe, each with her hands on her hips. Katie's long hair swirled around her; her lips formed a solid line. Her eyes stared, unflinching, at Kat.

Staring at her past self made Kat realize how much weight she had lost. Not that she was ever fat, but she had definitely toned down. Her body was lean and hard, compared to Katie's. She remembered how she loved having long hair, feeling like a princess from a fairytale. She had wanted hair as long as Rapunzel's, then to be swept off her feet by her prince charming, a cliché little dream that seemed to be every little girl's fantasy, to be rescued by her knight in shining armor. Nothing but a naïve dream that completely missed the point of the fairytale.

Well, her knight had rescued her, but there would be no happily ever after because real life was not as pretty as a fairytale. Kat clenched her jaw and forced the memories of her past to evaporate.

Katie looked up at the picture of Mrah.

"Get that ugly face off the sky."

"No," Kat dropped her voice, keeping it dangerously calm.

"Yes," Katie matched her tone.

"Fine," Kat's voice rumbled out of her chest like a warning grumble from a volcano. "Is this better?"

She waved her hand and changed the sky from Mrah's face to the meteor shower. Complete with the escape pods colliding and exploding. The familiar flowers of fire burst over their heads. Katie's face was a creepy theatre mask of reflected fire light and shadows. The wind kept blowing, and the meteors kept coming, but everything was bizarrely silent.

"If I'm you," Katie said; one corner of her mouth quirked in a half-smile. Her eyes sparkled mischievously, "then I can do it too!"

She waved a hand. Nothing happened. Katie's face hardened in concentration, she bit her lip and waved her hand again. Instead of fire, rainbows shot out of the center of the explosions. Each new rainbow cast colors across the plains, like an artist's psychedelic landscape. It was as if Katie had shot them into a nineteen seventy's tie-dyed t-shirt. Kat remembered seeing one once in a history book. The colors slid across Katie's triumphant face, rippling like a reflection of water.

Not taking her eyes off her counterpart, Kat snapped her fingers and changed it back to Mrah's hideous face. The colors faded away like a dying man's sight.

Katie, grinning, turned him into a fuzzy white kitten.

"Enough!" Kat cried. Her spirit crackled, filling with the angry energy she hadn't, yet, learned to control. If she wasn't careful, she might damage her past self. She lifted both hands and brought them down, hard. The shock wave sent ripples across the ground, knocking Katie off her feet. Katie's head bounced off the hard ground, leaving her looking stunned.

The ripples shot across the sky, like shaking out a blanket, snapping the kitten into oblivion. The ground shook, developing cracks that grew to large crevices. Dark, angry clouds filled the sky, followed by thunder and lightning. Kat swooped one hand through the air, bringing on a colder wind. The other hand followed suit and brought a heavy, pounding rain that beat the ground mercilessly.

The driving, icy rain had them drenched in mere seconds. Kat felt the cold seep into her bones, followed by an intense aching. Her fingers went numb, and her nose began to run. Kat lifted herself till she was hovering ten feet off the ground, looking down at Katie. Her arms outstretched, her feet pressed together and pointed down.

Katie lay sprawled in the forming puddle of water, the ground so hard and dry it couldn't drink the rain. She shoved her long wet locks out of her face and looked at Kat with wary eyes. Cracks formed all around Katie, creating an island from which there was no escape; they deepened, widened until there was no chance Katie could jump them. Lightning struck close to Katie's island. Katie spread her arms out at her sides and gripped the edges as the ground continued to shake.

"You cannot fight me," Kat's voice matched the thunder, rumble for rumble; it echoed into the distance. The lightning flashed like a strobe with no time to breathe before the crash of thunder. "I've survived more than you're even capable of dreaming."

She pulled another bolt from the sky. Katie flinched as it blackened the ground nearby. The only thing saving her from the current was the wide fissure.

"Make no mistake, I *will* succeed, and you *will* help me," Kat ordered.

"How?" Katie's teeth chattered as she spoke. She let go of the sides and sat up, wrapping her arms around her legs. She sniffed and coughed.

"Find Char."

"Who?"

"A friend," Kat answered.

"Where?"

Kat thought for a moment. She had never asked where Char lived. She didn't even know his last name. In all the time she had spent with him, she never once asked him about his past. She closed her eyes and thought back to when she first met him. He was in the observation base, at the military outpost. He must be in the military.

"I met him in Beta Alpha Quadrant Four in the Observation base," Kat said. "So, he must be military."

"How will I find him?" Katie asked. She dragged her soggy sleeve across her wet nose.

"Find him!"

≈Z≈

Kat watched Katie sit straight up in bed with a short, sharp scream. Her face glistened with sweat, her damp hair stuck to her cheek. She ran a shaky hand through her hair and looked around her room wide-eyed.

"Looking for me?" Kat asked, bemused.

"Kat?" Katie whispered. Her eyes darted around the room. Something in the room shifted. Katie jumped back, slammed into the wall, and screamed. More of her hair fell in her face, un-brushed and sticky; her wild eyes peeked out from the strands. She pulled her knees up and hugged them to her chest. She was breathing loudly.

"A little jumpy this morning?" Kat asked. Then after a pause, "Maybe, you should slow your breathing," Kat suggested. "You're going to hyperventilate."

The bedroom door burst open. Their mother raced into the room, tying her robe as she ran. She sat beside Katie and wrapped her arm around the shaking girl.

"Honey," their mother crooned. "What happened? Did you have a nightmare?"

"Mom," Katie burst into tears. She blubbered out the whole dream. Their mother listened and stroked Katie's hair, assuring her it was only a dream.

"It wasn't that scary," Kat rolled her eyes.

"Come on, honey," their mother soothed. "We'll go down and make some waffles with blueberry syrup. How's that sound?"

Katie sniffed loudly and nodded.

"Mom!" Kat cried. She hovered around her mother. "Don't coddle her!"

They, of course, couldn't hear her anymore today than they could when she had first arrived, and she couldn't manipulate the natural world as easily as she could the dreamscape. She had no choice but to follow the two downstairs and watch them make and eat the waffles. Katie was very quiet. Kat sat right beside her and talked in Katie's ear.

"Well," Kat asked. "What are you going to do?"

Boon's horn blew; Katie stood, slowly, and went out to see him. Her shoulders hunched as she walked, her head tucked down, staring at her feet as she shuffled along. Their mother told Katie to have a good day as she walked out. Katie didn't reply. Kat glanced back and saw the worry crease her mother's face.

"Stand up straight!" Kat snapped when she turned her attention back to the slouching Katie. Her spirit crackled again, sounded like sweaters fresh out of the dryer.

Katie flinched and spun around. Her mouth opened and closed, but no sound came out. She heaved a breath in but never let it out; her face went even paler. Her eyes bulged, searching everywhere.

"Katie," Kat ordered, "breathe!"

Katie kept searching but still didn't say anything. Kat stomped her foot in frustration. Boon honked the horn again, and Katie jumped. Her books slipped from her hands and skittered across the sidewalk. Loose papers fluttered in the breeze like a flock of listless white doves. She made no move to chase them.

Boon got out of the car, slamming the door harder than was necessary.

"Good, Boon, talk to her." Kat stepped toward him, half expecting him to stop, but he walked on past. She spun on her heel and followed at his side. "Calm her down. I'm afraid I overdid the effects last night."

"What's the matter?" He asked. His voice was low and gentle. Kat smiled at the sound of concern in his voice. Katie stared through him.

"Katie, talk to him," Kat said. "Tell him what's going to happen."

"Katie," He took her by the shoulders. Kat noticed the white lines outlining the red centers on his fingertips. She pursed her lips. Katie didn't flinch, but it must have been painful. "What's wrong?"

"Shh," Katie put a finger to her lips and whispered. "She might hear you."

"Who?" he asked.

"Me," Katie replied. A long lock of hair fell across her face. One wide eye stared out at Boon.

Kat slid her thumb and forefinger across her eyes and pinched the bridge of her nose, sighed, and shook her head.

"He's going to think you're nuts," Kat mumbled. "Especially when you look like you just escaped from a mental hospital; fix your hair!"

"What?" He asked. His eyes narrowed.

"I mean, future me," Katie said. Her eyes glanced over his shoulder. He followed her gaze. With his face turned away, he squeezed his eyes shut, then rolled them to the sky before turning back to her. He sounded tired and annoyed when he spoke.

"Get in the car, Katie." He stood and walked back to the car. Katie gathered her papers as if in a trance, then glided to the car and climbed into the passenger side. She pulled her seatbelt around her and clicked it into place as Kat crawled into the back.

"Great way to break the news," Kat said. "He'll never doubt you now."

"Boon?" Katie asked. She stared out the window as she spoke.

"Yeah?" He didn't hide his irritation.

"What's with the attitude?" Kat asked. She wanted to smack him in the head.

"Where's the compassion?" Kat continued. "Something is obviously upsetting her; you could at least hear her out."

"How would I go about finding someone in the military?" Katie asked.

"Why?" Boon put the car into gear and jerked it out into traffic. A car behind them leaned on the horn. Boon flipped it off. Tires squealed as the car zipped out around them and took off. Boon muttered an expletive.

"I just want to know." Katie seemed oblivious to what was going on around her. Kat leaned forward between the seats.

"I don't know." He replied as he barely slowed for the stop sign before hitting the gas and blasting through it.

"You really shouldn't drive when you're irritated," Kat said. "You're reckless."

"Who do you want to find?" he asked.

"A guy named Char," Katie said.

"Who's Char?" his voice was sharp. Kat raised an eyebrow.

"I don't know," Katie replied.

"Then why do you want to find him?"

"Because she told me to," Katie murmured. She stared out the window, unmoving.

"Maybe I did do some damage after all," Kat mused. "What if I caused myself brain damage? If I did do damage, though, wouldn't the effects be affecting me now?"

"Who told you to?" Boon asked as he flat out ran another stop sign, not even feigning a stop. An oncoming car screeched to a halt, horn blaring.

"Kat," Katie whispered.

"Not this again. Look," Boon's voice was stern. He looked at her long and hard, the car accelerated, but he never even glanced at the road. "Kat isn't real."

"Yes, I am!" Kat cried. "And watch the road!"

"I had another dream last night." Katie continued. Her voice was even, quiet, and barely audible.

He jerked the car to the side of the road and slammed on the brakes. Katie sucked in a sharp breath; white knuckles gripped the handle above the door. They both jerked forward and slammed back against the seats.

"Listen!" He hissed. He squeezed her arm. Her flesh bulged around his fingers. "It's just a dream! A stupid dream! There is no Kat! No Char! No end of the world or anything else your sick subconscious might have dreamed up!"

"But—"

"No! Drop it!" He didn't just let go of her arm; he shoved her away then whipped back out onto the road. "I forbid you to search for him!"

The rest of the ride was silent. Kat sat, with her arms crossed, seething.

～Z～

"You can do this," Kat encouraged, even though she knew Katie couldn't hear her. They walked into the army recruiting office. The room was small, with jail cell-gray walls and floor. Posters lined the walls, advertising the many branches of the military.

"Ugly little room, isn't it?" Kat asked. She scraped her foot across the dirty floor, but, of course, nothing moved.

Katie fiddled with a button on her shirt, twisting it until the fabric started to twist with it. She timidly crossed the room to the single desk. Kat followed at her side, wanting to slap Katie's hand so she would stop fidgeting.

Papers, brochures, and pens littered the desk. Kat could just see a phone peeking out from under a huge pile. A can of soda sat close to the edge of the desk, backed by a massive stack of brochures. The tower would topple and knock the can onto the floor if one gave way.

"You would think a military recruiter would keep his desk neater." Kat mused. "I mean, what would his drill sergeant think?"

There was a door to the right of the desk. Kat wondered where it went.

"Where's the recruiter?" Kat asked. A toilet flushed, the door opened, and in stepped an obese man. Kat groaned.

"We might as well leave now." Kat spit. "This guy's a pig."

He was a much fatter, sausage-arm guy, and he lacked the beard. His hair wasn't as greasy, and there was more of it. His eyes were still ice blue, not as menacing as when they last met, but she was sure it was the man from the plains.

"At least he isn't as sweaty this time," Kat muttered.

The fat man looked at Katie for a long moment before stretching out his hand to shake. Kat stepped back as Katie wiped her palm on her jeans then shook his hand.

"Oh, don't, I don't want his hand touching me," Kat moaned. Without realizing it, she was wiping her hand on her pants as if that would wipe away germs from years ago.

"What can I do for you, Miss?" He asked. His voice was professional and pleasant.

"My name is Katie," she replied, a little too fast. He motioned for her to sit, and she did. He hiked up his pants before sitting. His rotund belly caught the edge of the desk, showering the floor with papers. The can fell with the avalanche, making a hollow, tinny noise as it hit. He grunted as he leaned over to pick up the mess.

The avalanche revealed a picture in a plain black frame with a pretty blond woman holding a baby. She smiled for the camera, and the baby cried. He sat up, dropping the pile of papers on the picture.

"Sorry about that," he said breathlessly. "My name is Sergeant Doherty. What can I do for you?"

"Well, I'm looking for someone in the military," Katie said. She sat a little straighter and looked him in the eye. "And I was hoping you would be able to tell me how to go about doing it."

"I'm telling you, Katie, this guy is trouble," Kat whispered, then grinned. "What am I whispering for? You guys can't hear me."

"Well, if you tell me what branch of the service he's in, I can—"

"I don't know what branch of the service he's in." Katie cut in. Sergeant Doherty raised an eyebrow.

"All right, what's his name?"

"Char."

"Last name?" He asked. Katie grimaced.

"I don't know that, either; I'm sorry."

Kat paced behind Katie's chair. Why hadn't she thought to get all this information before she left?

"Do you know anything besides his name?" he asked. Before Katie could answer, the door opened, and in walked the pretty blond woman from the photo. She held the hand of a toddler.

"Hi, honey," her voice was zephyr-like. "I'm sorry to interrupt, but I wanted to let you know we were in the area, so we thought you might like to meet us for lunch."

The little blond girl let go of her mother's hand and toddled over to her father. She put her chubby little hands in the air, and he scooped her up into a hug. He tickled her belly, and she laughed loudly. Her laugh was a pure, sweet, uninhibited bubbling of joy. Kat smiled as he cooed over the child.

She stepped closer to them and put a hand on the little girl, sliding her palm over the shiny, corn silk hair. The girl didn't seem to notice, as Mary had. In a flash, she realized all he must have lost. He had been alone when they met on the plains. He must have watched his family die, as she had. She could just see his wife curled on the ground as her mother had. She couldn't even fathom the depth of his pain as he watched this sweet little girl, with her whole life ahead of her, perish. The innocent laughter was cut short by crushing pain then nothing; snuffed out so quickly, there wasn't time to adjust. Had he felt as helpless as she? Had he also groped in the air; tried in vain to pull his family back together from the dust that was not dust?

"I'm sorry," Kat whispered, remembering how she had beaten him, mercilessly, on the plains. "I had no idea... I never thought... I'm sorry I hurt you."

He gave the girl back to his wife, blissfully unaware of Kat's musings and apology.

"Give me half an hour," he told her. She nodded and left.

"I am sorry," Kat continued. "I guess I never realized you must have had a family too before the aliens came."

"I apologize," he said as he leaned back in his chair. "That was my wife and daughter."

"It's all right," Katie smiled. "Your little girl is precious." Her shoulders visibly relaxed, and she stopped fidgeting.

"Thank you," he said. "I don't think I can help you unless you can remember any more information about this young man." He told her. His voice was gentle and understanding.

Katie fidgeted with the button on her shirt again. She took a couple of deep breaths, not looking directly at him.

"I do know a little more, but..." she stopped.

"But," he asked. He spoke to Katie as if she were his daughter.

"I don't know if I should tell you."

"Yes!" Kat exclaimed. "Tell him! He may know what to do!"

"Go on," he urged.

"I've been having these dreams about a girl who looks like me; only, older, and with short hair. She tells me she's from the future, and she is me. She's here to warn us of an impending attack. The world turns green, then everyone on the planet dies. Last night she told me to find someone named Char." She stared at her lap. He stared at her, expressionless.

"I see," each word was slow and measured. He picked up a pen and scribbled something on a scrap of paper. "Call this number; they can help."

Katie took it and read the number. "Will they be able to stop the attack?"

"In a way," he replied. "They specialize in counseling troubled youth."

"What?" Her head snapped up; indignation flashed in her eyes.

"They do excellent work," His tone was too gentle. Katie pulled her shoulders back and stood. Her chair squeaked across the floor.

"She doesn't need a shrink!" Kat snapped.

"I don't need a shrink!" Katie snapped. She crumpled the paper and threw it at him. It bounced harmlessly off his chest. She turned and stormed out of the room.

"Wait!" He stood quickly, sending another shower of papers to the floor. He slipped on a document as he rounded the corner, catching his balance using the desk.

"I didn't mean to offend you!" But it was too late; Katie was gone. His shoulders slumped, and he went back to the desk. He grunted as he stooped to pick up the papers. Amongst the forms was the photograph of his family. He sat in his chair and sighed, holding the frame up to look at his wife.

"I'm afraid I didn't handle that very well, dear." His voice was heavy with guilt.

"It's all right," Kat assured him. "I understand. It is a hard story to swallow."

She left him to his cluttered desk and stepped out into the sunshine. She looked around, but Katie was gone. Cars drove down the street, people walked through her, unaware that she even existed. A woman on a cell phone chattered away, nearly colliding with a man in a suit. She grunted and kept walking, completely missing the irritated look on the man's face.

"You're all happily unaware of the danger in just a few days, aren't you?" Kat asked, unheard as always. She closed her eyes, tipped her head back to face the sky.

"How do I make them see?" She shouted at the sky. "And where is Char?"

She opened her eyes and gasped.

"How did I get here?"

CHAR

Char hovered somewhere between consciousness and the oblivion of sleep. He fought against the sedative-like tide in his mind. Willing himself to wake up, he kicked for the surface, only to be dragged down again by the waves rolling over his head. He hated the dizzy, swooping, falling sensation.

The spinning seemed to go on for ages, and the darkness wasn't cold, as it should be; it was hot. Flaming hot. Scalding hot. Char tried to roll over but hit a hot wall. He grunted and rolled away, but the hard surface he lay on was scorching.

The pain seeped into his body. With each new ache, each new stab, he knew another part of his body was intact. His spine throbbed up and down the whole column; the pain spread like an infectious disease. It drifted down his legs and arms. His knuckles ached like advanced arthritis.

He couldn't stretch his legs out, and the groaning he heard turned out to be his. He tried to force his eyes open, but his lids felt weighted down. Then his feet started to tingle, waking up. Thousands of needles stabbed at every inch of his feet. Then he accidentally moved one. He sucked in a lungful of scalding hot air and froze as thousands more needles attacked. It was a needle party, and they kept inviting friends.

Finally, he managed to crack a lid and peek through the slit. The room was blurred. He brought a hand up and rubbed his eyes, but the smudged world remained.

"Where am I?" he asked. His throat was raw, dry. He coughed and tried to swallow, but the sides of his throat stuck together. He tried to sit up, but the dizziness swooped back in to push him down.

It was so hot! He felt stifled in his heavy clothing. He ripped a sleeve off with his good hand and flung it away. He dropped his arms to his sides, exhausted. After a moment, he tried to rip the other sleeve off with his bad hand, but the pain nearly knocked him out. He sucked some air in through his nose, blew it out, sucked more in, held it, gritted his teeth, and, with a loud growl, pulled. His reward was a newly freed sleeve clenched in his fist.

He ran a hand over his chest to find something rough coiled around him. It didn't cover the entire surface. It was more like cords tied around him. He couldn't get his eyes to focus enough to make out what it was. He dropped his hand to his side and closed his eyes.

Kat! That one word cut through the fog in his mind, clearing it instantly. His heart picked up the pace as he realized he wasn't in the palace anymore. He pulled himself into a sitting position, fighting against the spinning sensation.

What had happened to him? The clarity didn't last. The fog that had just cleared from his mind gathered again, thicker than before. He rubbed his fingers across his forehead, squeezing his eyes shut. He vaguely remembered a Caparian and being thrown. He shook his head; why was it so hard to think? A flash of Mrah jamming the chair leg into Alex's chest flickered like a weak bulb in his mind before going out. Alex! Was he alive?

"If he's dead," he muttered, "Kat's going to kill me."

He drifted into a fitful sleep full of nightmares of being cooked by a yellow ogre with Mrah's face. When he finally, woke the spinning had eased enough for him to get up.

He was sitting in a small room with no door and no windows. The walls resembled lava before it developed the black crust. The floor and low ceiling looked just like the walls. The room had to be six foot cubed, with no furniture.

Char rolled onto his knees and pushed himself to his feet. This one motion caused his heart to beat as if he had just run a marathon. He had to stoop to keep from hitting his head and hobbled across the small room, which took about two steps. It was so hot! He should have been sweating. Why wasn't he sweating?

He put a hand on the wall and gasped as it burned him. He snatched his hand back and studied his palm. His hand was twice its normal size, and he could barely bend his fingers with his skin stretched so tight. His other hand was in worse shape with the underlying broken bones. He cringed as he remembered Mrah crushing his hand around the broken chair leg.

He gritted his teeth as he ran his good hand over the walls and ceiling, looking for a lever, a secret button to press to open a door. His neck ached, his eyes stung, and his vision wasn't clearing. His head pounded with a hangover-sized headache. His muscles cramped, sending sharp pains shooting throughout his body. He pressed an elbow to his side to dull a pain there and kept searching.

He pounded on the walls. He stomped a foot, then cursed in pain. He pushed on the ceiling. His energy was dissolving like a sugar cube in a hot cup of tea. His hands and feet went numb. He pressed the back of his good hand to his forehead. Dry. His skin was so dry.

"Dry heat," he mumbled. He looked at his hand again and noticed the tiny red spots on his arms. He ripped and pulled until he got the tunic off, no easy task with the cords around his chest. He tugged on his shirt till he could see the spots on his chest. They started to swirl and dance. He blinked, rubbed his dry eyes, and looked again, but they were still moving. The room spun, and he staggered a step or two.

"Why is it so hot?" He growled through gritted teeth. He squirmed inside his skin, tried to remain calm. Why was he suddenly so irritated? Furious, he ripped at his pant legs until he had ripped enough off to

make shorts. He punched the wall, but his energy was long gone, and his fist barely touched it.

"Let me out!" His throat was so dry his shout came out as a hoarse whisper. His head swooped again, and he had to sit down. His body weakened by the second. All of his muscles seemed to have turned to aspic. His stomach twisted in knots, lurched, sending bile up his scorched throat. He swallowed it back. Another sharp muscle spasm doubled him over. He crunched himself into the fetal position and groaned.

His lips were dry and cracked. Sharp pieces of lip skin poked his tongue as he licked his lips. His tongue stuck to his parched upper lip as if it were a frozen metal pole in winter.

He forced himself to straighten and look at the cords around his chest. Black ropes? No! Snakes! He had snakes squirming around his chest! Frantic, he jerked on them, twisted them, but he couldn't get them off. He scrambled back to his feet, trying to get away from the undulating black creatures. His heart was pulsing so fast now; he could feel the blood spurting through his carotid.

"Help!" His scream forced its way out of him, tearing through his throat and bursting forth like a living thing. He tried squeezing the snakes, but they wouldn't die! Why didn't they have heads? His scream became continuous as he thrashed at his chest. They constricted around his arms and legs. He pulled hard and heard them rip apart, but when he looked, they were still there. His vision blurred more, another swirling wave seemed to hit his whole body from the side, and he collapsed.

He lay like a slug. All his energy evaporated in this desert heat. He didn't even have enough left to blink. The floor was as hot as a sidewalk in a concrete city in the middle of July. His cheek pressed against the burning surface. Somewhere in his hazy mind, he thought he should roll away from the searing surface, but his body refused to move.

Tiny spots danced before his eyes. He couldn't remember where he was anymore or how he had gotten there. Then there was a face in front of him, a beautiful young woman with haunting ebony eyes shrouded in raven hair. She smiled at him but remained quiet.

"I'm sorry I let you down, Kat." He wasn't sure he had spoken the words aloud, and he wasn't sure it mattered. The face swooped away with the next tide he knew he had lost the battle. He closed his eyes and let the heat take him.

⇒Z⇐

Char heard a swooshing from above, but he didn't open his eyes. A burst of heat washed over him. The tattered remains of his clothing fluttered in the breeze. How can it be even *hotter?* He took a breath, feeling the heat sear his lungs, and immediately blew out that breath. He tried breathing in again, but the hot air was not satisfying. Almost against his will, he kept pushing out air. He squirmed with the effort to convince his lungs to suck in a breath.

Something grabbed the ropes on his back and jerked him up through the ceiling. He gasped; hot air filled his lungs while his bones seemed to bend unnaturally around the rope harness.

He managed, with effort, to open his eyes. The creature held him like a suitcase. Char hung limp, staring at the large bulky feet of his captor. He counted ten toes on each shoeless foot. Char's arms and legs hung like vines but didn't reach the floor. He wondered just how tall this thing was.

Sounds were eerily muffled. Blood pounded in Char's head, his temples pulsed with the rhythm.

"Let me go," was Char's feeble demand. He swung a fist at the knee of his captor. His fist bounced off. He might as well punch a boulder with a feather for all the harm it caused. He didn't even have enough energy for a second attempt.

His captor shook him hard. Char's body swung like a dead snake. He no longer seemed to have bones or muscles.

"Be nice, or I'll put you down." The creature's voice grated on Char's nerves. Char gritted his teeth and clenched a fist. There was no sound worse than that voice. The irritating sound distracted him from realizing the tiny universal translator Calypso had given him was working.

"Let. Me. Go." Char rasped.

"Fine," the creature said. Char dropped to the floor like a lumpy duffel bag. The floor was hotter than the room. His flesh sizzled on impact. He howled and tried to stand, but his skin was seared to the floor.

"Pick him up!" Another horrid voice bellowed.

The creature ripped Char from the floor; part of his skin remained behind. He stared in horror at the patches of sizzling flesh. Blood poured down his arms, but he couldn't feel it.

His head swooped again.

"I told you not to set him down!"

"Just teaching him a lesson, Sir."

"What lesson is that; how to fry like an egg?"

Char listened to them argue as one would listen to a video while dozing. He twisted his head until he could see the Caparian, not the one who had attacked him at the palace. This one had black hair.

"What do you want from me?" Char managed. His voice didn't sound much better than his captors. A cough rattled his dry lungs. The creature that held him shook him again.

"Show some respect," it said. "You're addressing Captain Warc."

"We'll talk as soon as you're feeling up to it," Warc said.

"So, you're not Mrah?" Char replied. But the Captain had already turned his back and was walking away.

"Sir, when can we turn the heat up again? The crew is freezing. We've had two reported cases of hypothermia."

Hypothermia? Char would have laughed if he could have found any air to use.

"When Char has had his bath, you can turn it up," Warc replied.

"Yes, Captain."

They walked on in silence. Char couldn't lift his head. He stared at the burning orange floor as they moved down a long corridor.

They turned down many passages, but the orange remained the same.

Finally, they entered a large room. Char couldn't look around, but he felt a spatial difference. There was an echo where none had been before.

"Set him by the pool." The Captain ordered.

"Yes, Sir!" The creature walked over to the pool and set Char down. The floor was cool to the touch, and the room was large and spacious. The main focal point was the invitingly blue pool.

He looked at his arms. He could see his muscles where the strips of skin had peeled away. His stomach lurched, and he gagged.

Warc gestured to the pool. "Get in."

"No," Char shook his head for emphasis. His body reacted to the image of water as if every cell had eyes to see it. He wanted nothing more than to submerge himself in it, but he didn't trust them. How did he know if it was indeed water?

"It will condition your body to the heat on this ship and our planet," Warc said.

"Why should I trust you?" Char asked. He stared at the clear liquid, mesmerized by the ripples. The lining in the pool was light blue, and in the center at the bottom was a round white disc.

"Your alternative is death."

"You'll kill me if I don't obey you?" Char asked; the disdain in his voice lost impact when it tripped over his swollen tongue.

"You are near death already. The human body cannot withstand the temperature of my planet. We have already lowered our temperature to dangerously low levels to keep you alive until you awoke. Now that you are awake, I need to think of my crew. Do this, or you will be dead within the next hour from heatstroke." Warc was matter-of-fact.

Char looked at his swollen hands, soaked in the blood from his wounds. He had never been so hot or dry in his life. Just glancing at the water made every fiber of his being ache for just one drop. It was more than want; he *needed* to taste it, pull it into him like a desert floor soaking up the meager yearly rainfall.

He rolled onto his knees, gasping in pain. The flesh was missing from his knees as well. He didn't have enough strength to stand, so he grimaced as he crawled across the rough floor to that beautiful oasis.

He hung over the edge and dipped in his hands to cup some of the water. He brought it to his lips.

"Don't drink it!" Warc snapped. "It isn't just water. You may have water after."

It took far more effort to drop the handful of water than it had to crawl to the pool's edge. Of course, he thought in his over-heated mind. Chlorine is poisonous. Don't drink chlorine.

He grunted as he spun himself at the edge to dip his feet in the water. The shock of the cold shot up his legs, iced his veins, and froze his lungs. All his insides shrunk away from the icy blast. His lungs tightened until he couldn't breathe. He opened his mouth wide and gasped, sucking in a huge lungful of air before blasting it out again. The contradictory lungful of hot air confused his already befuddled brain.

The cold raced through his parched body and rammed his foggy mind. The blast cleared the haze. He ripped his feet out of the liquid with more energy than he thought he had left and was surprised to find his feet dry.

"It's freezing!" he cried. "Are you trying to cause heart failure?"

"No, it is not," Captain Warc replied. "Get in."

"I can't! It'll shock my system! I could die!" Char tried again to stand but fell back to his knees.

"Get in!" Warc bellowed. His voice reverberated around the room. Char covered his ears with his shaking hands. His muscles twitched. He stuck his feet back in the liquid and slowly slid in.

The cold pierced his body like a thousand knives. His teeth chattered so hard his vision jumped—the liquid stained with his blood.

"H-how c-c-cold is this s-s-stuff?" Char chattered. He wrapped his arms around himself, but it was useless. The cold invaded him from every angle.

"A mere eighty-five Earth degrees," Warc replied.

"Is that Fahrenheit or Celsius?" Char asked.

"Fahrenheit."

"It can't be!" Char coughed. His lungs filled with moisture. "It feels more like twenty degrees!"

"It only seems that cold because you were going from one hundred thirty degrees to eighty-five."

The cold raced up his spine to fill his mind with frosty tentacles. He coughed again. He swung his hand through the liquid. It was thicker than water, with a consistency of honey.

"You must submerge, or you will not be properly protected," Warc said. "Dive to the bottom and touch the white disc."

"But how will I see it?" Char asked.

"You may open your eyes. The liquid will not hurt them."

"What is this stuff?"

"There is no sound in your language to pronounce the word. The closest translation is Temprafreeze."

"Temprafreeze," Char repeated. His joints ached.

"Take a deep breath," Warc continued.

Char took a couple of shallow breaths then sucked in a large breath before submerging. The cold froze the marrow of his bones. He had already forgotten what it was like to be as hot as he was just moments before. He feared he would never feel warm again. He swung his arms wide and kicked, keeping his eyes on the white disc, shimmering white against the blue.

He stretched out his hand to touch the disc and found a handle. He grasped the handle. Immediately the floor closed over his hand. He jerked back and struggled to stay calm. His lungs convulsed, demanding oxygen. Precious bubbles of air escaped, and he watched their assent.

Nobody was diving in to save him. He had been tricked.

He became weirdly detached from the situation as if he were watching a movie that had just slowed for dramatic effect. He turned his attention back to his hand and pulled again. His lungs pumped to draw in air, and he kept his lips tightly pressed together, fighting a losing battle. Soon his body would force him to breathe, and the honey-like liquid would fill his lungs.

He swung his feet down and pushed on the bottom, yet his hand would not slide free. Panicked, he twisted and jerked; more precious bubbles raced for the surface.

He was trapped.

KAT

Kat stood in a sanctuary with eight tall, white walls. A wooden pillar arched across the domed ceiling at each shallow corner, joining at a central point. Cylindrical lamps hung suspended from the ceiling, their cords woven through gold chains.

The dark green carpeted floor matched the green in the cushioned wooden pews.

Kat wandered down toward the pulpit, where a band was warming up. Against the wall, behind the band, stood a wooden table with an open bible and two tall white candles on either side. A single golden cross stood, unadorned, behind the bible. 'This, do in remembrance of me' was carved into the table's edge.

"Where am I?" Kat asked aloud.

"Testing, testing," a pretty brunette said into a microphone. "What would you like me to say? Or should I just ramble?"

Her voice was light and playful.

"Cause I could talk for hours. I could tell you stories all day long, I could—"

"That's good, now you, Bill," a voice from the back of the room responded. The brunette quit talking and took a sip from her cup. A young man with shaggy hair took his turn. His deep voice boomed overhead, everyone ducked.

"Sorry! Sorry!" the voice called again.

"What?" Bill held a hand to his ear, exaggerating his hearing loss. "I can see your lips move, Charlie, but I can't *hear* anything!"

"Charlie?" Kat spun around and looked up. There was an indoor balcony in the back of the sanctuary. Kat raced over to the steps, taking them two at a time.

"Oh, please be a nickname," she mumbled as she burst through the door. Two young women leaned over a computer, giggling and pointing at the screen. One had tightly curled blond hair that just managed to touch her ears. She was a little too round, her jeans and polo shirt a little too tight.

The other had flaming red hair, straight as an uncooked spaghetti noodle, with just a touch of brown. She wore white shorts and a green tank top.

A young man stood over a board with hundreds of knobs and switches. His hair was shorter than Kat remembered, but she recognized the red highlights. His hands flew over the board with an expertise that would intimidate a newbie.

"Char?" Kat asked. He didn't turn around. Kat went to the edge of the balcony and looked down at the stage.

"This is cool," she said.

"Tracy," a tall, lean man, standing behind a keyboard, called up. "Go ahead and run that first video clip, then just before the ending; I want to cut the video and go straight into the lyrics."

"No problem," Tracy replied. She moved the mouse, clicked the button, then jotted a note down on a tablet.

"Charlie, I need audio." She glanced at him as she spoke.

"You got it," he replied. He leaned to the right and pressed a button on another, smaller board with a handful of buttons and dials. The lights dimmed, and the screen on the wall above the band came to life.

A young man with earbuds strolled down a busy city sidewalk. He sang a popular Christian song. No one on the city street seemed to notice him.

Kat watched the video in silence. At some point during the video, the band started to play. Kat was surprised to hear the music continue when the video cut out. If she had had a spine, she was sure chills would be running down it.

Words replaced the video a moment later. The transition was smooth and powerful.

"Very nice," Kat approved.

"Good," the lean man said as they finished the song. "That's how I want it done on Sunday."

"Nick!" Tracy waved a hand to get his attention.

"Yes?"

"What are your lyrics for verse two?" she asked. She slid the mouse and clicked. Lyrics popped up on the screen. "This is what I have."

Nick looked at the screen.

"That's what I have," he called.

"Then why are you singing it differently," Tracy mumbled.

"You know Nick; can't let our jobs get too easy. We'd fall asleep at the mouse," the chubby blond said. "Even if we had it down to the letter, he'll switch it up Sunday to keep us on our toes."

"Tell me about it," was Tracy's good-natured reply.

Tracy's crystalline blue eyes glittered with amusement as she added another note to her tablet. She was about an inch shorter than Kat, with petite features and long hair that brushed her waist. But it was her eyes that made Kat wonder if she was related to Char. If she was, what had happened to her?

Kat turned her attention back to Charlie. She stood close to him, wishing she could touch him. He spun knobs and flipped switches. He grabbed a pair of headphones and listened intently.

"Char," Kat started.

"Charlie," A man in his early thirties stood at the top of the stairs, his hands on the door jam. He leaned in slightly.

"Yeah," Charlie turned to him.

"Pastor wanted me to tell you he can meet with you next Thursday at five." The man said.

"Thanks, Jim," Charlie said as he turned back to his board.

"Too bad Thursday never comes," Kat whispered. As always, no one heard.

༯

"So, you're involved with your church?" Kat asked as she watched Charlie fill the dishwasher.

"I would never have guessed that, from the way you acted when I met you," she continued. She paced around his kitchen.

The sand-brown tiles appeared coarse, but she couldn't feel them. The walls were a dark yellow, with a wallpaper border. The border had old-fashioned cook-stoves and fireplaces. Kat touched one of the stoves and remembered the one she had seen when she was seven. Her parents had taken her to a museum, and the stove had been part of a display.

The cupboards were golden oak, and the countertops were white marble. Kat wanted to touch the marble and see if it was real. She ran a hand over the countertop, imagining it was smooth.

"Wish I could feel," Kat mumbled.

Tracy bounced into the room.

"Hey," she smiled. "You comin' with me to donate blood next Monday?"

"Nope, next Monday doesn't come either," Kat said.

"What time?" Charlie asked.

Tracy grabbed an apple out of the basket and took a noisy bite. She hopped up on the counter and crossed her legs. The sunlight accented the fiery red in her hair, washing out the brown.

"After three, I don't get out of work till two-thirty," she said through a juicy mouthful. Kat realized she was insanely jealous of her ability to eat an apple. It had been so long since Kat had tasted an apple.

"Don't talk with your mouth full," Charlie said. "Yeah, I can go."

"I'll beat you this time!" Tracy declared as she hopped off the counter.

"Not a chance," Charlie shot back, "loser!"

"I'm sorry, what'd you say?" She leaned in and studied his lips as if she were trying to read them. She mouthed words then straightened, shaking her head. "You're going to have to work on that mumbling problem."

She leaped out of reach. His fist missed by a fraction of an inch.

"Ha!" She swung her foot around to kick his backside.

He caught her foot before it could make contact. She hopped on one leg to keep her balance.

"I always win," Charlie said.

"You know what that means don't you?" she asked thoughtfully. He released her foot. "You'd bleed to death faster than I would." She took another big bite of her apple.

"You won't even have time to bleed," Kat said as she touched Tracy's shoulder. Tracy didn't notice the touch.

"Pleasant thought, guess I'll have to be the one bandaged first," Charlie replied. He wiped the sink with the dishrag.

"I suppose," Tracy tossed her apple in the trash. "I've gotta go; I'm late!"

"Have a good night, loser!" Charlie called.

"You'll be the loser," was Tracy's distant reply before a door slammed.

Kat followed him up the stairs to his room.

He had posters of Jesus, Christian rock bands, and a cross adorning his walls. Kat ran her finger over a row of DVDs on a bookshelf.

"Antiques! I didn't know you collected antiques. How do you play them? Oh," Kat spotted a TV and DVD player stacked on a desk. She crouched and poked a finger at the DVD player. "That's how. Do they still work?"

"I didn't think you could get these anymore," her smile was sad. "Technically, you can't get anything anymore."

She shook herself and focused on Charlie.

He pulled his shirt off and flopped on his double bed. He had candles on every available surface of his room. None of them were lit. He sighed and closed his eyes. Kat watched him fall asleep, wondering if she could get into his dreams the way she had Katie's.

⁂

Kat paced around the darkness of Charlie's mind. She wasn't sure what scenery to put up for him. This was harder than talking to Katie. At least she knew Katie inside and out, literally.

"How about the church?" Kat asked aloud. She clapped her hands and watched the church materialize. It was just as she remembered it, only minus the people. She stood at the table, staring at the cross.

"Who are you?" Charlie asked from behind her. Kat was slow to turn, stalling for time.

Charlie wore faded jeans and a white t-shirt but no socks or shoes. Dreams were weird. The silver cross around his neck caught the light.

"My name is Kat."

He stared at her, taking slow, measured steps forward. He climbed the three steps and stopped in front of her. He raised an eyebrow as he stared into her eyes.

It was strange, in this dreamscape, she could feel her heartbeat, or was that his heartbeat?

"Why are your eyes black?" He asked, then leaned closer, noses inches apart. "Oh, I guess they're not completely black; there are tiny flecks of silver—very tiny flecks."

Kat thought she could feel a tiny vibration in the small space between the tips of their noses. She shook her head and stepped back.

"My eyes are not important. I have a message for you," she said. He waited.

She struggled for a way to explain without sounding like a lunatic or, worse, like a nightmare to be dismissed.

When she didn't answer right away, he continued, "A message?"

"Yes, in just a few days, the Earth will be attacked. Millions will die," Kat said. She hadn't meant to blurt it out like that. What was wrong with her? To Charlie's credit, he didn't laugh in her face.

"Who is going to attack?" he asked.

"An alien race called Caparians," Kat said.

"Aliens?" he asked, disbelief tainting his words. He walked over to the piano and leaned against it. Before she could continue, he blinked and straightened.

"Wait a minute, how did I get here?" he asked.

"I brought you here," Kat replied.

"What?"

"I chose this image because you were familiar with it. I have much more to show you, but I'm sorry it will not be as pleasant."

"Who are you really?" he asked.

"My full name is Katie, but you know me as Kat—well, you will, in the future."

"In the future," he repeated.

"Yes, I have come from the future to warn you about the attack."

A grin slid across his face, smooth as honey. He leaned back on the piano again and folded his arms.

"I'm dreaming, aren't I?" he asked.

"Yes, but that doesn't make this any less serious," Kat said. She was losing him; she could feel it. He ran a hand over his short hair and scratched the back of his head.

"I've had some weird dreams in my life, but this one tops them all," He said. "Wait till Tracy hears this!"

"This isn't a dream!" Kat snapped. Why was no one taking her seriously? She waved her hand, flattening the church in one motion. Hard, packed dirt stretched out around them in all directions.

Charlie, who had still been leaning on the piano, fell over now that it was gone. He hit the ground hard, leaving no mark and kicking up no dust. He leaped to his feet, his mouth hanging open, eyes wide.

"What did you do?" he asked.

"This is what the world looked like when we met," Kat said. She rolled her eyes, "Well, technically, it looked like this——" She swung an arm, and the exploding escape pods filled the sky.

"Whoa!" Charlie cried as he jumped out of the way of some falling debris, "stop!"

Kat turned her back on him and allowed the burning embers to fade, restoring the barren wasteland. She stared at the baked landscape and closed her eyes, feeling the hot wind on her face, tasting the grit in her mouth. Two years of grit coating her tongue, constantly crunching between her teeth, till she feared losing her sense of taste. She had to wonder, would that be such a bad thing? After all, she had only tasted dirt.

"We lived like this for two years," Kat whispered. "...and three years below ground."

"We?" Charlie asked.

"Everyone who survived the first attack."

"How much of the continent was hit?" he asked.

"All of it. It was a global attack." Kat replied, keeping her eyes closed as she spoke.

"I don't know who you lost or what you went through—we never really talked about that day," she continued. "So, I can't show you what you will lose. But I can say you were alone when I found you."

"You found me?" he asked.

"Yes, you were in the observation base, in Beta Alpha Quadrant. I found you standing by a window, watching more people die in the second attack."

"There were *two* attacks?" he asked. Then before she could respond, "I just *watched* them die?"

"Yes."

"How many survived the second?"

"Two."

"Two thousand? Two hundred?"

"No," Kat shook her head, "just two."

"Just two," Charlie whispered. His voice was heavy. "I assume we were the two."

Kat nodded. He walked up beside her. She opened her eyes to look at him. He swept his hand out in an expansive gesture at the land.

"And this is how we lived? Where are the plants?"

"Gone. All of it, gone. They call it the Particle Separator. It lights up the world in a hideous green light. Then everything starts popping."

"Popping?"

"Yes, every living thing, and non-living thing, all pop. Nothing left behind, not even dust."

"What about those explosions?" he asked.

"That was the second attack." Kat pushed the words out past the lump that filled her throat. She swallowed hard, forced it back down, and gritted her teeth. She had to keep it together; this was no time to break down.

"We lost the planet in that one."

"I see," his voice was soft. He put an arm around her, "And you went through this?"

She jerked away; her temper flared, her spirit crackled.

"Yes!" she hissed, "and so did you!"

"I'm sorry," he cried, throwing his hands up. "I didn't mean to upset you."

"Then stop talking to me like I'm five! I don't need to be *held*. I need to *kill* every Caparian I see! And I need your help to stop them!" Kat shouted.

He stared at her a long time before answering.

"Do you believe that is the right way to handle it?" he asked as the dreamscape began to melt.

"What?" she gasped, but he never had a chance to respond. Her words echoed, once again, unanswered.

⇒Z⇐

"Well, that went well," Kat growled as she fell out of Charlie. She hit the floor soundlessly. She floated, more than fell, and didn't feel the impact. She sat cross-legged on the floor, with her head resting on her fists.

Charlie leaped out of bed to shut off his alarm.

"Well?" Kat asked.

A sharp rapping interrupted their one-way conversation, and Tracy poked in her head.

"Come on, Charlie, we're going to be late."

"I had the weirdest dream, Trace," he said. He rubbed the sleep from his eyes. Her eyes widened, and she stepped into the room.

"Oh, no, you don't!" she pointed her finger at his chest.

"You promised me you would help me with the nursing home if I helped you in the booth at the church. You are not using that lame old excuse to get out of it." She punched his arm.

"I haven't used the bad dream/world ending excuse since I was seven! And I really did have a dream about the world ending," Charlie cried as he jumped back, too late to avoid the hit. She raised an eyebrow, not amused.

He grinned. "Don't worry. I'm still helping you at the nursing home today. So, un-ruffle your feathers so that we can go."

"What do I have to do to get through to you people?" Kat screamed at the ceiling.

CHAR

Char's lungs pumped hard, convulsed in his chest, demanded air. He quit jerking on his hand and floated still, conserving the little air he had left. He tried to think, but his thoughts were growing fuzzy, and all he could focus on was the pain of no oxygen. He couldn't free his hand, and he realized he was dying. He wasn't sure which was worse, baking to death or drowning. His body drifted up till he was upside down. His head swirled, and he nearly sucked in a lungful of Temprafreeze. His vision dimmed, and his bones were cold. Why would they pull him from a deadly heat just to drown him? Was this some alien ritual? Was he a sacrifice?

"Charlie," her whispered word was next to his ear.

He snapped his eyes open and looked for her. He searched the purple haze of the Temprafreeze for a glimpse of her flaming hair, always more red than his. He turned and twisted but couldn't see her.

"Be still and remember."

He opened his mouth, releasing the last of his vital air supply. Remember? What did she want him to remember? He stilled his mind and body and listened with his soul.

I will say of the Lord, "He is my refuge and my fortress: my God; in Him will I trust. Surely He shall deliver me from the snare of the fowler..." It had been years since he thought of that scripture. He repeated it in his mind, fighting off the darkness that crept into his consciousness. *He shall deliver me... He shall deliver me...* He found strength from the words. He pulled them deep into his heart, absorbed their power, and allowed them to fill him with peace. He grew calm, serene. He knew in his core that his God would not abandon him.

The sudden release of his hand startled him. For the length of a breath, he hovered above the white disc. He tucked his feet under him and pushed off the pool floor. He shot to the surface as fast as his buoyancy would take him.

He broke through the surface like a whale, sucking in a huge gulp of sweet hot air. He expected drops to rain around him, but there weren't any; the liquid slipped off him like butter melting on a hot cob of corn. The air didn't seem as hot either.

He swam to the edge of the pool and stood. His body was dry as soon as it was out of the liquid. He stared at his dry hand in amazement. He brought it to touch his chest. He ran his fingers across the dry cord wrapped around his chest.

"I'm not hot," he whispered.

"That's why I put you in the Temprafreeze. It conditions your body to our climate. Where we are going, your human body wouldn't have been able to survive the initial approach," Warc said as he approached. Char was happy to find out the Temprafreeze hadn't damaged the universal translator Calypso had given him.

"Where are we going?" Char asked. The numbing cold had already faded, and the pain from his wounds was pulsing back in full force. He forced himself to stand with his head held high, but internally he felt like curling into a ball and dying.

"Lebrac, my home planet, is not quite as hot as your sun but still hot enough to kill you. Come, we must tend to your wounds." Warc turned and walked out the door.

"Lebrac," Char repeated. He looked at the wounds on his legs. His stomach twisted at the sight of the meaty pulpy mess. He staggered when he took a step. The pain was excruciating. Was this how burn victims felt? His legs gave out, and he fell.

The same Caparian that had carried him into the room caught him before hitting the floor. The Caparian picked him up as if he were a child. He felt ridiculous, cradled in the arms of this massive creature. Following Captain Warc, they meandered down several halls before coming to one with a high ceiling and walls the color of dried blood. The Caparian set Char on his feet saluted Warc, and left when dismissed. Char leaned his good hand against the wall; feeling the warm crustiness, he pulled his hand back in disgust.

They faced a door that looked more like an inky black hole. Warc held out a hand, signaling Char to walk through. Char didn't want to touch the shimmering surface.

"Just step through," Warc said. "This is necessary before the battle." His voice still grated on Char's nerves; he wondered if he could ever get used to the sound.

"Will we go into battle?" Char asked, not because he cared but to delay stepping into the darkness.

"Oh, yes, we most certainly will. Mrah will stop at nothing." The way Warc said it left no room for doubt. As if he had known Mrah a long time.

Char swallowed and touched the undulating surface of the doorway. His finger slid into the shimmering mass. In seconds, the darkness wrapped itself around his hand, moving up his arm, pulling him forward. He felt the energy pulse through it, it was hungry, and it wanted him. Billions of tiny tentacles caressed his skin. It was gentle and urgent at the same time.

He pulled his hand back; the tentacles held on but finally broke away, slipping back off his hand, lingering as long as possible before letting go. It was soothing and scary all at once.

"What is it?" he asked, breathless.

"A healer from a dark planet. There is no wound it cannot heal. Step inside; you will be able to breathe," Warc replied.

"Does it have a name?"

"In your language, it would be called Wound Eater."

Char stepped into the strange creature. He felt the tentacles all over his body. They tickled a little. The energy pulsed all around him; it lifted and cradled him. Each silken thread pulsed against his skin. Their soothing touch was everywhere, all around him. He completely relaxed for the first time in five years. His muscles softened; he closed his eyes, and just drifted through this black sea of fluttering bliss.

His legs tingled; he thought about the jagged gash in his leg. How could the Temprafreeze change his skin so it wouldn't burn again? But it didn't matter. For now, he was safe. Nothing could hurt him in this soft cocoon.

He was rising and falling as if he were floating on gentle waves. He passed from tentacle to tentacle, like a weird game of hot potato. Finally, he oozed out of the darkness. The soft tentacles set him on the floor, where he folded up like a worn blanket. He felt the darkness slide off him, the feel of its fluttering fingers remained on his skin, and he was sad it was gone. He felt naked and alone on this strange ship and wanted to jump back into the sea of darkness.

"Come," Warc ordered. The voice set Char's teeth on edge. He suppressed a shudder and climbed to his feet. He looked at his arms and legs where the wounds had been and gasped.

"I'm healed!" Char couldn't believe his eyes.

"Yes, this creature feeds on wounds. It would die without them." Warc started walking.

"Where is Kat?" Char asked. He jogged a few steps to catch up. He felt oddly like a kid pestering his big brother. He tried to take long strides, but Warc still had to take baby steps to match Char's gate. Warc paused, then continued without looking at Char.

"You will see her soon."

They walked onto the bridge. Every Caparian looked alike at first glance. Char was determined not to show how small and insignificant he felt. He pulled himself up to his full six feet, four inches.

"Captain," one of the Caparians turned in his chair and faced Warc.

"Report," Warc said.

"Long-range tentacles show a ship closing in from behind."

"Time."

"Three units, Sir."

"Time out?"

"Two units, Sir."

Char looked from one to the other, wondering what a unit was.

"How long is a unit?" Char asked.

"A little longer than one Earth hour," Warc said. He turned back to the Caparian, "Push the hyper drive."

"Sir, that will show our location like a dying star."

"Yes, but it should also give us the edge we need to make it to the planet first," Warc responded. "I'll be in my quarters."

He motioned for Char to follow. "I have a surprise for you."

They walked into a large room with no furniture, no decoration. It had high ceilings and smooth blood-red walls. Red was quickly becoming his least favorite color. Like a splash of water in the middle of Death Valley, there stood Alex!

"Alex!" Char cried. Alex turned to face him with a grin as wide as Char's. They shook hands in the customary Earth way, grasping hands across the chest with a brief one-armed hug.

"I thought you were dead, man!" Char laughed, genuinely glad to see Alex. He pumped Alex's hand once more before releasing it and slapping him on the back. "I saw that chair leg go straight into your chest."

"Ah, my friend," Alex replied. "I have Droplet anatomy."

"Well, thanks for spelling that out for me." Char chuckled. "That clears things up."

"You see, our hearts are—"

"I'm sorry to interrupt, but we do not have time for an anatomy lesson," Warc said. "Sit."

Char looked around and shrugged. Warc started to sit, and a chair slid out of the floor as smooth as silk. Alex imitated him and sat. Char tried the same, and a chair formed for him as well.

"Where's Kat?" Char asked again.

"You will see her soon enough," Warc replied.

"She's safe," Alex said. Char looked from one to the other. The contrast was bizarre; the angelic blue-skinned Droplet against the dried mustard yellow-skinned Caparian. He looked at his hand and added the tanned white skin of the human to the mix.

"Why are you helping us?" Char asked, looking back up and more than a little irritated that neither would tell him where Kat was.

"Char," Alex said, "while you were still unconscious, we've had time to discuss the situation further. There is something you need to—"

"Please," Warc held up a hand. "We don't have time for back story. We need to get you to the planet."

"We have two units! And what good will getting me to the planet do?" Char asked. "And how do I know I can trust you?"

"He healed you," Alex said.

"So," Char said. "He could be 'fattening me up' for Mrah."

"I assure you, that isn't the case. We have a safe house for you on the planet."

"You have to know a safe house won't matter *at all* when Mrah uses his particle separator," Char argued.

"He isn't likely to attack his home planet," Warc said.

"What makes you so sure?" Char couldn't keep the bitter sound out of his voice. "He killed an entire planet just to kill Kat. Ironically, he missed his mark."

"That was different," Warc responded. "That was Earth. This is Lebrac. If he uses that separator on this planet, it will alert the high council; then he's as good as dead."

"What do you mean?" Char asked.

"The particle separator was never intended to be a weapon of mass destruction." Warc stood and walked to a table with a decanter and glasses. He poured clear liquid and handed a glass to Char. Char took it and sniffed the liquid. "It's water. You need it."

Char took a sip, realized it was water, and gulped it down. It felt so good sliding down his parched throat. He held his glass out for more. Warc filled it.

"The particle separator was designed to obliterate asteroids if they threaten a planet." Warc continued. "It comes standard in every ship but is forbidden under Caparian law to use for anything other than the destruction of space debris directly threatening an inhabited planet."

"So, Mrah is breaking Caparian law?" Char asked.

"Yes," Warc replied. "When a Caparian is discharged with honor from the military and intends to study life on other planets, he is given his current ship and crew for his private use. If the high council ever discovers Mrah's misuse of the particle separator, he will have his ship revoked, be stripped of rank, and put to death."

"The high council doesn't know he attacked Earth?" Char asked. He lifted his glass. Warc filled it and handed him the decanter.

"No," Warc said. "An honorably discharged Caparian is expected to maintain an honorable life. Having earned the respect and trust of his superiors, he is given free rein over his life. However, should any dishonorable actions be brought to light before the council, he loses his freedom by degrees. Depending on the offense, he may be monitored for the rest of his life with no chance of regaining that honorable status. The punishment escalates from there, up to and including death."

"Harsh society," Char mused. "So, why not just turn him in?"

He could tell there was something they weren't telling him. A flicker of a human-like emotion flashed across Warc's face. Was it sorrow? It was gone as fast as it appeared. He looked at Alex. Alex was unreadable.

"What do you know?" Char directed at Alex.

"I know enough to know you can trust Warc," Alex replied.

"That doesn't answer my question. What are you not telling me?" Char demanded. He squeezed his glass, forced himself to relax, and poured more water.

Warc stared at Char. He seemed to be struggling with a decision. He sighed, "Your universal translator does not have a word to describe it, but Mrah is something like my brother-in-law, though he is so much more and less."

"How did you know about the translator?"

"I had Calypso give it to you."

Char did not bother to hide his shock. "*You* had Calypso give it to me? Then she knew you were coming for me?"

"Yes, the attack was inevitable. She did what she had to do to save her people and her planet."

"She was supposed to protect us!"

"She did protect us," Alex said.

"Whose side are you on?" Char shot him a glare. "You do realize we're on a ship heading into the lion's den, don't you?"

Alex shrugged.

"If it were not for Aurora and her emotions, you would not be here," Warc said.

"What do you mean?" Char asked.

"Aurora has tried, unsuccessfully, to hide the fact she is not a full-blood Droplet. Though, I don't believe she knows she is not full blood."

"I don't understand." Char felt pain behind one eyeball.

"Aurora allows her emotions to cloud her judgment. She was dead set on revenge, and she used your friend as her weapon of choice."

"I thought Droplets are a peaceful species," Char replied. He pinched the bridge of his nose and squeezed his eyes shut.

"We are," Alex said. "But I suspect Aurora has Sprout blood in her, making her more susceptible to the want of power, greed, and selfishness."

"She is playing chess, and we are the pawns," Warc continued.

"You reference Earth a lot. How do you know so much about it?" Char asked. Warc, who had been leaning forward, leaned back in his chair.

"Yes," he looked at the floor but didn't seem to see it. "Mrah and I studied Earth for two hundred years. It fascinated us. We especially enjoyed the rise and fall of the United States. We firmly believe that if the War of 2018 hadn't resulted in the other continents sinking, creating the one massive ocean, what did you call it?"

"The Ocean of Atlantis," Char replied. "Named in honor of the continent of Atlantis, which the ocean had already claimed thousands of years before that."

"Yes, the ocean that eats continents. We believe the United States would still be around and the strongest country on the planet."

"You make Mrah sound like a scientist, not a villain." Char said, "And why was Aurora so bent on revenge?"

"Well, you see," Warc hesitated only for a breath. "Mrah killed Gasos, Aurora's mate."

Before Char could respond, the ship rocked with a hit. The shock of the news mixed with the cold rush of adrenaline. Char flew out of his chair and hit the floor, landing hard on his right side. The decanter shattered near his head, water and shards of glass peppered his face.

"What was that?" Char wiped his face.

"Damage report!" Warc bellowed.

If possible, his yelling voice was worse than his calm voice. Char was afraid the vibration would damage his ears. The answer seemed to come from the walls.

"Just a graze, Sir!"

"Get us out of here!" Warc ordered.

"Yes, Sir!"

The ship jerked again. Char pulled himself to his feet. Alex, who had not lost his seat, stood.

"Hit again?" Char asked.

"No, that was the warp drive kicking into gear."

"More Earth analogies?" Char asked. Warc grinned. It was a grin of nightmares. Every jagged tooth appeared, and saliva slid down the yellow surface of each tooth.

"I told you, Earth was my favorite planet, and I intend to see it restored," Warc said.

"If you and Mrah studied Earth for two hundred years, why did

Mrah waste his time killing grass? Surely, he would have known the two biggest threats on Earth would be disease and humans."

Warc nodded.

"He was toying with you. He wanted every human on Earth to feel the pain he felt."

"What pain?" Char asked. The pinpoint of pain behind his eye was blossoming into a full-blown migraine.

"After we finished studying Earth, we came home to Lebrac. Then Caparians began to die. The plague swept our planet like a wildfire," Warc said. "Mrah watched his wife and ten children die slowly, in agony. He was powerless to help them."

"What were the symptoms?" Char asked. Something churned in the pit of his stomach.

Warc stood, turned his back to Char, and stared into space.

"It came fast—first, fever, then body aches, swollen areas, and rashes. If the patient made it to the medical facility, closer inspection showed Meningitis, Encephalitis, or Meningoencehpalitis—to use your Earth terms. Sometimes, patients would be comatose for days or weeks before expiring. Some died so fast they hadn't had time to get a full diagnosis. Bodies piled up; we had to dig mass graves and eventually started burning the bodies. We couldn't keep up."

"Did you find a cure?" Char asked.

"No, one day, it was just gone. They called it the Walking Death because you could be fine and walking one day, and the next you would be dead."

Char closed his eyes, images flashing behind his closed lids, his grandmother urging him and his sister to walk faster. They must get out of the house. They must get away. They had thought they were safe. The plague had ended years ago, but a freak isolated case had his mother's beautiful face distorted and red with the rash, her neck, and underarms bulging. His father's labored breathing, the twitching muscles in his face, every ugly image from the plague pierced his mind.

"What year did you leave Earth?" Char asked, eyes still closed. He didn't want to know the answer.

"Earth year A.D. 2100," Warc said

Char opened his eyes.

"I thought I might know what killed your people, but it couldn't have been that," Char replied.

"What?" Warc asked.

"It's nothing. The plague that hit Earth didn't happen until 2103."

"I went back in 2103 for a follow-up visit," Warc said.

The words hit Char like a punch to his belly. The air whooshed out of his lungs in a loud gasp. Alex, quiet this whole time, let out a low whistle.

"What plague?" Warc asked.

"The West Nile Plague," Char replied. "It has all the symptoms you mentioned. It was first discovered sometime in the early 2000s; at that time, it was known as the West Nile Virus but wasn't lethal, at least not on a grand scale. A few died, but nothing drastic. It went dormant until 2103 when it suddenly mutated; became easily passed from human to human and ended up killing more people than the Bubonic Plague."

"If I'm correct, mosquitoes spread the disease, right?" Alex asked. "West Nile, not Bubonic," he quickly amended.

"Yes," Char's legs shook slightly. "One of you must have been bitten and inadvertently took the virus to Lebrac."

"But you never got sick," Alex said. "Which makes you carriers."

"Then, when I returned in 2103 for the follow-up visit, I brought it back to you." They stared at each other.

"Mrah's family died from the Walking Death..."

"So did my parents..." Char whispered.

KAT

"You haven't done anything!" Kat screamed at Charlie. He pulled his shirt over his head and dropped it on the floor.

"You didn't warn anyone. You ignored everything I said, didn't you?" She yelled. She stomped over to his bookcase filled with antique DVDs. Her spirit crackled, sparks of light spit like sparklers. She swung her hand and managed to fling a few DVDs across the room. She stared at her hand, no longer crackling with sparks.

"What the?" Charlie asked. He looked at the mess, then around the room, wide-eyed. He paled as if he had seen a ghost. "How did I do that?" She asked. Her anger dissolved in the light of her curiosity. She tried to hit the remaining DVDs, but they stayed on the shelf. "Sooo, I need to sparkle to move things?"

"Kat?" he whispered.

"Yes!" She leaped in front of him, but he looked right through her. He blinked and shook his head.

"Charlie, man, you're losing your mind." He picked up the scattered cases and put them back on the shelf. "You just need a good night's rest; you'll be all right."

He curled up in bed and closed his eyes. Within moments his breathing was deep and even. His age melted off him when he slept. He could have been a child curled there dreaming. A child that had never known a nightmare. But the world was full of nightmares, and it was time he accepted them.

"A good night's rest," Kat whispered as she slid inside. "We'll see about that."

⁓Ƶ⁓

"Well, did you have a good day?" Kat asked as Charlie walked up behind her. She sat cross-legged on the hard ground, staring into Neptune's Hollow. Charlie sat beside her.

"Wasn't too bad. A strange thing happened right before bed, though." His tone implied he expected her to be here.

"I know," Kat nodded. "I don't know how I did that. I was just so frustrated that you didn't take me seriously."

"For a second, I did think it was you, but I changed my mind," Charlie said.

"What can I do to convince you?" Kat asked.

"Don't know," Charlie shrugged. "What is this place?"

"The edge of the world," Kat replied. She stared across the massive canyon. She remembered stories of the Grand Canyon; this canyon would make the Grand Canyon look like a dried pond.

"Really?" Charlie asked. Kat nodded.

"We call it Neptune's Hollow. It's where the Ocean of Atlantis was before the first attack. Wait a minute!" Kat cried.

"What?" Charlie asked. The excitement caused Kat's spirit to pop and snap.

"I know how to convince you!"

He grinned.

"More parlor tricks?"

"No," she punched him playfully. "A few days before the first attack, a massive earthquake triggered a landslide in Crescent Bay.

They were never able to pinpoint the earthquake, but that doesn't matter; the point is, it caused an immense tsunami that flooded Crescent Bay."

"When does this happen?" he asked, a bemused smile on his handsome face.

"The tsunami will strike tomorrow morning at six, but they won't get it on public monitors until eight. The earthquake will register ten point one, the highest in recorded history, causing the record-breaking tsunami at six hundred meters high. It will kill two hundred forty thousand people."

He shook his head.

"What?" she asked. She got the feeling he still wasn't taking her seriously. He would, though. Once the tsunami hit.

"Just... I wish you were real."

"I am real!"

"Prove it; let me call you," He said.

She grinned; why hadn't she thought of that? The dreamscape started to melt around them. He was waking up.

She rattled off her contact information, but she wasn't sure he heard it.

Z

She watched Charlie wake. A slow smile spread across his face then his eyes fluttered open. He stared at the ceiling then looked at the clock.

"Quarter to eight... Tsunami has already hit," he snickered. "Right."

Kat groaned at his flippant attitude. He rolled into a sitting position and rubbed his face with both hands. Tracy poked her head in without knocking.

"Are you getting up? I made waffles." She shut the door without waiting for a response.

Charlie got dressed and hurried down the steps.

"Mind if we have the monitor on while we eat?" Charlie asked. Tracy raised an eyebrow.

"You hate the monitor," she said.

"I know, but today, I feel like looking at it." He flicked it on and sat down.

"You once compared having to look at it to having your arm ripped off and being beaten to death with it." She plopped a plate, loaded with waffles, down in front of him. She sat across from him and poured syrup all over hers.

"You always drown your waffles," he said, changing the subject as he drizzled his syrup.

"Keeps me sweet," she said as she stuffed a forkful in her mouth.

"Oh," he said as he offered the syrup, "you'll need more then."

She started to throw a chunk of waffle at him but stopped. Her eyes widened as she stared at the monitor. "Turn that up!"

"...tsunami that struck Crescent Bay early this morning around six a.m. is said to have been near six hundred meters high. This tsunami was caused by the largest earthquake in recorded history, registering a ten-point one on the Richter scale. There is no confirmed casualty count, but we will keep you posted around the clock. Again, the tsunami to strike......"

Charlie's hand shook as he shut the monitor off.

"What are you doing? I want to hear more," Tracy cried.

"Two hundred forty thousand..."

"What?"

"Died in the tsunami," Charlie whispered. He pushed his plate away. "Sorry, sis, it tasted great a moment ago..."

"I tried to tell you! Now call me, and you will know I'm telling the truth." Kat said, knowing full well he couldn't hear her. She sat at his elbow, touched his arm, and he shivered.

Tracy switched the monitor back on in time to hear the body count. She switched it off again.

"How did you know?" she asked.

"I dreamt it last night," he mumbled.

"You've never had prophetic dreams before."

"I know," he rubbed his face in his hands and left it there. His words muffled as he continued, "It wasn't truly prophetic."

He lifted his face to look at Tracy.

"I dreamed of a girl from the future, but I didn't believe she was real, so she told me about the tsunami. If she was right about that, what about the impending attack on the planet?" He knew he was mumbling to himself.

"A dream girl came from the future to warn us?" Her expression *defined* the word skeptical. "Why us?"

"I don't think it's because we're anything important. I think she knows me from the future or something."

"Then who is she? Does she have a name?" Tracy asked. Charlie shrugged.

"I don't know. I've never met her before. Besides, I didn't say *I* knew *her*; I said *she* knew *me*. And her name is Kat."

"Kat? Charlie, listen to yourself," Tracy softened her voice and leaned across the table to touch his hand. "It was a dream, a weird coincidence, but still a dream."

He nodded. Kat leaped to her feet.

"Oh, no, you don't!" Kat cried. "He's almost convinced! Don't you go spreading your poison seeds of doubt all over him!"

Kat balled her hand into a fist and slammed it down on the table. Nothing happened. Her temper simmered, and her spirit sparked. She slammed her fist down again, and this time, the dishes jumped, and so did Tracy and Charlie.

"What was that?" Tracy asked, one hand pressed to her chest.

"That was my dream girl," Charlie sighed, "literally."

"That's ridiculous. You must have bumped your knee under the table," Tracy insisted.

"No," Charlie shook his head. "The same thing happened upstairs in my room. A few of my antique DVDs suddenly flew off the shelf, and I was standing across the room."

"There has to be a logical explanation," Tracy said, but her voice lacked conviction.

"There is," Kat replied. "I'm real."

"There is," Charlie rushed out of the room, shouting the rest over his shoulder. "A girl from the future has come back to warn us about impending disaster!"

"Where are you going?" Tracy followed on his heels.

"What was that number?" Charlie mumbled, ignoring her question.

"What number?" Tracy asked.

"Charlie punched the letters into the keyboard. He tilted his head and tapped his fingers on the desktop.

"Charlie," Tracy shook his arm, her voice tense with frustration.

"Sssh," Charlie hissed. He clicked a few more keys, "What's the rest?"

"How should I know?" Tracy snapped. "I can't read the mind of a madman."

"Seven, one, zero." Kat willed him to hear her. She squeezed the back of his chair and hopped from foot to foot.

"Seven, ten!" He cried and punched the number into the keyboard. The computer was silent as it made the connection. The reoccurring avalanche indicated the computer was thinking.

"Hello," Katie said as her face materialized on the screen.

"Kat!" Charlie sounded surprised.

"No, I'm Katie—wait, did you say Kat?" she asked.

"Yes, I'm looking for a girl named Kat; she looks just like you, only with shorter hair. Do you know her? Are you twins too?" Charlie asked. Katie snorted.

"Hardly, and I only know her from my dreams. She's been haunting me for days."

"Your dreams?"

"Yeah, well, she was haunting my dreams—more like nightmares really—but she hasn't visited for a few nights," Katie mused.

"She's real. I can't believe she's real." Charlie looked at his sister, his eyes wide. He looked back at the screen.

"Who are you, and how do you know about Kat?" Katie asked.

"My name is Charlie, and she's been visiting me too," Charlie replied.

"Charlie? Hmm, does anyone ever call you Char?" Katie asked. Kat leaned over Charlie's shoulder just as he gave it a shrug. She could just see Boon entering the room behind Katie. He stepped through the door just as Charlie responded.

"Yeah, once in a while; why?"

"I've been looking for a man named Char. Kat mentioned him a lot and wanted me to warn him about an attack." Excitement crept into Katie's voice. She leaned toward the computer, her face getting huge on the screen. "I can't believe I found you!"

"What attack has she been warning you about?" Charlie asked.

Boon stood in the background. His eyes narrowed. His hands balled into tight fists. His jaw clenched.

"Who the *hell* is that?" His voice was deep and hard. Katie jumped in her seat and spun around.

"Oh, Boon, you scared me!" Katie cried. Her hand fluttered to her chest. Charlie tipped his head as if he could get a better view of Boon through the computer screen.

"Hello, my name is Charlie," Charlie said. His voice was steady and calm.

"So, you're the guy she's been looking for." Boon asked, "How the hell do you know my girl?"

"Not now, Boon," Kat scolded, though he couldn't hear her. She put a hand on Charlie's shoulder, which he never felt.

"Boon," Katie whispered, putting a hand up to stop him, but he leaned over her, his face expanding on the screen.

"I think you need to go, *Charlie*," his tone threatening. Before Charlie could respond, the screen went black. Kat sighed.

"What did I ever see in that guy?" She wondered out loud to no one in particular.

"Pleasant fellow, wasn't he?" Charlie asked, but his tone indicated he didn't expect a response.

"Charlie, what is going on?" Tracy folded her arms across her chest and tapped her foot. He kept his eyes on the dark screen as he replied.

"We have work to do."

CHAR

"We can't outrun him!"

Char hovered in the background while the chaos on the bridge played out like a movie. The red planet loomed on the screen. Various officers shouted orders and responses back and forth so fast his universal translator could barely keep up. It came out as a garbled mess of guttural sounds laced with fragmented English. Alex appeared beside Char but said nothing.

Captain Warc, seeming to forget about Char's presence and not noticing Alex's arrival, bellowed at his crew, "Report!"

"Captain Mrah is on our tail, and we don't have enough power to fight him off. We're not going to make it to the planet."

Warc sat silently for a moment.

"Orders, Sir?" barked an impatient officer.

Warc's thin yellow lips pulled back like an old rubber band, revealing his pointed yellow teeth. He pressed a button on the arm of his chair.

"Engine room."

"Sir!"

"Pool our power and funnel it all into the engines. There is no excuse for not making it to that planet!"

"Yessir!"

" And—set the charges according to what we discussed earlier."

"Is it that bad, Captain?"

"Just do it."

"Yessir."

"What charges? What's happening?" Char asked. Warc ignored him as he pressed a different button, and the loud speaker sprang to life.

"Attention all personnel: evacuate levels C, D, and E. Evacuate levels C, D, and E."

"Navigations officer," Warc bellowed. He was on his feet now.

"Yessir!"

"Land the ship."

"Yessir."

"Sir, Captain Mrah is hailing us."

"On screen," Warc replied.

Mrah's hideous face filled the screen. Saliva dripped off his mustard skin. His eyes burned hotter than coals.

"Hand them over, Warc." Mrah bellowed. Char fought the urge to dive behind the nearest Caparian.

"I can't do that, Mrah. You know this won't help anything. It won't bring them back. It won't bring *him* back."

"I don't want to have to kill you, too," Mrah replied. Warc stared at the screen, unflinching.

"Then don't," Warc said.

Mrah nodded at someone off-screen and, seconds later, the ship shook with a hit. Sparks burst from every direction. Knocked off his feet, Char made a grab at a chair, missed, and fell. He rolled and hit the wall. A sharp pain shot up his left arm. No one else on the bridge lost their balance, not even Alex. Char leaned on one elbow and craned his neck to see the screen.

"That was a warning shot. Surrender, and I will spare you and your crew," Mrah said.

"How gracious of you," Warc replied. "Why don't you drop this whole game?"

"Let me have them, and I'll drop it," Mrah responded.

"We are not objects!" Char shouted as he dragged himself to his feet. Warc shot him a warning look, and Alex caught his arm, but Char shook him off and ignored Warc. Fury drove him, "We are not yours to command. We are not spoils in this ridiculous pirate game you're playing."

Mrah pierced him with a glare, but Char took a step closer to the screen. "We have done nothing to you! *Nothing!* And you *will* leave us alone!"

"You betrayed me! You're murderers! All of you!" Mrah bellowed. His face was such a solid mask of loathing that Char took an unconscious step back. The murderous look in Mrah's eyes chilled him to the core.

Warc cut in before Char could collect himself enough to respond. How were they the murderers?

"This is not your decision," Warc said to Mrah. Mrah maintained his piercing glare at Char for several long seconds before turning his attention to Warc. Char took a breath, realizing he'd been holding it. He had never felt such hatred before. Malice so deep it was nearly tangible.

"Then you will not relinquish your claim?" Mrah asked.

"You know I won't." Warc's voice was softer than Char had ever heard from a Caparian.

"Then you leave me no choice," Mrah glowered. There was a weight behind his words. Not of anger or hate, but sorrow.

"Catch me if you can," Warc replied and shut the screen off. Char's heart thundered in his ears.

Warc turned to Char and Alex. Alex, whose expression never changed throughout the verbal parry with Mrah. Who never once flinched or lost his balance. Who stood calm and steady as any good Droplet.

"You may want to hang on to something." Warc turned back to his crew.

"On my order," Warc paused. Another hit rattled through the bridge. More sparks showered around them. *"Now!"*

Char had enough time to grab a pole before the ship lurched upon entry. And for the second time since leaving Earth, he watched as the burning red ground rushed up to meet them. He closed his eyes.

The ship hit hard. The downward force brought Char to his knees. He was acutely aware of the pole digging into his shoulder and that his hand felt molded to the metal. Then he was weightless for enough seconds to register the feeling before he slammed back into the floor. He bounced each time the ship hit as it skipped like a pebble across the surface of Lebrac.

Char's head bounced off the pole with each impact. Amidst the thundering, groaning hull dragging across the rocky ground, Char heard Warc shouting.

"Detonate!"

Before the ship had come to a rest, multiple explosions rocked it and deafened Char. He covered his ears and prayed for his protection.

He finally opened his eyes. An old Caparian, with black spots on his face making his skin look like a banana peel left out too long, knelt beside him. The stink of his breath enveloped Char like a fog. He suppressed the urge to gag.

"You all right?" he asked. Char nodded. The Caparian helped him to his feet, then hurried off.

"Well, that was fun," Alex said as he tilted Char's head to get a better look at where he had slammed it off the pole. "You've got a nasty bruise and a good-sized goose egg, but you'll probably live."

"Ow," Char growled and pulled his head away. "Thanks. How is it? I always end up tossed around like a rag doll, and you barely stagger?"

"Droplets are steadier on their feet?" Alex replied.

"You're half-human."

"Not the clumsy half."

"Come with me," Warc grabbed Char's arm and dragged him toward the door. Alex followed without a word.

"Where are we going?" Char asked as they raced down the corridors.

"We don't have much time. The false crash will not fool Mrah for long. He will send a team in to investigate soon," Warc replied. Char realized dozens of crew members were following them.

Warc stopped short and dragged Char into a wide, long room with a low ceiling. Warc's head just brushed the top. The room's only occupant was a shiny black coffin-like box hovering five feet off the floor. Char put his hand on the sleek, cold surface.

"Kat?" Char asked. Alex ran his fingers over the surface, looking thoughtful.

"Yes," Warc replied.

"She's dead?" Char felt the fear filling his body and struggled to choke it back down. It rose in him like a flood. In seconds it filled his throat and squeezed off his speech. It burned at the corners of his eyes. Was he indeed the last?

"No, this box regulates the temperature so she won't die," Warc said. He could almost feel the fear pouring out through his feet, leaving his body cold and weak.

Warc pulled on the box, and it floated along effortlessly. He released it and turned to pull two red cloaks off the nearby wall. He tossed one to Char and another to Alex. He took a third for himself. Char wrapped the coarse fabric around himself. It was lighter than he expected and felt cool on his skin.

"Keep the hood up," Warc said. He thrust a folded piece of paper into Char's hand. "We will get separated, but we will rendezvous at the safe house on that map."

He motioned for Alex to stand at the end of the box. "You push the box, and you," he turned to Char. "Walk underneath."

"What? Why?"

"You're the most easily spotted amongst us. Mrah could believe

Alex is just a short Caparian, but you look like a child." Warc explained impatience tainted his already irritating voice. "He *will* be watching. This is the only way to sneak you past. Trust me."

Char realized he did trust this Caparian, even more than he had the Droplets. He looked under the box, not much room. He was going to have to walk bent entirely over. It was going to be murder on his lower back. He crouched and positioned himself under the box.

"Ready," Char said; his head throbbed from the awkward position aggravating his headache.

"Positions," Warc cried. Dozens of crew members, each with an identical box, surrounded them. Warc also positioned himself behind one.

"You know the drill, box fan!"

"What?" Char shook his head. He didn't think Warc would hear him with his chin shoved into his collarbone under this coffin, but he did.

"I thought, being from Earth, you would appreciate the pun." Char could hear the grin in Warc's reply.

"You should know, Warc," Char said. "Few humans appreciate a good pun, and even fewer appreciate a bad pun."

Warc made a nightmarish noise which Char took to be a chuckle. "Very well, shall we?"

They started walking. Char had to crouch-run to keep up and more than once stumbled, nearly falling. Mrah would be on them like a killer hornet if he showed any part of himself. The cloak tangled around his feet, and he had to wad it up and cradle it in his arms as he ran. Soon the metal floor gave way to scorching sand.

From the corner of his eye, he saw the other decoys shoot out in all directions. He imagined, from the sky, they looked like a giant Chinese fan; box-fan, haha, Warc. Char shook his head, trying to focus. He stared at his feet. The red, dry dirt puffed up in his face and stuck to his sweaty skin. Even with his body temperature regulated by the Temprafreeze, and the cooling effects of this alien material, the heat on this red planet was unbearable. It was like sprinting across Death

Valley. He tried to look around but couldn't see anything except the blasted red dirt and his feet pumping back and forth.

He could hear the others. Every sound became acute. His ears were bombarded with the crunching dry ground, his labored breathing as he sucked in the hot air. He heard the thundering footsteps of the crew as they scattered with their decoy boxes.

The muscles in Char's calves burned with the effort to carry his weight in such a ridiculous way. His thighs quivered, and his back ached. His neck was tense, and his head throbbed. He tripped over a large stone and rolled across the ground. He scrambled to get back under the box as the direct sunlight scorched his exposed skin as if he was a vampire.

"No, no," Alex bellowed. "Just run!"

KAT

"What are you doing?" Kat shouted in Charlie's face, but, of course, he was oblivious to her presence. "I think it's great you want to save the people in your town, but you're, once again, not doing what I need you to do!"

Kat jumped up and down in front of him, but he walked right through her. She stood still for a moment, growled at the sky, then spun on her heel and followed him.

He grunted as he lifted the door to the shelter and stumbled down the steps, nearly dropping the large box of supplies he carried. Tracy let out a small laugh as he set the box on the floor, lost his balance, and nearly somersaulted over the box.

"That was graceful," Tracy snickered. "How many responses did you get?"

"Not enough," Charlie gasped. He sat on a crate to catch his breath. He ran his sleeve across his forehead, which left his hair matted to his skin.

"How many did you get?"

"Lots of children, but no adults. Are you sure this will work?" she asked.

"It's our only option. If we tell them we're going to be attacked by aliens, they'll think we're mental," Charlie replied. "But if they think we're just having a church social, and the bomb shelter is the theme, we'll get more people. It's our only shot."

"I suppose you're right, but what if no one wants to come? And what about the people who do go to church?"

"We'll just have to be extra convincing. Besides, they'll come flocking when the attack happens, *including* those who don't go to church," Charlie said. He sounded more hopeful than sure. "I don't know what else to do. There isn't enough time."

"No, no, no," Kat moaned. "You need to inform the military so they can blow them out of the sky!"

"Come on," Charlie sighed as he got to his feet. "There are still more boxes to get."

Tracy sauntered out the door, her energy bubbling out like fresh spring water. Charlie appeared tired, his face drawn with worry.

"You guys are driving me nuts!" Kat screamed. Her spirit crackled, and she swung at a stack of cans. The top can fell and rolled across the floor. Charlie whipped his head around and stared at the can for a moment. He scooped it up just before it bumped his foot. He turned the can of beans in his hand as he whispered.

"I know you're frustrated, Kat." He looked up as if he could see her. "But this is all I can do." He put the can back on the stack and walked out.

Kat squeezed her eyes shut. "I just want to go home," she moaned.

～Z～

When she opened her eyes, she was standing in her bedroom.

"Unh," Kat groaned. "I didn't mean right this second!"

Katie lay on her stomach with her face buried in her pillow. Her shoulders lifted and fell, followed by soft sobbing. Kat knelt by the bed and put a hand on the whimpering girl.

"Katie," Kat whispered, then rolled her eyes. "Why am I whispering?"

Katie rolled over, revealing her tear-soaked face. She sniffed hard and coughed. The whites of her eyes were painfully red, making the dark centers even darker. Kat stared into the obsidian depths, marveling at how black her eyes were. Seeing her eyes from the outside like this had a completely different effect than looking in the mirror.

"What happened?" Kat asked. The door to the room opened, and Katie quickly looked away.

"Katie?" Her mother's voice was soft. "Are you coming?"

"Yeah," Katie replied. It seemed to be a struggle for her to keep her voice even. "I'll be right there."

"Okay, hurry; your father and sister are out in the car already." The door closed with a soft click.

"What did he do to you?" Kat asked. Her spirit hummed with the first shot of her temper.

Katie sat up and dragged her sleeve across her nose. She washed her face and got ready.

"Shopping for the picnic," Kat said, remembering that day. "I'm running out of time."

CHAR

Char grabbed the box and ran, only mildly surprised at how little effort it took to pull. Alex still pushed from behind. Char looked around; the desert extended for miles. There was a large rock formation nearby, and he jerked the box in that direction. Mrah would know that's where they would go, but to go anywhere else would leave them out in the open. The outcropping, small in comparison to the desert, was massive. They could hide easily, and it was more defensable.

Each gasping breath brought searing hot air into his lungs. He would have been dead at his first breath if not for the Temprafreeze. He made a mental note to thank Warc for thinking in advance.

Boxes exploded left and right as Mrah attacked. Char cringed as black wood shrapnel peppered his skin. Crew members, thrown through the air at each blast, gave the impression of a flight of large spasmodic birds as the capes fluttered around them. Char could only hope in all the chaos, boxes, and hooded figures; Mrah wouldn't notice one "Hobbit-sized" human running with another cloaked figure who was slightly too short to fit the bill.

With all the cloaked figures blowing up around them, Char lost sight of Warc. He had no idea which one was Warc or if he was even still alive. The ground was a mix of rock and sand, as red as a Caparian's eyes and as hot as the sun. The deep sand swallowed Char's feet and slowed them down. Heat lifted from the ground in shimmering waves. Char blinked several times, knowing it was just the heat, but feeling as if his vision was blurred.

He concentrated on running, tried to ignore the smoldering heat, the sweat that ran off him in rivers. The cooling cloak flapped behind him, failing at its job. He wanted to look back to make sure Alex was still there but didn't dare take his eyes off the path ahead.

The sand had given way to solid rock allowing him to sprint faster. The mountainous rock formation loomed before them, its shadow reaching out to blanket them. It did nothing to relieve the oppressive heat. Char pushed himself to run harder, but it still seemed to take forever to reach the narrow path that led up and away. Char raced up it, wanting to put as much distance between Mrah and them as possible. He risked a glance back, and Alex was still with him. A burst of wind jerked Char's hood off his head. He reached back with one hand to pull it back on. It was twisted. He gave up.

Char slowed, then stopped. His chest heaved; he couldn't run anymore. Not only was the air so much hotter here than on Earth, but the air was thinner. Each suffocating breath fell far short of satisfying. He put a hand on the casket's lid but hissed as he snatched it back, "Hot."

"Do you think it's safe to stop?" Alex gasped, hands on his hips. Char held up a hand and shushed him.

"Listen," Char whispered. They stood quietly. Char struggled to hold his breath, but that didn't help his heart thundering in his ears. He willed his heart to quiet so he could hear. They leaned against the rock wall in a small alcove they found.

"I don't hear anything," Alex whispered.

"The explosions stopped," Char gasped as he released his pent-up breath. "We should check it out."

"Yes," Alex heaved a breath and exhaled the following sentence. "We should."

Alex's blue skin, which generally appears to move like water, seemed a little too fluid. Char held up a hand as if volunteering.

"I'll check it out. You guard Kat." He didn't wait for Alex to reply. He kept low as he made his way out of the alcove. The rock wall was high, but he didn't want to take any chances. He found a spot to poke his head up and survey the damage.

The ship lay in smoldering ruins, swarmed by Caparians like bees around a hive. There were cloaked bodies scattered everywhere like a battlefield. Only, this wasn't a battlefield, not in the true sense of the word. This was a slaughter. The splintered debris from the coffins littered the ground like *Pick Up Sticks*. More Caparians were picking through the bodies. Searching, no doubt, to confirm Char and his friends were dead.

Char crouched out of sight and slipped back along the path to the alcove. He found Alex sitting by the coffin with his knees bent and elbows resting on them. His head back and his eyes closed.

"Great way to stand guard," Char said.

"I could hear you were coming," Alex replied without opening his eyes.

"I think we lost them," Char said as he sat beside Alex. "At any rate, none of them are coming this way." Alex opened his eyes and looked at Char.

"What do we do now?" Alex asked. Char shrugged.

"I don't know."

"Do you still have the paper Warc gave you?"

Char nodded stuck a leg out straight so he could dig his hand into his pocket to retrieve it. He pulled his leg back up and wrapped the cooling cloak around him again. The cape was cooling him now that he wasn't running like a madman through the desert.

He unfolded the paper and stared at the map of Lebrac. Well, at least this area of Lebrac. He found where they were on the map and where Warc had marked the safe house. Char let out a low whistle.

"That looks like a long hike."

"Yes, it does," Alex confirmed.

Char squinted at the page. He looked up. "Is it getting dark already?"

"I believe it is. If I remember correctly, Lebrac has very short days."

"Then I vote we stay here for the night and get a fresh start in the morning," Char said. Alex nodded.

"Agreed."

The temperature dropped dramatically at night. The rocks still held their warmth from the day, so they each curled up on a rock. Char used his cooling cloak as a pillow because it was warmer without it. The alcove had an overhang, so he wasn't worried about being spotted by any flying patrols, but he did worry Warc was dead, and they wouldn't see him again. He didn't think he could sleep, but the exhaustion and heat took their toll.

He was sitting with Kat. They were back in that tent nestled in the lavender snow on the mountain on Zortentearth. She was laughing at something he had said, but he couldn't remember it. The wind outside the tent howled, but they were warm, huddled around the heating rock.

The wind grew stronger, whipping the tent back and forth. Concern clouded the joy on Kat's face. She spoke, but he couldn't hear her.

"What?" he cried.

Kat stood up as the tent ripped away. Lavender snow swirled in a frenzy around them. It blew away like sand. Below the snow was red, hot stone. Then she began to break. Her body fractured and scattered like snowflakes. Her voiceless words were unheard and unanswered.

Then Alex was there, furious, demanding to know why he let Kat die. He grabbed Char by the arms and shook him, screaming. His blue face was inches away, glaring in hatred. The blue dissolved, and mustard yellow skin and burning red eyes were underneath.

"Betrayed!" Mrah bellowed. "You betrayed me! You let her die!!"

Char awoke with a jerk. Sweat soaked his clothing, and his muscles still twitched from the nightmare. He rolled off the rock, unsteady on his feet. He staggered out of the alcove and to a nearby ledge, dragging his cloak behind him. He watched the sun peak over the horizon of Lebrac. Already the heat was scorching. He wrapped himself in the cape, willing it to cool him faster.

"I won't let you die, Kat," he swore. "I promise. No matter what. I. Won't. Let. You. Die."

He heard Alex wake and knew it was time to go.

✦

The journey was long and hot as they picked their way over boulders, down narrow paths, worked their way along high ledges and around obstacles. Would it be wiser to rest during the day and walk at night? Isn't that how you're supposed to cross a desert on Earth? Char didn't know, couldn't think; exhaustion was eating away at him. The days and nights were short. What little sleep he got was filled with fever dreams like the one he had on the first night. The days seemed to be about half the length of an Earth day. Char estimated they had been traveling for about a day and a half, maybe two Earth days.

He trudged along with Kat's box, appreciating again how light and effortless it was to move. His stomach twisted and gurgled. His tongue felt dry as sand. He tried to ignore how thirsty he was, but he could focus on nothing else with each step.

They approached an overlook. Before them, they found a forest of desert-type plants. None that Char had ever seen. Some of them were similar to cacti, but most were alien to him.

"Alex, we need to find food and water," Char said. His lips were dry and blistered. His tongue felt too big for his mouth.

"I know," Alex said. "We should find something in the forest."

"I don't know if you can legitimately call that a forest," Char replied. They made their way down the last sloping path.

"A forest doesn't have to have deciduous trees or even coniferous," Alex said. "My mother studied plant life on different planets. Part of my curriculum was the study of plants. Fortunately, Lebrac was part of my required reading."

Char heard the grin rather than saw it. "Well, that's convenient."

They wandered deep into the forest of nightmare plants. Many were as red as their soil, but some were yellow and orange, and a few were even green. All of them had deadly-looking thorns and jagged edges. Alex kept up a steady stream of information. "Don't touch that one; it's poisonous. That one will eat you alive. That one won't kill you, but don't eat it, or you'll be sick for days." Char kept his hands inside his cloak and tried to walk "skinny."

Finally, it was time to make camp. They found a clearing.

"Stay here. I'll find us some dinner," Alex said. Char was content to guard the coffin. He studied his reflection on the smooth black surface. He hadn't realized how much weight he had lost. His cheeks were hollow. What little clothing he had left sagged on him. His hair had grown back in and was now touching his shoulders. He had a beard and mustache too. It itched, and he didn't like it. He was always aware of it, but it was still a bit of a shock to see it.

"Good grief," Char mumbled. "I look like a mountain man."

He leaned against the coffin and closed his eyes, just for a moment.

"Great way to stand guard," Alex said. Char jerked awake and blinked several times. He fought a yawn as he replied.

"I could hear you coming."

"Right," Alex drawled. "Here, I brought dinner."

He dropped a slab of some yellow plant at Char's feet and set another giant seed-like pod next to it. He built up a fire and laid a thin flat rock across the flames. The temperature had dropped again while Char dozed. He shivered. The fire felt good. It would be a miracle if neither of them caught pneumonia from the radical temperature differences. Alex laid the slab of the plant across the rock to cook. A meaty smell arose with the sizzle.

"Here," Alex handed one of the pods to Char. He showed him how to crack it open. Char's attempt was clumsy but successful. Inside was sweet cool water. Char chugged his.

"Not too much too fast," Alex warned, "you'll make yourself sick."

"Sorry," Char gasped. "I'm just so thirsty." He set the pod down, determined to make the rest last. Alex piled some nuts by the sizzling plant and flipped the plant over.

"What is it?" Char asked as he glanced at his water pod.

"A meat-eating plant," Alex said. "It's a little like a large eggplant from Earth, and I mean *large* eggplant, but it's got a texture more like turkey."

"Meat-eating?" Char asked. "What kind of meat does it eat?"

"You don't want to know," Alex said as he sliced a piece off with a knife; Char didn't know he had. He laid the slice on a flat rock and added some of the roasted nuts to it. The whole thing smelled great.

His mouth watered as he brought the first bite to his lips. It tasted like wild turkey, and the nuts were so similar to what he would find on Earth that he could almost believe he was camping back home, albeit in Death Valley, but still somewhere on Earth.

⁂

"Stop," Alex hissed. Char almost jerked his arm out of his socket as he tried stopping the coffin. They were silent as they listened. A twig somewhere ahead of them snapped, then another. Soon it became clear there were a lot of footsteps up ahead.

"A patrol?" Char whispered. Alex nodded. He spun to face Char.

"Go back to that cave we saw. Hide there until it's safe."

"What are you going to do?" Char asked. Dread iced his veins.

"I'm going to distract them," Alex said. "Stay out of sight."

Alex started to leave, but Char grabbed his arm. "You can't do this!"

Quick as a viper, Alex spun and pinned Char up against the coffin. His arm pressed against Char's collarbone. He brought his face inches from Char. "Your *first* priority is *Kat*. If you try to follow me, so help me I will make sure you aren't around to endanger her ever again." He held his position, tense, angry. *"Keep. Her. Safe."*

His words were clipped. He bounced Char against the coffin for emphasis before releasing him. Without another word, he turned and crashed through the underbrush, intentionally making noise. He started singing something that sounded like a marching song.

Char pulled the coffin with him as he retraced his steps to the cave, moving as silently. Behind him, there was shouting and running, and Alex's song was cut short. Char felt gutted.

He found the cave and put the coffin deep inside. A cozy little place surrounded by moist rocks made the perfect hiding spot. He slipped the casket into the nook and laid a hand on it.

"Kat," Char whispered. His throat closed up. He shook his head. "I can't let him die for us. I know you would be the first to demand we go after him."

He paused and laid his forehead on the sleek surface. It burned.

"I don't want," he swallowed hard, barely able to force out the words, his voice thick with emotion, "I *don't want* to leave you, but I can't save him with this giant box tagging along behind me. Please, forgive me."

He pushed away and slipped out of the cave, looking back only once to ensure he couldn't see the coffin from the opening. It was black, and the shadows swallowed it up quite nicely.

The forest seemed more menacing now that he was alone. He couldn't remember which plants were deadly or just painful. The night was falling again, and the long shadows seemed to take on life. As if the plants were growing black tentacles from their bases to wrap around his ankles and drag him down. He wanted to take the cooling cloak off, but it provided the extra protection he needed against the thorns when he ventured too close.

He was suddenly angry, angry at this planet with its oppressive heat, short days, and killer plants. He was angry at Mrah for destroying his world, people, and friends. Why was he taking everything and everyone Char loved? Char furiously snatched up a stone and whipped it into the darkness.

Prior to this, he didn't remember hearing any animal noises, but now that he traversed this nightmare alone, his imagination worked overtime. He thought he heard twigs snapping, heavy breathing, a low growl. He imagined glowing eyes amongst the thick foliage, a flash of fangs. Any second, a massive beast, the like of which he had never seen, would leap out at him. It would devour him before he had a proper chance to introduce himself. He kept his hood up and pressed on through the fear. He imagined Kat slipping through the dark with him. She would be fearless and the first to scold him for being a sissy. The thought made him smile.

He broke through the foliage into a clearing. There was evidence of a struggle. Plants were bent down and crushed. One of the imprints looked like a body. Char would bet money that was an imprint of a Droplet's body. In fact, he would even bet it was a half-human Droplet. The smile shrank into grim determination as he followed the trail of damaged vegetation.

The trail led him to the forest's edge; before him spread a small village. Char couldn't believe his eyes. All the houses were small pyramids! They were missing their pointed tops as if beheaded, but they were definitely pyramids. Once out of the forest, the trail ended. Rock didn't record footprints.

He didn't see anyone in the village, but they had to be there somewhere. "I'm coming, Alex," Char said. "Like it or not."

He kept to the shadows as he snuck through town. He had no plan. How would he free Alex, providing he could find Alex? He peeked in lit windows and got a glimpse of family life on Lebrac. In none of the windows did he see Alex.

He came to a house with no lights. It appeared no one was home. The whole of the house had an abandoned feel. The windows, dark soulless eyes, seemed to stare at him. The silence whispered of a hollowness that could never be filled. He didn't realize he was reaching for the door handle until he touched it. It turned with little effort, and the door swung silently open. The silence was eerier than the loudest protesting hinge.

A sound like an exhale greeted him as the house released the breath it had been holding. Inside was surprisingly cool, given the hot days.

He shut the door behind him. The darkness was absolute. He put a hand on the wall for support, and light blazed through the entrance. As there were no windows in the entrance, he didn't worry about the light getting out.

The house smelled stale, musty, of disease and death. A narrow corridor extended into the darkness. Char held his breath as he walked. The walls were stone and painted with what looked like a type of hieroglyphics. He passed arched doorways beyond which were rooms he took to be the Caparians version of a living room and a dining room, though the furniture looked rigid and uncomfortable. One room contained a long table with twelve chairs. He passed what he assumed was the kitchen. Dirty dishes piled in the sink, overflowing onto the counter. Dried bits of alien food stuck to the plates.

He entered the room, which might have been a living room. The tables were designed to fit into the crook of the slanting walls without wasting space. Most of the room was spotless, save for a chair surrounded in garbage as if someone had camped out on it and just tossed his trash over the edge. He ran his fingers over the smooth marbled surface of a table near the wall closest to the chair. Instantly he was surrounded by holograms.

A woman with yellow skin and long thick black hair stood to his immediate right. She smiled. An invisible breeze gently brushed her hair back from her shoulders. Children of all ages ran around him, playing tag, perhaps? Their creepy soundless laughter gave him chills. The older ones stood stoically next to their mother. They were male and attempted to be more adult than their perceived years. Some things, it seemed, don't change throughout the galaxy.

The females in the Caparian race had a softer shade of yellow skin, less like dried mustard and more like sunflowers. Her black hair was thicker, less greasy, and her smile was gentle, kind, motherly. She was almost pretty. The overall effect was less frightening than a male Caparian.

Char took a step closer to the woman, oddly careful not to step on the hologram children. He tried to touch her face, but the hologram faded all around him, and he found himself alone once again. Though the hologram had made no sound, and the children issued soundless laughter, Char still felt the silence was deeper than before.

He continued his exploration. He found a ladder-like staircase at the end of the dark hallway. He placed a hand on the wall for support and climbed the steps. On the second, floor he passed room after room of tiny beds. He entered one. The bed was so small with a pink blanket. A doll lay on the pillow, waiting for the little girl to return. Unlike the mess in the kitchen, this room was spotless and had a shrine-like feel.

The whole house felt like a dusty old tomb. Ages since the owner had left, would he ever return? Though the furniture was alien to him, and he didn't know what most of it was and considered it rather ugly and uncomfortable, he still felt this had been a happy family. But what had happened? Where had they all gone? And why would this little girl, any little girl, leave her doll behind?

He left the room untouched and continued down the hall. The last bedroom was the largest and had a large bed. Half the room was in disarray. Bottles shattered on the floor, clothing strewn about, and dressers toppled over. However, on the other side was a shrine. A vanity mirror loaded with bottles and brushes sat untouched, albeit covered in dust, but nothing moved.

Dried flowers with drooping heads still sat in a vase on the bedside table—their decaying stench mixed with the lingering odor of disease. Something very wrong had happened in this house. Char backed out of the room and closed the door.

The room at the end of the hall caught Char by surprise. For a few minutes, all he could do was stare in wonder. It was Earth! Well, it could have been anyone's library on Earth. Shelves laden with books lined the walls. A desk, blanketed in papers, held a small Earth globe, or perhaps it only appeared small next to the enormous furniture. He certainly felt like a dwarf in this house. Char ran his fingers over the hard wood of the desk and touched the leather cushioned chair. A sextant, compass, and other nautical instruments sat amongst the books, which appeared to have originated on Earth upon closer inspection. They were in English.

Feeling like a kid, he scrambled up onto the oversized chair. He found a book of matches and struck one, inhaling the sulfuric fumes. He watched the tiny flame flicker and chew at the stick. An oil lamp sat on the corner of the desk. He lifted the glass globe and touched the flame to the wick. There was still oil in the lamp, and the wick greedily pulled the flame into itself. He shook the match and enjoyed the residual scent of burnt match. He replaced the globe and just stared at it for a few moments. He wanted to absorb this feeling. Outside that door was a typical home with carpets and painted walls. The moldings would be trimmed in white, and framed photos would line the walls. Outside the house would be green fields and full, rich trees. A gentle wind would rustle the leaves. Flowers would fill the air with their heady scent.

He shook his head; this was no time for nostalgia. He leaned forward again. The ink in the well had dried, and the pen lay beside it; the nib still coated in dried ink. Many of the items were from history long dead. Char sifted through the papers, not reading them. They were primarily scientific papers. Why were they written in English? Was the owner planning on writing a book about Earth?

A large brown leather book caught his eye. It was embossed in gold and held closed with a metal clasp which popped open easily. It was a journal! Char opened it to the first page; it was written in English. Why would a Caparian write in English?

Earth Year 2101, December 21st

We arrived home on the opening cusp of an epidemic. The first case was a day after our arrival. I've seen nothing like it on this planet and will be keeping detailed clinical logs at the lab. To date, every patient is confined to the lab to attempt to control the spread.

We are taking every precaution to keep this unknown disease from spreading to the outside. Those of us who are healthy work constantly, attempting to ease the suffering of those afflicted. I am head of a group that is tasked with finding a cure.
I worry for my family. I have been gone so long and, still, I can't go home. I must stay in the lab; no one is allowed in or out. We can't risk infecting those on the outside. I'm hopeful we will find a cure soon.

Char turned the page.

Earth Year 2101, December 22nd

We've had our first death from this illness. It strikes unbeliev-ably quickly. Despite our best efforts, more and more have fallen ill. It's strange how one moment they're fine and laughing, the next they're swelling and moaning, and by morning they're dead. The disease is spreading, and it's beginning to pick up speed. We've quarantined the sick to a separate room in the lab. No one may attend to them without full biohazard gear.
They're dying too fast to bury. We burn the dead in the incinerator.
There are no reported cases from the outside. For this, I am grateful.
What is it? Where did it come from?

Char felt sick and mesmerized at the same time. Is this what happened in this house? He flipped pages, jumping ahead in time.

Earth Year 2102, January 10th

I've spoken with my wife. She understands when I explain why I can't come home. She's worried; for my health, for the children, but I assure her I seem to have some kind of immunity. The children will be fine if we keep this within the lab.

So many have died in such a short time. I'm sure the sounds of the dying will haunt me for the rest of my life. Even now, as I write this, their moaning envelops my senses. I can smell the disease, the rot, the death.

We, who are not ill, get very little sleep. I grow weary with the constant care of the dead and dying. There's no cure, and the group assigned the task of finding it—most of them are dead.

Char paused, listening. Had he heard a noise? He tilted his head, willing his hearing to be more acute—silence, the same heavy silence as before. Beads of sweat broke out on his forehead and under his arms. He turned back to the book; flipped more pages, jumping ahead again.

Earth Year 2102, February 1st

The death toll is staggering. This place used to be so full of life. Thousands walked these halls; now, only a handful remain.

One of the men—an intern, I believe—escaped today. To date, he has shown no signs of the illness. I pray he is genuinely immune. God help us if this thing makes it out of the lab. I am so tired.

Char flipped more pages, reading faster now.

<u>Earth Year 2102, February 20th</u>

It's out! Oh God, we have failed to contain this scourge! They're dead! All of them! Dead! Only Warc and I remain in this tomb of a lab. We, alone, are immune to this plague!
My wife tells me it hasn't hit our neighborhood yet. She wants me to come home. Warc agrees it's time.

Char blinked and re-read the first paragraph. Warc? The owner of this journal knows Warc? He flipped more pages. A drop of sweat slid down his back, following the hollow over his spine.

<u>Earth Year 2102, February 24th</u>

My wife, my precious Myrna, why must it be you? She went quickly, as they all do. I thank God she didn't suffer as much as others.
She held my hand as she died. She made me promise. She made me swear to save the children. With her last breath, she squeezed my hand so hard. Her words still echo in my mind... "promise me... promise me..."
I promise, my love, I promise I will do everything I can to keep them alive. I promise. I promise. I promise.

Char closed his eyes. Something twisted in his stomach, and a sour taste touched the back of his tongue. How could she make him promise such a thing? He had a feeling this wasn't going to end well. He skipped ahead a few more pages.

Earth Year 2102, March 3rd

This plague, the Walking Death, as they have begun to call it, has spread across the whole of Lebrac. So many deaths. A shattering number. A heart-wrenching number. A genocide number. My family is no exception. It's pecking off my children one by one; God, my promise to Myrna. I'm failing her! I'm failing her!! My youngest, my little Natalie, remains healthy and strong. Natalie who is so like her mother. Natalie, the only Earth name Myrna would permit. She didn't love Earth as I do and wanted only Caparian names for her children, but she gave me this one, my Natalie.

Natalie tries to cheer me; she tries to make me laugh. She dances in the hall and sings silly songs. I try to smile for her. I try to be strong so she won't fear.

I am still so tired. She tells me not to worry; she will never leave me: my precious, the one bright spot in all this death. Dare I hope she has inherited my immunity?

"No," Char whispers. He flips pages growing sicker with every word. "Please... no..." Char jerked his head up. What was that? It sounded like the closing of a door. He slid off the chair with a thump and strained his ears. He tiptoed to the door and put an ear against it. Nothing. No sound whatsoever.

He cracked the door slightly and peeked into the hall. It was dark and undisturbed. He listened for what felt like an hour but was only about a minute. Still, the silence held firm. He shook his head.

"You're losing it, Char," he mumbled as he struggled back into the seat and picked up the journal. The leather was slippery with his sweat. He wiped one hand on his cloak, then the other, shifting the book from hand to hand as he did it.

<u>Earth Year 2102, March 17th</u>

They're dead. All of them. Even my little Natalie. Through it all, even through her suffering, she tried to make me laugh. Her last words to me before she died – Don't worry, Papa, I'll be all right. – She was only six. Only six. Only six. Only six.
Is this punishment? Were my sins so bad it warrants the deaths of so many? *Innocents! They were all innocents!! Take me! Take me! Take me!!!!!!*

Each "take me" was slashed so deep the paper was slit. His pain and frustration were tangible. There was only one entry left dated much, much later. He must have stopped logging everything. Char wondered, again, who this journal belonged to and wished he could do something to help the poor creature.

<u>Earth Year 2134, January 1st</u>

I know what I must do now. I met with Princess Aurora Jima of Zorten-tearth. She made it clear to me what I must do. I'm distraught that my family's killer is from another place that I hold dear to my heart.
It seems my punishment is not over. It's not enough to shatter my heart and soul, but I must now pulverize the remaining shards of my heart.
My precious Earth. My blue jewel in the darkness. It betrayed me. It sent the Walking Death to kill us! Betrayed! Betrayed! Betrayed!!
One last task. One last task. One last task. God willing, I will perish in the attempt. I can hear them now. I can hear their voices, their laughter. They are waiting for me, there, just on the other side. Wait for me, my loves.

<u>*I am coming...*</u>

Char closed the book. No more entries. There was no doubt about the owner of this journal. It was Mrah's. This was his house, his family, his tiny childless beds. It was his things thrown in frustrated grief. His pain. His sorrow.

"But why write it in English?" Char wondered aloud.

"Because," Warc stood in the doorway. Char gasped and jerked back against the back of the chair. The chair bucked and tilted but to rest on its castor's. "Earth was his favorite place, and English is not well known on our planet. You might say the book is written in code."

"You scared me half to death!" Char cried as he slid off the chair. His hand pressed to his heart. It beat fast against his palm. Then, almost to himself, he continued. *"I thought* I heard something."

"You're lucky I'm not Mrah, or you'd be dead."

"How did you know I was here?" Char asked.

"I didn't, but I was on the way to the safe house when I saw the lights and hoped to find Mrah." Warc entered the room and fingered the globe of Earth. Char snatched up the journal and shook it at Warc.

"I found this," he said. He opened it and fluttered the pages. "I read some of it. He mentions Aurora in the final passage."

Char flipped to the last entry and held it up so Warc could see it. "Aurora led him to believe the plague was some form of germ warfare from Earth! That we somehow knew he existed and attacked him without provocation."

Warc glanced at the page but said nothing. He turned to the bookshelf and ran a finger down one of the spines. He didn't seem surprised by the revelation.

"He attacked us because Aurora *lied,"* Char said.

Warc looked at the ceiling. "I know."

"How could he believe such a lie?" Char asked. His voice was getting louder, though Warc remained calm. "He had to know we didn't know you existed and that we didn't even have the power to attack him in such a way. We've barely made it to the moon for crying out loud! Is he an idiot?"

Warc spun on him; fury flickered across his face. "You've read his journal. Do you imagine he's thinking rationally? *Do you?*" Warc snatched the book from Char's hands and flipped through the pages. He stabbed a finger at the page. "Here! Do you see how he is repeating himself? Here! And here!"

He stabbed his finger at the page with each exclamation. Char fought the urge to flinch again.

"His anguish is so great his mind is *fracturing!*" Warc whipped the book away from him as if it had suddenly gotten too hot. It hit the book-case with an opened winged thwack and landed on the floor face down, pages bent. "I realize you have lost much, but he has also lost."

Warc crossed the distance between them in one lightning-quick motion, the enormous desk shoved to the side like a toy, pages fluttering to the floor, and pinned Char against the wall. "He is my *friend,* my *brother,* and my *family.* You have a chance to get back all that you have lost, but he will *never* get back what he has lost. He will *never* be given a chance to fix what he has wronged. *NEVER!!*"

Warc pushed away from him and stood with a rigid back facing Char. Char rubbed a hand across his neck where Warc had pressed his arm. He was shaking and desperately wanted to sit but didn't dare show his weakness.

"Where are Kat and Alex?" Warc asked, sounding tired.

"A patrol captured Alex, and Kat is hidden and safe." Char tried to keep his voice from shaking as hard as his hands. Warc gave him a sharp look.

"Safely hidden *where?*" Warc asked. Char cocked his head, unable to read Warc's tone.

"In a cave," Char said. Warc closed his eyes then opened them almost immediately.

"And Alex is captured?" Warc repeated. Char didn't say anything. "We'll have to rescue Alex first. Let's pray nothing finds Kat before we can get to her."

KAT

"You have to do more," Kat said. She sat on the edge of Neptune's Hollow, allowing the breeze to whip the short strands of her hair into her face. She felt the sting against her cheeks and in her eyes.

"What else can I do?" Charlie asked, not sitting. From the corner of her eye, she could tell he had his hands thrust into the pockets of his jeans. His shirt flapped.

"Try to contact the government. The army! Anyone! Everyone!" She climbed to her feet and faced him. He looked at her calmly.

"And tell them what?" he asked. "A *future* girl that only appears in my *dreams* told me *aliens* would attack us?"

"Of course not," Kat replied. "That makes you sound nuts. Make up a story, tell them something else, but make sure they feel the need to fight!"

"Do you hear yourself?" Charlie asked. He put his hands on her shoulders. "You don't know any more than I what we can tell them to make them believe. I'm having the dreams, and I hardly believe it."

Kat pulled away. A lump made it impossible to speak or even swallow. Her frustration reflected in the sparks emitted from her spirit. She balled her hands into fists; tears burned at the corners of her eyes. She was failing miserably and didn't know what else to do. She squeezed her eyes shut, forcing the tears back down. She didn't cry. She never cried.

He turned her to face him and wrapped his arms around her. She froze in shock as he pressed her head into his chest. She stiffened. He pressed his lips into her hair.

"You know this government as well as I do. If I were to warn them against this attack, they would lock me up for making terroristic threats, and I wouldn't be able to save anyone," he mumbled into her hair. She pushed him away.

"I'm sorry," she said, annoyed because she knew he was right. "I don't remember how to lean on anyone anymore."

"I'll try to do more." Charlie sighed, letting his arms drop back at his sides.

⌖

Charlie opened his eyes and sat up. Kat watched him rub the sleep out of his eyes and toss the blanket back. She followed him through his morning routine and said nothing as he ate his breakfast. There was nothing to say. He was right. There was nothing he could tell anyone that would convince them to fight an enemy they didn't believe existed.

Tracy walked in and plopped into a seat. "I got the last of the supplies last night. We can move them into the shelter today. I also got a few calls this morning before you woke up. People are excited about this shelter party of yours."

"I think we need to do more," Charlie said. Tracy grabbed the box of generic cereal and poured a bowl.

"Like what," she asked as she splashed milk over the cereal.

"Maybe we can get more towns involved," he mused. Tracy raised an eyebrow but didn't stop chewing.

"How many, and how?" She spoke through a mouthful of cereal.

"I don't know," he said. He put his spoon in the bowl.

"Charlie, if your girlfriend is right," Tracy pointed the dripping spoon at him. "We don't have enough time to organize such a thing."

"We have to do something. If we at least get the idea out there, then maybe God will move their hearts to try." Charlie pushed his chair back with a loud screech. He carried his bowl to the sink and let the water fill it till it overflowed. "We can't just let the rest of the world die."

"Well, I met a guy from a news station the other day. Maybe if we dress it up and make it a challenge, we can get more people involved. I'll talk to him," Tracy suggested.

"We'll do everything we can, and the rest is up to God," Charlie said.

For the first time in a long, long time, Kat allowed herself to feel hope.

CHAR

"How do you know he's going to be here?" Char asked as they approached the remarkably Earth-like building. The lab was all straight lines and glass and steel. They passed a sign sporting two languages announcing that this was the Institute of Earth Sciences. Char didn't recognize the second language but assumed it was the native tongue of Lebrac.

"I've worked with Mrah for many years," Warc replied as if that answered everything.

Char snorted. "Yeah, well, I *lived* with my sister for many years, and I still don't know where she would take a hostage."

"Silence is preferable," Warc said. Char felt thoroughly chastised and kept quiet as they approached the over-lit building. It sparkled like a diamond in the middle of a desert. They crouched behind a low rise.

"How do you keep the glass so clean with all this dust flying around?" Char asked. Warc rolled his eyes and released a soft sigh.

"I could leave you behind and do this on my own," Warc threatened. Char put his hands up in mock surrender. He mouthed the word 'sorry.' Warc turned his attention to the building.

Char noticed two guards by the door and two others walking the perimeter. He doubted they would be able to just saunter up to the door and knock. Warc watched the guards for a long time. Char wanted to tap him on the head and see if he was still awake. He decided that would be suicidal, so he didn't.

He wiped his sleeve across his brow; he was sweating profusely. Was it hotter than usual? The cooling cloak seemed like a joke in the growing heat, and the sand was sticking all over him. He could shower for a month, and still, there would be granules tucked in crevices better left un-sanded.

Warc motioned for him to follow and again to be quiet. They ran in a crouch closer to the building. The muscles in Char's legs quivered and ached. His back had developed a painful knot that he may never get unraveled. He wanted nothing more than to spend a few days soaking in a pool of cool water. He would demand nothing more of his muscles than an occasional swish through the refreshing liquid to stay afloat.

They kept to the shadows. Soon the sun would rise, and their cover would be scorched away, so they had to hurry. Warc led them to a drain with a wire mesh cover. Char looked from Warc to the drain and back.

"You're kidding, right?" Char whisper-screamed.

Warc shook his head as he produced wire cutters. Char mimed groaning.

"This only happens in movies," Char whispered. "This doesn't happen in real life."

Warc ignored him as he began cutting. Char wondered if they would be ankle-deep in sewage with rats chewing at their toes. The pipe looked big enough to stand, at worst, to be slightly bent. At least Char would be able to stand hunched over, but Warc would practically have to crawl.

Warc pulled him close, scattering his random thoughts. He thrust something into Char's sweaty palm. "Follow this map. I'll create a diversion." Warc pulled back a bit and looked more closely at Char's face. He put a hand on Char's forehead.

"How are you feeling?" Warc asked. Char shrugged.

"Hot," he said. "But that's normal for this place."

Warc shook his head. "No, the Temprafreeze is wearing off." Then, ominously, "We don't have much time."

Warc clipped through the wire mesh and motioned for Char to hurry. Char stuffed the paper in his pocket and squeezed through the small opening. His cloak got hooked; a tug and sharp rip had him free. The tunnels were dry with a layer of dust on the bottom, making sense since he hadn't seen any free-flowing water since coming to this cursed little ball of fire in space. He could stand if he kept his head cocked to one side. He didn't mind rats, but he was still relieved to see the lack of plague-carrying vermin. He pulled the paper out and found a small penlight wrapped up within it.

"That's helpful," Char mumbled. His voice, though low, echoed throughout the tunnels. He flinched at the ricocheted words; *he must remember to keep quiet.* He clicked the penlight on and studied the map. Oh good, a labyrinth. He had always wanted to try his hand at an impossible maze in suffocating heat on an alien planet while trying to rescue a friend and simultaneously not getting killed. He shook his head. He needed to focus, but it was so *hot.*

He hurried down the first tunnel. With each step, a loose thread from his now frayed cloak tickled his exposed calf. He kept imagining bugs crawling on his skin. He stepped high a few times and took a distracted swipe at the imaginary creepy crawlies while attempting to read the hand-drawn map.

He made the first turn, then the next. There was nothing in the tunnels to indicate he was closer to his mark or even if he was going in the right direction. Most of the tunnels were just underground tubes with no way out. The longer he ran, the hotter he got. The tunnels were like an oven, with little or no airflow. He felt he was suffocating and baking at the same time.

The darkness was absolute, and his little flashlight couldn't cut much of a line. It had an eerie horror movie vibe, and he kept expecting zombies to pop out of the darkness to attack. After several long minutes of imagining death by a zombie, he spotted a light from the ceiling of a tunnel. He took his time getting close. Any noise now might alert anyone above. He inched his way over to the ladder and took a quick peek through the floor grate. Not seeing any movement, he decided to risk the ladder. His climb was just as slow. The last thing he needed was to clang off this metal ladder.

The grate was small, but he was confident he could fit through. He did his best to scout out the room before lifting the lid. As far as he could see, no one was in the room. He pushed on the grate, but it didn't budge. He pressed harder, but it stuck fast. He wanted to use a few choice words on it, but he settled for glaring hard at it since he had to remain silent.

He shoved the penlight and paper back into his pocket and put his shoulder to the grate. He pushed it free with a growl and a loud metallic groan that echoed down the tunnels. He supported the weight for several moments listening for any sounds. Had he given himself away? The room above remained quiet, and the tunnels below retreated into silence. He tilted the grate back and was happy to discover it was on a hinge that kept it from falling back and making the loud noise that constantly gives people away in movies. Then he wondered when his life had turned into a movie?

He pulled himself into the room and looked around. It had beds lining the walls. Cabinets with red crosses lined another wall. A desk with papers and a lamp sat next to a door. The infirmary? Curtains shoved back to the walls waited to be pulled around a bed to give its occupant privacy. He closed the grate with only a little less groaning than when he opened it.

He tiptoed to the door and eased it open. At least the door hinges were silent. There appeared to be no one in the hall. He wondered what sort of diversion Warc had in mind. He consulted the map and decided going right was his best choice. His shoes squeaked, so he stopped and removed them. In stocking feet, he made his way down the hall. The floors were hot. Very hot. The socks offered little protection from the heat. He gritted his teeth and kept going.

Footsteps had him scampering to a door and ducking inside without checking to see if it was empty. He managed to close the door without a click. The dark inside was complete. He pressed his cheek to the door and waited for the footsteps to pass. Curiosity had him turning on his penlight and sweeping the room. Glass cabinets contained bottles of varying colors and shapes. A surgical table stood in the center of the room. A tray with surgical tools stood near the table; an I.V. stand still holding an I.V. bag was nearby; the tubes hung dejectedly to the floor. The air was stale with neglect. Another table stood near a wall, with boxes on the single shelf under the tabletop, and the top held jars filled with objects that Char felt better left unidentified.

He realized the footsteps had stopped, not passed. The hair on the back of his neck and his arms rose. He clicked his light off and let the ghosts of the past fade back into darkness. He crossed to the table in four quick strides and huddled behind. The latch on the door clicked loud enough to wake the dead, and Char nearly gasped audibly. An arc of light cut through the room and widened as the door opened. A flashlight beam created a circle on the opposite wall and swam across it like a stingray in water. It molded and formed to whatever surface it touched. It slid over the table and above his head. He crouched lower, just in case. After several long minutes, the flashlight switched off, and the door shut out the last of the light. He didn't move for an eternity after that. He still hadn't heard the footsteps leave. Sweat ran down his brow and into his eyes. He tried to wipe them away soundlessly.

At last, the footsteps moved away; he released the breath he held. He stood in the blackness, not daring to use his penlight again. He kept a hand on the table as he walked around it and headed for the door.

He eased the door open and peered down the hall. All was silent and clear, so he continued on his way. He was getting closer to the room; he was sure of it. The lights began to flicker. "Well, that's just creepy," he mumbled. "Seriously, why is my life suddenly a horror movie?" The lights went out.

"Great," he breathed. He backed up to the wall and waited. He could hear running footsteps, shouting, and general commotion. He wanted to turn on his penlight but feared that would give away his location. If this was Warc's great diversion, it was a lousy plan. He inched his way along the wall. He only needed to get to the next intersection and make a left. The room should be somewhere down that hall and guarded. It would be super great if he could see the guards.

A sudden scream sent his heart racing. It wasn't the guttural scream of a Caparian but the musical intonation of a Droplet. Alex! Char pushed off the wall and bolted for the intersection. He ran for a long time, expecting any moment to crash headlong into the wall.

Absolute darkness was weirdly disorienting. His other senses worked overtime. His ears strained to hear any noises but only seemed to pick up the beating of his heart. He was acutely aware of the pulsing in his neck and the soles of his feet burning. His nose was picking up a strange alien scent, like some kind of astringent and dust. His eyes, though blind, stretched wide in a vain attempt to be helpful.

He should have made it to the intersection by now. Had he gotten turned around? His shoulder grazed the corner; he stopped and placed a hand on it. He put his back to the corner and walked straight out, hands outstretched. His fingertips crashed into the opposite wall. Another scream, off to his left, oriented him. He turned toward the sound and followed it with a hand on the wall. His feet were so hot he was sure the sock had burned through At any moment, he would hear sizzling flesh. He remembered the Temprafreeze pool and tried not to fantasize about submerging himself in it.

Char found a recessed doorway and slipped inside just in time, as a red light started flashing and an alarm went off. The guards at the door, which Char was now able to see in flashing red, looked at each other then ran down the hall away from Char. A third stepped out of the room recently vacated by the guards, a menacing instrument still in his hands. He dropped it and ran after the guards.

Char ran to the room. He flattened himself to the wall and peeked around the corner. It was empty of any more guards, but Alex was bound to a table.

"Alex," Char whispered. He got to the table in two bounds and started working on the straps. He tried to ignore the white blood and blackened burn marks on the once beautiful blue skin; tried not to stare at the bald head that once had shining green hair, razor cuts still bleeding on his scalp. The remains of his long locks lay like a silken green puddle beneath the table.

"I told you," Alex scolded, "not to come."

The effort to speak seemed too much for him, for he released a sigh that half groaned and collapsed back on the bed. Char had the straps on his legs undone and started working on the one around his stomach. He accidentally dug a nail into a burn, and Alex flinched but didn't cry out.

Char grimaced, "Sorry."

"Leave," Alex gasped. "Me."

"No," Char replied. He began working on the chest strap. "I'm sorry. I am so sorry this happened to you. This wasn't your fight."

"It's everyone's fight," Alex rasped. "When a great wrong has is committed, it's everyone's fight."

Char shook his head. He gritted his teeth and worked the last strap. It popped free. He helped Alex sit up, then stand. He did his best to support the much larger Droplet. He forgot his burning feet as he helped steer Alex toward the door.

He didn't want to take Alex back to the drain, it was so far, and he was so weak, but as Warc hadn't given him a new rendezvous, he imagined Warc would expect him to get back out the same way. They hurried as quickly as possible, but the Caparians had done something to one of Alex's legs; he hobbled badly. His stomach twisted, bile rose to fill his throat. This was sick. It didn't matter what Mrah had gone through; there was no excuse for the torture of an innocent bystander.

"They wanted me," Alex gasped. "To tell them where you were. Where Kat was."

Char didn't respond.

"I didn't," he gasped again; pain tainted his words. "I didn't tell."

"You should have," Char was grim as he half dragged Alex down the last hall. A stampede of steps raced toward them. With a Herculean effort, he jerked Alex through the door to the infirmary. Alex collapsed to the floor while Char got the door closed just in time. He crouched out of sight and waited for the stampede to pass. Another alarm went off, this one with a blue light. They must have realized Alex was missing.

Char shoved his blistered feet back in his boots and jerked the grate up. With all the noise in the lab, he didn't worry about the squealing hinges. Alex managed to make it down the ladder without killing himself, and Char slid down after him.

Together they hobbled through the tunnels at a break-neck speed of —far too slow. Alex, for all his efforts, was gradually getting slower. He simply didn't have the energy to keep going. Alex had lost a lot of blood, and his Temprafreeze would also be wearing off. Char wasn't feeling the greatest either, but he couldn't give up. Kat wouldn't want him to give up.

Warc was waiting by the wire mesh cover when they finally made it out. He had to rip the whole mesh covering off to get Alex out. Alex slumped, on the verge of passing out, so Warc carried him like a wounded soldier off a battlefield. The three of them raced into the night, using the shadows as cover.

Char glanced back at the massive glass lab with its flashing lights and wailing sirens. It was too much like Earth for his taste. It reminded him of all that was bad about his long-dead home.

Z

"This is the cave," Char said as they approached the maw. He didn't wait for the other two before racing inside. Behind him, too distant, he heard a reproach from Warc. The cave exhaled, and a cool breeze lessened the smoldering heat. He headed straight for the nook where he had left Kat.

"No," Char gasped. He sucked in a breath, then another, and another, forgetting to release it. He felt the blood drain from his face, and a fresh cold sweat chilled him. The cave started to spin. He dropped to his knees, air whooshing out as he fell, grasping at his chest to press his heart back inside where it belonged, "Kat."

He felt, more than saw, Alex and Warc step up behind him. His mind refused to accept what he saw, or rather, didn't see. He knelt in the cold space where her box belonged. Something white fluttered in the breeze, stuck to the stone wall. Warc leaned over Char and snatched it.

"What does it say?" Char asked. He didn't turn to look, just listened to the rustle of paper, expecting Warc to read it aloud, but he was silent.

"Warc?"

Alex grunted. Char turned to see Alex's face turn grim as he read over Warc's shoulder. Warc lowered his hand without a word, and Char snatched the paper.

A single sentence was scrawled across the paper in handwriting recently made familiar to Char.

Did you really believe I wouldn't crack your code?

"...knew it would slow you down," Warc mumbled. Char barely heard him. The cold dread that just a moment before had covered him in sweat dissipated like steam. Dry heat filled his body till his head felt like a match head aflame. He felt his eyes roll back in his head, the room spun harder, and darkness came.

⁓Z⁓

Char woke to voices, the snapping of a fire, and the smell of meat. His mouth would have watered had he not been parched. His tongue felt three sizes too big, and he would swear there was sand in his throat. His face felt roasted. He wasn't entirely sure the smell of meat wasn't *his* flesh cooking. His mind was still foggy. He tried hard to remember where he was and what he was supposed to be doing. He managed to sit up, though he felt more like Sisyphus rolling a massive boulder up a very steep hill.

Alex and Warc spoke in low tones across the fire but stopped when he sat up and looked at them. They didn't need to say anything to trigger the memories. Mrah had Kat!

"What's the plan?" Char rasped. Alex handed him a water pod. He took a deep swallow reveling in the cold liquid as it coated his dry and dusty throat. Warc shrugged.

"We go save her."

KAT

"Did we remember to get bread?" Katie asked as she unloaded another bag of groceries. Their mother turned to her and smiled.

"You picked it up, remember?" she pulled a loaf out of the bag and tossed it to Katie. Katie caught it and set it on the counter.

"Oh, yeah," she shook her head, smiling.

"Turn the monitor on. I want to check the weather for the picnic."

"Okay," Katie switched on the monitor.

"And now we have a special message from a young man who has an unusual challenge for the public. We turn you to Nancy out in the field." The newscaster disappeared, and a pretty young woman with blond hair held a microphone close to her mouth. The wind was so intense her words were almost lost.

"Good morning; we are here to meet with Charlie Wessen, a young man who's decided to challenge the world to a competition. Charlie, what is this challenge, and what brought it about?" Nancy held the microphone out to Charlie.

"So, your last name is Wessen," Kat whispered.

"Well, my sister and I were planning a bomb shelter party. The bomb shelter was the theme, and while planning the party, we discussed preparation for the unexpected. We wondered how many people were truly prepared to survive should we be attacked unexpectedly," Charlie said. If he was nervous, he wasn't showing it to the camera. Kat stepped closer to the monitor and touched the screen, running fingers down Charlie's face.

"Thank you, Charlie," Kat breathed. Her spirit interfered with the monitor, so she stepped back.

"I'll go get your father," their mother said. "He'll be interested in this."

"And what did you come up with?" Nancy asked.

"Well, we felt a lot of people wouldn't be prepared at all. And given a limited amount of time, would people be able to get prepared in time? So, we decided to set a challenge for the public. Let's pretend we've gotten advanced warning of an invasion. You can pick the kind you want; part of the country attacking the other, creatures from the sea or even an alien attack; use your imagination. The game's parameters consist of surviving in a bomb shelter for at least three years. We will need to gather what we would need to survive."

"Why a bomb shelter?" Nancy asked.

"We figured just about every family would have a shelter on their property dating back to 2018," Charlie replied.

"Of course," Nancy said. "Almost everyone had one built during the War of 2018. So, when is the deadline?"

"We wanted to make it a tough and realistic challenge; I mean, how much warning could we get? So the deadline is—"

Boon reached around Katie and switched the monitor off. He crossed his arms and glared at her.

"Hey," Katie tried to switch it back on, but Boon blocked her. He brought his face close to hers, noses touching.

"Watching your little boyfriend," he growled. His lips peeled back from his teeth. Katie pulled back, but he held her firmly. "We are not playing his stupid little game."

"It's a good idea!" Katie argued. Boon raised a hand to backhand her.

"Hey!" Kat shouted. She stepped between them. "Don't you dare hit her! I mean me!"

Their mother came back, trailed by their father, and Boon dropped his hand, putting his arm around Katie as if nothing was wrong in the world.

"What happened to the monitor?" their mother asked. Boon shrugged and switched it back on.

"Sorry, I didn't realize anyone was looking at it." He left the room. He acted nonchalantly, but his posture was rigid.

The regular newscaster was back on. "Well, folks, it sounds like a fun challenge! I, for one, am going to give it my best shot. Remember, if you don't own a bomb shelter, talk to neighbors; you may be able to help them get theirs all set up."

"And don't forget the world party at the end, Bob," the other newscaster said. "I'm looking forward to the final day when everyone, everywhere, stays the night in their shelter, having a party to celebrate their accomplishment."

"That's right, Steve," Bob continued. "A worldwide bomb shelter party, it's unprecedented!"

"Can we do it, Dad?" Katie asked as she shut the monitor off. "It sounds like fun!"

"No," Boon said from the doorway. "It's a stupid idea."

"Shut up, Boon," Kat snapped. Knowing full well, he couldn't hear her.

"Well," their father said, looking at Boon out of the corner of his eye, then back to Katie. "Our shelter is already set up, but if you want to stay the night in it after the picnic, you may."

"No," Kat said. "You have to stay too. Katie, tell them!" She wanted to nudge her past self. Katie stood mute.

"Well, we'll talk about it later," their mother said, a little too much cheer in her voice to break the tension.

CHAR

"I realize I'm probably suffering from heat exhaustion or worse, but how do you suggest we rescue her? We have no idea when he took her or where." Char rubbed his face with his free hand; it itched. Sunburned, his sunburns always itched. What would happen when the Temprafreeze wore off completely? Would he die quickly? Would it be a slow process? Would he feel his blood boiling in his veins?

"Mrah and I designed those boxes. Each one has a unique electronic signature within the atmospheric stabilizer. We will be able to track it," Warc said. Alex stared at the fire. His wounds appeared worse by firelight. A white bandage wrapped his head like a turban.

"If you can track it, so could Mrah. Why would you put her in something he could track?" Char struggled to his feet. His legs shook, and he sat back down. "We were sitting ducks."

"No," Warc replied. "To access the electronic signature, you need a code."

"Wouldn't Mrah know the code?" Char asked.

"I changed it." Warc poked the fire with a stick. "I knew he would crack it, but it would take him a while. I just didn't think it would be this soon."

"So, let's go," Char attempted to get to his feet again, only to collapse back on the stone. He had never been so bone-weary in his life.

"We can't go anywhere tonight," Warc said. "Alex can't travel in his condition, and you are severely dehydrated. We need to take tonight to rest. We'll start fresh in the morning."

"But Kat—"

"He will not kill her yet." Warc held up a hand.

"How do you know?"

"I know Mrah," Warc shrugged.

"I don't think we have the time to waste," Char argued. "My Temprafreeze is wearing off."

"All the more reason to spend the night and drink. We need to get you hydrated." Warc pushed another water pod into Char's hand. Char drained it.

He would have argued further, but he didn't have the energy. He tossed his empty pod away and curled into a ball.

A series of fever dreams plagued his sleep—a mishmash of events that made no sense, but all happened. The anguish of the plague victims mingled with the horrors of the first attack. The flames of the exploding escape pods in the second attack rained down on the stoic Droplets as they lined up to die. He watched the long, painful death of a Caparian family he wept for but had never met. Throughout were the screams of the people he had let down. When he finally jerked awake, he noticed the mouth of the cave was already bright, and he felt like a dried lizard's skin.

Alex didn't look much better than the night before, but at least he was standing. Char joined him at the mouth of the cave.

"Where's Warc?" Char asked, looking back into the cave in case he somehow missed him.

"He said he needed to get a better signal." Alex sounded tired.

"How are you feeling?" Char asked. Alex looked at him as if that were the dumbest question on Lebrac.

"How would you say it on Earth?" Alex asked. "Like I've been struck by a train?"

"Are you going to be able to go?" Char asked.

"I have to," Alex replied. Then, almost to himself, "I can't let her die."

Char tried to ignore the statement. He echoed the sentiment, but it made him feel strangely angry to hear it come from Alex's lips. From the corner of his eye, he studied the Droplet. Gashes marred his otherwise perfect face. He was slightly hunched but appeared to be trying to hide it. Every so often, he would grimace. He seemed to be making every effort to mask his pain, and Char decided not to call him on it.

"I'm sorry," Char said. "I know you said this isn't your fight, but what he did to you…"

"Are we any different?" Alex asked. Char jerked his head back a little as if physically slapped.

"I'm sorry?" This time it was a question, not a statement.

"You seem ready to condemn him."

"Look what he did to you!" Char cried. Alex's flinch was almost imperceptible.

"God, be merciful to me, a sinner," Alex said. His eyes focused on some point far in the distance. It was his mouth moving, but it wasn't his voice. It sounded somehow deeper. It resonated with time ancient. It sounded much like the voice in the wind back in Coral City. *"Father, forgive them, for they know not what they do."*

"Alex," Char brushed Alex's arm with just his fingertips. Afraid to touch him. To break the trance, yet simultaneously wanting it to continue. "Are you all right? You're weirding me out."

A shudder visibly passed through Alex. He blinked several times. "What? Did you say something?" His voice was back to normal.

"Uh," Char felt his eyebrows knit together, mirroring his confusion. "No…" his voice was breathy, then pumping more energy than he felt into the words, "No, I was just thinking Warc sure is taking his time."

"Perhaps we should find him." Alex began walking without a reply. Char followed, still not understanding what had just transpired.

They found Warc at the edge of the forest. He was holding an instrument that resembled a flip phone. He turned a dial. The device was silent, but a light appeared on the screen. It left a green trail as it moved. Warc nodded, then nodded again before flipping the instrument shut.

"I've located them. They're on the move," Warc said. "We should be able to overtake them if we move quickly."

Char felt this translated into another mad dash across Death Valley. He wasn't looking forward to the run, especially with the Temprafreeze problem.

⌇Z⌇

Char believed his heart was perilously close to exploding. The human body wasn't made for long runs across burning deserts without water, and he had to run so much faster to keep up. Even Alex, with all his injuries, was outrunning him. Not that Alex was keeping up with Warc by any means, but still, to be outrun by a man closer to death than life was humiliating.

"Keep running," Warc bellowed. Char forced himself to focus. He tipped his head down and dug in harder, kicking up sand as he sprinted to catch up with the two taller beings.

"I really hate running in sand," he grumbled to himself. Warc put a hand up to stop them as they crested a dune. Char, happy to oblige, immediately bent at the waist and put his hands on his knees, heaving uncontrolled gulps of hot air. The other side of the dune was like an enormous slide and at the base was a group of Caparians running with the coffin. Leading the pack was Mrah. They raced toward a small pyramid, the only pimple on the horizon.

Warc pulled them to the ground. Char found it difficult to breathe while lying on his stomach, on burning hot sand. He wondered if his flesh was melting yet. Warc motioned for them to lean in closer.

"Here's the plan," he whispered. "Alex, you help me fight the guards. Char, your sole objective is to get Kat and take her to that pyramid."

"But there are *twenty*," Char said. He wanted to say he would fight too, but experience was a harsh teacher, and he fully remembered how under-matched he was with just one Caparian.

"I can handle it," Warc said.

"But you're a scientist," Char said. Warc rolled his eyes at Char.

"Human," Warc said. "I realize on Earth most scientists can get away with locking themselves up in a lab all day and may not actually have any combat training, but here on Lebrac, you have to earn the privilege to be a scientist, usually by way of enlisting in the military. Mrah and I have an *extensive* military background. Do not worry."

"What about Alex?" Char continued. He hated being the only weak member of the party. "He's injured and comes from a peaceful planet."

"My mother was half-human," Alex answered. "She felt it necessary for me to experience much of my Earth background. I was always partial to martial arts."

"But you were *captured* last time!" Char's whisper was harsh.

"Intentionally," Alex said.

"Maybe we should get some guns," Char suggested. Alex jammed an elbow into his side. Char grunted. Alex gave him a look and nodded toward Warc, glaring at Char.

"Oh, I didn't mean *you* needed a gun! I meant, I, uh, needed a..." His voice trailed off.

"As a matter of fact, *human*." Warc handed Char a gun. "I brought this for you. It's what we give to *children* before they learn to fight. Try not to shoot yourself."

Insulted, Char gritted his teeth; sand crunched between them. That's it! If he ever got Earth back, he was taking combat lessons! He wiped at the sweat on his brow, which left a streak of sand behind. Annoyed, he balled his hands into fists.

"Let's do this," he leaped to his feet and took one step.

"Wait— " Warc attempted to grab him. Too late, the sand gave way.

The whole side of the dune collapsed, taking all of them with it.

Char was rolled along under the sand. He kept his eyes squeezed shut and his mouth tightly closed, but sand got in his nose and ears. His whole body felt as if it were getting rubbed with sandpaper. He wanted to cover his face with his hands, but he flailed helplessly as he rolled. He couldn't tell where his arms were from one moment to the next, but he kept a tight grip on the gun. Something wrapped around his neck and tightened.

Through the muffled rushing sound of the sand, he heard his body thumping with each small impact. He seemed to fall forever before he finally stopped. His arms and legs felt stretched and cocooned in the soft, hot sand. It settled on him, getting heavier and heavier until the weight constricted his lungs.

He tamped down on the growing panic. He knew he needed to dig but didn't know which way was up. He once heard that you should spit if you're buried in an avalanche and see which way it goes. Of course, that usually applied to the snowy avalanches on Earth—and required spit. On Lebrac, after running a race across the desert, his saliva was non-existent. Then there was the total lack of an air pocket in which to spit, had he had the spit to spare. At least snow would stay firm while he dug a space; sand just rushed to fill the hole.

His lungs ached to breathe, but he didn't dare open his mouth. He tried taking shallow breaths through his nose, but even the slightest air movement pulled the fine grains into his nostrils. A few grains found their way deep inside him, and he coughed. The precious air he held inside slipped out with every convulsing shot of air from his lungs. He fought the urge.

He tried to move his arms, but it was worse than being buried in concrete. Not that he had ever been buried in concrete, but if he ever was, he imagined it would be something like this. Although, if he *were* buried in concrete, he wouldn't even try to move because he would know it was futile. Concrete is immobile; solid. Sand, on the other hand, by its very nature, is pliable. His mind demanded the sand to give, yet the reality refused to budge.

The immense weight pressed in all around him. He was alone in his grave. The gentle thump of his heart invaded his silent prison; the beat was steady and slow. It ticked away the last seconds of his life like a cursed Poe story. Thump, thump... Thump, thump... Thump, thump...

Then the awful hot darkness burst with the light of his dying thoughts. He envisioned Earth. He saw his home and his family. His sister was waving at him from the small concrete slab that functioned as their porch. She was young, only ten. He had been only half a person since the day she died. The door behind her opened, out stepped their grandmother.

"Grandma!" Char opened his mouth, and sand filled it. He was acutely aware of each tiny grain as they paraded into his mouth. They mingled with the stray grains he had crunched just before he fell. As the sand closed the gap at the back of his throat, he realized this was it.

He was dizzy; his brain fought against the desire to sleep. Over and over, his mind swooped, then jerked, swooped, then jerked. His heartbeat became fainter. The pauses between each beat grew longer. Each thump, he feared, was the last. He felt separated from his heartbeat, as if it thumped at him from across a chasm, distant and sad.

So, this is how it ends? He thought. *Buried in the sand on a planet where* he *was the alien.*

Something tightened around his arm. It squeezed like a python. A weak jolt of fear whipped through him. Was he now to be eaten by an alien sand snake? It was pulling him! Part of his body stuck fast inside the sand. His middle stretched and ached, feeling as if he would break in two, but his head popped out of the sand like a spring flower fighting through the last winter snow. His cloak was still buried and pulled at his neck. He couldn't move, couldn't breathe. Something metallic flashed in the light, blinding him. A quick tug and the sound of slicing fabric had his neck free from its accidental tourniquet.

From somewhere deep inside, his lungs found a tiny bit of air to force out, pushing all the sand out with it. The sand spilled forth like water from a fountain.

Warc pulled him out the rest of the way. Char rested on his knees as he sucked in a breath of hot air, hacking and coughing up sand. He blew air out his nose in short bursts, trying to clear the grit and attempted to spit, but didn't have enough saliva to do the job.

"Get up," Warc ordered. "They'll be upon us soon."

Warc dragged Char to his feet. Alex stood guard nearby, muscles tense for battle. Char's muscles and lungs ached. He thought of the healer on the ship. It had cradled him when he was wounded before, and how he wished he could go back and have it heal him again.

Warc stepped back, and Char noticed the wicked blades in his hands. "Remember, focus on Kat."

They turned to face the onslaught of guards. Alex leaped into the fray with wild abandon, an expression on his face, Char was sure, never appeared on the faces of an average Droplet. With almost impish glee, he fought two of the guards at once. His movements were lightning fast, the blows hard enough to crack bone. Two more joined the first two, but having four opponents at once didn't seem to faze or slow Alex.

Warc was more sinister in his attack. With razor-sharp blades flashing, he spun like a whirlwind, slashing into his opponents with the efficiency of a lawn mower.

"Char," Warc bellowed as he cut down another guard and squared off with Mrah. Char shook a little and ran for the coffin. He tried to ignore the clash of metal on metal as Mrah attacked Warc. He needed to get to Kat.

He saw where they had abandoned the box and ran for it. It was away from the pyramid, and as he raced for it, he heard Mrah bellow. He didn't dare look back. The sand thinned, and he felt stone beneath it as if there were a buried sidewalk. He heard footsteps behind him, and Warc shouted something, but he couldn't understand what he said.

Was Mrah following him? He would never be able to outrun Mrah, and the box seemed miles away. His lungs strained to pull enough air in to keep him going. His rasping breath came in short bursts; each torturous inhale threatened to shred his lungs. His, now exposed, skin blistered under the hot sun. He wasn't sure exactly when his clothing had become such a tattered mess. He wore what amounted to little more than shorts and a muscle shirt, and neither would pass for more than rags.

The thin layer of sand on the stone polished the soles of his bare feet with each scuffing step and felt the massive blisters forming. Sweat poured down his body, mixing with the sand, making a hot paste that stuck to his skin. He imagined the paste hardening. Caparians from all over the planet would come to see the 'statue' of the human.

The scraping steps came faster. Mrah was shouting something, but Char ignored him. Sensing him closing in, Char pressed harder on his poor feet. Where did his shoes go? Were they buried in the sand with his cooling cloak?

Char got to the box and jerked it along with him. The handle scalded his hand, but by sheer will, he held it. Never slowing, he made a wide circle and headed to the pyramid. Mrah was much closer than he realized. A healthy burst of adrenaline helped him go faster. Warc shouted something as well, but with Char's blood pumping in his ears, all he heard was his labored breathing.

The pyramid was so far away that Char knew, in his heart and soul, he wasn't going to make it. He shoved the box toward the pyramid and spun to face Mrah. Char fired off one shot before Mrah tackled him. He dropped the gun as he landed hard on his back. He couldn't tell if the shot hit Mrah or not. The ground burned even more than before. How could it be getting even hotter?

Mrah growled something in Char's ear, but he didn't understand it again. Was his translator broken? Or were his fear and the chase making it too hard for him to focus?

Char stared into the flaming depths of Mrah's eyes. The hatred still burned within, but Char now noticed a sorrow below the surface. There was a deep well of pain in those glowing red eyes. Char didn't want to empathize with this creature, especially as Mrah wrapped his long, bony fingers around Char's neck.

The dried yellow fingers seared like a branding iron. A scream built inside Char, wanting to burst out of him, but he suppressed it. He set his jaw and stared, unblinking, into Mrah's eyes. If Mrah were going to kill him right here, he would have to look him in the eye when he did it.

Mrah squeezed tighter and tighter. Char's vision began to blur. How much oxygen had his brain been denied in the past few minutes? In the past few days? How much more could his brain go without before damage set in, or had it already? He wrapped a hand around Mrah's wrists, but it was like moving a steel beam.

With his free hand, he searched the surrounding sand for the gun. Tiny dots filled his vision. He wanted to buck and thrash to throw Mrah off, but his weight kept Char wholly pinned. If he could just find the gun—found it! He pulled it up, pressed it into Mrah's flesh, and fired. Mrah roared in Char's face, his grip loosened.

With a grunt, Warc slammed into Mrah, flipping him off Char. The gun slipped from Char's grasp. Mrah's scalding fingers ripped viciously from his neck. He sucked in a lungful of the scorching air and ran his fingers over his neck, feeling the torn tissue. Strangely, he felt no pain. He pulled his hand back and watched his blood slide down his fingers and over his palm. There was a lot of blood, thick as honey and just as sticky. It dripped on the ground and sizzled.

"Go!" Warc growled. Char felt as if he were looking at Warc from across a dreamscape. That simple command held no meaning. Go? What was go? Go where?

Mrah shoved Warc off and scrambled to his knees, but before he got his footing, Warc was on him again. The blades flashed emerald now as they came down in a deadly arc toward Mrah. Mrah blocked it and sent a slice of his own at Warc. Metal screeched, and sparks flew.

Dazed, Char shook his head, trying to clear his mind. He needed to move. He felt blood pool at the hollow of his throat, overflow, and soak his shirt. Waves of heat lifted from the ground, distorting the world in a shimmering haze.

The battle raged around him, but he was only distantly aware of it. Somewhere off to the side was a blue streak battling an impossible number of yellow things, and two more yellows decided they didn't like each other and clashed repeatedly. The building... what was it called?

He couldn't remember. Mythological dog-headed gods filled his mind, but not the name of the building that rippled in the heat.

Char rubbed his eyes, smearing blood across his face, and climbed to his feet. He staggered a step and looked at his fingers. They looked strange, alien to his body, and they were cold. Why were they cold? He flexed them, admiring how much longer and more slender they appeared while cloaked in the crimson sheen.

He blinked and shook his head. He had to focus! He scanned the area for the precious black box that contained his sleeping beauty. He let out a hoarse giggle at the wild notion that *he* could be *her* prince! All their hopes rested on her pale shoulders while he failed time and again at his one duty. He clenched his fist and felt the blood squish between his fingers. He would *not* let her down! With renewed determination, he staggered toward the box.

The farther he walked, the more distant the box seemed to get. Kat was teasing him. She danced on the horizon, always out of reach, always beckoning.

"Kat," he mumbled. His feet had gone cold as well. Was the Temprafreeze working again? He reached for the box. Just as his hand wrapped around the handle, it vanished only to reappear a little further ahead. He pressed his other hand to his wound, with each beat of his heart, another spurt of blood pushed back. The blood was warm on cold fingers. Blood doesn't warm a body as well from the outside as it does from beneath the flesh. He literally felt his life slipping away. From somewhere in the back of his addled mind, he heard his sister's voice teasing him about how fast he bleeds. That day they agreed to donate blood seemed a lifetime ago.

"Char!" The name sounded familiar to Char, but he couldn't quite put his finger on why; familiar yet wrong. He wasn't Char—he was someone else. No, that someone else was dead. He died with *her*. The name repeated, drifted across the empty ravine of his scorched mind. He tilted his head to hear better but kept his eyes on the teasing box that was just about within his reach.

"*Char!*" This time the voice was loud in his ear. It snapped him out of his daze; he realized he had climbed halfway up a dune, chasing *a mirage!* He looked back down the hill and spotted the box hovering by the pyramid's door.

Mrah lay motionless on the ground. He looked more like a pile of tattered rags than a body from this distance.

"Look at me!" Warc demanded. He forced Char to look him in the eye. Warc studied Char's face for a moment before nodding. "That's what I thought; the Temprafreeze has near worn off completely." He shook Char a little. "Listen to me! You have to fight the heat!"

Char stared at Warc. He raised his fingers and touched Warc's mouth. He knew what Warc was saying, but he couldn't seem to get his head to acknowledge the statement. Warc shook him again. Char's teeth chattered. Fight the heat? He didn't feel hot. He felt cold.

"Cold," Char mumbled.

Warc's eyes narrowed. "You're losing too much blood." He guided Char back down the dune.

"Is he..." Char tried to ask, but his voice cut out on him. Not so much from emotion as from lack of water and intense heat. He couldn't seem to keep his thoughts in check.

"No, he's just unconscious. I'm trying to avoid killing him." Warc explained. They had reached the door of the pyramid. Char leaned on a wall. His energy was quickly being sapped by loss of blood and scorching sun.

Warc opened the door, a burst of cool air rushed over Char. It should have felt better, but it merely chilled the last vestiges of body heat. He felt light-headed, and the tickle in his chest imitated a chest cold. He resisted the urge to cough. He and Warc pushed the box inside the sanctuary.

"Where is Alex," the words nearly lost in the chattering of Char's teeth.

"Here," Alex replied as he put his shoulder into shutting the door. Stone scraped on stone as the last bit of burning light was snuffed. The deep thud resonated inside the pyramid.

KAT

Kat stood in the water, wishing she could feel its strength pressing against her legs. How many would play the game? How many would the challenge save? Would it even be enough to save those she held most dear?

She watched as Katie knelt by the stream and held her hand in the water. Kat remembered how cold it had felt that day, so many years ago. She remembered how her bones had ached. Now she was just a spirit watching her own death; memories of the pain, but suffering no actual discomfort.

Katie pulled her hand from the water and wiped it on her jeans. A breeze brushed her hair from her shoulders. Kat closed her eyes and remembered the feel of that breeze. A cold ache shot through her ankle and raced up her leg. She gasped and leaped out of the water. Back on the grass, she stared at the ripples. Had she truly felt that?

Katie had already run to the grassy spot by the blanket their mother had laid out for the picnic.

Kat walked over to her father, sprawled under the old oak. Kat put a hand on the trunk, the bark was coarse, and her fingers felt the grooves and imperfections. She looked down at her father. He opened his eyes and stared up into the branches. He seemed to be looking right into her eyes.

"I'm sorry, Daddy," Kat whispered. A lump filled her throat. "I failed."

Kat felt a burning sensation at the corners of her eyes, but no tears came. This was nuts! She can't feel! She's a ghost! A spirit! An echo from the past! A gasp from the future! Insubstantial, incapable of feeling, yet—she felt. It could be phantom pain, memories of past hurt. Still, this bark was real, and her fingers *felt* the texture.

"I don't understand." She looked at her fingertips as if they held the answer but refused to tell her.

Mary weaved in and out of the trees, giggling madly, darting toward their mother only to turn just before getting caught. The lump in Kat's throat swelled till it threatened to burst through her neck.

She looked back at Katie. Katie stared at the road, waiting for Boon.

"Where's Boon?" Kat asked as she stepped up beside the younger version of herself. "He should have been here by now." Katie, of course, didn't answer. She let out a small sigh and walked toward the road.

Kat followed her gaze. Boon had finally arrived.

"Hey," Katie's voice was even. Her red eyes were the only sign she had been crying.

"Hey," Boon replied, his voice just as even.

"Look, I'm sorry I reacted as I did about that guy," Boon said. But before Katie could reply, the world was thrust into darkness, so black it felt thick, then the sickly green light.

"They're here." Kat's spirit sparked and crackled. Under it all, she thought she felt her muscles tense, which was still crazy since she had left her muscles back on Zortentearth five years in the future. No time to worry about improbable ghostly feelings now; she had to warn them.

"Run!" Kat cried desperately. "Everyone run!"

Katie looked at her hands, then at Mary and Boon. She touched Boon's cheek.

"You're glowing," she whispered.

"Yes, everyone is," Kat said. "Now run!"

"So are you," Boon replied.

Their parents walked over.

"Mom? Dad?" Katie asked. She held up her hands as if they couldn't see the green. Something slowly started to dawn on Katie's face.

"What's going on?" Mary asked. Katie took her sister's hand.

"I told you about this!" Kat cried. She looked at Katie. *"Remember."*

It was an order, not a question. "I *showed* you this!"

"This is weird," Boon said. "Look!"

He pointed to a fat squirrel that had just fallen out of the old oak. Katie stared at the squirrel, a growing look of horror on her face.

Kat turned her eyes away from the squirrel and focused on Katie. She could feel her own heartbeat. Kat put a hand on her chest, amazed at how much it hurt. She shook her head and leaned in to talk to Katie.

"Yes," Kat hissed as she studied the shocked expression on Katie's face. "You remember, don't you?"

The squirrel erupted with the horrible moaning screech that had pierced Kat's ears so many years ago. Katie slapped her hands over her ears; her eyes grew larger, her jaw went slack.

"What's wrong with it?" their mother cried.

"I don't know," their father shouted. He had his face inches from hers when he answered. The squirrel gave one final shriek, then a soft popping sound, and the squirrel was no more. There seemed to be a fine powder in the air for a split second, then nothing.

Kat stood with her mouth inches from Katie's ear and shrieked with all the pent-up fear and rage inside her, *"Run!"*

Katie jerked and leaped away. She stared at Kat, stuck her arm out, swinging it back and forth. Her arm swished through Kat's middle.

"What are you doing?" Boon asked.

"The aliens," Katie mumbled. She looked from one face to the other. "Run!"

Katie picked up Mary and started running for the shelter. Kat let out a whoop and leaped for joy. Maybe it wasn't too late to save them! The old oak groaned and burst just like the squirrel.

"Katie, wait," Boon cried. He caught her by the arm. "I admit this is weird, but it isn't aliens!"

Katie jerked free. "This is exactly what I've been dreaming!" she screamed.

Mary whimpered and buried her face in Katie's shoulder. The individual blades of grass began popping. The birds shrieked and fell from the sky but never hit the ground.

They had to shout over the deafening wailing.

"I think she's right," her father shouted. "We need to get to the shelter."

Their mother pressed her hands to her head.

"Mom!" Kat cried. She put her hands on either side of her mother's face. Her spirit sparked again. She breathed hard, remembering the fear and panic from the first time she lived this nightmare.

"The pressure..." she gasped.

"I know, Momma," Kat whimpered. She wanted so much to take the pain away, to save her mother. She squeezed her eyes shut, swallowed the lump. Still, her voice came out breathy when she looked back into her mother's tortured eyes. "I'm sorry, Momma. I'm so sorry."

Her father took her mother's arm. Kat broke away.

"You have to get up; you have to try," he pleaded. She shook her head, dropped to her knees, and howled. She curled into a ball and screamed into her knees. Then she lifted her head and looked at Katie.

"Baby—," she popped, just like the tree. Like the squirrel, a hint of dust, like blowing off an old book, then nothing.

"Mom," Katie and Kat screamed in unison. With Mary still in her arms, Katie stood staring at the spot their mother used to be. She shook her head, slowly, from side to side. Tears streamed down her face.

Kat stared at Katie, watched her dark eyes get wider and wider. Her head shook faster, her mouth opened wider, and she started screaming. Mary, startled by the sudden outburst, started wailing.

"Do something," Kat demanded. "I don't want to watch them die *again!*"

It was so unfair! She had to live through this twice! First her mother and then...

"Daddy," Kat wailed. Her father was holding his head now.

He threw his head back and howled. Then he was gone too. All the pain from the past flooded her soul. She no longer cared if it was phantom pain or real; it filled her like hot air into a balloon. She felt stretched and swollen with the pain. Then anger. Rage. Fury. She had warned Katie! She balled her hands into fists, felt nails digging into her palms. She spun on her heel and stormed over to where Katie stood, stunned.

"I told you!" Kat growled. She pulled her hand back and swung hard.

"Now run!" The flat of her hand made contact with the side of Katie's face. Katie's head swung hard to the side. She whipped back around, a lock of hair plastered across her face, staring at the nothing before her. She spun and ran for the shelter; Mary bounced on her hip. Boon followed on her heels. Boon!

"Wait," Kat cried. She had forgotten to warn Katie about the keypad!

She raced with them. Boon got to the door first and jerked it open. He pushed Katie and Mary toward the black hole.

"Don't want to go down there," Mary whined. "I want Momma!"

"So do I," Katie sniffed hard. She dragged her sleeve across her nose.

"Move," Boon bellowed as he pushed his way in behind her.

Kat stood on the outside, watching from a distance; her spirit sounded like a roaring campfire.

"I'm sorry, Boon, I'm so sorry," Kat murmured. He pulled the door closed. Kat waited, knowing he was trying the keypad. He'd curse under his breath. Katie would ask what was wrong. He would try to tell her the keypad won't work, but he wouldn't be able to finish his sentence.

Won't what? Kat mouthed the words she had said to him. He wouldn't tell her; he would just kiss her and dive through the door before she could react.

The door burst open; Boon leaped out and slammed it shut. He punched the code into the keypad. The door locked. She was safe, and he would die. He leaned his head against the door. Kat wandered up beside him.

"Now, *I'm* the hero," he whispered.

"What?" Kat asked. "Did you just say now you're the *hero?*"

He grunted, grabbed his head, and dropped to his knees. Boon, Kat mouthed the word. Whatever his reasons, he still sacrificed himself to save her. She knelt by him, putting her arms around him. She knew he couldn't feel it, but she could feel him. The scent of his cologne invaded her nostrils. He whimpered and cried.

"I don't want to die," he sobbed. He dragged himself closer to the door, slipping right through her spirit.

"Let me in." He tried to pound on the door, but his strike was too weak. He curled into a ball and stretched one weak arm toward the door; his nails scraped across the surface. "Please... don't... let me die..."

"Boon..." Pain stretched and thinned her words till they were barely audible. She wrapped him in her arms again. He squirmed and cried for a long time before finally succumbing to the pressure and vaporizing in her arms with one last heartbreaking whimper.

She curled around the empty air he left behind, head between her knees. Hot boiling anger, the like of which she'd never felt, shot through her. Her spirit exploded in a fiery blaze. White-hot flames covered every inch of her. Blue sparks shot past the flames like sparklers.

Her climb to her feet was slow and deliberate; her feet spread, her arms out at her sides. She tipped her head back and stared unblinking into the green sky.

She drew every ounce of power she had from across the years; sucked the energy out of the very air around her, letting it pool deep inside her like a well. Her eyes felt cold and dark. When she spoke, her voice resonated with time and doom. Her words echoed across the distance, and she was sure she would hit her mark.

"*Mrahhhhhhhh!*"

CHAR

"Quickly," Warc urged. They pushed the box across the room. The ceiling was high; images of the crucifixion adorned the walls.

"Where are we?" Char asked. He fought against the tremors the cool air was invoking; clenched his teeth against the chattering, and squeezed the box handles to stop his hands shaking. He turned at the sound of ripping fabric.

Alex was folding the piece of cloth he had just torn from what remained of his clothing. He offered it to Char. Char pressed the soft cloth to the wound on his neck and wondered if the bandage on Alex's head had fallen off in battle.

"Mrah and I built this church. It was just another way of honoring your planet," Warc said.

"Too bad he doesn't honor it anymore." Char didn't attempt to hide the bitterness in his voice. The room was as ornate as a Catholic Church. It was strange to know this room was in a pyramid. A pyramid should have mummies and hieroglyphs, not crosses and holy water.

"We can claim sanctuary," Warc continued, ignoring Char's comment. His voice dipped deeper, "But not for long."

"Why?" Alex asked. "On Earth, sanctuary lasted as long as the person needed it."

"She is running out of time," Warc said. "Besides, I said we built this to *honor* Earth; it isn't a church. It just looks like one. Sanctuary will last until Mrah gets inside and finds us."

"I'm pretty sure it won't take long to find us since we're standing in the middle of an open room." Char spread his arms wide, winced, and pressed the bandage back to his wound.

Warc crossed to the closest wall and pressed the base of one of the Crucifixes. A trap door slid open in the center of the room.

"Come," Warc ordered. Char and Alex guided the box down the narrow flight of stone steps. The deeper they went, the colder it got, and Char could no longer stop his teeth chattering; his vision bounced. His fingers were numb, he could no longer feel his toes, and all the blisters on his feet had broken open. He glanced back at the bloody footprints he was leaving. *Oh, yeah, Mrah would* never *find them now!*

At the bottom of the steps, Warc pressed something on the wall, and the trap door slammed shut overhead. The sudden darkness had Char widening his eyes until it felt as if the corners would tear.

Warc lit a lamp. The friendly blue light blinded Char. He blinked several times before his eyes adjusted. The lamp turned out to be a floating, glowing orb. It drifted down the corridor like a ghostly companion.

Char didn't know how long they walked, but he was running low on his energy reserves. He couldn't remember the last time he had eaten or had something to drink. His tongue felt too big for his mouth. He couldn't swallow, not that there was anything to swallow. He pushed the box by rote.

Alex didn't look a whole lot better. Green and white blood stained his tattered clothing. He didn't appear to be as cold as Char, but he hadn't lost as much blood either. Char was sure most of the blood that covered Alex belonged to a particular group of yellow bodies lying out in the desert sun.

"Here we are," Warc opened another door.

"Does Mrah know where we are?" Char asked.

"Indubitably."

"Great," Char mumbled.

"We have to hurry, or there won't be a Kat for Mrah to kill." Warc ushered them into the room. Char's heart picked up the pace at Warc's tone.

"What do you mean?" Char asked.

"She's dying," Warc helped them lift the lid. Char gasped and leaped back. Alex stood stoic.

Kat's body twitched and convulsed. Her eyes burst open then rolled back into her head; just the whites, rimmed in long black lashes, showed. Her mouth opened in a silent, choked scream. Her face contorted until she didn't even look human. Her back arched, her fingers clenched, half bent.

Warc whisked the box out from under her. She hovered, her body jerking with each spasm. The blood vessels in her eyes darkened until the whites looked more red than white.

"What's wrong with her?" Char cried. He raced forward to embrace her.

"Don't touch her," Warc ordered. Char halted mid-step.

"Why?"

"You could kill her." Warc slid a stone table beneath her. She still floated ten inches off the table. The sand-like substance slid off her like a gritty waterfall, each crystal ticking away another second of her life, her own personal countdown to death.

Sweat glistened on her exposed skin; her hair damp at the roots. She began to make choking noises, sucking in a shot of air then pushing it back out as if it were poison. Yet, she did not wake up.

"She's pulling too much power! She'll kill herself early!" Warc cried.

"Do something!" Char yelled. He grabbed Warc by the tattered remnants of his collar. He wanted to yank Warc down to his level, but he didn't have enough strength even to budge the much taller being. He ended up feebly tugging on the fabric.

"I can't. The only one who can bring her out of this trance is a Zortentearthian."

"What?" Char cried. Fury fueled him to pull harder, and he did manage to pull Warc's face to within inches of his own. Nose to nose, Char growled, "Then why *the hell* did you take us off that planet?"

Char swung his fist at the ugly yellow face of his supposed friend, but Warc caught his fist easily and held it. Each word was slow and measured.

"I bought you time."

KAT

When Kat opened her eyes, she was standing on the bridge of the Caparian warship. There he sat, at the controls of his death laser, the particle separator. Oblivious of her arrival, his boney fingers danced across the control panel. None of his crew seemed aware she stood amongst them, just like her family.

"Mrahhhh," the exhale of her breath like a cold hollow wind. A burst of hot energy shot out of her core. Control panels and monitors nearest her exploded, spraying the officers running the controls with white-hot sparks.

Mrah spun in his chair, burning red eyes wide. He stared unflinchingly but surprised into her eyes. *He could see her!*

He spoke; his hideous voice scraped her nerves like a cheese grater. She didn't understand his words, but the few crewmen still on deck left. A nearby officer seemed to argue with him, but he barked a command. The officer, cowed, left with the others. Mrah turned his attention back to her. Again he spoke.

"Die," she said, took two swift steps forward, and leaped. She soared through the air like a blazing phoenix. He put his hands up in defense, which of course, was useless. She was insubstantial. She was breath and fire. She was wind and sea. She was revenge and punishment.

She dove inside his body as if it were a swimming pool. She shoved his spirit aside like a meddlesome curtain. Inside his body, was hotter than the surface of the sun. His scorching blood fueled the fire in her soul. She sapped his body of its heat and energy.

She whipped open a dreamscape. It was different this time. This time she possessed a conscious mind. Though the dreamscape lay before her, bleak and sad, she could still see the outside world through Mrah's eyes.

The dreamscape was not what she had expected. The dry black ground was interrupted by wilted grey spider plants and low ferns for miles. A webbing of fissures broke up the ground, leaving jagged shapes in the hard shell. Every step felt unstable, the ground hollow as if it might crumble from beneath her.

Black and gray mottled clouds filled the sky and hung low and angry, full of rain that would not fall. A flicker of lightning and a peal of thunder in the distance made the whole effect more oppressive.

A gust of wind hit her in the face. It brought a voice like Mrah's, but twisted, deeper, darker, "I told you she would come. I told you she wouldn't lie."

She understood him! How? Because she was in his mind? Her spirit must have tapped into his speech banks to communicate, like a computer.

From another direction came a response; the voice was less sinister, more clinical, and—younger, "She did lie. I already told you she lied."

Kat noticed a shape huddled in the ferns. For a moment, curiosity replaced her anger. She approached slowly, not sure what to make of it, a yellow skeleton in ragged clothes, its head twitching as if shaking away dark thoughts.

"Stand and face me, Mrah," Kat commanded. She allowed her words to fill with the limitlessness of space. They rumbled through the sky like thunder. The twitching head stilled, paused, then the lean body of her enemy unfolded. He rose before her like the 'ghost of Christmas yet to come.' He turned his burning red eyes on her. They glowed from the depths of his hood. Like nothing she had ever heard, his voice issued forth and sent chills down her spine. It was deep and dark, yet child-like with glee.

"Kitty," He cooed. "Kitty has come to play."

His hood blew back from his head. He glared with hatred that belied his gleeful tone. His head twitched again as if he had been on antipsychotics for too long. His grin peeled back like the thin membrane of an onion.

"Hello, Kat," he took a step toward her. "I've missed you."

His head twitched, his smile dissolved, he knitted his brows in concentration. "No, I don't miss you. *I don't miss* ***you.***"

Kat pulled her shoulders back, tipped her head down, and looked up at him through her lashes. She glowered; refused to be intimidated by his strange behavior. "Playing crazy will not earn you sympathy from me. You killed my family!"

"You killed my family!" Once again, his childish voice took over; his face softened briefly before taking on a superior look. The phrase was mocking, "You killed my family!" He danced away, laughing. He swung his arms out and shouted at the sky, "You killed my family!"

Then his mood took a darker turn. He faced her, locked eyes with her, mocking turned to accusing, "You killed my family! ***You*** *killed my* ***family!!***"

He shoved her. She staggered back a few steps. She whipped her hand around before he could strike again, and he flew backward. He hit the ground hard and skidded to a stop by a tall blackened tree, a survivor of a forest fire?

"It had to be done," Mrah said as he rolled onto his knobby knees. He sounded more like himself than he had the entire conversation.

"Why?" Kat asked. Her tone was deadly calm.

"To stop the deaths..." he kept whispering, "So many deaths... So many deaths... So many deaths..."

"You wanted to stop death," Kat spread her arms wide, daring him to attack, "By *murdering innocents?*"

He didn't know the dream realm as well as she. She was confident she could take him. He cocked his head and grinned.

"They weren't innocents," his tone was playful. He could have added the word 'silly' to the end of the sentence. His head twitched. His attitude went dark.

"Germ warfare," he growled. "Fight back; must fight back."

Another twitch and the young clinical voice took over, "No, they didn't know we were there. They couldn't know we were there. How could they? How could they?"

"Who didn't know you were there?" Kat asked. "What are you talking about?"

Mrah didn't seem to hear her. His voice went high, much too high for his species. Was he imitating someone? "Of course, they knew you were there! Humans are devious. They fight with germ warfare. It's all through their history."

He began pacing and chanting, "Germ warfare! Germ warfare! Germ warfare!"

He stopped and turned—another grin spread across his hollowed face. The smile, though not as maniacal as before, was still revolting.

"You look nothing like yourself," he whispered. Then, in a single blink, she saw herself through his eyes. It lasted only a second, but it was enough to send a chill through her soul.

She appeared as a sexless body, covered in white-hot flames, rimmed in neon blue sparks. She was a sparkler out of control. Her eyes were huge and completely black. Then she was gone, and he remained.

"Are you trying to blame us?" she ignored his comment.

"What?" he asked.

"Why did you obliterate my planet?" she shrieked.

"I didn't obliterate it. I merely killed a few people." He waved his hand as if this were nothing worth noting.

"Don't lie!" She swung her arm again. He slammed into the same charred tree. The tree gave a loud crack before splitting in the center and toppling on him. He lay there for a few moments before stirring.

She realized he wasn't lying because he hadn't yet returned to finish off the planet. He was still working on his first attack. Well, she would just have to remedy that. While he was trying to free himself from the tree, she focused on looking outside his body.

She felt big and bulky as if she were wearing five thick wool sweaters. She examined the hands now extended before her, his hands with long fingers with fat arthritic knuckles and talon-like nails. The hands moved across a smooth metal plate. There were no buttons, levers, or anything that would suggest a control panel, yet the ship reacted to the areas his hands passed over. Too late, she realized he was still controlling the particle separator.

"No!" Kat cried. The ship rocked as it let loose the evil green light that evaporates people without prejudice.

"I have to," Mrah was by her ear, whispering, his breath stunk like moldy food too long in the refrigerator. Though his voice still sounded like a smoker with a trach tube, his tone had a touch of despair. She shook her head.

"I won't let you," she concentrated and lifted one of those claws. She turned it, palm up, staring at the surprisingly smooth palm. No lines or creases as her human hands had had.

"Well, look at that," Kat breathed.

"What are you doing?" Mrah asked. There was a struggle as Mrah tried to lower the hand. Kat fought to keep it aloft. His body jerked and swung violently, first one way, then the other.

"Stop," he grunted.

"No!" The body tipped over and fell to the floor. It was a bizarre weightless feeling for a moment as the physical body fell; the two souls inside seemed to hover in the center before landing. The dreamscape shuddered like an earthquake, and they both fell. Kat scrambled back to her feet first and manipulated the body to climb to its feet.

"So, I can control you," her giggle was dark and evil. "Let's go for a ride."

"You don't know how to fly this ship," Mrah replied as he staggered back to his feet.

"No, but you do," Kat said. Suddenly the smooth top control panel looked like an old friend. She knew precisely how to manipulate it.

"Now, where is your home planet?" She paused; the answer seemed to just float into her mind. "Lebrac, is it?"

"No!" Mrah cried. His head twitched again. He fought for control of his body, but her anger lent her strength. Inside the dreamscape, she gripped his shoulder, squeezing with all her strength; he didn't grimace. She looked him dead in the eye.

"Ah," she cooed. "There it is."

Still holding his shoulder, she turned her attention back to the outside world. She manipulated the controls, and the ship pulled away from Earth. Mrah jerked himself backward, his shoulder ripped from her hand. Her nails left green gashes in his yellow flesh. The poison green blood sizzled on her blue and white flames.

The dreamscape pulsed, colors rippled across the sky, keeping time with the beat. Kat looked up. The pulse was familiar and strong.

"Is that—your heartbeat?" Kat asked. "Interesting, you have a heart."

Mrah pressed one clawed hand to his open wound and glared at her. His head twitched again. Another quick shake, as if annoyed by a troublesome fly. He cocked his head as if listening. His eyes rolled skyward but then down to stare at her. He tipped his head down then looked up at her with his eyes.

"Sssseeeeee," he hissed. She could imagine a forked tongue flicking at her from between his teeth. "I told you she would do thisssss. She didn't lie. She can't lie."

His head twitched again, his glare melted, replaced by profound sorrow. "I don't want to..."

Another twitch and the sorrow crushed under the hatred, "*Now!*"

Before she could respond, he leaped at her. They hit the ground hard. He rolled on top of her, his hands around her neck. He squeezed.

She gasped and choked. His eyes widened, his breath came in short gasps as well.

She drew power from deep inside her and shoved him off. He rolled across the ground. In a flash, she was on her knees, raised both hands, felt her stomach muscles stretch, made one big fist, and slammed it into the ground. Mrah, climbing to his feet, lost his balance when the shock wave ripped through.

The widest fissure grew. He was on one side of the gap, she on the other. She didn't dare take her eyes off him to see what was at the bottom of the ravine. He wiped his mouth with the back of his hand. A long glistening string of saliva stretched between his hand and the corner of his mouth.

"Why," Kat demanded. "Why kill innocent people just to get to me?"

"I didn't know it was you!" He spit on the ground. "Why did you kill my family?"

"I didn't kill your family!" Kat growled. "You killed mine!"

She pulled more energy out of the air. It was so much easier inside this body with the tremendous heat that fueled her, feeding her growing desire to kill.

She spread her arms, looked up, and levitated, shooting at least ten feet straight up. She looked back down at him. The dark clouds gathered over her head; thunder rumbled in the distance. The ominous sound reverberated throughout the dreamscape.

She called the wind and rain to do her bidding, and they did. The wind scoured the land like a hurricane as rain pummeled the few withered gray plants into oblivion.

Mrah stood steadfast through it all. He appeared even more emaciated with his wet ratty clothing clinging to his body. His head twitched.

"I know something you don't know." He sang like a child. He grinned; water dripped off his pointed teeth.

Kat ignored him. She clapped her hands together, leaving them in prayer. A bolt of lightning shot out of the darkest of the clouds and hit

Mrah square in the chest. He flew backward twenty feet, sliding through the mud on his back.

Kat felt a massive blow to her chest and flew out of the sky at the exact moment Mrah was hit. She hit the ground hard, skidded to a halt by another charred tree, and lay in the mud with the rain pounding on her face gasping for breath. What happened? She curled into a ball. Was this what it felt like to die?

The black ground felt more like a sponge than solid ground. The rain battered her mercilessly. The irony was she had sent the rain to torment Mrah, and she was the one afflicted.

She squeezed her eyes shut, trying to concentrate on drawing in all the power she could, but the lightning bolt that hit Mrah had also left her weak. Why had she felt it? She dug her fingers into the soft black mud. Her skin was a shocking white in contrast.

The heartbeat that shook this dreamscape became erratic. Was Mrah dying, or was she? More power; she needed more power.

"You realize you won't make it, don't you? You'll be long dead before you ever see my planet," Mrah whispered. His voice had softened; the edge was gone. He sounded almost human.

Kat jerked her head up to glare at Mrah. He sat cross-legged on the soggy ground, a puddle formed around his hips. He dipped his fingers in the water and swirled it.

"Watch me," she dared. New energy surged through her spirit, though not as strong as the first. She pulled herself to a sitting position and stood, tried to appear strong, and focused her attention on the outside world.

"Let me see your planet," she whispered. Then, there it was. She could picture its surface, the red ground, and the glaring red sun. She closed her eyes and focused all her energy on getting to that spot. The problem was, she had never tried to take anything with her when she teleported somewhere. She didn't even fully understand how she teleported anywhere.

She tried to imagine the ship as an extension of herself. She willed it to come with her. Whether it was her own power or the extra heat from this physical body that gave her the strength, she never knew, but when she opened her eyes, the planet Lebrac loomed before her, and the ship was with her!

She wavered. Her hands flickered. She felt distant, detached. *No! I can't die now!* She stumbled toward Mrah, her energy seeping out like air through a crack.

"Not before I finish you..." she said. Her voice had an odd tone, unlike anything she had ever heard before. She reached for the sky to pull another bolt down to pierce his heart.

"If you do that, you'll die too," Mrah said. His voice still had a soft tone, entirely unlike his original voice.

"I'm dead anyway." She lifted an arm to gather the clouds to strike, but a sharp pain shot through her. She clenched all over, dropped to the ground, choked, and gasped but couldn't breathe.

She watched her hand fade before her eyes. Her last thoughts were of her failed mission.

CHAR

Kat's body shook harder, twisted further than a human body should. It was a scene straight out of a possession film. Char couldn't stand to look at her in such agony. His only hope was she couldn't feel it since her spirit was in the past. He wanted so much to touch her, to ease her pain. But the slightest wrong move could end her life prematurely.

Alex stood on the other side of the table, looking upon Kat with a tenderness that twisted in Char's stomach, turning it sour. He clenched his fists. This was not the time nor the place for jealousy. Besides, how many times had Alex helped them? How many times had he saved them?

"Well," Char's tone came out sharper than intended. He forced his fists to relax. "Are you going to do it?"

Alex's eyes widened, his mouth opened and closed. He blinked, shook his head, and continued, "What am I supposed to do?"

"You're a Droplet, aren't you?" Char asked. "Bring her out of it!"

"It isn't that simple," Alex replied. "I'm only half Droplet."

"So," Char said. "Use that half."

"It isn't as if I can turn one half on and the other half off," Alex cried. "That isn't how it works."

"You don't have to 'turn off' any half; just do whatever it is Droplets do to get her out of this mess!" Char snapped.

Alex went rigid; his jaw muscles pumped as he fought to maintain his composure, the legendary Droplet composure which had them lining up for slaughter without a fight.

"Even if I had the equipment," Alex growled through gritted teeth, "which I don't, a mere half-blood like me wasn't taught the ritual. I am forbidden certain things because my blood isn't pure."

"That's a stupid law! Why can't you learn like everyone else?" Char cried. He realized he was gripping the edge of the table. His knuckles were white.

"It isn't just a law," Alex replied. His fury seemed to drain away as quickly as it had come. "You need a direct line of communication to God for it to work. He has to give His blessing. My human blood prevents that direct line to my God. It blinds me to His will."

The fury seeped out of Char as well. "Then there is nothing we can do."

He let go of the table; his fingers ached and didn't want to bend right away. More sand slipped from Kat's body to pile on the table below. Char tried to catch them all and put them back on top as if that would help anything. He wanted to brush her hair back from her face but dared not touch one strand.

"Hurry, Kat," Char urged, close to her ear. "There is no time."

"Buy her time," Warc said. He stood close to the door, waiting for Mrah. There would be nowhere to run if he found them. Of course, he would find them. Only an idiot would lose a trail of bloody footprints in a narrow hall. They were trapped.

"How can we do that?" Char asked. He was feeling weaker by the second. He felt his own life slipping away with each grain of sand that shortened Kat's life. Perhaps they would die together in this hole in the ground, this secret cellar beneath a fake church on an alien planet. When it came time for the last grain to fall, he would gather her in his arms so she wouldn't be alone in death. He would close his eyes and die with her, a twisted Romeo and Juliet; the last two humans, the end of a species.

"Pray," Warc didn't turn to look at them.

"What?" Char stepped back from Kat's body. His heart fluttered at the idea, praying, after all this time... would God even listen?

"Pray," Warc repeated, "to God."

"I don't pray anymore," Char whispered, his fingers already searching for the absentee cross that had hung from his neck. He stared at the wall, but he didn't see the wall; he saw his sister. He felt the tug of the chain, the pressure on his neck, then the release as it snapped. He never saw the cross again, nor his sister. He had prayed for days. Days turned into weeks, which turned into months—praying in the dark, begging and pleading that somehow, someway, she had survived. Still, when those doors had finally opened, letting in the scorching sunlight, his sister was not waiting for him on the other side. She wasn't hidden away safe in some other shelter. She wasn't anywhere. She was dead; he was alive. That was the day he had stopped praying.

"You reach for a cross that no longer hangs from your neck. You say you do not pray, but your instinct to reach for God is still strong within you," Warc said. He kept his eyes on the door, but his words were directed at Char.

"God will hear you," Alex looked Char in the eye.

"Pray!" Warc bellowed.

Char flinched. He looked at Kat. How? What could he possibly say to solve this situation? Kat's body had lowered. She was only an inch or two above the table now. Another sign that time was running out. Alex stretched his hands over Kat, palms up. He nodded at Char.

"I will pray with you," Alex said. "Perhaps my half Droplet side will help us make a better connection."

Somehow, Char knew that wasn't needed. Alex was trying to make him feel better. He stretched out his hands and took Alex's. *For where two or three gather in my name, there am I with them.* The voice echoed inside his mind. A shiver raced down his back, causing him to convulse visibly, his palms damp with sweat. He had heard that voice before in Coral City and the cave coming from Alex. Was this the voice of God?

He broke his hold on one of Alex's hands, and against Warc's warning, he took one of Kat's hands. Her ivory skin almost glowed against his. Her hand was moist with sweat, the muscles were all tense under her skin, but her skin was still smooth as silk. Alex followed his lead and took Kat's other hand.

Char bowed his head, wanting to kneel, but her body floated too high. His mind went blank; he was acutely aware of Warc's eyes on him and the two hands he held. What should he pray? Start with something simple. He took a breath, the inside walls of his throat stuck together. He cleared his throat. He used to do this all the time! Why was he so nervous now? *Concentrate!*

"Our Father, which art in heaven, hallowed be thy name, thy kingdom come, thy will be done, in Earth..." No, we're not on Earth, Char thought; I'll have to adjust.

"Thy will be done, in the *universe,* as *it is* in heaven. Give us this day, our daily bread, and forgive us our trespasses, as we have forgiven our..." but we haven't forgiven those who have trespassed against us.

He paused for a long time. He thought of home and family and love. He thought of the teachings of Jesus, teachings he hadn't thought about in a long, long time. Jesus was persecuted, tortured, and killed to save us. Yet, He still forgives us our sins.

We mock Him, turn our backs on Him, and analyze every word for hidden meanings; secret agendas, and yet He still forgives us. Thousands of years of sin; all the sin ever committed, all the sin that will *ever* be committed was slashed into His flesh to save us, all He asked in return was our faith and love.

A flash of cold heat shot through him as he realized what he should have been doing the entire time. Once again, he proved to be a poor shepherd. He let his sheep drift away. God took away the *entire planet,* gave him only one sheep to guide, and he couldn't even handle that!

He squeezed the hands he held.

"Father," he cried in earnest. "I need you! We need you! I am a poor shepherd. I can't fix this myself."

Tears stung the corners of his eyes.

"You are the only one who can touch both sides of time. Please give Kat the strength she needs to accomplish her mission! Open her eyes to the truth. Help her see what I've only just now grasped. Please, Father! We can't do this alone!"

Char sank to his knees; his hands slipped free, landing uselessly in his lap. Tears slid down his cheeks. His strength slipped away with each new tear that fell. He had nothing left to give. He was wrung out, used up. He was an empty water flask, a threadbare old blanket with no warmth. Warc shook Char's shoulder.

"Get up," Warc demanded. "Get up and see what God has done."

Warc dragged Char to his feet; he gasped. Kat's body was calm, her face relaxed with a serene smile. He checked for a pulse; her heart still beat!

"She's out of danger, for now," Alex said.

KAT

Kat's spirit re-ignited in a single brilliant burst. She sat up and looked around. Mrah had crossed the ravine and was sitting next to her, watching and waiting. He still looked a little weak from the lightning strike. She climbed to her feet and found she could do so easily.

"Thank you, God," she whispered. Would she be able to manipulate anything, though? She tried something simple, waved her hand, a willow tree sprouted and grew to full size in seconds. She smiled, waved another hand, and it burst into flame.

"Well, I guess I'm feeling better," she said. Mrah stood.

"Good."

She glanced at the outside world then looked back at him.

"Why didn't you kill me when I was down?" She tried to split her focus; she would manipulate his physical body while keeping him distracted with the conversation.

"I never wanted to hurt you," he replied forlornly. His head twitched, his eyes narrowed, a sneer twisted his mouth. "Shut up!"

"I didn't say anything," was her absentminded reply. She managed to gain control of Mrah's physical hands and activated the particle separator.

"Not *you*," Mrah growled. He blinked, "What are you doing?"

"What goes around...," Kat mumbled as she took aim and fired. The red planet ignited with the macabre green light. Screams wrought with pain pierced her ears. That couldn't be! She was too far away. How could she hear the screaming? She squeezed her eyes shut, shook her head. Is this what Mrah had heard while attacking her planet?

Quickly, she aimed and fired again; more screams. She slapped her hands over her ears. Stop!

With a roar that would rival a lion in Africa, Mrah tackled Kat. They hit the ground and rolled. Kat's head bounced off the spongy ground; the rain pelted her face. Mrah turned her head with his claw-like hand, pressing the left side of her face into the mud. Why hadn't she thought to stop the rain?

"See!" he hissed in her ear. "I told you she would do it! I told you she didn't lie!"

The mud was cold on her cheek; black water ran up her left nostril. Her cheek squished open; the bitter inky mire infiltrated her mouth. It oozed across her tongue, tasting like beetles and sand. His weight crushed the air out of her lungs. She couldn't breathe. He seemed to be having trouble breathing as well.

His head twitched; the clinical voice was back. "No, no, it's a trap! It's a trap!"

His head twitched again, "Shut up! We lost everyone! *Everyone!*"

Another twitch, "Punishment. We deserve it for what we did."

"*Shut up!*" he roared. He pressed Kat's face harder, even though she hadn't said a word.

She pooled a little power and thrust it upward with all her might. Mrah flew straight up; she held him there for a moment before flinging him to the side. He hit hard, landing on his shoulder. A sharp pain shot through her shoulder, leaving a throbbing pain in its wake. She sat up, spit, and wiped the back of her hand across her mouth.

"Why is this punishment?" Kat asked. Mrah ignored her and

turned his focus to the outside world. He tried to take back control of his body. He managed to shut the laser down. Kat noticed another ship approaching them.

Mrah activated the monitor. Another Caparian emerged. He was just as ugly as Mrah.

"Have you lost your mind?" The Caparian on-screen shouted.

Kat snorted, "Yes." She wasn't surprised she could understand him. She seemed to be tied entirely into Mrah's body now. Perhaps too tied in, she wondered if she would be able to get back out.

Mrah tried to speak, but Kat took control back.

"Try and stop me!" Kat made Mrah say to the Caparian on the other ship. Warc, yes, that's his name. Kat seemed to be tapping into Mrah's memory with greater ease. Now, if she could just tap into his memories permanently, she would be able to use his memories against him.

"Mrah," Warc began, but Kat cut him off. Mrah snatched control of his body and passed his hand over the control panel before Kat could stop him. She regained control and shoved Mrah away. He came dangerously close to sliding over the edge of the gorge. What would happen if he fell into a crevice within his own mind?

She turned back to the outside world and started up the laser again. She no longer wanted to kill Mrah's planet, but she came here to do a job, and she would see it through. She was able to send out two hits before Mrah struck her from behind. She hit the ground again, sliding across the top of the mud as if it were black ice.

"Oh, that's it!" she cried, irritated. She swung her hand as she stood. The rain and clouds scattered like dried leaves in a strong autumn wind. She waved the other hand and covered the ebony ground with sparkling green grass and trees. A snap of her fingers brought blue skies and white clouds.

She turned her attention back to the outside world, but Mrah tackled her again. They rolled across the soft grass, leaving wet black streaks behind.

"I don't want to hurt you!" Mrah cried.

"Ha! You don't want to hurt me!" Her laugh was wild and high. *"You* don't want to *hurt* me!"

"I prayed it wasn't Earth!" he shouted. He pushed away and stood with his back to her. He sounded normal, for a Caparian anyway. No trace of the clinical scientist or the demon.

"Ha," her laugh turned bitter, "as if you pray."

She added more earthly decoration to her scenery. Soon, she had the dreamscape looking just like Earth.

"Stop," he whispered. He spun in circles, taking it all in. She added flowers, butterflies, and a small stream cut its way through the trees.

"You killed all this," Kat replied, bitter. "But you didn't want to *hurt* me."

Mesmerized, he wandered over to a tree and touched the trunk. A Caparian stepped into the picture, one that Kat did not create; she recognized him as Warc.

Suddenly, Mrah was talking to Warc. They discussed the food chain on Earth.

Kat watched them with interest, and Mrah seemed to forget she was there. A bird landed on a branch nearby; she also did not create the bird. This—was a memory.

"I'm telling you, Mrah; they have a very delicate balance on this planet. It could be catastrophic if even one species goes extinct," Warc *said. He held a bee in his hand.*

"I disagree," Mrah *countered.* *"Look at all the species that have already gone extinct; that wasn't very catastrophic."*

"Yes, but they went extinct by way of natural selection," Warc *replied. He had wandered into a swarm of mosquitoes; he brushed them away. They flew over to Mrah. Mrah slapped his hand on his arm.*

"Not all of them went by way of natural selection. Some of them were hunted to extinction," Mrah *continued.* He suddenly seemed aware of himself, and he shook his head.

"No!" the scene evaporated. Mrah's eyes, if possible, turned an even brighter red. He charged like a mad bull.

"You didn't want to hurt me?" Kat mocked him. "You killed everyone I've ever loved!"

He plowed into her. They hit the ground hard. The air whooshed out of her lungs. She shoved him off but hung on as they rolled. She straddled his waist.

"You have no idea what it's like to watch your family die!" She screamed in his face. "But I do! I had to watch it *twice!*"

He slammed his palm into her chin. She rolled across the grass and up onto her feet. Tiny floating spots impeded her vision. She blinked, turned her attention to the outside, and gasped when she saw Warc.

"Where did he come from?" she asked. Mrah was getting to his feet, breathing hard.

"How did you get aboard?" Kat made Mrah's physical body demand to Warc. Warc looked confused. She got a weird echo each time she made Mrah's physical body speak. She heard her voice then echoing the words was Mrah's voice. It was more maddening than when her cell phone would repeat her own words back at her.

"Same way I always board the ship," Warc said. "What the hell are you doing?"

Mrah shoved Kat. His physical body jerked as he retook control.

"Warc, I—," Mrah's body jerked again as Kat regained control.

"What does it look like?" she asked sweetly. She aimed the laser. Her finger poised to fire.

"Stop it, Mrah," Warc demanded. "I've disagreed with everything you've done to Earth, but I've stayed out of it till now. I cannot stand by while you destroy our planet as well."

"Then don't stand by," Kat said. Warc grabbed the wrist she held over the control panel. He jerked her until she was facing him. His eyes appeared more sad than angry.

From inside, Mrah shoved her hard. She skidded across the ground and over the edge of the ravine. She scrabbled for the edge as she went over; her arms jerked hard as she caught hold at the last second. She grunted as her body slammed against the side. Heat wafted up from below. She chanced a glance down and saw the glowing red molten rock. *Who has lava in their brain?*

"Warc, I need help," Mrah cried.

Kat gathered her energy and exploded over the edge. Rather than hitting him again, she grabbed him and threw him like a football. He landed on the other side of the ravine and didn't move. The blow nearly knocked her to the ground as well.

"Say goodbye," Kat gasped. She yanked the arm out of Warc's grasp and started to fire.

"Stop," Warc cried. He leaped forward and tackled her around the waist. She found Mrah's body had a great deal of strength. They rolled across the floor of the ship together. She felt every blow, every knock as if this was her natural body.

She managed to pin Warc down and raised her fist. This body had strength, but she lacked the years of control Mrah had with it. The fist felt heavy and cumbersome. Warc blocked her punch as if he were swatting a fly. He shoved her off and pinned her next. Once again, her face crushed into the floor. She imagined the imprint of the grating in the floor on the cheek of this ugly devil that she possessed. It might be an improvement.

"This won't bring your family back," Warc said in her ear. Kat paused. She twisted the large bulky head and peered at Warc out of the corner of her eye.

"How do you know about my family?" she asked, forgetting for a moment that he thought he was talking to Mrah. Warc jerked his head, shocked.

"I was there."

"No," Mrah said behind her. She looked back at him. His typically yellow face was about three shades lighter.

"Yes," Kat said. "I want to see."

The Earth-like scene faded, replaced by an alien planet. Everything seemed to be red and radiating heat. The sand burned Kat's feet through her shoes, and she wondered how a dream could burn. Then there was a small pyramid, the size of a two-story house. It didn't seem complete with its top missing.

Kat boldly walked into the pyramid, partly out of curiosity and partly to get out of the killer heat. Even though this was a simple memory, the effects were real.

"Don't go in there," Mrah said, his voice faint. He put up a hand in a half-hearted attempt to stop her. She brushed on past and slipped inside.

She followed the narrow corridor. Horrible sounds seemed to come from every direction at once. She noticed Mrah had not followed her into the house. The house seemed familiar and foreign at the same time. She had walked this hall hundreds of times before; no, *she* hadn't walked it; *he* had. It was familiar because it was *his* house!

She passed the kitchen and living room, all empty of life. The noises, she realized, were coming from the second floor. She climbed the steep staircase to a narrow hall lined with doors. Horrible noises emanated from behind each one. She ignored the closed doors and headed for the one open door.

Mrah knelt by a large bed. He held the slender hand of another Caparian. Kat inched closer.

"Myrna," Mrah moaned. His shoulders shook as he bowed his head against her hand. Kat leaned over him to peek at Myrna and gasped. Her yellow skin was inflamed with a rash, unlike anything she had ever seen on Earth. She had massive lumps, one under her arm, another protruding from her neck, and the third behind her knee. Her body glistened with sweat, matting her thick black hair to her head. Her eyes barely flickered as she tried to turn her head, but the lump left little room for movement. She moaned in obvious discomfort.

Mrah lifted his head to look at Kat; his red eyes shone with unshed tears. He blinked, and a single tear sizzled as it streaked down his face.

"She's so warm; I can't cool her off." His already grating voice broke as he tried to speak. "Warc, what can I do? What can I do?"

Behind Kat stood Warc, solemn and silent. He didn't speak, but the pain in his eyes spoke volumes. She turned back to see Mrah leaning over Myrna. He ran a gentle hand over her wet hair. She cringed at the touch.

"I can't even touch her," he whispered.

"Father?" Kat spun around to find a small child standing in the doorway. Mrah made no move to get up. Maybe it was because she was in Mrah's mind, but she saw the little girl through Mrah's eyes. She was the most beautiful little girl she had ever seen. She had long black curly pigtails, and her yellow skin wasn't the dried mustard yellow of her father's but the color of sunflowers. She looked so much like her mother. A wave of love for the little girl nearly crushed Kat. This little girl—Natalie—was brave and caring, sweet and gentle.

Kat furiously shook her head. She couldn't afford to get attached to these creatures. She had to stop them!

"Don't come any closer," Mrah ordered without looking at her. "I don't want you catching this."

"But, Mother," Natalie whimpered. Warc picked the little girl up. He hushed and rocked her. She pushed away enough to look at Warc. "Gildae isn't feeling well."

"We'll go see to Gildae, then, shall we?" Warc whisked Natalie out of the room.

Kat inspected Myrna closer. The rash covered her from head to toe. The little clothing she wore seemed only to cover unmentionables. Kat touched the woman's head and immediately snatched her hand away. This woman was burning up! Kat looked more closely at the bulge protruding uncomfortably from the neck. If she didn't know any better, she would think this Caparian was suffering from the most recent plague on Earth. But that was impossible. They were light-years from Earth!

She stepped away, giving Mrah space. Myrna started to convulse. Mrah squeezed her hand, but there was little he could do but hold her head as her body jerked and twitched. It came to rest, and she lay so still, Kat thought she had died. Myrna's eyes snapped open and rolled to the side.

"Promise me," she wheezed. "You'll find a way to save the children."

Mrah squeezed her hand, eyes tight shut, tears burning tracks down his hollowed cheeks. He bared his teeth in an anguished grin that wasn't really a grin.

"I promise," Mrah forced the words between clenched teeth, his voice tightly controlled.

"Swear it," her words came out as more of a gurgle.

"I swear," his voice was barely above a whisper.

She arched her back, her mouth opened in a silent scream. The whole effect was eerie, with her emaciated body nearly overcome by the enormous bulges; her sunken face made her eyes bulge from their sockets. She sucked in a sharp breath that sounded like sandpaper scraping across rough wood.

"Mrahhhh," she used the entire breath in that one ghostly word. Kat felt a chill. Suddenly all three bulges burst, leaking green blood and yellow pus. Kat slapped a hand over her mouth and gagged. She knew she was in a memory and didn't have a stomach to empty, but somehow she couldn't shake the sick feeling.

Warc stepped into the room, gently pulling Mrah to his feet and leading him away from the body. "I'm sorry. I'm so sorry, but your children need you."

After the Mrah of the past left the room, the actual Mrah appeared beside her.

"Why are you making me remember this?" he asked. He looked haunted, not angry.

"Because I want to understand," Kat replied. She was surprised she felt the sudden urge to hug him.

"What's to understand," he asked. "She died, and I couldn't save her."

He turned to face Kat; his eyes narrowed slightly. "Do you want to watch as each of my ten children die? Do you want to know what my little Natalie said as she lay distorted by boils and dying?"

Kat swallowed and shook her head. She didn't want to see the little girl with pigtails die.

He looked towards the door; his voice became distant. "I don't even know what it was."

"You don't?" Kat asked. He shook his ugly head, which somehow wasn't quite as ugly as before.

"No, we'd never seen it before."

"It looks a lot like a pandemic we had on Earth."

At the mention of Earth, his head twitched, his expression became more sinister. He snarled at her, and the scene melted back into the barren black plane.

"So, you sent us the pandemic to kill us off," he accused. He hit her hard; she skidded across the ground.

"No," she growled as she climbed to her feet and checked for blood on her face. "I saw you get bitten by a mosquito in one of your other memories. I'll bet my planet you contracted it then and brought it here with you."

"*Liar,*" he bellowed. His head twitched, the scientist spoke.

"No, no," he shook his head, took a single step to the side. "It makes sense."

His head twitched again; the demon was back. A long black spear formed in his paw, "If I kill her, I won't have to listen to her lies."

He threw the spear with all the accuracy of a master.

CHAR

"He's here," Warc said. Alex leaped to his feet, and Char tensed. They had pushed the table to the farthest wall from the door. Warc stood by the door while Char and Alex guarded the table. The cloth Char had been using to staunch the flow of his precious blood was now saturated.

"Just a little more strength, Father," Char prayed as his head spun.

The sudden banging on the door shot adrenaline coursing through his body. He was soaked in sweat and crusted in the dried blood of three different colors. The danger had not passed, but already Char felt the rush of adrenaline leaving his body. He simply didn't have much left.

"Let me in!" Mrah shouted.

"Sanctuary," Warc bellowed. Char found the voices getting more irritating with each passing moment. Mrah's sinister laugh seeped into the room and hovered around them.

"A silly Earth claim," Mrah said. "If you haven't noticed, we're not on Earth anymore."

"You always adhered to Sanctuary," Warc countered.

"That was a different time; I was a different *man,*" Mrah said the final word as if it were poison on his tongue.

"It was your idea to adopt it on this planet," Warc said. "So, I'm invoking it now."

Something sharp scratched across the outside of the door, metal on stone. It was slow, deliberate. Char cringed.

"So," Mrah's voice was soft, near a whisper. "You want me to act more *human?* Is that right?"

"I want you to acknowledge the right of Sanctuary," Warc replied. He shifted his stance, ready to fight. Alex did the same, and Char braced himself for the attack.

"Human..." Mrah cooed, making his voice even creepier in the process; another long, slow peal of metal on stone. "Humans make deals and break them all the time. They give gifts filled with death. The Trojan horse, smallpox infested blankets," then he shrieked, *"The Walking Death!"*

"I made the rule; I can break it!" As the final word left his lips, the door exploded. Pieces of debris shot into the room. Alex was struck in the shoulder by a chunk of the door. Char dropped to the floor; pebbles bounced across his back, and dust coated his body. He silently cursed himself for not covering Kat. Mrah stood in the doorway, looking pleased.

"Hello," he said sweetly. His voice did not convey sweetness very well.

At least one of Char's shots had hit its mark. A wet patch of green blood stained his left side. Warc put a hand on Mrah's arm.

"Stop," Warc said.

"They've come to kill us, and you want to *spare them?*" Mrah cried.

"You know they would never have destroyed us," Warc argued. His tone implied they had had this argument before. "They had nowhere near the technology to even make it to our planet, let alone wipe us out."

"Shut up! Human lover!" Mrah lashed out with his left arm, slamming Warc against the wall. His head made a sickening crack on

impact. He shoved off the wall and tackled Mrah around the waist. They hit the floor and rolled. Alex leaped out of the way. Char backed up and bumped into the table. More sand slid off Kat's body; her face cringed then relaxed.

"Why do you defend them?" Mrah growled.

Warc blocked Mrah's fist with his forearm as he swung up with the other fist and caught Mrah in the ribs. Mrah grunted and staggered back a pace.

"Because," Warc gasped, green blood trickled down his neck. "They are innocent."

"Innocent?" Mrah's head twitched, and a snarl twisted his face. "You know nothing of innocence."

Warc swayed and tilted his head as if it took all his concentration to look at Mrah. Mrah whipped a foot around and caught Warc on the side of the head. With a wicked snap, Warc slammed against the wall. He crumpled to the floor, unmoving. One of his swords spun across the floor, coming to rest near Alex's feet. Mrah didn't notice or didn't care.

Char felt what little blood remained in his body drain from his face. His heart skipped a beat. He prayed for Warc to move, to jump to his feet, but he lay still as death.

Mrah stood over the lifeless body, drew his sword, and raised it above his head. "My little Natalie knew of innocence... She *was* innocence..."

"Innocence... innocence... innocence..." He whispered the word repeatedly like a chant and swayed to the rhythm. His voice cracked, and he shook his head; a tear rolled down one yellow cheek.

Mrah was about to bring the blade down on Warc when Alex, in one smooth motion, scooped up the fallen sword and brought it up under Mrah's blade. The clanging of the metal echoed in the room. The scraping of the blades set Char's teeth on edge.

"I don't think you want to do that," Alex glared at Mrah without the slightest fear. Mrah bared his teeth at Alex.

Char looked at the inert body of Warc, torn between guarding Kat and checking to see if Warc had a pulse.

"Ah, half-blood," Mrah said. He pushed, and the swords cried as they pulled apart. "Tell me, are you ashamed to share the blood of such a hateful species?"

"Hateful?" Alex asked. They circled each other. "Why are they hateful? Because a bitty little plague killed your family? I have news for you; a virus, not a human, killed them!"

Char reached a hand back and placed it on Kat, reassurance that she was still there as he glanced at Warc for any sign of life.

"The humans *sent it!*" Mrah bellowed as he swung his sword. His blows drove Alex back across the room. Alex was graceful, agile, and soon danced away from the wall back into the open center of the room.

"The humans didn't send it," Alex gasped, but Mrah cut him off with another attack.

Watching Alex fight was mesmerizing. His skin, which had always seemed to move like ripples on the water, appeared even more fluid. Several shades of blue pulsed all over his body, and when he dodged, twirled, or danced out of the way, he was like a wild river.

They fought like Earthlings. Both opponents being well versed in Earth life, it was hardly far-fetched that their studies would have rubbed off to such a degree. Mrah's style had more of a medieval knight feel, while Alex's style had more the flavor of a samurai. Once in a while, Mrah would get off an otherworldly move. An attack that Char had no name for, but Alex seemed just as well versed in Caparian battle skills as he was in Earth's and was able to dodge or block it.

"It was *you, Mrah!*" Alex shouted. Mrah stopped. His sword hovered, ready to strike. He froze and stared at Alex. After a long pause, he shook his head, blinked, and shook his head again.

"What?" it came out as a whisper, a thread of breath. Mrah's eyes glazed over, staring into the middle distance.

"You brought the Walking Death," Alex said. "You brought it from Earth, and Warc took it back to Earth three years later."

"Liar!" Mrah bellowed. His attacks became more intense. Alex was sweating profusely; his deep blue skin was paling. He became more the shade of a summer sky.

"I. Don't. Lie." Alex fit a word in between each sword strike. "Aurora lied!"

Something about how Mrah's head twitched, how his eyes darkened, how he focused on Alex, let Char know he was about to end it. With certainty beyond explanation, Char knew this was it. He wanted to shout 'Alex,' but it came out as a breathy whisper. He raised a hand and took a single step forward, but it was too late.

Mrah spun and rammed the blade deep into Alex's belly. Alex's eyes went wide, shock spreading across his beautiful face. His sword clattered to the floor. Time slowed, and Char became hyper-focused on how the sword rocked, the tip making little scratching noises.

Alex staggered back, and Mrah's blade slid out of him. White blood coated the blade and oozed out of Alex.

"No!" Char cried. "Alex!"

Time sped up, and Char caught Alex as he fell. He didn't have the strength to support the much taller being, so they sank to the floor. Char cradled him like a brother. Tears blurred his vision. Already the fluid skin was settling. Alex tried to talk, but he only managed a faint gurgle.

"Shh," Char whispered, his throat closing up, making it difficult to continue. He choked, "Please, God... no..."

He pulled the soaked bandage from his neck. It was stained a deep red from his blood. He didn't want to use it, but it was all he had. There wasn't enough of his clothing left to tear apart. He pressed the scarlet bandage to the belly wound. The white blood mingled with the red turning it pink. He hated pink.

"Do..." Alex broke off in a coughing fit. It wracked his whole body.

"Don't try to talk." Char pressed harder on the wound; he had to stop the bleeding. There was so much blood, like spilled milk pooling on the floor beneath them. Alex groaned and wrapped a hand around the one Char pressed into the wound.

"Everyone has a time," Alex sounded every bit the calm, accepting Droplet. "This... is... my time."

Another round of coughing and white blood splattered across Char's chest.

"No," Char croaked, tears flowing freely now, "You can't die... please... you have to stay..."

Alex shook his head; a small smile played around his lips. "Do... what you can... leave the rest... to God..."

Alex went limp in Char's arms. The black of his pupils faded till they matched the pale gray of the rest of his eye, leaving the sharp contrast of the blue irises. The green stubble of his hair, where the razor hadn't cut quite so close to his scalp, faded to the color of spring grass. The rippling color of his skin went smooth as glass and faded like an old photograph. There is no more fluid-like motion, no more raging river, just a mirror surface with no reflection.

Char shook his head then harder. Not again. This wasn't happening again. He didn't notice the bandage fisted in his hand nor the pink blood squeezing between his fingers. He didn't feel the tears as they coursed down his face, nor that he was rocking. He didn't realize he was tugging on the limp body in his arms as he howled.

"Wake up," Char moaned. He bent and pressed his face into Alex's chest. "Please, wake up..."

He didn't even notice as Mrah towered over him and raised his sword for a final killing blow.

KAT

Kat formed a staff to deflect the spear just as it was about to pierce her heart. She expertly sent it spinning into the ravine.

Mrah, furious, formed a staff of his own and raced toward her. She dropped back into a defensive maneuver as he approached. He swung his staff at the side of her head. She brought hers up to block. The two stave's hit with a loud crack.

He brought the other end around to hit her ribs, and she also blocked that. He was fast and skilled. At first, she could only block, but soon she saw openings in his defense and was able to attack.

Her staff vibrated with each impact; it rattled through her bones and into her skull. Her teeth rumbled against each other as she blocked a powerful blow.

Mrah's eyes were hard, determined. A snarl etched into his gaunt face. Each swing, each strike was stronger than the last. His anger and hatred fueled his attack.

She took a step back. Her heel hooked on something she couldn't see, and she fell backward. She landed hard on her rear, and her staff fell to the ground. Mrah laughed. Not a deep chuckle, not a gleeful giggle, but a sinister cackle. He formed a blade on the tip of his staff and raised it high.

Kat thought of her family, sister, world, and Char. Char, who was waiting for her back in 2140. Who had stood by her through the end of the world and the planet that had followed. She would not let him down. She would not let the world down. She would *not die this way!*

"No!" she cried. A burst of energy exploded from her core. Mrah flew backward and slammed into a tree. The staff spun and embedded itself into Mrah's shoulder, pinning him there.

Kat grabbed her shoulder and screamed. She curled around the burning pain. She had never been impaled before. The pain traveled down her arm and through her fingers. It burned across her chest and ached in her neck. It turned her stomach; nausea built inside her, and it took every ounce of concentration to keep it at bay. Mrah's scream mirrored her own until she couldn't tell one from the other.

She pulled her hand back and looked for blood, but her hand was dry. The pain was in her mind—in his mind—it wasn't real. It felt real. Still, the 'pain' had her holding her arm close to her side. Her sister once asked her if people die in their dreams, did they die in real life? Kat had said they would never know since everyone who dies in their sleep never talk about their dreams. She was on the verge of finding out the answer to that question.

She used her good arm to sit up, but her head swirled with the motion. She sat still until the dizziness had passed. Mrah was pinned to the tree and attempting to pull the staff out of his shoulder.

Kat realized, outside the body, that Mrah's face was still pressed into the floor, and Warc had been talking to her this whole time. She took control of the body and bucked hard. Warc rolled away.

"Why didn't you stop me?" Kat asked as she rolled over and sat up. She rubbed the imprint from the floor off her face. She knew Warc still believed her to be Mrah, so she played the part.

"What are you talking about?" Warc asked. "I *did* try to stop you. You cut yourself off from everyone."

"You let me go to... to... a fortune teller to seek advice?" Kat asked.

"I tried to talk you out of it," Warc cried. "I thought you had a lot of nerve going to *her* to seek guidance after what you did to her."

"What did I do?" Kat asked Warc. She turned her attention inward and addressed Mrah. "What did you do?"

Mrah's head bowed; his stringy hair hid his face. He pulled the staff from his shoulder with a solid jerk and dropped to his hands and knees. Kat felt the pain as the blade left his shoulder. She gritted her teeth against it; her good hand came up to press on her shoulder. He didn't look at her.

"Don't tell me you don't remember," Warc said. He sat back against a wall and pulled his knees up, resting his elbows on his knees. "You don't remember Gasos."

Kat ignored Warc and kept her attention focused inward on Mrah. He heaved a deep sigh. All his fight seemed to seep out of him at once.

"Many decades ago," Mrah's voice was deep with defeat. All trace of the demon was gone. The clinical voice was absent; his normal guttural voice filled the silence. As he spoke, the dreamscape conformed to his memory. "Warc, Gasos, and I began a study on a new un-named planet. This planet was previously unexplored, and certain precautions had to be taken to limit our footprint on the planet, so to speak."

The barren black plane of his mind burned away under a glare of crystal white. Huge mountains marked the surface of this white planet. Kat walked amongst the strange crystalline plants. Some towered over her like the sequoia of Earth; others were like blades of grass. They crunched under her feet. Her breath appeared before her in dewy white puffs.

She touched a slender icy leaf. It snapped under the slightest pressure. It was ice clean through. These were not plants covered in ice; the ice *was* the plants! Everything was translucent or opaque and glittered like a world full of diamonds. There was no snow, no drifts, and no piles of soft white anywhere. Everywhere there were sharp points of icy stalagmites. The 'trees' didn't look like trees but massive spires of ice aimed at the sky like missiles ready to launch.

"We each had our little jobs." Mrah continued in his ever more haunted voice. "Mine was the mirage cloak."

Kat was amazed at the three figures as they slipped silently through the underbrush. How were they able to walk without crunching? Kat recognized Mrah and Warc; she assumed the Droplet was Gasos. They gathered samples and examined the foliage. From their actions and smiles, she believed they had been good friends. Gasos and Warc seemed to be debating an issue when Mrah wandered away. He stared, transfixed, at the world around him.

"It was the first time I had ever seen anything so white," Mrah said. He stood by Kat and watched his past self.

"It seems very cold," Kat mused. "Why weren't you freezing?"

"Temprafreeze," Mrah said as if that explained it all. He narrowed his eyes at his former self and pointed. "See here; I'm not paying attention to my job. I let the mirage cloak fade."

There was a shimmer around them, and they became clearer. Kat hadn't realized the haze surrounding them until it faded, and she saw them in sharp focus. They were too engrossed in their study to notice the cloak had disappeared. It left them easy prey to the native patrol coming round the bend.

The natives were bundled in fur and seemed excessively large, yet small hands held spears. They were shorter than the three intruders but didn't seem afraid. They quickly overpowered the scientists and hauled them back to their tiny village.

"Why didn't you fight?" Kat asked. Mrah shook his head.

"It's against Caparian law. The punishment for getting caught is bad enough, but also breaking the law by fighting..." Mrah trailed off.

The scene faded, and the mouth of a cave appeared. The scientists were in a holding cell made of bone, tied with some type of twine but not like any twine Kat had ever seen. Mrah and Warc were curled up on the floor, shivering. Their teeth chattered, and their yellow skin had a purplish hue. Gasos appeared in better health and was sitting, watching.

"Why is your skin purple?" Kat asked. "Were you beaten?"

"No," Mrah said. "We were freezing."

"The—Tempra—freeze—was wearing off?" Kat asked. Mrah nodded.

Night had fallen, and the temperature was dropping. She felt the cold though it was only a memory. Gasos had a sharp eye and waited until one of the three guards wandered too close to the cage. He reached his blue arm through the bars and snatched the knife from the native's belt. The native never noticed.

When the guards finally slept, Gasos used the knife to cut the bindings that held the door closed. He freed Warc and Mrah and helped them to stand. Neither one appeared to have the strength to stand, let alone run, but Gasos managed to spirit them out of the shallow cave.

"How were you three communicating?" Kat asked. Through this whole memory, not once did she hear any of them speak. They used hand signals and facial expressions, but never words.

"Cerebral communicators," Mrah said. "The mirage cloak hides us from prying eyes but would not muffle our words. The closer you are to someone, the better the communicators work."

"Distance, or emotionally?" Kat asked.

"Emotionally," Mrah replied.

So they were good friends. Kat mused.

They followed the three through the woods as they made their escape. An alarm sounded in the village. The three stopped and looked back; they looked at each other and ran.

"We got separated," Mrah said. There was a level of pain in his voice. Kat had to look at him to see if he was crying.

Kat watched as the past Mrah stumbled out of the cave and into a tall sparkling "grassy field." The night air filled with the snapping and crunching of his clumsy footsteps. He was slowing with every step. He rubbed his hands together and slapped his sides, each breath a puff of white. He dropped to his knees and coughed. Each burst sounded deep and painful, like bronchitis, and a bit of green blood spotted his palm when he pulled his hand away from his mouth.

Gasos burst from the tall grass and spotted Mrah. He helped Mrah to his feet, and half carried, half dragged Mrah with him. One of the natives discovered them and aimed his arrow at Gasos. Mrah tried to raise his hand, but the effort was too much, and it fell to his side. Gasos pushed Mrah to safety but took the arrow in his stomach. The natives swarmed the body of Gasos like ants.

Mrah, forgotten by the natives, crawled away.

"Enough!" Mrah bellowed. The memory burst like a soap bubble. Kat looked at him, startled. Tears pooled in his red eyes. He swallowed a few times as if his throat could push the pain back down.

"I wanted to save him," he whimpered. He was talking more to himself than to Kat. He looked at his hand, turned it over, and stared at his palm. "I wanted to... I tried..."

He shook his head.

"That was not your fault!" Kat cried.

"Through my inactivity, he died," Mrah clenched his jaw and fisted his hands.

"You were half frozen!" Kat tried to get him to face her, but he shook her off and stepped away.

Kat turned her attention back to the outside. "Warc, tell him!"

Warc looked at her as if she had lost her mind.

"Who?" Warc asked, his tone slow and careful.

"Tell Mrah that it wasn't his fault," Kat said, completely forgetting she was *in* Mrah's body and that Warc thought he was talking *to* Mrah.

"Mrah," Warc said. "It... isn't... your fault?"

Mrah's body twitched as he regained control.

"Nevermind," Mrah said. "It was nothing. Forget it."

Kat tried to take control back, but Mrah turned on her. Eyes blazing, he pinned her to a tree with one hand around her throat.

"You do not understand," Mrah snarled.

"It wasn't—," Kat choked, but Mrah squeezed to cut off her words.

"He doesn't need to know what a coward I am," his nose touched the tip of hers. Spittle flecked from his mouth, spraying her lips. The pressure was building in her face, red then purple. She needed air. Her fingers scrabbled at his hand, but he didn't even notice. Spots floated in her vision. She made desperate little choking sounds, but he didn't care. The demon was back; his hatred burned her as much as her lungs burned for oxygen.

"Mrah," Warc's voice echoed across the dreamscape. "We can get you help."

Mrah looked up at the sky as if that was where Warc was hiding. He looked back out at the outside. Warc was there; concern etched into his face. What did Warc see when they were fighting each other in this dreamscape? Was Mrah's body just staring into space, like a catatonic patient?

Mrah's head twitched; his grip loosened, then released. He turned all his attention to the outside as Kat dropped to her knees, sucking in huge gulps of air. He was shouting something at Warc, something about not being crazy. She could barely hear over the roaring in her ears.

How did he do that? How did he strangle her without feeling the effect? What had he done differently?

She got one foot under her, paused, breathed, took a deep breath, and pulled herself to her feet. She staggered to Mrah.

"Not..." Her voice rasped. She cleared her throat. "Not your..."

He spun around and hit her hard. The world narrowed until all she knew was the pain in her head where he hit her. She didn't feel herself flying through the air. She didn't feel the impact as her back slammed into a tree. She collapsed in a heap beneath the charred branches. She barely even noticed as the darkness swooped in to claim her.

CHAR

"You didn't have to kill him," Char croaked. He swallowed hard and glared at Mrah through the blur of unshed tears. Mrah held the blade above Char, ready to bring it down and end this. Char went unnaturally calm inside. He sat straighter and squared his shoulders.

"This wasn't his fight," Char said. "There was no reason to kill him."

"There was *every* reason," Mrah growled. "He helped my enemies."

Warc arose behind Mrah with the sword raised. Char's expression must have given him away because awareness spread across Mrah's face a split second before he spun and countered the attack. The swords screeched upon impact.

Green blood coated Warc's face and soaked the tattered remains of his clothing. He bared his teeth at Mrah and growled like a feral animal. Mrah growled back. They pushed each other away and clashed again. Their movements were too fast for Char to follow. He didn't know anything about fighting styles, but some of their moves he recognized from movies. They jumped from one fighting style to another, an attempt to confuse and throw their opponent off balance, perhaps? They not only switched fighting techniques but mixed them as well. Moves he recognized mixed with alien styles he didn't.

Warc landed a solid kick to Mrah's abdomen. Mrah doubled over, and Warc brought a knee up and cracked Mrah's chin. Mrah's head snapped back, and he tipped backward. His head bounced off the wall with the sickening thud of melon on stone. He straightened, shook his head, and swayed slightly on his feet.

"End this," Warc demanded. "Drop this grudge! It's based on false information."

"Never," Mrah gasped. He pointed his blood-soaked blade at Kat. "She must die, or we all die."

"She doesn't need to die!" Warc bellowed. He lunged, and Mrah blocked him, but only just.

Char looked at Alex's still body, his blind dead eyes staring at nothing. Char closed the lids, so Alex could rest and was gentle as he laid Alex's head on the floor.

"I am sorry, my friend," Char whispered, placing a hand on his chest. "I never should have let you get involved."

He climbed to his feet. He had been sitting with Alex's weight on him for too long. His bones didn't feel as if they fit together anymore. He hobbled a little till they worked themselves back together. His fingers were thick and clumsy as he pried the sword from Alex's hand. He wouldn't be able to fight for long, but perhaps he would be able to defend Kat long enough to give her time to succeed. He staggered over to the table. There wasn't even a handful of sand left on her. Her body was near to touching the table again.

He wanted to pull her in his arms and protect her. To whisk her away someplace safe. A place without monsters bent on revenge. A place where they could rebuild the shattered remains of their life. Perhaps they could find a planet like Earth? But he knew that would never be. They would die here, in this room, and he would not hurry her death along by touching her. So, he turned his attention back to the battle.

Warc was showing signs of fatigue. His strikes slowed and didn't seem to carry the same power as before. Mrah was tiring, but he didn't suffer as many injuries as Warc.

"This won't make you feel any better," Warc heaved a deep breath and let it out in a whoosh.

"I'm doing this to save our planet," Mrah said.

"Our planet was never in danger," Warc said. Warc lowered his sword as if it was too heavy to hold. There was green blood everywhere; it coated his arms and legs, splattered the walls, and dripped from the blades of the swords. It was impossible to tell where Warc's wounds were through all the blood, but his blood loss was obviously significant.

He brought his sword up to block Mrah's next attack, but the sword was knocked from his hands and clattered to the floor. Char shook his head, but it was all he could do to stand and hold the sword. There was nothing he could do when Mrah brought the blade down on his last friend.

"She lied," Warc said, but Mrah still drove the blade into his neck. Warc twitched, eyes wide, but said nothing else as his body crumpled to the floor.

"No," Char whispered. The yellow body of his friend lay in a heap like an old pile of bones. Mrah turned to face Char.

"Now it's just you and me," Mrah's ghoulish grin revealed blood-stained teeth.

KAT

The rumbling of an earthquake woke Kat. She opened her eyes, but the light pierced her skull, and she squeezed her eyes shut again. Her head throbbed, her shoulder ached; she just hurt all over. She wanted nothing more than just to lay there and die, give up this fight and let Mrah win. The ground shook harder. She forced her eyes open.

Mrah focused on the outside world. He was shouting at someone, but Kat couldn't make sense of the words.

She grabbed the tree and pulled herself to her knees. A jolt of pain shot up her back, but she ignored it and forced herself to her feet. She swayed heavily and leaned against the tree for support. The throbbing in her head was worse now that she was standing. Her jaw felt like it was on sideways. She wiggled it with her hand, but that only increased the pain.

She told herself this pain wasn't real. She was a spirit and therefore couldn't feel pain, but it was difficult to convince her mind she wasn't really in pain when the pain was coursing through her body like poison.

She peeked at the outside world and realized the "earthquake" was really Mrah and Warc fighting! She had to stop them. They needed to understand. She needed to tell Warc it wasn't Mrah's fault. He didn't murder Gasos; he simply couldn't save him.

She needed to pool more energy, but she was sapped. All her anger, which had fueled her energy before, was gone. She no longer felt hatred for this poor creature but pity. He had suffered such guilt for so long, then lost his whole family. Warc was right. Earth would never have attacked Lebrac.

"We didn't even know we weren't alone in the universe," Kat mumbled. Mrah didn't turn around. He must not realize she's awake. She closed her eyes. "Please, God, help me right this wrong."

She felt a fresh sizzle of energy. This rush was pure and white. This was the burn of love rather than hate. Her head cleared, and her body stopped hurting. She strode forward and touched Mrah.

"Stop," she said. Her voice carried weight and authority beyond her capability.

Mrah stopped and looked at her, surprised. She caught a glimpse of herself through his eyes. Her body glowed with a golden light. The image faded, and Mrah's stunned face replaced it.

She held his face in her hands, looked him in the eye, and a burst of her energy coursed into his body. He stiffened and arched his back, choked on a scream, and went limp. She lowered him gently to the ground.

She turned her focus back to the outside world. It was time to leave this body. Walking out of the body was like walking through a massive spider web. It clung to her, but she pushed her way through, and it fell away. Warc gasped as she emerged.

He looked from her to Mrah, to her again. His mouth opened and moved with silent half-finished words. "I thought he was going crazy."

"He was," Kat said. "But he should be better now."

"Who are you, and how long have you been inside him?" Warc demanded. Kat waved a dismissive hand.

"My name is Kat; I'm from the future; there isn't time to explain. I need to tell you something before he awakens." Kat explained what happened on that un-named planet so many years ago.

"So, he didn't kill Gasos," Warc whispered. He shook his head at Mrah's slumbering body. "Why didn't you ever tell me?"

Mrah stirred. He sucked in a deep breath, and his eyes fluttered open. His eyes flicked back and forth between Kat and Warc. Warc helped him sit up. They both had wounds from their battle, but neither seemed seriously injured.

"It's good to have you out of my head," Mrah grumbled.

"She told me," Warc said. Mrah glared at Kat.

"Why did you tell him?" he cried.

"Mrah," Kat said. "He needed to know. And I think I can help."

"How can you possibly help?" Mrah asked.

"I time jumped once," Kat replied. "I don't have much time left, but I think I can jump one more time."

"How will that help?" Warc asked.

"I can go back to when Mrah was distracted by the planet and stop him from letting the mirage cloak fade."

"Why," Mrah asked, "would you do that for me? After all, I've done?"

"Because," Kat smiled. "I forgive you."

CHAR

Mrah raised his sword.

Char looked at the weapon clutched in his pale hand. He could barely hold it, let alone swing it. He glanced at Kat before turning back to Mrah. He lifted the sword, which seemed to weigh so much more than it should.

Mrah grinned, a laughing sort of grin. He was humoring Char. They both knew that Char didn't stand a chance in a fair fight.

"Little human," each word dripped with condescension. He spread his arms wide, opening up his body for an attack. "Take your best shot."

Char looked at the sword in his hand again. What was his best shot? With all his skill in the different fighting arts, Alex could not kill this creature. Warc, with all his talent and inside knowledge of Mrah's fighting tactics, could not kill him. A man who had never drawn a sword and had lost as much blood as he stood absolutely no chance of fighting, let alone winning. If he fought, he would lose, and they would still die. This battle was already over.

He closed his eyes; Calypso's words returned to him; 'When your heart is tugged with compassion, or when you feel the urge to say something you may feel is out of place in a conversation, God is guiding you.' How long had it been since they had sat in that quiet garden where he could hear God's voice?

Put your sword back in its place, for all who take the sword will perish by the sword, words from the book of Matthew. Char knew God was trying to tell him something.

Char looked Mrah in the eye and dropped the sword. He would trust God.

"Pick up your weapon," Mrah demanded. Char shook his head.

"I understand why you did what you did," Char said. "I believe you to have been manipulated by another being."

"Shut up," Mrah growled. His paw squeezed the hilt of his sword.

"And," Char was calm as a Droplet. "I forgive you."

Mrah roared and shoved Char against the wall hard enough to break his spine. He lay in a heap on the floor, unable to move even a single finger. Still, he was calm as he watched Mrah stand over Kat. Mrah raised his sword high above his head.

"I'm sorry, Kat," Char whispered. Tears rolled down his cheeks, but inside he still felt calm. This was how it was supposed to end; he was certain of it. His only regret was that he couldn't be by Kat's side as Mrah took her life.

The last thing he saw was the blade plunging into Kat's chest.

KAT

Kat gasped and clutched her chest. It felt tight like a heart attack. She could barely draw a breath; she collapsed. Mrah and Warc leaped forward to catch her as she fell. She looked into their faces; faces she once considered so hideous now looked more like concerned faces of old friends.

"It seems," Kat wheezed. "I've run out of time."

"Hold on," Warc said. "You'll be all right."

"You'll rally again, like before," Mrah was earnest. Kat shook her head.

"No," Kat huffed like an old smoker. "I fear my friends have failed."

She felt engulfed by their arms. They were so much larger than she; it left her feeling like a baby in the arms of adults. They cradled her like a child. She failed her mission. She couldn't save the Earth, but maybe she could still do something for this one poor tortured soul. She put a hand on Mrah's cheek. His skin was smooth, which surprised her. She expected it to feel coarse as sandpaper. She looked into his red eyes and saw the love in them for the first time. He loved her, and she had no doubt he had loved the Earth. She felt a burning at the corners of her eyes, and for the first time since her family died, she cried. She didn't cry for herself, the loss of her planet, or even the extinction of her race; she cried for Mrah. She cried for everything he had lost, his family, and the guilt he had felt and would feel that no words could ever ease.

"Tell her," Kat whispered. Her silent tears rolled down her cheeks and into her ears. Her head was spinning. She needed to hold on just a little longer. "Tell Aurora the truth. She deserves to know... to know Gasos died... saving his friends..."

The coughing was uncontrollable, and it ached. Each burst felt like someone was squeezing her lungs. She felt her diminishing heartbeat in her very soul. She flickered with each beat, and they were getting farther apart. Not much time left...

"Mrah," Kat clutched his shoulder and tried to pull up. He leaned down to listen. His tears dripped onto her cheek. "Know that... I... forgive you..."

The darkness swirled in to claim her for the final time.

KATIE

The rock burned Katie's hands as she pulled herself up onto the plateau. The sharp edge cut into her palms, but she ignored the pain and grunted as she dragged herself over the edge. Her Kur turned its head in her direction for only a moment before looking away. The climb out of Neptune's Hollow got harder every year.

"Katie," Mary called. She sounded frustrated. Katie laughed as she reached down to help Mary up. Her sister had handled the past five years well. She was only fourteen, but hard life had toughened her, made her older. Katie had tried to give her a childhood, but that wasn't possible with how the earth was now.

She turned her attention to the limitless horizon, hating the flat bleakness of it. No clouds protected the poor bruised Earth from the sun's scorching rays. Nothing grew. The land was barren, dead, and even the sky was a flat immovable gray. A harsh and constant wind scoured the land.

She had accomplished nothing. Sure, she had saved Mary, but everyone else still died. Sometimes she thought it all must have been a dream. Kat had never appeared to her again after the attack. Her memory of the explosions was still vivid in her mind. This was the year something else was supposed to happen, a second attack. But Kat hadn't returned to tell her what to do. Perhaps it was all just a dream and nothing more. Still, she had a nagging feeling she should do something, warn someone, before the next attack.

"Earth to Katie," Mary waved a hand in Katie's face. Katie blinked.

"I'm sorry, what?" Katie asked.

"I said we should build stairs or something," Mary huffed. "It's nuts to climb this every year."

"If we build stairs, people will find it," Katie replied. "And we have this conversation *every* year."

Mary offered a mischievous grin. "And we'll keep having it until I wear you down."

Katie shook her head and guided her Kur back toward home. They walked in comfortable silence the whole way back to the bomb shelter, which had been home for the past five years. They left their Kurs standing outside and descended into the cool depths of the shelter. Katie found the torch and touched its globe to light it. She went back out and tossed their supplies down into the shelter where Mary caught them.

Together they loaded the shelves with their treasures. Katie opened her personal bottle of water and took a sip. She felt the cool, clear water slid down her parched throat and trace an icy path to her stomach. Her body demanded more, but she put the cap back on her bottle. Mary chugged hers.

"Mary," Katie scolded as she put her bottle back on the shelf.

"I know," Mary gasped as she pulled the bottle from her mouth.

"You know better than that," Katie said.

"I know," Mary chirped. A noise had her looking up, and they locked eyes. They both stilled and listened. She motioned for Mary to stay quiet and found her staff. Mary grabbed her sword. Katie raised an eyebrow; Mary shrugged and grinned. Katie shook her head and motioned for Mary to stay behind her.

She listened for a breath longer, but the rattling chains of her distressed Kur shot her into motion. She leaped from the darkness into the light with a shriek, extending her staff simultaneously. With her own shriek, Mary was right behind her, her sword at the ready.

She saw the wagon, the two extra Kurs, and a lean man in a quick sweeping glance. She paused. He had obviously lost some weight and had a beard, but she was sure she had seen this man somewhere before. His blue eyes regarded her with caution.

"Daddy," a little blond head popped out of the wagon. Her smile was bright as the sun.

"Get back in the wagon, sweetheart," the man said, without taking his eyes off Katie. Concern on her face, a pretty blond woman, peaked out, but she pulled the little girl back inside. The blue-eyed man held his hands up, palms out.

"I mean you no harm," he said.

"You seem familiar," Katie lowered her staff. She looked at Mary, who lowered her sword.

"I believe we've met once before, Katie," he smiled.

"You're the recruiter!" Katie gasped. She held out her hand, and he shook it.

"I wanted to apologize for the way our last meeting went." He looked back at his wagon, then back at her. "I thought you were crazy, but when that guy challenged the world to prepare for some kind of attack, I felt it might be more than a coincidence. If you hadn't tried to warn me, I might not have taken him seriously, and my family would have died. As it is, I owe you my life and the lives of my wife and daughter."

Katie waved a dismissive hand, "It's all right. I'm sure I sounded like a lunatic."

"I was hoping I would get the chance to thank you one day." He went back to his wagon and dug around in a box. His wife whispered furiously to him, but he waved a calming hand. She glanced at them again before disappearing inside the wagon.

"Ah-ha! Here it is!" He came back and pressed a medallion and key into her hand.

Katie looked at it. She recognized the symbol for Zortentearth, and the triangular key belonged to an escape pod.

"Take these," he said warmly. "You allowed me to save my family."

He climbed back onto his wagon, waved, and drove away. The little girl waved frantically out the back. Mary waved back as Katie studied the medallion.

"What was he talking about?" Mary asked.

"I don't know," Katie replied, but she did know. She read the tag on the key and looked at the horizon. Why did Beta Alpha Quadrant Four sound so familiar?

"Katie," Mary asked. "What's wrong?"

"I think we need to take a little journey."

⇥Z⇤

The hustle and bustle of the colony were familiar to Katie, as most large colonies crowded with people. She told Mary to stay close. Mary was more than old enough to handle herself, but she was still that scared little nine-year-old crying for their dead mother in Katie's eyes.

She had only heard Kat reference this place once in regards to Char. She didn't even know if he would be there. She wasn't sure she would recognize him, even if she walked right by him.

Mary stopped at every stand to look over the merchandise. She loved to shop and dicker with the merchants. She was good at it too. She could talk any merchant down to a reasonable price. Katie was careful to teach Mary never to lower the cost so much that the merchant lost money on the deal.

The siren sounded, and Katie tensed. People began shouting and running. She pulled her staff from her belt and extended it; Mary had a hand on her sword.

"What's that?" Katie cried. Is this the second attack Kat had warned her about?

"I don't know," Mary craned her neck, trying to see over the river of people. They were jostled from behind and swept away. The traffic flow took them to the edge of the colony out near the landing fields.

A light like fire and black clouds billowed across the sky. The loud rumble like thunder shook the ground. A single Caparian warship entered the atmosphere. The downburst from the monstrosity knocked more than a few people down. Katie extended one blade on her staff and impaled the ground; she held tight and leaned into the blast. Mary did the same with her sword. Katie's long braid wrapped around her neck, but she didn't dare let go of the staff to fix it.

"What's a Caparian warship doing here?" Katie shouted over the din. She sucked too much dust into her lungs and coughed. The wind died down as the ship landed and the doors opened. Katie felt strangely light as pressure eased, and she no longer had to strain to stand. She tugged her braid from her throat. Mary jerked her sword from the dirt and looked at Katie. Katie shrugged, pulled her staff from the ground, and retracted the blade but didn't put it away.

Two Caparians stepped out of the warship. Katie recognized the face of Mrah. It was the same hideous face Kat had shown her in the dream. She stepped closer to Mary.

"That's Mrah," Katie whispered.

"You weren't exaggerating about his looks," Mary whispered back.

Katie didn't know what to do. This wasn't the rain of fire Kat had shown her, but something must have gone wrong if Mrah was still alive.

"May we have your attention, please?" The Caparian who wasn't Mrah asked. "My name is Captain Warc of the Planet Lebrac."

Katie glanced around the crowd. No one appeared aggressive, but judging by their faces, these Caparians were not welcome. Who could blame them after what the Caparians had done to this once beautiful planet?

"I have with me, Captain Mrah," Warc continued. The way Warc pronounced the name was far different from how Kat had pronounced it. His was a deep, drawn-out, guttural sound, which made the name sound complete, as opposed to Kat's pronunciation which made the word sound short and clipped as if it were missing a syllable. Warc looked at Mrah. Katie wasn't sure, but she thought Warc looked concerned. Mrah nodded to him. "He would like to say a few words to you."

Mrah stepped forward.

"My name is Mrah," He looked across the unfriendly faces of the remaining people of Earth. "I am responsible for the attack on this planet."

Everyone began talking at once, drowning out his following words. Mrah held up a hand. The crowd quieted enough for him to continue.

"I believed this planet was responsible for an attack on my home planet, Lebrac, and without further research, I retaliated," Mrah continued. "I am solely responsible, and I am prepared to accept the consequences of my actions. Do with me what you will."

The roar of the crowd was deafening. A lone ball of some alien food launched through the air and hit his shoulder with a brown splat. He didn't flinch as another gray glob of something hit him square in the chest. Warc stepped forward, but Mrah held a hand up and shook his head. The crowd surged forward and seized him. Katie and Mary pressed their backs to the hot wall of one of the domes.

The crowd parted, making a clear path for the men who had captured Mrah to parade him past. Someone had found ropes and the men bound Mrah's hands. He kept his head held high, even as the onslaught of alien foods found their mark. Mrah made eye contact with her as he passed. His expression remained unchanged, but there was a slight widening of his eyes when he made eye contact with Katie.

Katie looked back at the ship where Warc stood stoic.

Katie felt sick. She understood the need for revenge. She knew why her people wanted to punish him for everything he did, but she couldn't get Kat's angry look out of her mind. Kat had become so cynical, so angry over everything she'd lost. Katie knew she was only a breath away from turning into that girl from her dream. She had made a vow to herself never to become so angry she couldn't see what was right and good. She tightened her grip on her staff and raced for the ship.

"Where are you going?" Mary asked as she caught up with her. Katie ignored her as she pushed her way through the last of the crowd.

"What don't we know?" Katie asked. Warc appeared startled.

"Kat," he asked.

"No," Katie shook her head. "I'm Katie. You know Kat?"

He nodded slowly. "She died."

Somehow Katie knew this must be true. Why else would she not have come back to tell her what else had to be done? It was a strange feeling knowing part of her had died. True, she was just a spirit from the future; she was a different Katie from another time, but to know that Kat had died saddened her. She wanted to cry for the girl who had lived her life alone; for the girl—who couldn't cry for herself.

"It doesn't make sense," Katie continued. "For him to attack our planet then come back so *we* can have *our* revenge. So, what don't we know?"

The muscles in his jaw pumped. He stared across the flat land before turning back to Katie. "We came back because of Kat."

"What did she do?" Katie asked. Tears glistened in Warc's eyes; one escaped and slid down his yellow cheek. He sniffed hard and blew out a loud breath.

"Healed him." Emotion thickened the words.

"What does that mean?" Mary asked. Katie let that thought swirl around in her head. What *did* that mean? Healed him? She didn't know what had happened to Kat, and she didn't know what healing him meant, but she felt certain if Kat had taken the time to heal him in any way, she wouldn't want the people of Earth to hurt him again.

"Come on," Katie barked as she bolted for the town square. Mary was on her heels.

"What are we doing?" Mary asked.

"I don't know," Katie shook her head. "But we have to do *something*."

The crowd had Mrah on his knees in the center of the square. His head was bowed, hands were tied behind his back, and he dripped with various alien foods.

The crowd was shouting and throwing things at him. Several purplish bruises had already formed, and a large goose egg was already swelling on the back of his head.

"What shall we do to this creature?" One man stepped up beside Mrah and poked him with a stick. Mrah didn't flinch. He remained motionless.

"Hang him!"

"Burn him!"

"Whip him!"

Katie couldn't believe her ears. Had they fallen into the dark ages? Katie tightened her grip on her staff. She must be nuts.

"Stop!" she shouted as she leaped out of the crowd.

"Katie!" Mary cried. The man with the stick swung it at her. She knocked it from his hand and pushed him back toward the crowd with her staff. The crowd hummed like angry bees.

"Get back, lady," a faceless voice ordered.

Mary joined her by Mrah. He still hadn't moved. Mary had her sword ready. She leaned over and mumbled, "Have you lost your mind? You're going to get us killed."

"I don't know why, but I feel Kat wouldn't want it to end this way." Katie looked across the crowd, but she didn't see one friendly face. "Keep watch."

She turned and knelt by Mrah. She realized it wasn't only food coating him but also green blood. She placed her hands on either side of his face, and he raised his head to look at her.

"Kat," Mrah whispered. A single tear cut a line down his cheek. "I thought you died."

"I'm Katie. Kat did die."

"I'm sorry," he whimpered. "I am so sorry I couldn't save you."

"I will get you out of this," Katie said. He shook his head.

"Leave me," he lowered his head. "I deserve whatever they deem worthy. Even if it is death—*especially* if it is death."

"No," Katie replied, her voice grim. "There has been enough death."

She tried to force her muscles to stop twitching as she stood to address the crowd. Kat had always seemed so strong, so calm, but Katie felt neither. She felt scared and small in the face of so many people who hated.

"Good people," she held her staff in the air. The crowd quieted. "We may not have seen rivers run red with blood. We have not had to sift through the bodies of the dead on a battlefield. We have not had to dig mass graves nor burn the bodies of our loved ones because they died too fast for burial. We may not have hills filled with tombstones. We don't have gruesome images burned into our minds. We have none of these markers to remind us of the cost. These deaths came too swiftly and left behind no trace."

She paused, waiting for some reaction. The crowd remained silent. "Perhaps that is why it is so easy to forget how many died. We've all lost families. We all lost friends. We all lost those we held dear, but will killing him," she gestured to Mrah, "really bring them back?"

"No," she continued before anyone could interrupt. "It won't bring them back. It won't bring back a single lost soul."

"It'll make *me* feel better!" a voice cried.

"No," she replied. "It won't. You think it will, but taking a life leaves you with a bigger hole than before."

"Let's kill him and find out," another voice shouted. The crowd rumbled an agreement. She was losing them; she could feel it.

"Well, this is working well," Mary mumbled. Katie shot her a look. Mary shrugged and maintained her battle stance.

"Has there not been enough death? Has there not been enough killing?" Katie shouted.

"Listen to her!" A man's voice cried above the clamor. Katie looked across the sea of faces to find the voice. It sounded so familiar. There he was!

"Charlie," Katie whispered. He pushed his way through the crowd.

A girl with flaming red hair followed on his heels. His smile lit up his whole face as he approached.

"I knew I would find you someday," he said as he shook her hand. "I just didn't think it would be in the midst of a blood-thirsty mob."

"You're a difficult man to find," Katie smiled.

"Not half so difficult as you," he replied.

"Charlie," the redhead tugged his sleeve. She pointed toward the restless crowd. "Perhaps we can save the small talk until we've gotten out of this mess."

"Please," Charlie raised his hands to quiet the crowd again. "Allow me a few words."

He looked at Katie. She spun her staff, nodded, and faced the crowd again. She was relieved to have someone else on her side and happy to hand the speech over to him. She had never liked giving speeches.

"We have been given a great gift." He paused, "God has blessed each of us with free will. This means we are not automatons. We are not preprogrammed to say or do anything specific. We are free to choose how we want to live."

Katie glanced back at Mrah. He had raised his head and was listening to Charlie.

"We cannot control the actions of other people. We can, however, control how we react to those actions."

Mrah's eyes widened. Charlie turned back to Mrah and helped him to his feet. Mrah stared at him wide-eyed like a child.

"Mrah, here, believed this planet was responsible for an attack on his planet. He had a choice to make. He could either investigate this theory or choose to attack without asking questions. The result was that millions of innocent lives were lost. What would have happened if he had asked questions? Would those lives have been spared?"

"We have a chance," Katie spoke up. She glanced at Charlie; he nodded. "This is our chance! We have the same decision to make. Do we retaliate without question, as he did, perhaps regretting it forever, or do we first ask why?"

"Ask why," Warc bellowed. The crowd turned to look at him. A few alien foods flew through the air, but he dodged them. The crowd parted as he pressed on through.

"Warc," Mrah growled. "I told you to stay out of this!"

"No," Warc cried. "Not this time! I will not watch you suffer again for something that wasn't your fault!"

"What do you mean, not his fault?" Mary asked. She eyed a big burly man who kept inching his way closer. Katie spun her staff as a warning and glared at the man. He noticed her and took a step back. She heard metal slide from a sheath, and she turned to see the redhead had pulled a dagger from her boot. Charlie was the only one who didn't draw a weapon against the crowd.

"Tell them, Mrah," Warc said. He reached them and hesitated as he looked at Mary's sword. The crowd looked at Mrah in one motion, like fish in a tank following the hand that feeds them.

"I will take my punishment," Mrah growled.

Warc uttered a word in his language that sounded like an expletive. "Mrah! Tell them!"

Before Mrah could answer, another siren blared. The sky burned again, only this time it was a Zortentearthian Royal Ship entering the atmosphere. It did not land, but a small pod disengaged and landed on a side street. Three Droplets emerged. Katie glanced at the crowd, making sure no one was using this distraction as a chance to attack, but their attention was consumed by the arrival of the Royal Princess of Zortentearth.

Katie knew Calypso by reputation, but she didn't know who the other two were. Calypso smiled as she stepped up beside Warc. Her blue skin rippled in the light, her emerald green hair would have dragged on the ground behind her, but her silver gown was so long the hair rode on the folds of fabric. When she spoke, her voice was the sound of silvery bells and baby birds.

"My name is Calypso Jima of the planet Zortentearth. This is Captain Gar and Alexander." She gestured to each of them in turn. "It has been brought to our attention that the previous attack on Earth was initiated out of revenge. I am ashamed to say it was brought about by one of my own people."

There was a rumble of confusion from the crowd.

"What does that mean?" someone shouted.

"Yeah, if a Droplet is to blame, why is this Caparian taking the punishment?" a woman shouted.

Calypso held up a hand. The crowd stilled. Calypso seemed to emanate serenity, and Katie suddenly felt foolish for drawing her weapon. She collapsed her staff and stuck it back in her belt. Mary slid her sword back into its sheath, and Katie heard the dagger slide home as well.

"The Princess Aurora Jima manipulated an emotionally unstable Mrah to do her bidding. In her twisted mind, she hoped Mrah would attack Earth, and in return, Earth would fight back and kill him for an imagined slight against her." Calypso spoke without accusation.

"So, revenge," someone said. "She wanted revenge on this guy, Mrah, and rather than do her own dirty work, she used him to invoke us to kill him."

"That is correct," Calypso said. Gar stood at her elbow like a guard, but he seemed to carry no weapon.

"The question still stands," Katie blurted without thinking. Everyone looked at her. She felt the heat building in her face. She couldn't believe she had just cut in on one of the Royal family! She bullied on through the burning in her cheeks. "We still have a choice to make. Will we kill him? Thus giving Aurora exactly what she wanted, playing into her hand like pawns, or shall we foil her plans and forgive him?"

Silence. Her face burned hotter. The silence stretched. No one seemed to be breathing.

"I vote," Charlie said, "forgiveness."

"As do I," the redhead said.

"Me too!" Mary said.

"A show of hands," Katie called, "for forgiveness!"

Calypso raised her hand, then Gar, Warc, and Alexander. The crowd stayed still.

"Well... I won't be a pawn in someone else's game," the burly man grumbled and raised his hand.

"Neither will I," a woman raised her hand. One by one, hands went up all around the crowd. A bubble of joy expanded inside Katie with each hand that went up. She felt she would burst.

Not all the hands went up, but the number that did far outweighed those do didn't. Katie saw discontent on many of the faces that worried her, but they seemed to decide a fight wasn't worth it.

She turned to Mrah. He had food stuck to his face. She took the edge of her cloak, wiped it away, and smiled at him.

"We forgive you," she whispered. Tears spilled from his eyes as she cut his bindings.

"Thank you," he hugged her. She helped him to his feet, and he faced the crowd. "I cannot convey how truly sorry I am for what I have done. I cannot bring back your loved ones, but I have studied Earth for two hundred years. If you allow me to live, I will make it my life's work to restore this planet to its former glory. I will also pledge my continued protection from outside forces. No one will harm this planet again as long as I draw breath!"

The crowd cheered. Hats flew in the air. People hugged, cried, and laughed, and eventually, the crowd dispersed. Some approached Warc and Mrah to discuss how to rebuild the planet. The rest drifted back into town.

Calypso approached Katie. "May I speak with you?"

Katie nodded, and they stepped away from everyone else. Katie tried not to fidget. She didn't remember Kat being such a scaredy-cat. The thought made her smile, and she felt a little calmer.

"Katie," Calypso's voice was like a bubbling brook, a soft breeze through spring leaves, and gentle music. "For what you have done for us in the past, the future, and in the present, God has granted you a great gift, if you would like to have it."

"I didn't do all that much," Katie said. She wondered if Calypso was referring to Kat. "What gift?"

"You alone will have the opportunity to remember."

"Remember what?" Katie asked. Butterflies fluttered in her chest.

"Everything," Calypso smiled. "Kat died, but she can live on in you if you are willing."

Katie's hand fluttered to her chest. Live on through her? Would this be like before when Kat haunted her dreams? Would she develop a split personality? Kat *was* her, and she *was* Kat. "What does that mean?"

"Do not fear," Calypso said. "You will not go crazy."

Did she want to remember? What of her promise to herself to not become like Kat. Would she not become as cynical if she remembered what Kat went through? Katie looked at Mrah and realized that Kat may have changed. Why else would she let her enemy live? Curiosity won out, and she nodded.

Calypso placed a hand on either side of her head. A ghostly voice whispered inside her mind. *"Katie, remember..."*

Katie felt a burst of heat rush through her. The sky brightened, blinding her, and the air was sucked from her lungs. Images flooded her mind like a movie on fast forward. Faces she had never seen but saw with fond memories. Everything from the destruction of Earth to a Caparian woman taking her last breath. Mrah's agony as he lost his family and farther back as his friend died saving him. Finally, Kat's final battle within Mrah's mind and him holding her as she spent her last breath on forgiveness. The light faded, and Katie nearly dropped to her knees. She blinked, tears rolling down her face.

She looked up into the friendly face of Calypso. Now, she glanced around, recognizing everyone for who they were; her friends Alex, Mrah, Warc. Captain Gar was alive again! No, he never died, but he had in this *other* lifetime.

And Charlie! Charlie, who had been by her side every step of the way, she *remembered!*

"But," she turned tear-filled eyes back to Calypso. "They don't remember me, do they?"

"Charlie won't remember," Calypso said. "And neither will Alexander, but Mrah and Warc remember you."

"How do you remember me?"

"God gave me the knowledge," Calypso said.

"I still feel like me." Katie raised an eyebrow.

"You are still you, Katie," Calypso said. "You just have Kat's memories."

"So..." Katie paused, unsure how silly this would sound. "It's like a second life?"

"In a manner of speaking," Calypso smiled. "But don't expect nine, Kat."

Katie laughed. Calypso turned to Captain Gar, and Katie walked over to Mrah and placed a hand on his arm. He no longer appeared hideous to her. "What happened to Aurora?"

"I did as you requested," he paused. "Well, I did as Kat requested and went to Aurora to tell her the truth about Gasos. Instead of making her happy or more accepting of the situation, she flew into a passion and screamed about how her plan had failed, and I was supposed to be dead, my planet was supposed to be dead—she was raving."

"I was there," Alex said. "I had been summoned to discuss the plants and the possibility of replanting the Earth when she lost it. She was taken into custody under suspicion of being a half-blood. Imagine that the queen was a half-blood like me!"

"She broke away and ran," Warc said. He looked a little sad.

"I chased her through the palace," Alex continued. "I tried to stop her; I really did."

"She made it to the highest tower, jumped, and fell to her death," Mrah finished.

"Shortly after that, Calypso assumed the throne," Alex said.

"Mrah," Katie turned to him. "I remember everything."

"What do you mean?"

"I have all of Kat's memories," Katie said. "I am willing to do the time jump she offered just before she died."

"No," Mrah shook his head. "I can't ask you to risk that."

"Why not?" Katie asked. "I'm the same soul. I should be able to do it."

"No," Calypso said behind them. Katie jerked, startled.

"Why?" Katie asked.

"We all have a time to die," Calypso said. "It was Gasos' time. He was meant to die saving Mrah. If Aurora had been a full-blood, she would have understood this."

"Rather than time jump for me," Mrah said. "Why don't you help me catalog the desert plant specimens we've collected from your planet?"

"Don't forget the desert animals we collected," Warc pointed out.

"And I have tons of plants and animals from Earth that need to be cataloged," Alex smiled.

"Looks like we have our work cut out for us," Katie laughed.

KATIE

Katie crashed through a bush and shoved a low-hanging tree branch out of the way. A vine wrapped around her ankle, trying to trip her, but she rolled with it and was back up on her feet without a thought. She heaved a deep satisfying breath. It felt so good to run! She reveled in the knowledge that there would be more than enough air to fill her lungs when she needed that next deep breath.

She inhaled the heady scent of flowers, Earth, and alien. Small animals skittered away through the underbrush. She sent a flock of birds flying as she shoved her way through another bush. She just caught a glimpse of a whitetail as it leaped over a log and disappeared into the forest. The distant sound of a raven brought a smile to her face. The raven; she still remembered every word written in that book from her previous life. It's strange to have memories rattling around in her head that are so real, so vivid, but none of them have happened in this lifetime.

She burst through the tree line and skidded to a stop at the edge of a precipice. She took huge gulps of air as she looked out over Neptune's Hollow, no longer hollow.

She'd missed the idea of oceans, so she had them plant the tall blue grass she remembered from Zortentearth. It looked like ocean waves from this height, and they swayed in the breeze giving life to her fake ocean. It was dark now, too dark to see the "waves."

She sat at the edge of Neptune's Hollow and waited. She didn't turn at the sound of crunching leaves. She knew who it was before he sat beside her.

"You made it," she said.

"Wouldn't miss it," Charlie replied.

"Are they coming?"

"You know they will."

"We're here!" Mary chirped as she sat on the other side of Katie. She tugged Alex down with her.

"Where's Tracy?" Katie asked. Charlie shrugged.

"She said she wanted to sleep in."

"And miss this?" Katie gasped.

"I changed my mind," Tracy laughed. Charlie almost fell off the edge. Tracy and Katie grabbed him and pulled him back.

"Dang it, Sis," Charlie cried. He took a swing at her legs, but she jumped back. "I'm going to put a bell around your neck!"

"Shh," Katie laughed. "It's starting!"

The horizon glowed with the coming day. It warmed the sky with orange and red. A few wisps of white clouds smudged the colors. As the light spilled across the waves of alien grass, it shimmered and rippled like water. A breeze rushed through the grass, causing a sound almost like waves. Behind them, the green trees rustled, and birds woke up to sing.

Tears filled Katie's eyes, "It's good to be home."

Dear reader,

I just wanted to say thank you for taking a chance on me. It's always a gamble when picking up the first book of a brand new author. The cover might be fantastic. The title might be intriguing. Even the description might be engaging, but—what if the book is a flop? What if all the pretty little details pump you up for something far better than what actually lies between the pages? Then you're left feeling disappointed, even ripped off. You spent hard-earned money on this pack of papers with the promise of a good ride, and here you are at the end wondering if it would be too much like sacrilege to burn the book.

I sincerely hope this is not the case, as you have just turned the last page of my story. I hope you feel exhilarated, maybe even exhausted, as you have just run this race with my friends, Kat and Char. Perhaps you are sad or happy or, at the very least, satisfied with the ending.

Or, if I've done my job, you feel like you don't want the story to end. Perhaps, you are clutching this book or e-reader in the hopes that I will tell you there will be another book—A continuation of Kat and Char's story. You're hoping for a whisper of a promise that this is not the end.

And I would have to say—I wrote this book, initially, as a stand-

alone novel. I had no intention of writing a sequel. For me, the story was done. But—by now—we both know how hard it is to tell Kat what to do. She's been telling me there is more to her story. I argue that I have other stories to tell. Other characters who want to be heard, but she insists I listen to her! She's so bossy!

I don't know much yet, but I know that Katie isn't handling Kat's memories very well. She seems to be losing touch with herself and her reality. That Mrah is still hiding a dark secret that might just tear the Earth apart. And that the only one who has a chance at saving them is the girl who died.

Until then, I invite you to visit my webpage , where you'll be able to find links to my book, and Facebook page, where you will find updates on my stories and can ask me questions. I look forward to meeting you!

God bless,

H. L. Anderson

REFERENCES

Bartlett, J. (2002). *Bartlett's Familiar Quotations 17th Edition.* New York: Little, Brown and Company

NIV Bible. (2001) *NIV Study Bible.* United States of America: Zondervan

Poe, E. (1827-1849). *The Complete Works of Edgar Allan Poe.* United States of America: Tally Hall Press

ACKNOWLEDGMENTS

Acknowledgements
Special thanks to Tim Chizmar for pushing me to take the next step so that my book would finally see the light of day, and always being there with great advice and an encouraging word – or outright shoving me in the direction I needed to go. Not to mention, without you, I wouldn't have met Stacey Smekofske!

Thank you, Stacey, for being such a brilliant and energetic editor. Your enthusiasm is infectious, and I look forward to working with you on future projects! Without you, my book wouldn't shine as brightly.

Last but certainly not least, thank you to Shaina Riordan for helping me get a picture of me where I don't look like an ogre! You are one of the kindest and most beautiful people I have ever met, and I am incredibly blessed to call you my best friend.

Once upon a time, there lived a little girl named H.L. Anderson. She loved to tell stories and would follow her mother around the house, spinning endless yarns and driving her mother crazy.

One find day, H.L. Anderson learned how to write. Joy of joys! Now she could put every thought on paper, and her mother could enjoy the blissful sound of silence.

But, little H.L.Anderson was not just a storyteller. She was a girl of  many passions. She also liked to draw and fancied herself quite good at it. She knew there would come a day when she would have to choose which path to take, art or writing.

So, one day she decided she would draw. She even took commercial art classes thinking this would be a practical way to earn money with her art. But the lessons taught her this was not the path for her. It was too much like work and took the joy out of creating her art.

Though she still focused mainly on her art, she kept writing. She couldn't help herself. The stories would fill her mind until she had to put them down or run mad. She worked on her style and voice and read voraciously. She learned from other writers and read books on writing. Until one day, she realized what she really wanted was to write.

So, she went to college for writing. Her classes focused on writing for children, but she decided that was not for her. She had spent so many years learning to add detail and texture to her stories that stripping it all out for a children's story hurt. The stories felt naked and thin. No! She needed room to create worlds and creatures! Thin lines of children's stories would not limit her!

Finally, finally, little H.L.Anderson, who had spent so many years honing her craft, published her first book. She enjoyed every second of writing it, and now she invites you to enjoy reading it!

www.hlanderson.com

facebook.com/H.L.Anderson2014